With her roots firmly planted in the South, #1 *New York Times* bestselling author **Sherryl Woods** has written many of her more than one hundred books in that distinctive setting, whether it's her home state of Virginia, her adopted state, Florida, or her much-adored South Carolina. Now she's added North Carolina's Outer Banks to her list of favorite spots. And she remains partial to small towns, wherever they may be.

Sherryl divides her time between her childhood summer home overlooking the Potomac River in Colonial Beach, Virginia, and her oceanfront home with its lighthouse view in Key Biscayne, Florida. "Wherever I am, if there's no water in sight, I get a little antsy," she says.

Sherryl loves to hear from readers. You can visit her on her website at www.sherrylwoods.com, link to her Facebook fan page from there or contact her directly at Sherryl703@gmail.com.

New York Times bestselling author **RaeAnne Thayne** finds inspiration in the beautiful northern Utah mountains, where she lives with her family. Her books have won numerous honors, including four RITA® Award nominations from the Romance Writers of America and a Career Achievement Award from *RT Book Reviews*. RaeAnne loves to hear from readers and can be reached through her website at www.raeannethayne.com.

#1 *New York Times* Bestselling Author

SHERRYL WOODS

A LOVE BEYOND WORDS

HARLEQUIN® BESTSELLING AUTHOR COLLECTION

ISBN-13: 978-0-373-01037-0

A Love Beyond Words

Copyright © 2016 by Harlequin Books S.A.

The publisher acknowledges the copyright holders of the individual works as follows:

A Love Beyond Words
Copyright © 2001 by Sherryl Woods

Shelter from the Storm
Copyright © 2007 by RaeAnne Thayne

PLEASE RECYCLE
THIS PRODUCT IS RECYCLABLE

Recycling programs for this product may not exist in your area.

This edition published by arrangement with Harlequin Books S.A.

For questions and comments about the quality of this book, please contact us at CustomerService@Harlequin.com.

® and TM are trademarks of Harlequin Enterprises Limited or its corporate affiliates. Trademarks indicated with ® are registered in the United States Patent and Trademark Office, the Canadian Intellectual Property Office and in other countries.

HARLEQUIN®
www.Harlequin.com

Printed in U.S.A.

CONTENTS

Also by #1 *New York Times* bestselling author
Sherryl Woods

Chesapeake Shores

WILLOW BROOK ROAD
DOGWOOD HILL
THE CHRISTMAS BOUQUET
A SEASIDE CHRISTMAS
THE SUMMER GARDEN
AN O'BRIEN FAMILY CHRISTMAS
BEACH LANE
MOONLIGHT COVE
DRIFTWOOD COTTAGE
A CHESAPEAKE SHORES CHRISTMAS
HARBOR LIGHTS
FLOWERS ON MAIN
THE INN AT EAGLE POINT

The Sweet Magnolias

SWAN POINT
WHERE AZALEAS BLOOM
CATCHING FIREFLIES
MIDNIGHT PROMISES
HONEYSUCKLE SUMMER
SWEET TEA AT SUNRISE
HOME IN CAROLINA
WELCOME TO SERENITY
FEELS LIKE FAMILY
A SLICE OF HEAVEN
STEALING HOME

The Perfect Destinies

DESTINY UNLEASHED
TREASURED
PRICELESS
ISN'T IT RICH?

For a complete list of all titles by Sherryl Woods,
visit sherrylwoods.com.

A LOVE BEYOND WORDS

Sherryl Woods

To Pat and Mark and all the others
who went through the travails of
Hurricane Andrew right along with me...
here's to clear skies from now on.

Chapter 1

Help me. Please help me. The words echoed in Allison's head, though she had no idea if she had actually spoken them aloud.

Everything around her was eerily silent, but it had been that way long before Hurricane Gwen, with its 130-mile-an-hour winds, had struck Miami just after midnight. In fact, her world had been silent for nearly fifteen years now, a long time to go without hearing her parents' voices, a long time for someone who had studied music to miss the lyrics of a favorite love song…an even longer time to adjust to a life of perpetual quiet.

Watching the newscasts about the approaching storm, she had read the lips of the veteran meteorologist and sensed, rather than heard, his increasing panic over the size and force of the storm and its direct aim at Miami.

Then the power had gone out, and she had been left in total darkness to wonder what was happening outside. She'd tried to tell herself it was beyond her control, that she ought to go to bed and attempt to sleep, but for some reason she had stayed right where she was, on the living room sofa, waiting for morning to arrive. Unable to listen to a radio for updates on the storm's progress, she had simply replayed the last reports over and over in her mind and prayed she had done everything she could to protect herself and her home.

Anyone who'd lived in South Florida for any length of time knew the precautions to take. From the start of the hurricane season in the spring until it ended in November, they were repeated with each tropical storm that formed in the Atlantic.

Allie had arrived from the Midwest only a few months earlier, but she was a cautious woman. After living her whole life with the surprise factor of devastating tornadoes, she was grateful for the advance notice most hurricanes gave from the instant they began to brew off the coast of Africa. Unlike some newcomers, she took the potential threat of these powerful storms seriously.

At the very start of her first hurricane season, she had read every article on preparedness. She had installed electric storm shutters on her pretty little Spanish-style house before she'd spent a dime on the decorating and landscaping she wanted to do. She had a garage filled with bottled water, a drawer jammed with batteries for her flashlight, plus stashes of candles and canned goods. She had double what anyone recommended, enough to share with neighbors who weren't as prepared.

She suppressed a hysterical laugh as she wondered where all of those precious supplies were now, buried right here in the rubble with her, but defiantly out of reach and useless. As for the house in which she had taken such pride, there appeared to be little left of it but the debris that held her captive. Obviously, despite all she'd done, it hadn't been enough.

It was pitch-dark, though she couldn't tell for certain if that was because of the time of day or the amount of debris trapping her. She suspected the former since every once in a while rain penetrated the boards and broken furniture that were pinning her down in painful misery.

Every part of her body ached. She had cuts and scrapes everywhere. The most intense pain was in her left leg, which was twisted at an odd angle under the weight of a heavy beam. She had no idea how long she had been unconscious, but sensed it couldn't have been more than minutes. Her stomach still churned from the sudden shock of shutters ripping loose, windows blowing in and walls collapsing around her.

There had been no time to run. Perhaps if she had heard the wind and lashing rain, things would have turned out differently. Instead, out of the blue she had experienced the odd sense that the walls were quite literally closing in, and then everything had begun to break apart around her. Her house had seemingly disintegrated in slow motion, but even at that, she hadn't been able to move quickly enough.

She had taken one frantic step toward the safety of a doorway, then felt a wild rush of air as the roof lifted up, then shattered down in heavy, dangerous chunks. Those expensive shutters—which had wiped out the last of her savings—had been no protection at all against the fury of the storm.

She remembered the slam of something into the back of her head. Then her world had gone blissfully dark for however long it had been. When she'd come to, there had been nothing but pain. A foolhardy attempt to move had sent shafts of blinding agony shooting up her leg. She had passed out again.

This time she knew better. She stayed perfectly still, sucking in huge gulps of air and fighting panic. She hadn't been this terrified since the day nearly fifteen years earlier when she awoke in the hospital and realized that everything seemed oddly still and silent. Sensing that something was amiss, she had flipped on the TV, then tried to adjust the volume. At first she had blamed the television, assuming it was broken, but then she had inadvertently knocked over a vase of flowers. It had crashed to the floor without a sound. And then she had known.

Panicked, she had shouted for her parents, who had come running. They had brought the doctors, who had ordered a barrage of tests before concluding that nerves had been damaged by the particularly virulent attack of mumps she'd contracted.

For a while they had hoped that the effect would be reversible, but as time passed and nothing changed, the doctors had conceded it was likely that her world would forevermore be totally silent. It had taken days before the devastating news finally sank in, weeks more before she'd accepted it and slowly learned to compensate to some degree for the loss by relying on her other senses.

Now, because she couldn't see what was happening, it was as if she had suddenly lost yet another of her senses—her sight. She wasn't sure she could bear it if the inky darkness that was her world right now was permanent.

Frantic, Allie again shouted for help, or thought she did. In that great vacuum of silence in which she lived, she had no idea if anyone could hear her and was responding. She didn't even know if anyone was searching the area for casualties or whether the worst of the storm had passed or was still raging overheard.

She had no idea if the dampness on her cheeks was rain, blood or tears. On the chance that it was the latter, she scolded herself.

"Stay calm," she ordered. "Hysteria won't accomplish a thing."

Though, she conceded, it might feel good to give in to a good bout of tears and rage about now.

That wasn't her style, though. She hadn't valued or even tested her own strength before she'd lost her hearing. At nineteen she had cared more that she was pretty and popular, that her college studies in music education came easily. Then, in an instant, none of that had mattered anymore. She had been faced with living her life in total silence and she had been terrified. What would she do if she couldn't share her love of music with others? Who would she be if she couldn't perform in the occasional concert with the local symphony as she had since her violin teacher had won an audition for her when she was only fourteen?

For a time Allie had quit college and withdrawn into herself. Once gregarious, she had sought isolation, telling herself it was better to be truly alone than to be in a room filled with people and feel utterly cut off from them. Her parents had hovered, distraught, taking the blame for something over which they'd had no control.

Then one day Allie had taken a good, hard look at her future and realized that she didn't want to live that way, that in fact she wasn't living at all. Her faith had taught her that God never closed one door without opening another. And so, she had gone in search of that door.

Not only had she learned sign language, she had studied how to teach it to others. She might have lost something precious when the raging infection had stolen her hearing, but she had gained more. Today she had a career that was full and rewarding, a chance to smooth the way for others facing what she had once faced. The hearing-impaired children she worked with were a challenge and an inspiration.

The strength it had taken to view tragedy as an opportunity would get her through this, too. She just had to ignore the pain, the nearly paralyzing blanket of darkness, and stay focused on survival.

"Think, Allison," she instructed herself, calmer now.

Unfortunately, thinking didn't seem to be getting the job done. Determined to make her way to safety, she tried to maneuver one of the smaller chunks of debris on top of her, only to realize that the action was causing everything to shift in an unpredictable, potentially deadly way.

This time when the tears came, there was no mistaking them. They came in tandem with the pain and fear.

"I am not going to die like this," she said, then repeated it. She thought it was probably just as well that she couldn't hear the quaver she could feel in her voice. "Just wait, Allie. Someone will come. Be patient."

Of course, patience was not a virtue with which she was very well acquainted. Once she had accepted her hearing loss, she had moved ahead with learning sign language and lip reading at an obsessive pace. She seized everything in life in the same way, aware of just how quickly things could change, of how a sudden twist of fate could alter a person's entire vision of the future.

Now, just as it had been when the doctors had been unable to battle the infection that had cost her her hearing, it appeared her fate was in someone else's hands. She could only pray that whoever it was would hurry up.

"Come on, Enrique," Tom Harris taunted. "Let's see those cards. I could use the down payment on a new car."

"In your dreams," Ricky retorted, spreading his full house on the bench between them.

The other firefighters had gathered around to watch the high-stakes, winner-take-all hand between two men who were intense rivals for everything from women to poker winnings in their spare time, but dedicated partners when it came to rescue operations. Ricky's grin spread as Tom's face fell.

"Come on, baby. Show 'em to me," he said, tapping the bench. "Put those cards right down here where everyone can see."

Tom spread three aces on the bench, then sighed heavily. Just as Ricky was about to seize the cash, Tom clucked disapprovingly.

"Not so fast, my man. This little devil here must have slipped my mind." He dropped another ace on top of the other three, then grabbed the pot. "Come to Daddy."

The other firefighters on the search and rescue team hooted at Ricky's crestfallen expression.

"Next time, *amigo,*" Ricky said good-naturedly.

There would always be a next time with Tom. About the only thing Tom liked better than playing cards was chasing women. He considered himself an expert at both pursuits, though even he grudgingly admitted that Ricky was the one with a real knack for charming any female between the ages of eight and eighty.

"You may be lucky at cards, but I am lucky at love," Ricky boasted.

"It's those dark eyes and that hot Latino blood," Tom replied without rancor. "How can I compete with that?"

"You can't, so give it up," Ricky retorted, as always. "You can't match my dimples, either. My sisters assure me they're irresistible."

"Your sisters aren't exactly unbiased. Besides, they have spoiled their baby brother shamelessly," Tom retorted. "It's no wonder you've never married. Why should you when you have four women in your life who wait on you hand and foot? I'm amazed their husbands permit it."

"Their husbands knew I was part of the bargain when I allowed them to date my sisters," Ricky said. "And there are five women, not four. You're forgetting my mother."

"Saints forgive me, yes. Mama Wilder, who comes from the old school in Cuba where the husband is king and the son is prince. She's definitely had a part in shaping you into a scoundrel."

Ricky grinned. "I dare you to tell her that."

Tom turned pale. "Not a chance. Last time I offended her precious son, she chased me with a meat cleaver."

"It was a butter knife," Ricky said with a shake of his head at the exaggeration. His mother might be a passionate defender of her offspring, but she wasn't crazy. Besides, she considered Tom to be a second son, which she felt gave her free rein to nag him as enthusiastically as she did Ricky or his sisters. She was still lecturing Tom about his divorce, though it had been final for three years now. If it had been up to her and her meddling, he would have been back with his wife long ago.

"Hey, guys, cut the foolishness," their lieutenant shouted, his expression somber as he hung up the phone. "We've got to roll. There's a report of houses down."

"Casualties?" Ricky asked, already moving toward his gear.

"No word, but it's the middle of the night. Some people might have gone to shelters, but outside the flood zones where evacuations were required, most stayed home to protect their belongings. Worst-case scenario? We could have dozens of families whose ceilings came crashing down on top of them as they slept. Clearly the construction in that part of town was no match for Mother Nature."

"Multiple houses?" Ricky asked. "I thought we'd lucked out. I thought this sucker had all but ended. Was it the hurricane or a tornado spawned by the storm?"

"No confirmation on that. Either way, it's trouble," the lieutenant said.

Within seconds the trucks were on the road, traveling far more slowly than Ricky would have liked. The main street in front of the station was ankle deep in water and littered with debris. Rain was still lashing from the sky in sheets, and the wind was bending nearby palms almost to the ground. Other trees had been uprooted, their broken limbs tossed around like giant Pick-Up Sticks.

Street signs had been ripped from the corners, making the trip even trickier. With signs down and landmarks in tatters, it was going to take luck or God's guidance to get them where they needed to be, even though it was less than a mile from the station. He murmured a silent prayer to the saints that they would reach the devastated street before someone died in the rubble.

As if in answer to his prayer, the rain and wind began to die down. In a few hours the street flooding would begin to ease, but that was no help to them now. They crept along at a frustrating pace.

The scene that awaited them when they eventually reached the middle-class Miami neighborhood was like a war zone. Power lines were down, leaving dangerous live wires in the road. Here and there a home had miraculously escaped the worst of the hurricane's wrath, but those were the exception. Most of the two-story houses had been leveled by the winds or by an accompanying tornado. Those that hadn't collapsed completely were severely damaged. Roof tiles had been stripped away, glass was shattered and doors had been ripped from their hinges. Another testament to lousy inspections and shoddy construction, Rick thought wearily as he surveyed the damage. Hadn't the city learned anything from the devastating hurricanes they'd had in the past?

There was no time to worry about what couldn't be changed. With the precision of a long-established team, the firefighters assessed the situation, then split up. A call was placed to the electric company to get a crew on the scene. In the meantime, barricades were set up to prevent people from stumbling onto the area around the live wires.

A few people were walking around dazed and bloody, oblivious to the light shower that was now the only lingering evidence of the hurricane. Some of the paramedics set up a first aid station and began to treat the less severely injured, while others took their highly trained dogs and began to search for signs of life.

A woman who looked to be in her seventies, clutching a robe tightly around her, hobbled up to Ricky. She seemed to be completely unaware of the bloody gash in her forehead, though her expression was frantic.

"You have to find Allie," she said urgently.

"Your daughter, ma'am?"

"No, no, she's my neighbor." She gestured toward a severely damaged house. As Ricky and Tom headed in that direction, she trailed along behind. "She's a wonderful young woman and she's already been through so much. This house was her pride and joy. She just bought it a few months ago, and she's been spending every spare minute fixing it up, putting in flowers all around."

Her eyes shone with tears. "None of that matters, of course. Houses can be rebuilt. Flowers can be replanted."

"You say her name is Allie?" Ricky asked.

"Allison, actually. Allison Matthews."

As Tom went to get the equipment they'd need,

Ricky surveyed the collapsed structure in the early-dawn light. He opened his mouth to shout, but the woman's frail hand on his arm stopped him.

"Calling out won't help," she said urgently. "She won't be able to hear you. Allie's deaf."

As if the situation weren't complicated enough, he thought, then reminded himself to treat it as he might a rescue in a foreign country where he didn't know the language. It wouldn't matter that he couldn't communicate with this Allie in the usual way. He just had to find her.

He circled the twisted pile of debris, looking for any sign of the woman, any hint of where rooms might have been. Would she have been in an upstairs bedroom or downstairs?

Shadow, the highly trained dog at his side, moved gingerly through the rubble, sniffing. Rick stood where he was, waiting, letting Shadow do his part. This was always the hardest part of a rescue, hanging back, leaving it to the German shepherd to pinpoint signs of life.

Finally Shadow stilled, whimpered, then barked.

"So, you found her, did you, boy? Good dog."

Shadow yipped excitedly, but didn't move, as if he sensed that one tiny shift could be fatal.

"Let's get her out of there, boy," Ricky said. He paused long enough to give a reassuring smile to the neighbor. "Looks like we've located your friend. We'll have her out of there in no time."

"Thank God," she said. "Allie's one of those special people put on this earth to show others the meaning of goodness. She's an angel, sure as anything."

Ricky didn't know a lot of women who could live up to such high praise. He tended to gravitate toward women who could best be described as free and easy with their affections, the kind who placed no demands on him, who knew that his job came first. Definitely not the sort of women to take home to meet his mother, who bemoaned his failure to marry on an almost daily basis. The only time she let up was when he brought Tom home for a meal of her famed pork roast, black beans and rice. Then she served up marital advice along with the food. Tom enjoyed her cooking too much to complain.

Of course, right now it didn't much matter whether Allie was a saint or a sinner. She was someone who needed his help, and that was all that mattered.

He intently studied the collapsed home again, looking for the best possible access, using Shadow's watchful stance as a guidepost to Allie's location.

"Shouldn't you hurry?" the elderly neighbor asked, wringing her hands anxiously.

"Better to do it right than rush and cause more injuries than whatever she's suffered so far." Thinking of his grandmother and how she would feel under these circumstances, he took a moment to cup the woman's icy hands. "It's going to be okay."

No sooner were the words spoken than he heard a feeble cry for help from deep within the rubble. The sound tore at his heart. Knowing that there was nothing he could say, that words of reassurance would quite literally fall on deaf ears, he settled for reassuring her friend instead.

"See, there? She's alive. We'll have her out of there in no time," he said optimistically. "In the meantime, why don't you go over to the first aid station that's been set up and let somebody take a look at that cut on your forehead. Looks as if you might have a sprained ankle, too."

"At my age, hobbling's normal. As for the cut, it's nothing," she said, facing him stubbornly. "I want to be right here when you bring Allie out. She must be terrified. She'll need to see a familiar face."

Ricky recognized the determined set of her jaw and gave up arguing. Like his *abuela,* this woman knew her own mind.

He looked around until he caught sight of Tom, who had assembled the necessary rescue equipment and was ready to get started.

"All set?" his partner asked.

Adrenaline kicked in as it always did when the hard work was about to begin. Ricky nodded.

"Let's do it," he said with an eagerness that always struck him as vaguely inappropriate. Yet it was that very anticipation that had driven him to take on such highly dangerous work in the first place. True, what he did sometimes saved lives, which was incredibly rewarding, but it also tested his skill and ingenuity at outwitting the forces of nature and near-certain death in the aftermath. A part of him craved that element of risk.

Often he was halfway across the world. Today, however, he was in his own backyard, so to speak. Somehow that raised the stakes.

He thought of the elderly woman's assessment of Allie and grinned. He had to admit that his anticipation was heightened ever so slightly by the promise that when this particular rescue was over, for the first time he might be face-to-face with an angel.

Chapter 2

Allie fell in and out of consciousness. Or maybe she only slept. She just knew that every once in a while her eyes seemed to drift shut and her pain faded away. When she awoke, there was always the throbbing, more intense than ever.

"Help!" she cried out again. Surely by now there were rescuers in the area. If they could hear her, they could find her. Gasping at the pain, she steadied herself, then shouted again, "Help!"

When her shouts were met with nothing but more of the same silence, she felt as if she were calling into some huge void. As her cries continued to go unanswered, she began to lose hope. What if they never found her? How long could she stay alive in this unrelenting heat without water? Despair began to overwhelm her.

Then, suddenly, just when she was about to give up, she thought she caught sight of a faint movement far above her. Was it possible? In the pitch-blackness, she couldn't be sure. Had there been a glimmer of light?

"Here," she called on the chance that it hadn't been her imagination playing cruel tricks on her. "I'm down here."

A chunk of what once had been her roof—or maybe a wall, considering how topsy-turvy everything was— was eased away, allowing her a first glimpse of sky. Ironically, given the storm that had raged so recently, the sky was now a brilliant blue, too beautiful by far for anyone to imagine that such destruction had been wreaked by the heavens only hours before.

Relieved that she still had her sight, she wanted to simply stare and stare at the sunshine, but she was forced to close her eyes against the brilliance of it. Still, she could feel the blazing heat on her cheeks and vowed she would never again complain about Miami's steamy climate. It felt wonderful.

When she finally dared to open her eyes again, there was a face peering back at her, the most handsome face she had ever set eyes on. Of course, at this point, she would have been entranced by a man with whiskers down to his knees and hair the consistency of straw if he'd come to save her. This man was a definite im-provement on that image.

Even with his hard hat, she could see that he had black hair, worn a little too long. He had dark, dark eyes and a complexion that suggested Hispanic heritage and dimples that could make a woman weep. It was all Allie could do not to swoon and murmur, "Oh, my."

He was too far away for her to read his lips with any

accuracy, but she could see his mouth slowly curve once again into that reassuring, devastating smile. She clung to the sight of that smile. It was a reminder that life could definitely be worth living. No man had smiled at her like that in a very long time, if ever.

Or maybe she just hadn't noticed, she admitted candidly. From the moment she'd lost her hearing, her life had taken on a single focus. Everything had been about learning to adjust, learning to cope, opening that new door...and forgetting about the social life that had once consumed her. She discovered that not many men were interested in a woman who couldn't hang on their every word, anyway.

For fifteen years now she had had male colleagues, even a few men she counted as friends, but not a single one of them had made her blood sizzle the way this one had just by showing up. She figured it had to be a reaction to the circumstances. After all, this hardly seemed to be an appropriate time for her hormones to wake up after more than a decade in exile.

As time slid by, she kept her gaze locked on that incredible face. She sensed from the way the debris was slowly shifting above her that there was a scramble to free her, but that one man stayed right where she could see him, easing closer, inch by treacherous inch.

"Hi, Allie," he said.

By now, he was close enough that she could read his lips. And she guessed from the way he'd spoken, being so careful to face her, that he knew she was deaf.

"Hi." She breathed the word with a catch in her voice, even as relief flooded through her. It was going to be okay. As long as he was there, she knew it.

"Can you read my lips?"

Eyes glued to his face, she nodded.

"Good." He reached out his hand. "Can you take my hand?"

She tried to move her arm, but it felt as if it, too, were weighted down, just like her pinned leg. She almost wept in frustration.

"That's okay," he said. "Hang in there a little longer. You're being incredibly brave, and if you give us just a little more time, I'll be able to reach you and this nightmare will be over."

She nodded.

"Anything hurt?"

"Everything," she said.

He grinned. "Yeah, dumb question, huh?"

He turned his head away. She could see a change of expression on his face and guessed he was speaking to someone out of sight.

More debris shifted and bits of plaster rained down on her. She yelped, drawing his immediate attention.

"Everything okay?" he asked, his expression filled with concern.

She nodded, her gaze locked with his worried brown eyes.

"Good. Then here's the deal, Allie. I imagine you want to know what we're up to out here, right?"

"Yes." She wanted to know everything, even if she didn't like it. She'd learned a long time ago that she could cope with just about anything as long as she knew what she was up against.

"Okay, then. I'm going to disappear for just a minute. We're not happy with this approach, so we're going to come in a different way. It'll take a little longer, but there's less risk. Are you all right with that?"

She wanted to protest the delay, but he was the one who knew what he was doing. She had to trust him. Gazing into his eyes, she found that she did. And even though she didn't want him to move, didn't want to lose sight of him, she nodded again. "Okay."

She turned her head away to hide the tears that threatened. Suddenly she felt what seemed to be a deliberate dusting of powder sprinkle down on her face. She glanced up to find him watching her anxiously.

"Sorry," he apologized. "I needed to get your attention. I promise you'll see me again in no time. I never leave a pretty woman in distress."

She almost laughed at that. Even when she wasn't under a ton of debris, no one in recent years ever said she was pretty. Now she imagined she must look a fright. She had been dressed for bed when disaster struck, wearing a faded Florida Marlins T-shirt and nothing else. At the end of the day, her hair was always a riot of mousy-brown curls, thanks to Miami's never-ending humidity. She imagined she looked pretty much like a dusty, bloody mop about now.

"Go," she told him. "I'll be here when you get back."

He chuckled. "That's my girl."

And then he was gone, leaving Allie to wonder if it was possible that angels ever came with dancing eyes... and looking like sin.

Ricky was still chuckling as he eased his way off the mound of debris. Allie Matthews was something, all right. Scared to death but doing her level best not to show it. He'd caught the occasional glimpse of panic in her amazing blue eyes, but not once had she complained. She had to be in pain, as well, but beyond her one joking admission, she'd never mentioned it again.

"You find something funny about this?" Tom asked, regarding him with curiosity as he leaped to the ground beside him.

"You probably had to be there," Ricky admitted.

"How's she doing?"

"Her sense of humor's intact, but she can't move. No way to tell if that's because she's pinned down or because of an injury. Bravest woman I ever saw, though. She's not hysterical, but those eyes of her are killers, blue as the ocean and shimmering with tears, though she's fighting them like crazy."

Tom shook his head. "Leave it to you to go all poetic about a woman's eyes in the middle of a rescue."

"I was hoping to motivate you," Ricky claimed, though the thought of Tom getting ideas about Allie bothered him more than he cared to admit. It was crazy to be jealous over a woman to whom he hadn't even been introduced.

He gazed at the rubble with frustration. "Any idea how we can get in there without bringing this mess tumbling down around her?"

They stood surveying the crazy haystack of debris. It was far from the worst they'd ever seen. There had been whole apartment complexes to dig through in earthquake disasters. But Ricky had never felt a greater sense of urgency. Something about Allie's spirit and bravery had caught his attention in a way that few women did. In just a few minutes he had felt some of that strength and resilience that her neighbor had bragged about.

For the next few hours Ricky, Tom and the others

worked with tedious patience to reach Allie. When they finally had a clear view of her through a tunnel that seemed safe enough, Ricky was the one who inched forward on his belly, clearing more debris bit by bit until he could reach out and touch her hand. Again those huge, luminous blue eyes latched on to him and held him captive.

He passed a water bottle to her, but she couldn't seem to negotiate it to her mouth. She stared at her immobile hand with evident frustration.

"It's okay," he soothed. "I'll get it to you. Hang in there."

He eased forward an inch at a time, waiting between movements to make sure that the precarious arrangement of debris wouldn't shift. Finally he was close enough to touch the plastic straw to her lips. She drank greedily, her gaze never leaving his face.

"Is Jane okay?" she asked the minute she'd satisfied her thirst.

"Jane?"

"Next door. Mrs. Baker."

He thought of the woman who'd guided them to Allie. "About seventy-five? Five-two? Feisty?"

"Yes, yes, that's her. She's okay, isn't she?"

"A cut on her forehead and possibly a sprained ankle, but you're the only thing that seems to concern her," he said. "She hasn't budged since we started trying to reach you. She found a lawn chair down the block and planted it right out front so she can keep an eye on us."

Allie grinned. "That sounds just like her. And the rest of the neighbors? How are they?"

"We're checking on all of them now," he said, unwilling to mention that so far there was one dead and several unaccounted for. Fortunately, she seemed to take his response at face value.

"How long have I been down here?" she asked.

"Not so long. A few hours. We got the call shortly before six a.m. It's just about noon now," he told her. "Must seem like an eternity to you, though."

She nodded.

"Well, it's almost over. You stay perfectly still, *querida*. I'll have you free in no time," he promised.

"Couldn't move if I wanted to," she said as a tear slipped down her cheek. "I—" her voice faltered "—I think I might be paralyzed."

"Now, don't go getting any crazy ideas. Looks to me as if it's just because of the way you're wedged in here," he reassured her. "No need to panic. Once you're out, I'll take you dancing."

The teasing drew a watery smile. "You'll regret it. Even before this I had two left feet. On top of that I can't exactly hear the music."

"I'll take you someplace where it only matters if you can swivel your hips."

"Ah, salsa," she said knowingly.

"With a little tango mixed in," he said. "You'll just have to hang on and follow my lead."

She gave a decisive little nod. "I can do that."

"Then it's a date."

All the while he talked, chattering nonsense mostly just to keep her attention focused on his face, he cleared debris from on and around her. When he saw the bloody gashes in a long shapely leg, he had to fight to keep his expression neutral.

That was the worst of it, though. If he could free

her leg, he thought he could get her to safety. He just had to keep his mind on what he was doing and off the fact that she was all but naked. The T-shirt she'd presumably worn to bed was shredded indecently. She apparently hadn't noticed that yet or else she was more brazen than he'd imagined.

"Make sure there's a blanket ready and waiting when we come out," he murmured into the radio tucked in his pocket, his head turned so she couldn't read his lips. She tapped his shoulder, her expression frustrated. He smiled. "Sorry. I was talking to my partner. I just wanted to be sure he'd be ready for us when we blow this cozy little cave under here."

It took another hour of careful excavation around her leg before he felt confident enough to move her.

"You ready?"

"Oh, yes," she breathed softly.

"I'm not guaranteeing there won't be some pain."

"What else is new?" she said bravely.

"You want something for it?"

"Just get me out," she pleaded.

He cradled her as best he could, aware of every bare inch of skin he was touching, then slowly worked his way back the same way he'd come. It seemed to take forever, but at last he saw Tom's face peering at them intently.

"You have that blanket?"

"Right here."

Ricky reached for it, then wrapped it around Allie as best he could in the confined space, before shimmying the rest of the way out.

Allie blinked against the brilliant glare of sunlight

and continued to cling to Ricky as if he were all that stood between her and an unfamiliar world.

And, of course, the neighborhood must seem strange—nothing like what it had been the last time she'd seen it before the storm. Ricky could only imagine how it must feel to emerge and find everything changed. He'd seen that same sense of shocked dismay on the faces of other victims of other tragedies as they realized the extent of the damage around them and the likelihood of casualties among their friends and family.

As for the way Allie was looking at him and holding on, it wasn't the first time he'd seen that reaction, either. The bond between victim and rescuer could be intense, but in most instances it wasn't long before familiar faces arrived and the bond was broken.

This time, though, only the elderly neighbor stepped forward to give Allie a fierce hug, even as the paramedics moved in to begin their work. Allie was on a stretcher and headed for an ambulance in no time, Jane right beside her, giving instructions. Ricky grinned at the bemused expressions of the paramedics at taking their orders from a pint-size senior citizen in a flowered housecoat and bright-pink sneakers.

"Wait," Allie commanded as they were about to lift her into the ambulance. Her gaze searched the crowd.

Ricky felt a quick rush of heat at the precise moment when she spotted him. Her gaze locked on his.

"Thank you," she mouthed, too far away for him to actually hear the words.

"You're welcome," he said, then deliberately turned away from the emotion shining in her eyes to move on to another complicated search taking place a few houses away.

"You going to see her again?" Tom asked as they began work on the recovery of a victim who had been less fortunate than Allie.

"I wasn't down there making a date," Ricky retorted.

"I was asking about your intentions."

Those blue, blue eyes came back to haunt him. He wondered if he might not have to see her again before he could get them out of his head.

"I promised to take her dancing," he admitted, earning a punch from Tom.

"Next time there's a pretty woman involved, I get first dibs," Tom said. "There's nothing like a little gratitude to get a relationship off to the right start."

"And what would you know about relationships, Mr. Love 'em and Leave 'em?"

"More than you," Tom said. "I was married."

"For about fifteen minutes."

"Three years," his friend corrected.

"And in that time you learned what?"

"That women get all crazy once you put a ring on their finger."

Ricky chuckled. "Are you referring to the fact that Nikki thought you ought to stop dating other women after the wedding?"

"Very funny. You know it wasn't that. I might have looked, but I never went near another woman during that whole three years. Nikki just got all weird about the job. She knew what I did for a living when we met, but for some reason after we got married she seemed to think I'd give it up and go to work for her father." He shuddered. "Me, behind a desk. Can you imagine it?"

No more than he could imagine himself there, Ricky conceded. "Mama says Nikki still loves you."

"Not enough to give up that crazy idea," Tom said, a hint of something that might have been sorrow in his eyes. But it was gone in a flash, replaced by an irrepressible glint of laughter. "That divorce was the best thing that ever happened. Women figure if I got married once, I might risk it again. You'd be amazed what a woman will do when she's optimistic about your potential. You should consider it."

"What? Get married, just so I can divorce? Not me. If and when I ever take the plunge, it's gonna have to be forever. Between Mama and the priest, my life wouldn't be worth two cents if I even breathed the word *divorce*."

"Which is why you never date a woman for more than two Saturday nights running," Tom concluded. His expression turned thoughtful. "I wonder if Allie Matthews could make you change your mind."

"Why would you even say something like that? I barely know the woman, and you didn't exchange two words with her."

"I got a good look at her, though," Tom said. "A man doesn't soon forget a woman who looks that incredible even after being buried under a collapsed building. Besides, if her neighbor is right about what an angel she is, she's nothing at all like your usual dates. Did you ever consider that you make the choices you do precisely because you know they're not keepers?"

Ricky scowled at the analysis of his love life. He had a hunch it was more accurate than he wanted to believe. "We've got more houses to check out," he said, stalking away without answering Tom's question. His friend's hoot of knowing laughter followed him.

What if he did protect himself from winding up

married by dating women he would never, ever spend the rest of his life with? What was wrong with that? It wasn't as if he led any of them on. As Tom said, Ricky rarely went out with the same woman more than once or twice, and he always put his cards on the table, explaining that in his line of work he was on the go way too much to get seriously involved.

Maybe it was a pattern he'd developed to avoid commitment, but so what? It was his life. He liked living alone. He liked not being accountable to anyone. After spending his first eighteen years accountable to an overly protective mother, an iron-willed father and four sisters who thought his love life was their concern, he liked having his freedom. His nieces and nephews satisfied his desire for kids, at least for the moment. He got to play doting uncle, soccer coach and pal without any of the responsibility that went with being a dad.

There wasn't a woman on earth who could make him want to change the life he had.

Satisfied that Tom was totally and absolutely wrong, he dismissed his taunt about Allie Matthews. He'd probably never even see her again, never make good on that promise to take her dancing. She wouldn't even expect him to.

He was still telling himself that the next day, but he couldn't seem to shake the image of Allie's cerulean gaze as it had clung to his. If what he'd seen in her eyes had been expectations, he might have run the other way, but that hadn't been it. There had been gratitude, but underlying that there had been a vague hint of loneliness.

He tried to imagine being rescued from the debris of his home, having only an elderly neighbor for support, rather than the huge, extended family he had. He couldn't. He knew without a doubt that his hospital room would be crowded with people who cared whether he lived or died, people who would help him to rebuild his home and his life. Who would be there for Allie?

He spent an hour telling himself that surely a woman described as an angel would have dozens of friends who would be there for her, but he couldn't shake the feeling that Allie might not.

"Damn," he muttered, slamming his coffee cup into the sink and grabbing his car keys.

On the drive he told himself that if he got to the hospital and found that Allie had all the support she needed, he would just turn right around and leave. That would be that. End of story. End of being haunted by those big blue eyes.

Unfortunately, something in his gut told him he was about to go down for the count.

Chapter 3

Allie hated the hospital. The antiseptic smell alone was enough to carry her straight back to another time and place when her life had been forever changed. This time she was an adult and her injuries weren't either life-threatening or permanent, but the doctors still had no intention of releasing her until she could tell them she had both a place to go and someone to care for her.

Unfortunately, there was no one. She knew only a few of her neighbors, and their lives and homes were in as much a shambles as her own. Her parents had offered to fly down immediately and stay with her, but the expense of paying for hotel accommodations for all three of them struck Allie as foolish. In addition she knew that they would hover just as they had years ago. She didn't need that. She needed to get back into a familiar routine as soon as she was physically able to. She had promised to let them know if she couldn't come up with another solution. There had to be one. It just hadn't occurred to her yet.

"What about that lovely young woman at the clinic?" Jane asked helpfully. She had been to visit the night before and was here again, taking a bus from her sister's, where she had been staying since the storm.

"Gina has a brand-new baby and a two-bedroom apartment. I couldn't possibly impose on her and her husband," Allie said, though her boss had indeed come by and issued the invitation.

"I would insist that you come to Ruth's with me, but she's not in the best health herself and, to be perfectly honest, she's a pain in the neck," Jane said.

Allie bit back a laugh. Jane's opinion of her sister was something she had heard with great regularity since she'd moved in next door to the elderly woman. They barely spoke, because Jane thought Ruth spent way too much time concentrating on her own problems and not nearly enough thinking of others.

"Old before her time," Jane often declared. "She was a cranky old woman by the time she hit fifty. Dressed like one, too. I tried to talk her into a snazzy pair of red sneakers the other day. You would have thought I was trying to get her to wear a dress with a slit up to her you-know-what."

Now she sighed. "The minute I get that insurance check, I'll move to an apartment, so I won't have to listen to her complaining all the livelong day."

"She did open her home to you," Allie reminded her. "She was right there as soon as she heard about what had happened."

"Yes, she was," Jane admitted. "Of course, she said

it was her duty. She wouldn't have come, I promise you, if she hadn't worried what her pastor would think of her if she left her only sister on the street."

Jane waved off the topic. "Enough of that. We need to decide what's to be done about you. If I thought we could find an apartment in time, you could move in with me until you rebuild, but there's no way I can get settled someplace that fast."

"It's very sweet of you to want to do that, but this isn't your problem," Allie told her. "I'll figure something out."

Jane looked as if she wanted to argue, but eventually she stood. "Okay, then," she said with obvious reluctance, "but I'll be back tomorrow. Same time. You have my sister's phone number. If anything comes up and you need me, you call, you hear me? Anytime, day or night."

Her elderly neighbor bent down and brushed a kiss across Allie's cheek. "I think of you as the granddaughter I never had, you know. I hope wherever we end up, we don't lose touch."

"Not a chance," Allie promised, squeezing her hand.

She watched as Jane left, admiring her still-brisk step in her favorite pink shoes. She wore them today with an orange skirt and flowered shirt. A bright-orange baseball cap sat atop her white hair. It was an outfit that could stop traffic, which Jane counted on, since she hated wasting time on a corner waiting for a light to change. It was a habit that scared Allie to death.

All in all, her neighbor was a wonder, interested in everything and everyone. Allie saw her pause in the hallway and watched her face as she carried on an animated conversation with a nurse she'd befriended on her first visit. Jane had all of the doctors and nurses wrapped around her finger. Allie didn't doubt that Jane was the reason they'd been taking such extraspecial care of her, bringing her treats from the cafeteria and lingering to chat to make up for the fact that she'd had so few visitors.

Once Jane was gone, Allie struggled to her feet, determined to take a walk around the room at least to begin to get her strength back. She closed the door on her way past so no one would witness her awkward, unsteady gait.

She was still limping around the confined space, filled with frustration, when the door cracked open and eyes the color of melted chocolate peered at her. When her visitor spotted her on her feet by the window, a grin spread across his face.

"You're awake. They told me not to disturb you if you were sleeping."

"Come in," she said, glad to see her rescuer again so she could thank him properly for saving her life. "I just realized that I don't even know your name."

"Enrique Wilder," he said. "Ricky will do."

"Thank you, Enrique Wilder."

He looked almost embarrassed by her thanks. "Just doing my job."

"So you spend your life scrambling around like a cat saving people?"

"If I'm lucky," he said.

She shuddered a little at the implications of that. "Well, I'm grateful."

He moved carefully around the room, his gaze everywhere but on her. He seemed so uneasy, she couldn't help wondering why he had come. He paused to gaze out the window, and after a moment she tapped him on the shoulder so he would face her.

"Why are you here?" she asked finally.

"To tell you the truth, I'm not entirely sure."

"So this isn't follow-up you do on everyone you've pulled from a collapsed structure?" she teased lightly.

He looked away. She could see his lips moving, but because of the angle of his head, she couldn't read them. She touched his cheek, turning his head to face her.

"Oh, sorry," he apologized. "I forgot. I just came to make sure you're okay. No lasting damage?"

"None. You can check me off as one of your success stories."

"When are they springing you?"

"Not fast enough to suit me," she said.

"I thought the goal these days was to get people out as quickly as possible, too quickly sometimes."

"That's the general rule, yes, but these are unusual circumstances. It seems I don't have a home to go to, and they don't want me alone."

"You don't have a friend you could stay with?"

"None I feel I could impose on. I haven't been in Miami very long. Most of my friends are neighbors." She shrugged. They both knew the situation most of her neighbors were facing.

"Of course. How is Mrs. Baker, by the way?"

"Living with her sister and grumbling about it," Allie said with a chuckle. "Jane is very independent. She thinks her sister is a stick-in-the-mud. A half hour ago, you could have heard all about it."

His devastating smile tugged at his lips. "She was here?"

"Yesterday and today. She says it's to check on me, but I think she's just desperate to get away from her sister."

"I know the feeling," Ricky said.

"You have a sister?"

"Four of them."

Fascinated by the idea of such a large family, Allie sat on the side of the bed and regarded him eagerly. "Tell me about them."

He looked doubtful. "You can't really want to hear about my sisters."

"I do," she assured him. "I was an only child. I've always been envious of big families. Tell me about your parents, too. Is your mother Cuban?"

"How did you guess?"

"Your coloring and your first name are Hispanic, but your last name is Wilder. Those looks had to come from somebody."

He laughed. "Ah, deductive reasoning. Yes, my mother is Cuban. She met my father at school when she had just come to the United States. She swears she fell madly in love with him at first sight."

"And your father, what does he say?"

"He says she didn't look twice at him until they were twenty and he'd used up all his savings sending her roses."

Allie chuckled. "Maybe she just liked roses."

"That was part of it, I'm sure, but Mama has always understood the nuances of courtship. She might have been madly in love, but she wanted my father to prove his love before she agreed to a marriage that would be forever."

"And the roses proved that?"

"No, but the persistence did."

"And she passed all of this wisdom on to her children, I suppose, assuring that all of you have nice, secure relationships."

"Let's just say that my sisters each made their prospective husbands jump through hoops before they said yes. On occasion I felt sorry for the poor men. They had no idea what they were getting into. Sometimes I tried to warn them when they showed up for the first date, but it was too late. My sisters are very beautiful, and the men were already half in love with them before they arrived at the house."

"How about you? How have you made your mother's wisdom work for you?" she asked, surprised by how much she wanted to know if Ricky Wilder was married or single and how very much she wanted it to be the latter.

"I haven't. Haven't met a woman yet I wanted to impress."

"But I'm sure you're swimming in eager admirers," she said, teasing to hide her relief.

"What makes you think that?"

"Please," she chided. "Look in the mirror."

His grin spread. "Are you trying to say that you think I'm handsome, Allie Matthews?"

"Facts are facts," she said, as if she were stating no more than that. She hardly wanted him to know that he was capable of making her blood sizzle with little more than a glance. "Back to your sisters. Tell me about them."

He settled into the room's one chair. "Let's see, then. Maria is the oldest. She's thirty-six and has four children—all boys, all holy terrors. Each of them is fascinated by bugs and snakes and chameleons. To her horror, they're constantly bringing their finds home and letting them loose in the house. I told her it's penance for all the rotten things she ever did to me as a kid."

Allie laughed, sympathizing with the other woman's dismay. "How does she handle it?"

"She gives her husband and the boys exactly five minutes to find the missing creature and get rid of it."

"And if they fail?"

"She leaves and goes shopping. She can buy herself a lot of perfume and lingerie in a very short period of time. She claims her skill with a credit card is excellent motivation for her husband."

"I don't know," Allie said doubtfully. "Some husbands might consider the prospect of a little sexy lingerie as a benefit, rather than a threat."

Ricky grinned. "I know. I don't think she's figured that out yet." His expression sobered. "Then again, maybe she has. Maria is a very sneaky woman."

"And the others?" Allie prodded.

"Elena is next. She's thirty-five and is married to a doctor. They have only one child so far, because they waited until her husband's medical practice was well established before starting a family. My mother prayed for her every day. She will not be happy until there are enough grandchildren to start their own school."

"Are the other two sisters cooperating?" Allie asked eagerly, already able to envision the noisy family gatherings.

"Daniela and Margarita are twins. My mother despaired of ever getting them both married, because they took their own sweet time about it. Neither married until they turned thirty and had their own careers. Daniela is a stockbroker. Margarita is a teacher. Daniela has two daughters and insists that she's through. Margarita has a son and a daughter, but she's expecting again and the doctor thinks it might be twins. Needless to say, my mother is ecstatic."

"I think I would love your mother," Allie said wistfully. "And your sisters. I love my parents dearly, but they never anticipated having children at all. They're both college professors and loved the quiet world of academia. I came as a total shock to them. Not that they didn't adore me and give me everything a child could possibly want, but I always knew that I was a disruption in their lives. They would be horrified if they knew that I'd sensed that."

Ricky's gaze narrowed. "Do they know you're in the hospital?"

"Yes, and before you judge them, they did offer to fly down, but it's the beginning of the fall semester."

"So what?"

"I couldn't ask them to do that. It would disrupt their classes."

Ricky stared at her incredulously. "You can't be serious. That's why they're not here?"

"They're not here because I told them not to come," Allie said defensively. "We would have ended up in a hotel, anyway. It just didn't make sense."

"You've just been through a terrible storm," he said indignantly. "Your house was destroyed. You're in the hospital. They should have been on the next plane, no matter what you said."

Allie refused to admit that a part of her had hoped they would do exactly that, but she had known bet-

ter. They had taken her at her word, because it had
suited them. It didn't mean they didn't love her. They
were just practical, and they'd never been especially
demonstrative except for those weeks after she'd lost
her hearing. That it had taken such a thing to get their
attention had grated terribly.

"I won't defend my parents to you," she said stiffly.

He seemed about to say something more but fell silent instead, his expression troubled.

Allie waited, and eventually he met her gaze.

"What will you do?" he asked.

"Stay here a day or two longer, I imagine. Then the
insurance company will no doubt insist the hospital
kick me out no matter what. Or I suppose they could
send me to an intermediate treatment center of some
kind for rehab if the insurance would cover it."

"A nursing home? At your age?"

"There aren't a lot of options," Allie said. "Besides,
I don't think it will come to that. I'm getting stronger
every minute."

"I saw you limping when I came in here. You're
probably not even supposed to be on your feet, are
you?"

The doctors had insisted on a few days of bed rest
for her ankle and knee, but she didn't have the luxury
of waiting. She had to prove she was capable of managing on her own. "It's nothing," she insisted.

"I could ask your doctors about that," he challenged.
"Would they agree?"

She frowned at him. "Really, you don't need to
worry about it. You did your job. I'll manage."

"Allie—"

"Really," she said, cutting off his protest. "It's not

your concern. The social worker is looking into some possibilities."

"I can just imagine," he said dryly. He stood up, then moved to the window to stare outside as if something out there fascinated him.

Allie used the time to study him. Even if he hadn't been the one to rescue her and carry her out of the rubble, she would have recognized his strength. He was slender, but the muscles in his arms, legs and shoulders were unmistakable in the snug-fitting jeans and T-shirt he wore.

More important, there was strength of character in that handsome face.

As she watched, it was evident that he was mentally struggling with himself over something. She didn't doubt that it had to do with her. He seemed to be feeling some misplaced sense of responsibility for her predicament and nothing she'd said thus far seemed to have lessened it.

Finally he faced her and spoke very deliberately. "I have a solution."

"To what?"

"Your situation," he said with a touch of impatience.

"Which is?"

"You need a place to stay."

She told him the same thing she'd said to Jane earlier and to him repeatedly. "It's not your problem. I'll work it out."

"I'm sure you will, eventually, but you'd like to get out of here now, right?"

She couldn't deny it. "Of course."

"Okay, then. You could come home with me."

She wasn't sure which of them was more startled

by the invitation. He looked as if he wanted to retract it the instant the words left his mouth. If she wouldn't impose on her friends, she surely wasn't about to impose on this man whose duty to her had ended when he saved her life.

"That's very kind of you, but—" she began, intending to reassure him.

"It's not like I'm there a lot," he said hurriedly, cutting off her automatic protest. "But I'd be there enough to satisfy the doctors, and it would be a roof over your head till you figure out what you want to do."

Before she could follow her first instinct and turn him down, he seemed to reach some sort of decision. His chin set stubbornly.

"I'm not taking no for an answer," he said, then headed for the door. "I'll speak to your doctors."

She launched herself off the bed and managed to get between him and the door. Her ankle throbbed with the effort. "You will not," she declared, trying not to wince at the pain. "I have no intention of being a burden on anybody, much less on someone I barely know."

"I don't think you have a choice," he said, his gaze unwavering.

"Of course there are choices," she insisted, even if most of them were impractical or unpalatable to someone who treasured her independence and didn't want to lose it even temporarily.

"Give me one."

"I'll go to a motel and hire a nurse," she said at once, grabbing at the first idea that came to her.

"Why waste that kind of money, when you can come with me? Do you have money to burn?"

"My homeowner's insurance will pay for the motel,

and my medical coverage will pay for the nurse," she said triumphantly, praying it was true.

"And where will you find this motel room?" he asked.

"Miami's a tourist destination. There are hundreds of hotel rooms."

"And most of them are either packed with tourists willing to pay two or three hundred dollars a night or are filled up with insurance adjusters, fly-by-night contractors who've swarmed down here hoping to make a quick killing doing repairs or people just like you who've been displaced by the hurricane and who got there first."

Allie sighed. He was probably right. "Then I'll go into a treatment center. How bad can it be? I'll only be there a few days."

Ricky shrugged. "If that's what you want," he said mildly. "Institutional food. Antiseptic smells. A hard hospital bed. If you prefer that to my comfortable guest room and my mother's home-cooked meals, which I'm sure she'll insist on bringing over, then go for it."

He wasn't playing fair. This room was already closing in on her. She doubted a change to another medical facility would be an improvement. And she'd definitely had her fill of bland, tasteless meals. Cuban food was her very favorite. Her mouth watered just thinking about sweet, fried plantains.

But could she move in with a man who was virtually a stranger? Especially one who stirred her hormones in an extremely disconcerting way?

As if he sensed that she was wavering, he gave her an irrepressible grin. "I won't even try to seduce you, if that's what's on your mind."

"Of course that's not on my mind," she protested a little too vehemently, even as a guilty flush crept up her cheeks. "Don't be ridiculous."

His grin spread. "If you say so, *mi amiga*."

Friend? she translated derisively. That's all she was to him? For a man she'd barely met forty-eight hours ago, it was actually quite a lot, but for reasons she probably shouldn't explore too closely, she found it vaguely insulting.

As if to contradict his own words, he lifted his hand and caressed her cheek, allowing his thumb to skim lightly, but all too sensually across her lips.

"Come on, Allie. A few days. It's a way out of here. That's what you want, isn't it?"

She swallowed hard. More than anything, she thought. More than anything, she wanted not just out of the hospital, but to go home with Enrique Wilder. The powerful yearning terrified her.

Not once in recent years had she given in to her own desires. She had become cautious and practical and self-protective. Heaven help her, without even realizing it, she had turned into her parents.

And two nights ago she had almost died. Maybe it was time she got back to living every single minute of every day.

"If you're absolutely sure that it won't be an inconvenience," she said finally, trying to ignore the wave of heat that continued to build simply from that light touch against her cheek. "And it's just for a few days."

His gaze locked with hers. "A few days," he echoed softly. He bent his head, his mouth hovering a scant inch above hers.

She yearned for him to close the distance, prayed

for it, but he jerked away instead, his expression suddenly troubled.

"Sorry," he said roughly. "I'll go find the doctor."

And then he was gone.

Sorry, Allie thought, sinking gingerly to the side of the bed. He was *sorry* he'd almost kissed her. She was trembling inside, filled with anticipation, and he was *sorry?*

If she could have backed out of this deal of theirs right now, she would have, but he would have no trouble at all guessing why. It would be too humiliating.

She could keep this crazy lust under control for a few days, especially if he was gone most of the time as he'd promised. It was probably no more than some out-of-whack hormonal reaction to coming so close to dying. It probably had nothing to do with Enrique Wilder at all.

He walked back into her room just then, and her pulse ricocheted at the sight of him. Okay, she thought despondently, it had everything to do with him.

But she could control it. She had to.

"All taken care of," he announced. "Let's get you out of here and go home."

Just the mention of the word did her in. Two days of pent-up emotions crowded into her heart. Allie thought of her own home, unrecognizable now, and had to fight the sting of tears. Ricky regarded her with alarm.

"What's wrong?" he asked. "What did I say?"

Before she could respond, he gave a low moan and knelt in front of her, taking her hand in his. "Home? That's it, isn't it? I'm sorry. You'll rebuild, Allie."

"Of course," she said with sheer bravado. "It just

caught me by surprise for a second, realizing that I don't actually have a home anymore."

"Well, for now you have a home with me," he reassured her.

The promise gave her comfort. It might be only a stopgap solution, but it was enough for now. For the first time since the whole ordeal began, she didn't feel quite so terrified and alone.

Chapter 4

Ricky wasn't sure exactly what had possessed him to insist on taking Allie home with him. He'd never in his life lived with a woman, had always assumed he wouldn't until he got married. He'd never been serious enough about any female to allow her into his world. A few had slept in his bed, but all had left the next morning, most never to return.

He protected his freedom with blunt words and clean breakups, when necessary. No woman had helped him decorate, not even his mother or sisters. From the color of the paint to the spread on the bed, he had chosen it all. It was a haphazard decor, because he'd made impulsive choices depending on what struck his fancy or what he'd been able to find when he'd had a few minutes to shop.

The house itself was small compared to the homes

in the area where Allie had lived—two bedrooms, a living room and dining area, one bath and a kitchen that could best be described as cozy. He could stand in the middle and reach the stove, the refrigerator or the table without taking a step. He considered the setup efficient, when he thought about it at all.

The house might not be fancy, but it suited him, because the backyard was filled with trees—grapefruit, avocado, mango and orange. There was nothing better than walking outside first thing in the morning and plucking fresh fruit for his breakfast. Once he'd seen those trees, nothing else had mattered.

The fenced-in yard was also perfect for Shadow. On the first day Ricky brought him home, the shepherd had chosen a favorite spot in the shade, which he guarded as zealously as Ricky did his privacy. Eventually Shadow had allowed Ricky to put a lawn chair in the vicinity to share it. They spent a lot of relaxing hours out there, Shadow dreaming his doggie dreams about chasing squirrels, and Ricky sipping a beer and thinking about as little as possible.

How was Allie going to fit into their bachelor life? Surely in just a few days—which was all he'd bargained for—she wouldn't get any ideas about putting artificial flower arrangements all over the place or sweet-smelling soaps in the bathroom.

Suddenly an image of lacy underwear and panty hose hanging over his shower rod popped into his head. But rather than making him shudder, he found himself eagerly anticipating the intrusion. Did she wear skimpy little scraps of sexy lingerie or practical cotton panties? The speculation heated his blood by several degrees.

"Geez," he muttered under his breath. "Get a grip."

He glanced over guiltily, relieved to see that her gaze was directed out the car window. Obviously he was losing it.

No, the truth was, he had lost it earlier, back at the hospital. When Allie had faced him in that faded hospital gown, looking battered and bruised and vulnerable, he hadn't been able to stop the invitation from crossing his lips. Even if he'd managed to keep silent initially, the impulse would eventually have overwhelmed him. He knew he could never in a million years have made himself walk out of that room without insisting on taking her along. The more she'd resisted, the more determined he had become. The woman got to him, no doubt about it.

Still, this wasn't a permanent living arrangement. It was only a temporary solution to an emergency, he reassured himself. It was nothing personal, though that didn't seem to stop his body from reacting predictably every time Allie so much as glanced his way. If he'd spotted her in one of the clubs on South Beach, he doubted he would have given her a second glance. She was too all-American, too petite for his taste. So why did he want her so badly? Because he'd mentally declared her off-limits the second he'd invited her into his home?

He felt a light tap on his shoulder, and his body jolted. He made himself turn, his gaze clashing briefly with troubled blue eyes.

"Are you really sure you want to do this?" she asked.

"I said I did, didn't I?" he said, grateful that she couldn't hear the tenseness in his voice.

"But you managed to get me sprung from the hospital. I'm sure I could manage on my own, if you wanted to drop me off."

"Where?" he asked testily, then cursed himself when he saw the quick rise of hurt in her eyes. There was the problem. She might not be able to detect the nuances of his voice, but she could obviously read his expression. And her every emotion was in her eyes, right there for even an insensitive jerk like him to see.

"I'm sorry," he apologized. "I shouldn't be reminding you that you don't have a home of your own."

"No, I'm the one who's sorry. You're being kind enough to do me a favor and I must seem incredibly ungrateful."

He reached for her hand, gave it a reassuring squeeze until they reached a red light and he could turn his head to face her so she could easily read his lips. "Allie, we're going to make this work, okay? Having you at my place is not going to be a problem," he lied, because to even hint otherwise would send her running and they both knew that, for now, she had nowhere else to go.

And, if he were being totally honest with himself, even if she had, he would have wanted her with him. The troubling question was why? Duty and obligation didn't seem to cover it. And any other possibility was unacceptable.

Allie desperately wanted to believe that Ricky meant what he said, because he was right—for the moment she had nowhere else to turn. She vowed, though, to cause as little disruption to his life as possible.

She had to admit to being curious about how a man like Enrique Wilder lived. He was all male, and she imagined that, despite his disclaimers earlier, he had his share of women. Would they have left their imprint on his home? Would his sisters have descended on the place to see that their baby brother had all the material comforts a man required?

She fought a smile as she realized that unless he had made a rushed phone call from the hospital, there had been no time for him to invite in a swarm of people to tidy up and ready the house for her arrival. His invitation had been too impulsive. She would be seeing exactly how Ricky lived, for better or for worse. The thought of tossed-aside shirts and damp towels on the bathroom floor, an atmosphere more male than any she had ever experienced, gave her an inexplicable little quiver of anticipation.

As Ricky turned onto a street in an older section of Coral Gables, Allie eagerly studied the neighborhood for clues about his personality. Small, modest homes sat cheek by jowl with brand-new mansions. She knew the area had strict rules for everything from setbacks to the color of paint that could be used, which somehow made the mix of old and new work.

She was relieved when Ricky pulled into the driveway of a stucco house with a tile roof and a lush front lawn, covered with a thick, green carpet of grass. Towering palms and dense shrubbery lined the walkway from the garage to the house. Bright-purple bougainvillea climbed up the sunlit walls of the garage. Other than a few stray branches and a littering of leaves, it didn't even look as if it had been touched by the hurricane. The landscaping seemed to have been in place for years, unlike her pitiful attempts to turn her yard into something more verdant than the small plots of green sod and one pin oak sapling the developer had considered sufficient for each property.

"It's lovely," she told Ricky, captivated by the effect.

When he would have led her inside, she stalled, peppering him with questions about the names of the various plants. To his credit, he not only knew, but responded with patience and increasing amusement.

"Allie, don't you think we could do this another time, perhaps when you're not in pain?" he finally asked. "I'll write it all down for you."

For a few minutes in her excitement she had actually forgotten about the pain and about the awkwardness of the circumstances. Now it all came flooding back.

"Sorry," she said, avoiding his gaze. "It's just that I love to garden and everything down here is so new to me. I'm still trying to figure out what works in this climate. Did you do this yourself?"

She had to make herself look at his mouth, so she could understand his response. Gazing at those sensual lips was not exactly a hardship, but she was beginning to realize that it was dangerous. The more she focused on his mouth, the more she wondered what it would feel like against her own.

Suddenly she realized she'd done it again, gotten lost in her own wicked thoughts, and had paid no attention to the words he was uttering.

"What?" she asked, an embarrassed flush climbing into her cheeks. "Could you say that again?"

"Am I talking too fast?"

"No, I just got distracted for a moment."

His eyes twinkled with knowing laughter. "Really? By what?"

She frowned at the teasing. "Never mind." She looked away.

He tucked a finger under her chin and turned her to face him. "I said that I did some of it. Fortunately, if you pick the right plants, the tropical climate takes care of the rest. Except for mowing the grass, I don't spend a lot of time worrying about upkeep."

"I imagine you don't have a lot of free time."

"No, and sometimes I can be gone for a couple of weeks at a stretch with virtually no notice."

"When there's an earthquake," she guessed.

"Or a flood. Any kind of natural disaster, really."

"I don't know how you do that. All that devastation and human suffering. It must be such sad work."

"Sometimes it is," he agreed. "But there are moments when we find a survivor against all the odds. That's what we have to focus on, the unexpected miracles."

He put his hand in the middle of her back and guided her up the walk. He unlocked the front door and opened it, then steadied her when a German shepherd bounded toward her. At a command from Ricky, the dog promptly sat, tail wagging as he stared up at her. Allie regarded the big dog warily.

Ricky caught her attention. "Allie, this is Shadow. He helped us to find you after the storm. Shadow, this is Allie. You remember her. Can you shake her hand?"

The dog raised his paw. Allie took it, then hunkered down to scratch the dog's ears. "Thank you, Shadow. I owe you."

"Offer him a doggie treat every now and then, and he'll be your pal forever," Ricky said. "I'll show you where I keep them. Just remember not to overdo it.

He doesn't need one every time he looks pitiful and begs. It works on my nieces and nephews, so he tries pretty regularly."

Allie chuckled. "I'll keep that in mind."

"Ready for a tour of the house?" Ricky asked. "It'll take about two minutes. Then, if you'd like to lie down for a while and rest, I'll try to come up with something for dinner."

"I've rested more than enough," Allie said. "I can help with dinner."

"Not tonight," he contradicted. "I promised the doctor you'd stay off that ankle as much as possible for the next couple of days."

Her gaze clashed with his. "You shouldn't make promises you can't keep."

"Oh, I think I could find some way to keep you in bed if I absolutely had to," he said.

His eyes smoldered in a way that made Allie swallow hard and look away. Surely he didn't mean… She met his gaze again. Oh, but he did. She could recognize the desire even without hearing the likely sensual undertone of his voice.

"About that tour," she said, all too aware that her voice probably sounded breathless.

He grinned. "Right this way."

From the moment they stepped into his living room, she knew that Ricky—and no one else—was responsible for the decor. The overstuffed sofa looked comfortable and very masculine. The leather recliner that faced the television sat next to a small table that was littered with newspapers.

The walls had been painted a bright yellow with white woodwork. One large, unframed oil painting hung on the wall behind the sofa, a scene of the Everglades at sunset with a vibrant poinciana tree in the foreground. The streaky orange shades of the sunset and the red blossoms of the tree were so vivid they seemed unreal, but Allie knew the artist had gotten it exactly right, because she had seen the setting herself. She stood in front of the painting, as awed by it as she had been by the real thing.

"It's magnificent."

"Thank you."

His vaguely embarrassed expression caught her attention more than the polite response. "You painted it?" she asked, astounded.

"Yes," he admitted with a diffident shrug.

"Ricky, it's amazing. Have you done others?"

"One or two. Nothing much."

"Why on earth not?"

"It's just dabbling," he protested.

Her gaze narrowed as she studied him. "I imagine someone told you that real men don't paint."

His lips quirked ever so slightly. "My father did express some concern about it."

"Then your father is an idiot."

He placed a hand over his heart in exaggerated shock. "Don't let my mother hear you say that."

"I'll say it to her or to him," she said fiercely.

"Allie, it's okay. It's not as if I grew up desperate to be an artist. I wasn't prevented from pursuing it. I paint when I have the time or inclination."

"You're wasting an incredible talent."

"I'm not. I love my career. I am exactly where I was meant to be with my life, doing something that really matters." He rubbed a thumb across her cheek. "Thanks for being so ready to defend me, though."

She restrained herself from arguing. Perhaps he *was* doing what he'd chosen to do with his life. After all, she barely knew him. She was in no position to judge his choices, to assume he was a firefighter because his father considered that more appropriate for a son than being a painter.

Maybe she had been so quick to do battle on his behalf because fate had taken her own choice away from her. Still, losing her music to fate was one thing—losing it to a domineering parent would have been quite another. Had she been in Ricky's position, she would have fought like anything to keep her music in her life.

As they completed the tour, she discovered a few more examples of his work in the other rooms of the house, all vibrant with color, all capturing scenes of the unspoiled Florida landscape. The paintings, even the small ones, dominated the rooms in which they were hung. Wisely, though, Allie kept from forcing another debate of the wisdom of his decision to relegate painting to the status of a hobby.

The guest room he showed her to was spotless and uncluttered. There was a small dresser and a comfortable bed with a dark-blue spread that picked up the exact shade of the tumultuous ocean in the painting that hung above the headboard.

"There should be room in the closet," he said, opening the door to demonstrate.

Allie managed a tremulous smile. "For what?" It was hard to believe that all she owned were the robe, underwear, sneakers, jeans and T-shirt Jane had bought and taken to the hospital.

Ricky looked disconcerted, then apologetic. "I'm sorry. I wasn't thinking. I'll put out a call to my sisters. They can bring you a few things or go shopping for you, whichever you'd like."

She gestured toward the outfit she was wearing. "As long as you have a washer and dryer, I can make do with this for a day or so. Then I'll go shopping."

"Trust me, they all have clothes to spare, some no doubt with the price tags still on them. Maria and Elena are always battling their weight. They buy things too small, counting on them as an incentive to lose a few pounds. I'm sure they will be delighted to get them out of their closets, so the outfits no longer mock them for their failure."

Allie chuckled, totally understanding their feminine logic. Ricky, however, was clearly mystified by it. "Will you explain to them that you only want to relieve them of the clothes that are too small?" she asked.

Ricky looked justly horrified by the suggestion. "Are you crazy? I value my life too much to even hint at such a thing. Let me call, Allie. You'll feel better when you have some things of your own. A few days from now, next week, when you're feeling stronger and have your insurance money in hand, you can shop to your heart's content."

Years of struggling for independence made her want to refuse, but common sense told her he was right. "Thank you, but please, don't let them overdo it. One or two things will be plenty. The insurance adjuster promised to have an initial check for me by next week, so I won't have to rely on my credit cards to shop."

He nodded approvingly. "I'll call now, but I'll tell them not to come by until morning, when you've had a chance to settle in. Anything else you need—a favorite hand lotion, shampoo, cosmetics?"

"I have a few things from the hospital that will do for now."

"You're sure?"

"Absolutely," she said, determined not to put him or his sisters to any more trouble than she already had. "By the way, when you speak to them, how will you explain me?"

"You mean the fact that there's a beautiful woman living in my house who happens to be all but naked?"

"You can't say that," she protested, even as laughter bubbled up. She had a feeling he was scoundrel enough to make exactly that sort of outrageous remark.

"Of course I can," he said. "Then again, that will bring them flying straight over, so I won't. I'll simply tell them the truth."

"And what will they think?"

"That you must be an astonishing woman for me to break my rule."

"What rule?" she asked with a frown.

His solemn gaze locked with hers. "Never to let a woman move in with me unless I intend to marry her."

Allie had to struggle to keep him from seeing how shaken she was by his admission that he didn't make a habit of inviting women into his home to stay. Why her? she wondered.

Because he pitied her, of course. Nothing else. How *could* it be, when he hardly knew her. Still, she couldn't stop the feeling of disappointment that washed over her.

Ridiculous, she chided herself. This was a temporary haven. It had been offered as such, and what kind of idiot would she be to wish for anything more?

But she did, she admitted. She liked the lingering looks they'd shared, looks that sizzled with tension and promise. She liked the little shivers of anticipation that his unexpected touch sent through her. She liked the male scent of him, the hard feel of his muscles.

She simply liked Enrique Wilder, because for the first time in years, she felt completely and totally like a woman. Even if nothing more happened between them, even if all he offered from now on was a room and a roof over her head, he had given her an incredible gift. He had reminded her that she had lost her hearing years ago, not her life.

Until she'd met him, she had convinced herself that what she had was enough. That because her days were crammed full of activities, she was living. Now she knew better.

Because none of that had made her feel half as alive as one glance from her new roommate.

Chapter 5

"Could you repeat that?" Maria asked when Ricky called and gave his oldest sister a shortened version of Allie's clothing predicament.

He should have known there was going to be trouble. "Which part of 'She needs clothes' didn't you understand?" he asked impatiently.

"Forget the clothes. I'm still on the part where you asked this total stranger to move in with you."

"Temporarily," he reminded her.

"She must be gorgeous."

He saw no point in denying the obvious, since his sister would see Allie for herself before another day was out. He thought of her pixie face, her untamed curls, the killer eyes. "She is, in an all-American way."

"Not your usual leggy brunette?"

He hadn't realized that his habits were so predictable that even his big sister knew his type. "No," he admitted.

"But you are attracted to her?"

"That's not the point."

"What is the point?"

"She's all alone with nowhere to go. I have room for her. It's not a big deal, Maria. I'd do the same for anyone."

"Did you happen to rescue anyone else the other day?"

Ricky saw exactly where she was heading with the question. "Yes," he replied warily. "But it wasn't the same. Most of those people had family."

"And Allie doesn't?"

His blood still boiled when he thought of her parents staying wherever the hell they were, rather than coming to be with her. "Not in Miami," he said tightly.

"Uh-oh," his sister muttered.

"Uh-oh what?"

"You've gone all protective, haven't you? I can hear it in your voice."

"What if I have? Somebody has to look out for her."

"You don't think you're carrying this hero-to-the-rescue tendency of yours a little too far?"

"No, I don't."

"How old is this woman?"

"I don't know. Twenty-nine, thirty, maybe."

"Ah," she said dryly. "An actual grown-up. And you don't think she can look out for herself?"

Ricky ignored the implication that he usually dated women who were less than mature. Instead, he tried to imagine how Allie would react to any suggestion that she couldn't manage on her own. He tempered his response accordingly. "Well, of course she could, but why should she have to, when I can pitch in for a little while?"

His sister muttered something in Spanish suggesting he was delusional, then added, "I'll be there in an hour."

"Not tonight," he countered. "In the morning. She's exhausted."

"There you go again, being protective of her."

"Doctor's orders," he contradicted, grateful to have them to fall back on. He could produce a list of very specific instructions if he had to. "He wants her to rest."

"Of course," Maria said with a laugh. "I wonder exactly how much rest she'll get in your bed."

"Dammit, Maria, she is not in my bed. She's in the guest room."

"For how long, I wonder?"

Ricky bit back a curse. "Maybe you should just stay away," he said. "I'll call one of my more understanding sisters."

"When it comes to speculating on your love life, *niño,* no one is more understanding than I am. I'll be there first thing in the morning."

"On good behavior," he instructed.

"I won't embarrass you," she promised.

"And you'll call the others?" he asked, not sure he was prepared to endure three more inquisitions, much less his mother's cross-examination once she got wind of Allie's presence. His mother would make this conversation with Maria seem like little more than idle chitchat.

"With pleasure," Maria said.

Ricky could all but see the grin spreading across her face. "Don't bring all of them in the morning," he warned. "Just a few clothes."

"Oh, Ricky, Ricky, Ricky," she chastised. "Do you really think I'll be able to keep any of them away?"

"Try," he pleaded. "Allie's not up to it."

"Allie or you?" she taunted.

"Both of us, okay. Just you, Maria, and I will be forever in your debt."

"Really?" she said, sounding suddenly more co-operative. "And in return for my help, you'll keep the boys for a weekend? All of them?"

He sighed, knowing what an incentive that would be for her to keep his other sisters away from his house. "I will," he agreed. "Two weekends if you can keep Mama away from here, as well."

Maria laughed. "Now, that, little brother, is beyond even my powers of persuasion. I'll have to settle for one weekend alone with my husband."

"At least try," he pleaded again. "I'll even go to Pedro's next three concerts."

Everyone in the family dreaded the concerts, because seven-year-old Pedro and his classmates had more enthusiasm than musical talent. The events were torture, and excuses not to attend inventive and wide-spread. And poor little Pedro was beginning to catch on. To have his heroic uncle Enrique attend would go a long way toward improving his status among his classmates. Maria knew it.

"I will convince Mama to stay home tomorrow if I have to tie her to a chair," she said with grim determination. "And the next concert is on Thursday. Plan to be there."

Ricky grimaced. "You do your part and I'll put it on my calendar," he promised without enthusiasm.

Satisfied that he had done what he could to keep Allie from being intimidated by a gathering of the Wilder females, he hung up and turned his attention to dinner. He had steaks in the freezer and plenty of vegetables for a salad. It wouldn't be fancy, but it would be filling. Allie needed to get her strength back, and he was going to need all of his to keep fending off his mother and sisters.

While Allie rested, he started the charcoal on the grill, defrosted the steaks in the microwave, then made the salad. He set the table on his patio and made sure the steaks were safely indoors and out of Shadow's reach. He'd learned his lesson the hard way. There wasn't a lot of human food the dog liked, but steak topped the list. Shadow could accomplish astonishing feats when there was a nice juicy slab of meat involved.

"Outside," he ordered the disappointed dog.

Shadow stood on the opposite side of the screen door, an expression of betrayal in his eyes.

"You're not going to make me feel guilty," Ricky added.

"Guilty about what?" Allie asked.

She had managed to slip into the kitchen without Ricky even being aware she was in the vicinity. He was going to have to remember that she moved so silently and watch what he said. Of course, unless she was right in front of him, he was safe enough, but it would be wise to remember it just on general principle.

"I thought you were sleeping," he said. "Wasn't the bed comfortable?"

"The bed was fine. And I did rest for an hour."

"Are you hungry?"

"Starved, actually. Everything they say about hospital food is true. It's tasteless. Wouldn't you think a place where the doctors keep telling you to eat to keep your strength up would do a better job of preparing something worth eating?"

"You would," he agreed. "Is steak okay? And I've fixed a salad."

"Perfect. What can I do to help?"

"That depends on what you'd like to drink? Iced tea? Coffee? Water? Beer?"

"Iced tea sounds wonderful. Shall I make it?"

Because she so obviously needed to make some sort of contribution, he pointed out the location of the teakettle and the tea bags. Unfortunately, the size of the kitchen all but guaranteed that they would keep bumping into each other as they moved around. Each brush of hip against hip, thigh against thigh made Ricky's blood sizzle. He was so aware of Allie, so blasted tempted to stop her in her tracks and kiss her that he finally grabbed the steaks and backed out the door.

"I'll be outside," he said. "Cooking."

She looked as relieved as he felt. "Will we eat out there?"

"Yes. The table's all set."

"I'll be out with the tea in a few minutes, then."

Ricky moved to the grill, closed his eyes and took a deep breath. It didn't calm the flutter of nerves at all. He couldn't imagine what was wrong with him. Women didn't make him nervous. In fact, he loved women. All women. He could flirt with the most intimidating female on earth without so much as a tingle of unease. He could dance slowly, sensually with the sexiest woman alive and experience no more than the expected stirring of arousal. So why was he acting like a love-struck teenager around Allie Matthews? Why was his body behaving as if he hadn't had sex for months?

Whatever the answer, Ricky was pretty sure he was going to hate it.

After Ricky went outside, Allie stood perfectly still and forced herself to draw in a deep, calming breath. No man had rattled her like that in years. Her only comfort was the fact that he had seemed as disturbed as she was.

"It's the situation," she muttered. "Of course we both feel a little awkward. He's apparently not used to having a woman underfoot, and I am definitely not used to bumping up against anyone so...*male* every time I turn around."

But what she felt wasn't awkwardness. Not exactly. What she felt was an edgy need, a hunger for something more than the whisper of his thigh against hers in a glancing contact that had lasted no longer than a heartbeat.

She had lost her virginity years ago, to a man she had thought herself in love with. Maybe she'd forgotten over time, but she couldn't recall that he had ever made her feel this wicked sense of anticipation, this unspoken awareness.

She had been nineteen when she had met Jared Yardley in one of her music classes. Only a few months later they'd had sex for the first time. She recalled feeling grown-up and vaguely thrilled by the decision that she was ready to take such a step. She didn't remember feeling much of anything during the act itself. Not that first time, which had been rushed and uncomfortable.

Nor any of the times after that, now that she thought about it. Once she'd lost her hearing and left school, they had broken up, and there had been no one in her life since. Living with the memory of that single experience of having a lover, she had assumed that was just the way sex was, and she couldn't imagine what all the hoopla was about. Now she was beginning to see that she might have gotten it all wrong.

If Ricky could make her feel hot and shivery at the same time with a casual touch, she had to wonder what he could do if he put his heart and soul into it.

She was so distracted by her speculation that she forgot to keep an eye on the teakettle. She was startled when Ricky came inside and stepped up to the stove to take the kettle off the burner.

"It was whistling," he explained, when she regarded him quizzically.

"Sorry. I wasn't paying attention. I usually watch for the steam."

"No problem."

"You can go back outside, if you want. I'll pour it over the tea bags."

"Trying to get rid of me, Allie?"

She swallowed hard at the teasing glint in his eyes. "Of course not. Why would I want to get rid of you?"

"I have a feeling I make you nervous. Do I?"

"Not you," she insisted. "The situation. I've never stayed with a man."

"Have you ever had roommates?"

"In college."

"Then think of this as the same thing."

She tried to compare living with Ricky to sharing space with the two giggling adolescents who'd been her freshman roommates. She shook her head. "Sorry, I don't think that's going to work."

"Why not?"

"Did you have roommates in college?"

"I didn't go away to college. I went right here in town. Later, though, I shared an apartment for a year."

"With a guy?"

He nodded.

"Was it the same as this?"

"Hardly," he said at once, then sighed. "Yeah, I see what you mean."

"So what are we going to do about it?" she asked, determined to discuss the situation sensibly and get it under control.

Ricky's expression turned thoughtful, then impish. "I do have one thought."

"Which is?"

He took a step closer, which had Allie instinctively backing toward the counter. He put a hand against the counter on either side of her, effectively trapping her.

"This," he said, lowering his head until his lips hovered just above hers.

Allie could feel the heat from his body reaching out to her. His breath fanned across her cheek. Anticipation stirred inside her as she waited and waited for him to close that infinitesimal distance.

When he did, when his mouth settled on hers, an amazing sense of calm and inevitability spread through her. The action was bold and unexpected, but the kiss itself was as light as the caress of a butterfly. It was unimaginably tender, shocking from a man who exuded such overwhelmingly masculine strength. Because it was so deliberately gentle it made her yearn, made her want things she had never imagined wanting, filled her with a sense of wonder.

Her pulse scrambled. Heat spread through her. And through it all there was the sensation of that wickedly persuasive mouth against hers, asking for more, hinting at everything but demanding nothing.

When he pulled back slowly, unwillingly, Allie uttered a harsh, "No," before she could stop herself. She felt his lips curve into a smile as they returned to hers for one more lingering caress.

She sighed when he abandoned her again, then avoided his gaze, until he captured her chin and gently forced her to face him.

"Better now?" he asked.

She blinked and tried to interpret the question. "Better?"

"Now that we've gotten that out of the way," he explained. "It was bound to happen sooner or later."

Was it? Allie hadn't guessed that when she'd agreed to move in temporarily. Hoped for it, maybe, but she assured herself she definitely hadn't grasped the inevitability of it.

"Because you can't go for more than a few hours without kissing a woman who's in close proximity," she said with what she hoped was just the right amount of teasing inflection.

Looking vaguely hurt by the question, he stepped away from her, leaving her feeling suddenly bereft.

"It won't happen again," he informed her, his expression serious and determined. "We'll just make sure not to come into the kitchen at the same time."

"Why?" she asked, before she could stop herself.

"Because I don't want you to think that I invited you here so I could take advantage of the situation." He ran a hand through his hair. "I thought it might relieve the tension to get the kiss out of the way. That was probably a mistake."

She could never bring herself to think of anything as wonderful as that kiss as a mistake. She studied him curiously. "Did it?"

"Did it what?"

"Relieve the tension for you?" It surely hadn't for her. If anything, she was more restless than ever, more anxious to know where a devastating kiss like that could lead.

Ricky looked shaken by the question. "Dammit, Allie, you don't ask much, do you? How can I answer that without causing you to run for the hills?"

"The truth might be a good place to start," she suggested.

He shook his head. "I don't think you're ready to hear the truth," he said, slamming through the back door and leaving her to stare after him.

She couldn't stop the smile that began at the corners of her mouth and spread. So, she thought with a touch of feminine satisfaction, it had gotten to him, too.

Knowing that made it a whole lot easier to pour the just-brewed tea into a pitcher, add a tray of ice cubes and carry it outside where she would have to face him. He was concentrating on the steaks with a frown knitting his forehead. She had a feeling that frown didn't have anything to do with worries over whether the meat was going to turn out rare or well-done.

He glanced up warily when she held out a glass of iced tea. "Thank you."

"You're welcome." She nodded toward the grill. "The steaks smell wonderful."

"They're almost done."

"Anything I can do?"

"Just have a seat," he said, then added pointedly, "over there."

Allie bit back a grin. Was he afraid she'd edge too close and distract him again? Maybe she should, but she wasn't bold enough for that. Instead, she dutifully settled into a chair at the round redwood picnic table, sat back and sipped her tea. Shadow came over to rest his head in her lap so she could scratch behind his ears. Or maybe he just meant to ingratiate himself in hopes of getting any leftover steak later.

"Did you speak to your sister?" she asked when Ricky eventually joined her at the table.

"Oh, yes," he said, his expression bland.

"Did she have a lot of questions?"

"My sister could put an investigative journalist to shame," he said, a grin tugging at his lips.

"Was she satisfied with your answers?"

"Temporarily," he admitted. "And she promised to hold off all the others for a day or two in exchange for me babysitting her sons for a weekend."

Allie laughed. "You bribed her?"

"You wanted peace and quiet, didn't you?"

"Not half as much as you did, apparently," she teased. "You don't think your sisters are going to make too much out of my presence here, do you?"

"Oh, yes," he said fervently. "You have no idea."

"Then I guess they'd better not catch us kissing," Allie said.

His frown returned. "There will be no more kissing," he declared with grim determination.

"Too bad," she said mildly, surprised at her own daring.

He carefully placed his fork on his plate and leaned toward her. "Allie, don't do this."

"Do what?" she asked innocently.

"Tempt me."

"Is that what I'm doing?" She truly hadn't been sure it was working. She was relieved to know it was.

"Blast it, you know you are," he said with evident frustration. "Stop it."

"Why?"

He blinked and stared. "Why what?"

"Why stop?"

"You know perfectly well that wasn't part of the deal."

"True," she agreed. "It's just a bonus."

"You don't have to feel obligated," he began.

Before he could continue, Allie felt something akin to fury begin to stir inside her. She wasn't totally familiar with the sensation, because she'd always been very slow to anger. Now it bubbled up, hot and urgent.

"Obligated," she said, her voice rising sufficiently to draw a warning *shush* from Ricky. She allowed her voice to climb one more decibel as she repeated the word.

Ricky winced.

"I do not feel *obligated* to do anything," she snapped. "When you kissed me, I kissed you back because I wanted to, not because I felt *obligated*. Since when did that word have anything at all to do with me moving in here? Were you thinking that sooner or later I'd feel *obligated* to do more than exchange a few little kisses? Despite your earlier denials, is that what this invitation was really all about?"

Ricky rubbed his hand across his face. Clearly, he hadn't expected her to tear into him. "Look, that is not what I meant," he declared, his expression defensive. "Of course, you don't owe me anything for letting you stay here. There are no strings at all. None. That was exactly the point I was trying to make, when you got all hot under the collar. Maybe you misunderstood what I said."

"Maybe I couldn't hear you, but I could read your lips just fine. This isn't about me being deaf."

He winced. "No, of course it isn't. I'm sorry if I sounded as if I thought it was. It's just that there are going to be some adjustments here. We hardly know each other. There's bound to be some miscommunication. It doesn't have anything to do with whether or not you can hear."

Allie sighed. Perhaps she had overreacted...on that point, anyway. She did tend to get defensive occasionally when dealing with the hearing world.

"Maybe we should start over, establish some boundaries," she suggested.

"I thought that was what I was trying to do when I said there would be no more kissing," he said with evident frustration.

"I suppose that would be a good place to start," she said, hiding her reluctance to agree to any such thing.

Of course, despite the relief that spread across Ricky's face, she already had a pretty good sense that any such agreement was absolutely, positively doomed to failure.

Chapter 6

Ricky had never been so relieved to get an emergency call in his life as he was when Allie was sitting right across from him, all but daring him to kiss her again.

Oh, she was saying all the right words, agreeing that there would be no more moments like that one in the kitchen when he'd discovered that she tasted better and was far more intoxicating than wine. But her eyes held a challenge. In fact, he was pretty sure that she was going to dare him to break their agreement before the bargain was even sealed.

And he would do it, too, because he wanted her, now more than ever. He'd convinced himself for about ten seconds that it was circumstances and proximity that had him aching with need, but he was pretty sure now that he knew better. It was Allie, pure and simple. Intentionally or not, she was going to drive him crazy.

So when his cell went off, he all but bolted, not just from the backyard, but from the house. He kept right on going to the station even before he'd heard the message with the details of the emergency. For all he knew, it could have been Tom wanting to sneak in a quick game of poker. It didn't matter, as long as it got him away from temptation.

As it turned out, the lieutenant had called them in on standby because of an imminent hurricane threat to the Louisiana Gulf Coast. That meant another long night of waiting, just in case there was devastation similar to what had happened in Miami. Normally the waiting made Ricky restless, but tonight the effect was compounded by the fact that he'd left Allie waiting for him at home.

He reached for the phone, then realized belatedly that he could hardly call. She wouldn't even know the phone was ringing. And he had no other way to get word to her about when he might get home again.

"Blast it," he muttered, slamming the receiver back into place. He tried to tell himself that he owed her nothing, but he simply couldn't leave her there to wonder what had become of him.

"What's wrong with you?" Tom asked, regarding him curiously. "Did you have to cancel a hot date?"

"No, it's Allie," he responded without thinking.

Tom's eyes lit up. "Allie, as in the beauty you plucked from the rubble the other day? What about her?"

Ricky had really hoped not to get into this with his partner. Tom would make way too much out of it, and Ricky would wind up as the butt of endless good-natured joking around the station. Not that the ribbing would be a new thing, but for some reason he didn't want Allie's name tossed around as if she were just another conquest.

"Never mind. It's nothing," he said. "I'll figure something out."

Tom regarded him with feigned hurt. "Who better to help than me, your buddy, your pal, the man you trust with your life?"

"You can't help. You're in the same boat I'm in, right here, waiting to sail, so to speak."

Tom straddled a bench and beckoned to Ricky. "Sit. Talk to me."

Ricky surmised his friend wasn't going to let the subject drop. With a sigh he sat. "Allie's at the house," he began.

"Your house?" Tom asked, eyes wide with shock.

"Yes, my house," he retorted impatiently. "Whose did you think I meant?"

"You could have meant your mother's."

Which probably would have been the smart place to take Allie from the outset, Ricky concluded. Neutral turf. Oh, his mother might have pestered him with questions, but at least his denials that Allie meant anything to him would have been more believable if she was staying with his family, rather than him.

It would also have made it more difficult for those sizzling kisses to lead them both into more dangerous territory. Under his mother's watchful gaze, he would have been lucky to steal a peck on the cheek.

Oh, well, he thought with a sigh. It was too late now.

Tom regarded him with approval. "So, the beautiful Allie is at your house. Very smooth, Enrique. Quick work."

"She didn't have anyplace else to go," he said defensively. "None of which is the point."

Tom grinned, obviously enjoying Ricky's discomfort. "Then explain the point. I'm all ears."

"I left tonight before I knew we were going to be stuck here indefinitely. Now I don't have any way to get word to her."

"You can't…" He glanced toward the phone, then nodded with sudden understanding. "Of course you can't."

Since leaving her there wondering and worrying, particularly after the way he'd bolted, was completely unacceptable, Ricky concluded he had only one choice. "Can you cover for me?" he asked Tom. "I'll run home, explain things and be back here in twenty minutes. We won't take off that fast, even if a call comes the second I'm out the door."

For once Tom didn't indulge in his usual taunting. He just nodded. "Go."

"Thanks, pal. I owe you one. I'll be back in twenty minutes, tops."

Ricky was halfway to the door before Tom hollered, "Just don't hang around for any hanky-panky."

"Allie and I are not engaging in any hanky-panky," Ricky retorted. *Not yet, anyway.*

He actually made it home in five minutes and was surprised to find most of the house in darkness except for a lamp in the living room. The remains of their dinner had been cleared away, the dishes washed. He headed down the hall to the guest room, then cursed when he saw the light was out. Allie was probably asleep and he was going to have to wake her, no doubt scaring her half to death in the process.

Leave her a note, a little voice murmured in his head. He acknowledged it might be the thoughtful, sensible thing to do for both their sakes, but that didn't seem to slow his progress toward her room.

He eased the door open and peeked inside. The instant the light from the hallway flooded into the room, Allie sat straight up in bed, her eyes wide with alarm.

"Ricky?"

He flipped on the overhead light, then stepped inside so she could see his face. "Sorry," he said, chagrined. "I didn't know whether to wake you or not. I'm going to be stuck at the station for hours and I might have to go out of town. I couldn't think of any other way to let you know."

He tried not to notice that her tousled hair was skimming shoulders that were bare as she clutched the sheet to her breasts. Sweet heaven, the woman was naked. His imagination seized on that and stripped away the sheet before he could get a tight rein on it. Fortunately her gaze was locked on his face, so perhaps she didn't notice the unmistakable sign of his arousal behind the zipper of his suddenly uncomfortable jeans.

"A hurricane?" she guessed. "The one heading for Louisiana?"

"Exactly."

"I saw the news reports. Is there anything you want me to do for you here if you have to go? Shadow...?"

"He'll stay with me. Just keep an eye on things," he said. "Make yourself at home. And don't forget that Maria is coming in the morning. She has a key, so don't be startled if she just walks in. She knows you won't hear her knock."

She nodded. "I'll be waiting for her."

He dragged his gaze away and took a step back. "I'd better go. Good night, Allie."

"Good night. Stay safe."

He turned off the light and carefully shut the door, then leaned against the opposite wall and waited for his pulse to stop racing. He was in trouble here. Big trouble.

All the way back to the station he thought of her last words to him. *Stay safe.* She had said it as if she actually might worry about him. When was the last time someone had done that? Oh, of course his family worried, but they'd had years to get used to his comings and goings, to accept the risks he took. Allie was the first woman he'd allowed to get close enough to be affected by his well-being, the first one he'd left behind to worry.

He told himself not to let that matter. If his mind was on Allie at all, he could lose concentration on whatever job had to be done. That would put not only his life but Tom's at risk, to say nothing of whatever victim they might be attempting to rescue.

He had to forget all about her, block her from his mind, and that was that. Unfortunately, as he'd already discovered in a few brief days, that particular feat was going to be easier said than done.

Allie had stayed awake for a long time after Ricky left. She'd been stunned the night before, not by him walking into her room, but by his thoughtful return to let her know that he might have to leave town. She doubted he was used to being accountable to anyone.

She was sitting at the kitchen table, stirring sugar into her coffee, when she glanced up and saw a beautiful, dark-haired, dark-eyed woman surveying her intently. The family resemblance would have been unmistakable even if she hadn't seen a photograph of all the Wilders the night before.

"Hello," she said tentatively. "Maria?"

A grin identical to Ricky's spread across the woman's face. "And you must be Allie. I hope I didn't scare you. I tried not to sneak up on you."

"Unfortunately, having people sneak up on me is pretty much a given in my life. At least my heart doesn't leap out of my chest anymore."

Maria chuckled, then sobered as she stared longingly at the pot of coffee. "Thank goodness. Can I have some of that? We were running late this morning at my house and I left to take the kids to school before I could get my first cup."

Since she was already reaching into the cupboard for a mug, Allie concluded she didn't really expect a response. Because she knew what it was like to need a jolt of caffeine to feel civilized, she waited as the other woman poured the coffee, stirred in three heaping teaspoons of sugar, then took her first sip.

"Ah, heaven," Maria murmured, her expression content. She glanced around. "So, where's my brother?"

"He was called in to work last night. He thought he might have to go to Louisiana."

"He left you all alone on your first night here?"

Allie grinned at her apparent indignation. "He does have a job. I doubt his boss would care that he has a temporary houseguest."

Maria's gaze narrowed. "Then this is only temporary?"

"Of course. He just offered to let me stay here so

I could get out of the hospital. The doctors wouldn't release me until I knew where I was going and had someone around who could make sure I rested. Your brother took pity on me. As soon as I make other arrangements, I'll be moving out."

Maria laid her hand on Allie's. "Do me a personal favor, okay? Don't be too quick to go."

Allie regarded her with confusion. "Why?"

"My brother might not admit it, but he needs someone in his life."

"But what makes you think *I* should be that someone? You don't really know me. He doesn't, either, for that matter."

"He invited you to stay here. That alone tells me quite a lot. As for me, you can spend the next hour satisfying my curiosity."

"Oh?" Allie said cautiously.

"I want to know everything about you, all the deep, dark secrets, all the hopes and dreams."

Startled by Maria's unrepentant determination to dig into her life, Allie fell silent.

"Uh-oh, I've come on too strong, haven't I?" Maria said. "Sorry. It's big-sister syndrome. I usually don't get this much privacy with Ricky's women, so my curiosity is never satisfied. It's very frustrating. I suppose it doesn't really matter, because they're usually gone in no time at all."

She smiled warmly. "Something tells me, though, that you have staying power."

Allie was stunned by the assessment. How could Maria come to such a conclusion based on a meeting that hadn't even gone on for fifteen minutes yet?

"Sisterly instinct?" she asked.

"Exactly. You're beautiful. You're vulnerable."

When Allie would have protested, Maria held up her hand. "Maybe not typically and not for long, but for the moment you definitely require a little extra pampering, a certain amount of macho protectiveness." Her smile turned smug. "And you are in his house. I rest my case." She took a mock bow.

Allie chuckled. "Very confident, aren't you?"

"Very." Her smile faltered. "Unless you're not interested in him. You do find our Enrique attractive, don't you?"

"I'd have to be blind, as well as deaf, not to find him attractive," Allie admitted without hesitation. "Beyond that…?" She shrugged. She was not going to bring up those kisses. She was not even going to think about those kisses, much less discuss them with his sister.

"It's a start," Maria declared with evident satisfaction. "Now then, do you want to take a look at the clothes I brought along? I stopped short of raiding my sisters' closets, so what you're getting comes from mine. It was easier than trying to explain to them why they couldn't come along this morning. Ricky was afraid that you would find all four of us at once to be overwhelming."

"Are the others like you?" Allie asked.

Maria chuckled. "I like to think they're worse, but yes, pretty much."

"I can't wait to meet them, then," Allie said honestly. "But Ricky was right. All of you at once would have been a little terrifying."

Maria regarded her with understanding. "Your whole world must seem a little off-kilter now. I can't imagine going to bed in a home, with belongings that you treasure, and then waking up to discover that everything, including the house, has been destroyed. Was anything at all salvageable?"

"To tell you the truth, I don't know. I came here straight from the hospital, so I haven't been able to go back and sift through the debris to see if anything's left."

"Would you like to do that now?" Maria offered. "I could take you. You might feel better if you could find some things of your own."

Allie desperately wanted to take her up on the offer, but she knew she wasn't strong enough physically for the ordeal. "I'm afraid I don't have the stamina just yet. And my ankle and knee are still in pretty bad shape."

"Of course. What was I thinking?" Maria apologized. "You let me know whenever you're ready. If Ricky doesn't have time to take you, I will. Or the family and I can go for you."

"I couldn't ask you to do that. You've already done too much."

"I've taken a few things out of my closet. What's the big deal? To tell you the truth, I'm glad to be rid of them. I bought them too small and they're mocking me."

Allie tried unsuccessfully to hide a grin.

"I see Ricky told you about my habit of deluding myself when it comes to my weight," Maria said. "A woman in this family has no secrets. Well, no matter, you will put them to good use, so there was a reason I bought them, wasn't there?"

"Before we look at the clothes, could you do me a favor? I'd like to let my former neighbor know where I am. Otherwise, she'll waste a trip to the hospital."

"Give me the number and I'll call right now."

Once the call to Jane was made and Maria had managed to satisfy her elderly neighbor that Allie was in good hands, Ricky's sister took her into the guest room. To Allie's amazement she found a huge pile of clothes on the bed. There were shorts, slacks, blouses and dresses, all still tagged an optimistic size eight.

"I know," Marie said ruefully when she saw Allie examining a tag. "These hips haven't been in a size eight in ten years, but I can dream, can't I?" She surveyed Allie. "Will they be too big for you?"

"No, perfect, I imagine. I'll choose one or two to get by with—"

"Don't be ridiculous. Keep them all. If there are any you don't want, give them back later."

"Then let me pay you, at least."

"Absolutely not. They might not even be to your taste. The important thing is that they'll do in a pinch."

"I insist on paying you for anything I keep," Allie repeated firmly. "That's only fair. Then you can buy something else."

"Whatever," Maria said dismissively, sifting through the stack until she hit on a bright-blue sundress. "Try this. It will be gorgeous on you. Very sexy."

Because she'd never had anyone to go on shopping excursions with her and had always envied the fun it would be to try on clothes and giggle over the ones that looked absurd or get advice on the ones that looked best, she reached for the dress.

It wasn't her style. It was too revealing by far, but the color would be nice with her eyes, she thought, as she stripped to her underwear and slid the dress over her head.

It fit like a dream. She could tell even before she turned to look in the mirror. The silky fabric fell like a whisper to caress her thighs before ending just above her knees. It clung to her breasts, barely held in place by spaghetti straps.

Her gaze shifted in search of Maria's reflection in the mirror only to find Ricky's stunned face instead. She could see the muscles in his neck work as he swallowed hard. Her own mouth went dry and she pivoted slowly to face him.

"I was just…"

"You look…"

She grinned, anxious to know what he had been about to say. "You first."

"Amazing," he said, his gaze still riveted. "You look amazing. That dress was made for you."

"I don't really have anyplace to wear it."

"Sure you do," he contradicted. "We have a date to go dancing, remember?"

She was surprised that he remembered the promise he'd made when she was so terrified that she might be paralyzed. "I thought you'd probably forgotten all about that."

"I never forget an invitation to hold a gorgeous woman in my arms."

They were both startled when Maria waved a hand between them to get their attention. "I'll just be going now," she said, barely containing her laughter as she added, "As if either of you will care."

"I heard that," Ricky said, his gaze returning to Allie.

Allie felt her skin begin to burn under the intensity of his scrutiny.

"You're back," she said, then winced at the statement of the obvious.

His eyes twinkled. "I am."

"You didn't have to leave town?"

He shook his head. "The storm weakened and veered back out to sea. Unless it strengthens and turns again, Louisiana should be in the clear. Then we'll have to wait to see about Texas or Mexico."

"That's great."

He blinked, then tore his gaze away. "I'm going to take a shower. Did you have breakfast?"

"Yes, but I can make you something."

He shook his head. "I ate at the station."

Allie nodded, feeling yesterday's awkwardness stealing through her again. What would he normally do with the rest of his day? She didn't want to interfere with whatever plans he might have made.

"Look, you do whatever you want to do. I'll probably go out back and read for a while, then take a nap."

"In that dress?" he inquired, his expression amused.

She glanced down, stunned to see that she was still wearing the sundress. "Of course not. I'll change." She gestured toward the pile of clothes. "Your sister got carried away."

"So I see."

Fumbling a little as she tried to untangle the hangers, she began putting the clothes in the closet without even examining them. A moment later she felt a tap on her shoulder.

"Yes?" She faced Ricky. Hands jammed in his pockets, he looked uncomfortable.

"Want to go somewhere for lunch?" he asked. "If you're not too tired."

She nodded. "That would be nice."

"I have to go to my nephew's soccer game after that. You can come along if you're up to it, or I can bring you back here."

Allie desperately wanted to go along, to feel as if she were becoming a part of this huge extended family of his, but the fact was she still tired easily.

"Can we play that by ear?"

"Absolutely."

Then he was gone and she was left clutching an armload of clothes. Her decision to stay here was getting more complicated by the second. The undeniable heat between them, his sister's generosity, a lifelong yearning for boisterous siblings and close family ties, it was all too alluring. She was very much afraid she might start wanting something that wasn't in the cards.

But years ago she had vowed never to let fear control her life. This experience might be totally unexpected, it might come to a painful conclusion, but in the meantime, she was going to savor every second of it.

Chapter 7

Ricky took an icy shower to cool down enough to face Allie again. That dress his sister had brought over ought to be banned...except in the privacy of his home. He wouldn't mind seeing Allie in it night and day. It was only a sundress, nothing fancy, but it did devastating things with her already potent eyes, drew attention to every dip and curve of her body, revealing way too much satiny skin in the process. He'd promised to take her dancing so she could wear it, but he already hated the prospect of other men ogling her.

When he went looking for her after his shower, he was relieved to find that she'd changed, though the white shorts and T-shirt she had on now weren't much of an improvement. She still looked way too tempting. Apparently his displeasure was evident, because she frowned when she saw the way he was studying her.

"Is everything okay?"

"Fine," he said tersely. "Are you ready to go?"

"Whenever you are," she said at once.

He gestured toward the door, then followed her out, trying to keep his gaze focused on something other than the sway of those slender hips and the bare expanse of shapely thighs. At this rate he was going to have to start buying his jeans in a larger size.

"Any preferences for lunch?" he asked when they were in the car.

"It's up to you. Whatever works with your plans."

"Are you always so agreeable?" he inquired irritably.

Her gaze seared him. "I thought I was being considerate," she said stiffly. "If there's a problem, I can stay here."

Ricky sighed. "Absolutely not. The only problem is me. I'm tired and cranky and taking it out on you."

"Maybe you'd rather take a nap than go to lunch," she suggested as if he were an irritable toddler.

Ricky ground his teeth together. "We're going to lunch," he insisted, glad she couldn't hear his tone of voice, which was less than gracious. "I know the perfect spot. It's guaranteed to put me in a better mood."

She gave him a wry look. "Then by all means, let's go there."

Even as he drove across the Rickenbacker Causeway, Ricky could feel the tension slipping away. With the sky a brilliant blue and the water of both Biscayne Bay and the Atlantic sparkling, it was hard to think about anything other than how lucky he was to live in such a place.

He glanced at Allie and saw that she, too, looked more relaxed as she studied the narrow strip of palm-tree-lined beach and the water beyond. He tapped her arm, drawing her attention.

"Can't beat the view, can you? Look back toward the city," he suggested, indicating the Miami skyline over his left shoulder.

Allie nodded. "I know. It's my favorite drive. I come to Key Biscayne almost every weekend."

"Have you been to the restaurant in the state park?"

"The one at the lighthouse?"

He shook his head. "The other one."

Her expression brightened. "I didn't know there was another one."

"You'll love the setting," he promised.

A few minutes later, after driving through the small village of Key Biscayne, with its stretch of oceanfront condos and hotels on one side and mansions on the other, they reached the state park at the tip of the island. Ricky paid the admission, then made a right turn that took them to an inlet referred to as No-Name Harbor.

Built on stilts so that it sat above the water was a small, no-frills restaurant with an outdoor deck that faced back toward the southwest. The view was best at sunset, but even at midday it was like being on an isolated island, rather than just minutes from downtown Miami. A few boats bobbed at anchor in the harbor and a few diners sat with beers and fresh fish, enjoying the mild breeze that offered relief from the steamy early-October heat.

"Like it?" he asked Allie.

"It's wonderful," she said.

"A little rustic, but the fish is fabulous. You have the feeling they just threw in a line and caught it about the same time you placed an order."

Once they'd ordered their own fish sandwiches and drinks—a soda for her, a beer for him—he sat back with a sigh. A moment later he felt Allie's gaze on him. She gave him a slow smile.

"You look better already," she said.

"I feel better. Sorry about before."

"Want to tell me why you were so uptight?"

"Not especially."

"It did have something to do with me, though, didn't it? Ricky, if our arrangement isn't working for you, just say so. I can find someplace to go. I don't want to take advantage of an impetuous offer you'd rather you hadn't made."

"It's not that," he protested. "I just hadn't counted on…"

"Yes? Talk to me. We have to be able to communicate."

Her gaze was so trusting, so expectant, that he knew he'd never be able to lie to her face just to save them both a little awkwardness. "Okay, you want the honest-to-goodness truth?"

"Of course."

He thought of half a dozen ways to put it before finally settling for being blunt. "I'm attracted to you."

To his astonishment, she feigned an exaggerated sigh of relief.

"Thank goodness," she said. "I was worried it was my imagination."

"It's not funny, Allie."

She placed her hand on top of his. "Ricky, we're both adults. I'm not going to jump in bed with a man just because I'm attracted to him, but that doesn't mean I'm not going to admit the obvious."

His gaze narrowed. "Which is?"

"That I'm attracted to you, too."

He wasn't sure whether he was relieved or appalled by her admission. It definitely made things more complicated.

"I just want you to know that I'm not going to do anything to take advantage of the situation," he said.

Amusement flickered in her eyes. "Good, because I wouldn't let you even if you tried."

She said it with absolute confidence, as if she had loads of experience protecting herself from men like him. Ricky doubted that she did, but he had to admire her faith in her own values. Or maybe it was a lack of faith in his powers of persuasion.

He seized the hand that had been resting atop his. "Careful, angel. Some men might consider that to be a challenge."

"Are you one of them?" she asked, clearly more curious than fearful.

"On occasion," he admitted. "I've rarely been one to turn down a dare."

To his amazement her lips curved into a slow, provocative smile. "Then it will be very interesting to see how you handle this one, won't it?"

He groaned at the blatant taunt. Every time he turned around, Allie Matthews was surprising him. Something told him that for the first time in his life he had met his match.

Allie watched the play of expressions on Ricky's face and took a great deal of satisfaction from clearly having stunned him. She knew she was playing with fire, but she also trusted him more than anyone she'd ever known. He had said he wouldn't take advantage of their situation, and she believed him. That gave her the freedom to test her powers of seduction.

She studied Ricky's now-wary expression and congratulated herself. So far she seemed to be quite good at it.

It also seemed like a smart time to scale back the game. "Which nephew is playing soccer this afternoon?"

Ricky stared at her blankly. "What?"

"I was asking about the soccer game. Is it one of Maria's sons who's playing?"

He nodded. "Tomás. He's actually quite good."

"How old is he?"

"Six."

"They have a soccer league for six-year-olds?"

"They do indeed. Of course, the kids are a little older before the game actually resembles real soccer, but they have a great time, and they're very enthusiastic. My brother-in-law coaches."

"Why not you?"

He grinned. "I coached for one week, but I kept forgetting they were only six. My competitive spirit kicked in and I put way too much pressure on them. After the first game my sister threatened to ban me from the stands as well as the sidelines. We compromised. I can sit in the stands, but I have to keep my mouth shut. Maria sits next to me to make sure I don't forget. I'm pretty sure she and her husband have a bet on how long my silence will last."

Allie chuckled. "Who's betting on you?"

"No one," he admitted, his expression rueful. "The only question seems to be when, not if, I will break my promise." He studied her. "How are you feeling? Do you think you'll be up to stopping by? Your color is better today."

"I feel better," she admitted. "But I don't know if I can last a whole game, and I don't want you to have to leave before it's over."

"Haven't you been listening? You'll probably be doing everyone a favor if you get me away from there. You will earn Maria's undying gratitude, to say nothing of little Tomás's."

"Then I'd love to go," she said, looking forward to seeing Maria again and to meeting her family. "Will the other boys be there?"

"Absolutely, though they're usually running around and getting into mischief."

A half hour later, Ricky pulled into a parking lot beside a soccer field. The game was apparently already under way, because the attention of the adults in the stands was riveted on the field.

As Allie and Ricky walked in that direction, three dark-haired boys, who seemed to range in age from seven or eight down to three or four, spotted him and raced in their direction.

"Guess what?" the oldest one shouted, his face flushed with excitement. "Tomás scored a goal, all by himself."

"Only because the goalie ran off the field to go to the bathroom," his younger brother countered.

Ricky laughed. "That does make it easier," he said, then turned to Allie. "At six, the finer points of waiting for substitutions or time-outs seems to elude them."

"I can imagine," she said dryly. It would drive a

particularly competitive coach to distraction. "Glad you're not coaching?"

"Glad I'm not coaching the other side, anyway."

The littlest boy was tugging on his hand. "Uncle Ricky. Uncle Ricky."

"What is it, *niño?*" he asked, scooping the boy into his arms.

The child pointed at Allie. "Who's she? Is she the one everybody's talking about?"

Allie was a bit disconcerted to discover that she'd been the topic of conversation in the family, but Ricky didn't seem the least bit surprised.

"Yes, she is," he told his nephew. "This is my friend, Allie Matthews. Allie, this little munchkin here is Miguel. His big brother is Pedro. Pedro is a budding musician."

Pedro politely extended a hand. "Hello."

Allie regarded him with immediate interest. "What kind of music do you like?"

"I play the violin," he told her shyly.

"I used to play the violin, too," she told him, aware that Ricky was staring at her with surprise that swiftly changed to sympathy as he realized the full implications of the revelation. "In fact, until I lost my hearing, I was going to be a music major. Sometimes I even played with a symphony orchestra."

Pedro's eyes widened. "Wow, that is so cool. How come you didn't tell us that, Uncle Ricky?"

"Because until just now I didn't know it."

Allie felt a tug on her arm and looked down into an upturned face.

"I'm a big brother, too," the remaining boy protested. "I'm Ramón, but my friends call me Ray. I'm five."

Allie grinned. "I'm glad to meet you, too, Ray."

"Is it true you were almost buried alive?" Pedro asked, clearly fascinated by the gruesome prospect.

Allie couldn't prevent the shudder that washed over her.

Ricky winced. "Sorry," he said to her, giving her hand a squeeze. He turned to his nephew. "Pedro, you don't ask people a question like that."

"But Mama said—"

"I don't care what your mother said. It's not polite to ask about something that would be very upsetting if it were true. Would you want to talk about it if you'd been trapped in a building that collapsed?"

Of course, a seven-year-old couldn't really imagine exactly how dire a circumstance that might be. Pedro's expression turned thoughtful, then decisive. "I think it would be cool."

"It would not be cool," his uncle declared.

"But you rescued her, didn't you? She's okay, and that makes you a hero. All my friends are talking about you. I can't wait till you come to my concert on Thursday so they can all meet you."

"Enough," Ricky said, ending the discussion, clearly embarrassed by the talk of his heroics.

"It's okay," Allie said. She smiled at Pedro. "I can imagine it must seem pretty exciting, but believe me, it wasn't. It was scary until your uncle came along. He really is a hero."

"I knew it!" Pedro shouted exuberantly, and went racing off, no doubt to repeat the story. Miguel and Ray scrambled to keep up with him.

"Obviously you've made a conquest," Ricky told her. "Why didn't you tell me about your music before?"

"It never came up," she said with a shrug. "Besides, I try not to think about it too much."

"I'm sorry. Losing something you loved like that, something you'd intended to spend your life doing, must have been as hard as losing your hearing."

"It was," she said in a way that she hoped would end the topic.

Ricky took the hint and led the way to the stands. Allie noticed quite a lot of speculative looks aimed in their direction as they climbed up to join Maria. Ricky tried to maneuver Allie toward the space next to his sister, but Maria shook her head.

"Oh, no, you don't, Enrique. You sit next to me so I can clamp a hand over that big mouth of yours, if you forget yourself." She regarded Allie apologetically. "It's not that I wouldn't rather have you beside me."

"I understand," Allie said with a grin. "Completely."

"He told you, then, about his abominable behavior."

"He swears he has reformed," Allie confided.

"Ha! That I will believe when I see it."

"Okay, when you two have finished having your fun, I'd like to concentrate on the game," Ricky said.

Maria clucked disapprovingly. "It is the concentrating that is the start of the trouble. We are here for fun. That is all."

"There is nothing wrong with wanting to win," he countered defensively.

"Only when you wish to win at all costs. Now behave. You are making a bad impression on Allie."

He scowled at his sister. "And that would matter to you because...?"

"Because I like her," she said, winking at Allie.

Ricky draped an arm across Allie's shoulders. "I like her, too," he said, his gaze locked with Allie's.

"At last, something we can agree on," Maria said.

The warm acceptance of Maria and the flash of lust in Ricky's eyes combined to make Allie feel as if she had stumbled into her heart's desire. This was what she had always craved—the teasing, the sense of belonging. If the hurricane had been her worst nightmare, this... this was her dream.

She sighed. Ricky instantly cupped her chin and studied her face.

"Everything okay? Are you too hot? Tired? Would you like something to drink? There are sodas available."

The barrage of solicitous questions made her smile. "I'm okay. Stop worrying. I'll tell you if I need something or if I want to go."

She caught the smirk of satisfaction on Maria's face and had to resist the urge to return it with a smug grin of her own.

"So, Enrique," Maria began, her expression suddenly innocent. "Will you and Allie be coming to Mama's for dinner tomorrow?"

Allie held her breath as she waited for him to reply. Was he ready to subject himself to the speculation of the rest of his family? Was she, for that matter?

"What do you think, Allie?" he asked, his expression neutral.

"I think it's up to you. This is your family. Maybe we should discuss it when we get home."

He brightened at the reprieve. "Good idea."

"Well, I hope you'll be there, Allie," Maria said. "Everyone else is dying to meet you."

"I can just imagine," Ricky murmured, his voice apparently too low for his sister to hear, because she didn't react.

Allie, however, grinned. "Maria might not have heard that," she said. "But I did."

"It's not bad enough that I have a mother who, I swear, has eyes in the back of her head? I have to meet a woman who can read my mind?"

"It wasn't your mind," she said. "It was your lips."

"Whatever," he said miserably. "I'm doomed."

Maria, her eyes full of mischief, turned in their direction. "Yes, little brother, I think maybe you are."

In the end Allie opted not to go to the Wilders' for dinner. Ricky swore that he wanted her to come if she felt up to it, but she was beginning to sense that he was totally bewildered by how quickly things were happening between them. The truth was, she was no less confused. She concluded that a day apart would be good for both of them.

"But you'll be all alone," he protested.

"Not if you'll call Jane and give her a ride over here."

She couldn't deny that he had seemed relieved by the compromise. And Jane had been ecstatic at the idea of getting an afternoon away from her sister. She had arrived with a picnic hamper packed with food.

"But I'd planned to fix something," Allie protested when she saw it.

"You need to rest more than you need to be standing over a stove. Besides, it's not much."

Allie had to laugh as she began removing the contents of the hamper. Her former neighbor's idea of "not much" consisted of fried chicken, potato salad, coleslaw and a homemade key-lime pie, which she knew was Allie's favorite.

"Well, I see you're not going to starve," Ricky said, studying the food with obvious envy. "Maybe I could…"

"Stay," Jane invited. "There's plenty of food and I have a few questions I'd like to ask you."

He regarded her warily. "About?"

"Your intentions toward our girl, for starters."

He cast a frantic look at Allie, then backed up. "I can get those questions at my mother's."

Jane gave him an unrepentant look. "And she'll probably let you brush her off, won't she?"

"Hopefully," he agreed, then dropped a kiss on her cheek.

"Well, I'm made of tougher stuff, young man. You can get off the hook today, but I'll be watching you."

Allie laughed at his horrified expression. "She will be, too."

"I don't doubt it," Ricky said. "I'll be back in plenty of time to drive you home, Jane. Don't even think about calling a taxi or taking the bus."

She chuckled. "Are you kidding? When I'll have the whole drive home to ask you all those tricky questions I've been storing up?"

"On second thought, maybe I should leave cab fare," Ricky countered.

"Too late now," Allie told him as she walked with him to the door. "Have fun with your family."

"You have fun with Jane. I'll be back soon."

After he'd gone, she turned to find Jane studying her. "You're falling for him, aren't you?" her friend asked worriedly.

"Only a little," Allie admitted.

"Be careful," Jane warned. "That one has the devil in his eyes."

"But the heart of an angel," Allie reminded her. "And the arms of a hero."

"Oh, baby," Jane said. "Don't go mixing up heroics with love."

"I didn't say anything about love," Allie insisted.

"You didn't have to say it. It's written all over your face."

If that was true, Allie could only pray that Ricky wasn't nearly as adept at reading people as Jane was.

Chapter 8

By midweek, Allie was going stir-crazy. She desperately wanted to get back to work, but both Rick and her doctor were vehemently opposed to the idea.

"I promise I'll stay off my feet," she said while both men regarded her with skepticism at the conclusion of her follow-up appointment on Wednesday. She scowled at them and repeated, "I will."

"Not good enough," the doctor said, then glanced at Ricky. "See that she stays at home at least through the weekend. After that I suppose it won't hurt for her to go back part-time." His gaze shifted to her. "A half day, is that clear?"

The restriction grated even worse than his attitude. "I teach sign language, for goodness sakes, not aerobics. I can hardly wear myself out doing that."

"You teach kids, correct?" Ricky asked.

"Yes."

He glanced at the doctor. "Have you ever known kids to sit still?"

"Not mine," the doctor said.

"Not the ones I know, either," Ricky said.

"Well, my students are very well behaved," she argued. Judging from the look the two men exchanged, she was wasting her breath. "Never mind."

She walked out of the office without another word. By the time she reached Ricky's car, she was steaming.

"You do know that this is none of your business, don't you?" she said as she got in the car and slammed the door.

He didn't seem to be overly impressed by the reminder.

"Want to go to lunch?" he asked as he settled behind the wheel. Clearly he had no intention of getting into the fight she was itching to have.

"No, I do not want to go to lunch. I want to go to work. My students need me. It's disruptive for them to adjust to someone new."

"Sorry. You heard the doctor. Not till next week."

"You sold me out. You know I'm well enough to go back."

"Hey, it wasn't my call," he said, feigning innocence. "That's why they have follow-up visits, so the doctor can decide what the patient is capable of doing."

"I could have talked him into it, if you'd kept your big mouth shut."

"Doubtful," he said. "Now, about lunch…?"

"Forget lunch," she all but shouted. "You won't be able to stop me if I decide to go back tomorrow."

"How will you get there? Your car is still in the

shop. So are a zillion others, waiting to see if they can be repaired. I figure you're pretty much at my mercy for the time being."

"I can rent a car or take a taxi, if necessary. And you can't watch me every minute. Sooner or later you'll have to go to work."

He beamed at her. "Actually, unless there's a natural disaster somewhere, I have the rest of the week off."

That didn't please her nearly as much as it might have a couple of days ago. He seemed to be intent on seeing to it that she didn't do anything the least bit taxing. Ever since he'd taken Jane home on Sunday, he'd devoted himself to hovering. He was worse than her parents had been when she'd lost her hearing.

Maybe if there had been anything the least bit lustful in his attention, she would have been pleased, but he'd been treating her like a sister, and a pretty mindless sister at that.

She stared at him and noted the unrelenting set to his jaw. Okay, then, if that was the way he wanted to play it, she had an idea of a sneaky way to get even.

"As long as we're out, there is something I need to do," she began innocently.

"Name it," he said at once, clearly relieved to have the topic of work tabled for the moment.

"Shopping. I want to pick up a few things."

"Clothes? Makeup? What?"

"All of it," she said, watching with amusement as the enthusiasm drained out of his face. He was such a man. By the time she finished with him, he would regret his part in keeping her away from her job. In fact, he might take her straight to the clinic and leave her there.

"What about all that stuff Maria brought?"

"She was very generous, but there are still things I need."

"Fine," he said, his expression grim. "We'll go to the mall, but just for an hour, Allie. That's all I'll agree to. You shouldn't be on your feet any longer than that."

"An hour will be just fine," she said, beaming at him.

Once he'd parked and they'd walked inside the mall, she aimed directly for a lingerie shop. Let him sweat, she thought triumphantly when she caught his pained expression. He was clearly torn between whether to accompany her inside or find a bench a safe distance away.

"Coming?" she inquired pleasantly, making absolutely sure he understood it was a dare.

"Sure." He trailed along reluctantly.

He stood amid the racks of lacy bras and bikini panties looking as terrified as if she'd just left him to fend for himself in a nursery of screaming babies.

Allie grinned at the twentysomething sales clerk, who couldn't seem to stop herself from casting surreptitious glances at Allie's very male companion. She turned her back on him finally and said in what was probably an undertone, "How'd you ever get him in here? Most men won't come near this place."

"Bodyguard," Allie confided. "He can't leave my side."

The young woman's eyes widened. "Oh, wow. I don't know what he's protecting you from, but I'd risk it to have him around day and night."

Allie raised her voice. "Trust me, honey, it's not nearly as much fun as you'd think."

Her words had the desired effect. Ricky's head

snapped around in her direction just as she held up two pairs of bikini panties and inquired of him, "Which do you think?"

A dull red flush climbed his cheeks, but then his gaze locked with hers and it was as if he could read her mind. She could tell the precise instant when he figured out what she was up to.

"Why not try them on and model them for me?" he suggested. He reached out to a selection of lacy bras on a nearby display, sifted through them and plucked out a handful. "These, too."

Check and checkmate, Allie thought with a sigh. She wasn't nearly daring enough to take him up on the taunt.

"I'll take them all," she told the clerk, handing over the two pairs of panties, along with several other pairs that were less provocative. Then she sorted through the selection of bras Ricky had grabbed and chose three of those. She tried not to notice that he'd somehow gotten the size exactly right.

She moved to the counter to pay for the purchases, but a prickling sensation on the back of her neck told her that Ricky had followed. She glanced up into twinkling brown eyes.

"These, too," he told the clerk as he handed her a matching bra and panties in black lace. "But I'm paying for them."

Allie swallowed hard at the challenging glint in his eyes, but just as she was about to protest, he said mildly, "Save your breath, *querida*."

As she watched in dismay, he glanced around at the displays, wandered over to an extremely skimpy negligee in turquoise and brought that back to add to the pile. He winked at Allie. "I can't wait to see the color on you."

The clerk seemed oblivious to Allie's increasingly irritated reaction. She was too busy ringing up the additional sale.

"Thank you," she chirped as they left. "Come back again."

"Not in this lifetime," Allie muttered.

Ricky grinned. "Something wrong?"

"Not a thing," she snapped.

"You got what you went in there for, didn't you?"

And more, she thought darkly.

"Anything else you wanted to get while we're here?" he inquired cheerfully.

"No, I think I'm finished."

"Good, because I'm starving. All that shopping worked up an appetite."

His gaze locked with hers in a way that made her feel as if steam must be rising from her skin.

"How about you? Hungry?" he asked, though it was plain that food was the last thing he craved. "Or would you rather go home and go to bed?"

Allie very nearly choked. "Excuse me?" she said, when she could catch her breath.

"I was just asking if you were too tired to stop for lunch," he said, not even attempting to fight the grin that was slowly spreading across his face.

"Lunch sounds good," she said.

And the first thing she was going to do was order a huge glass of iced tea for her suddenly parched throat. Of course, if she were smart, she probably ought to get a pitcher of ice water and dump it right over her head. Maybe that would chill her steamy thoughts and clearly overheated hormones. It would also serve as a harsh reminder not to play provocative games with a man who understood the rules far better than she did.

Ricky should have been feeling very smug, but instead he was all hot and bothered, and it was his own blasted fault. He might have been the victor in that little game in the lingerie store, but Allie was definitely having the last laugh.

She was seated across from him in the restaurant looking thoroughly cool and collected, while all he could think about was getting her home and into— and then out of—those sexy little numbers he'd purchased. Definitely bad planning on his part, since he had made her a promise that things were going to remain strictly platonic between them. He was going to honor that promise or die trying, which he was fairly sure was a distinct possibility.

He tapped her hand to get her attention, then gestured toward the menu. "What are you having?"

"I feel like something spicy," she said slowly, her gaze lingering on his mouth. "What about you?"

Ricky had a hard time getting his brain to kick into gear.

"There should be plenty of jalapeños in the *quesadilla*," he said finally, pretending that he hadn't even noticed the deliberately suggestive note in her voice. "Want to share that as an appetizer?"

"Sure."

"What else?"

"I'd say a cheeseburger, but I don't think I could eat a whole one," she said.

"We'll split that, too."

"Will that be enough for you?"

"Absolutely," he said. "Especially if we have dessert."

"You're on your own there," she said. "With all this inactivity, I don't dare."

He could think of one way to burn off a few calories, but he resisted the urge to mention it, even in jest. He wasn't even supposed to be thinking about such things. Of course, that was a little like telling a jury to ignore inflammatory testimony after they'd already heard it. After telling himself to keep his thoughts on the straight and narrow where Allie was concerned, erotic images taunted him nonstop. He forced his attention back to the matter of their lunch.

"We'll see how you feel after the burger," he said, then beckoned for the waitress and placed the order.

After the waitress had gone, he realized Allie was studying him. "What?" he asked.

"Can I ask you something?"

He nodded, though the expression on her face made him a little wary.

"You don't subscribe to the idea that if you save someone's life, you're responsible for it, do you?"

"Of course not," he said without hesitation.

"Then why are you being so protective where I'm concerned?"

He tried to shrug it off. "Habit, I suppose. I always tried to look after my sisters. That's just the way I was brought up. My father ingrained it into my head that it was a man's job to protect the women in his life— mother, wife, sisters, whatever."

Her gaze remained doubtful. "And that's all it is?"

Ricky was no more convinced of the honesty of his

answer than she was, but he didn't want to admit that it could be anything else. He certainly wasn't about to tell her he'd never before felt this need to watch over a woman, to protect her—even from himself. What he felt around Allie was a far cry from anything he'd ever felt for the women in his family. Maybe because protectiveness and jealousy and lust were somehow getting all mixed up together.

"Of course," he said, lying brazenly. "What else could it be?"

She shrugged. "I have no idea, but it's a relief that that's all it is, because then I don't feel quite so bad telling you that I find it extremely annoying."

He'd gotten that earlier, back in the doctor's office and later in the car. "So I gathered."

"Then you don't care that I find your attitude irritating?"

"Not if it gets the job done," he said. "Talk to me again in a week, when you're back on your feet. Maybe you'll be able to convince me to back off."

"I *am* back on my feet now."

"To some degree," he acknowledged. "But if I weren't around, you'd be pushing yourself to do too much. You'd be back at work and hunting for a place to live and wearing yourself to a frazzle worrying about Jane and all your other neighbors."

"How can you say that? You barely know me."

"I know enough. And what I didn't figure out on my own, Jane explained."

Indignation set off sparks in her eyes. "The two of you are in cahoots?" she asked.

"You bet. And before you ask, I've also spoken to your boss. I got the skinny from Gina, too. You're an overachiever, Allie Matthews. That's a very admirable trait under most circumstances, but under these—" He shrugged. "Let's just say I've decided to save you from yourself."

"You had no right to run around behind my back, prying into my life."

"Sure I did."

She scowled at him. "How can you say that?"

"Somebody had to." He patted her hand consolingly. "It could have been worse."

"I don't see how."

"I could have brought in the big guns."

She regarded him in confusion. "Big guns? What does that mean?"

"I could have put my mother on the job. You'd still be flat on your back in bed and watching soap operas in Spanish."

A chuckle erupted before she could stop herself. Ricky grinned.

"Have I made my point?" he asked.

"Oh, yes," she said.

"You are in my debt," he added, heaping it on.

"Apparently so."

He leaned forward. "So, what do I get for my trouble?"

Allie was clearly struggling with herself. She moistened her lips, started to lean forward as if to meet him halfway, then sat back with a heavy sigh.

"I'll have to think about it," she said.

He winked at her. "Let me know if you can't come up with anything, because I have a few ideas myself."

"Yes," she murmured. "I imagine you do."

"Great ideas," he emphasized, keeping his gaze

firmly fixed on her mouth, even as he told himself he was being a louse...again. The flirting was as ingrained in him as breathing. He couldn't seem to stop himself.

Allie didn't so much as bat an eye. Rather she met his gaze boldly and directly. "Care to elaborate?"

"Oh, I think it will be a whole lot more fun if we both just rely on our imaginations."

"Something tells me yours has been in overdrive," she said wryly.

"Since the moment we met," he conceded. "Since the moment we met."

By the time they got home and Allie had gone to her room for a nap, Ricky was in such a state of arousal he changed clothes and went outside to mow the lawn, hoping to exhaust himself before he had to see Allie again over dinner.

He was hot and sweaty and covered with grass clippings when he heard the slam of a car door. He moaned as he considered the possibilities. Whoever it was, he didn't want to see them.

"Hey, Enrique, you out back?" Tom shouted as he rounded the side of the house clutching a six-pack of beer.

Ricky assured himself that his receptiveness increased only because of that beer. He nabbed one before his friend could settle on the chaise longue next to his.

"You're a mess," Tom said after a casual survey. "How do you expect to land the fair maiden looking like that?"

"Actually, I'm hoping to look and smell so disgusting, she won't come within a foot of me," he said.

"How come?"

"Because she's dangerous," he said before he thought to censor himself.

"Dangerous how? Is she sleepwalking with a butcher knife or something?"

"Hardly."

"What then?"

"She just exists, that's all," he grumbled, taking a deep swallow of the cold, refreshing beer.

"Oh, boy," Tom said with a hoot. "You have it bad, my friend."

"I do not."

"Of course you do. You have gone way beyond just scheming to get her into your bed, haven't you?"

Ricky scowled at the suggestion. "Don't be ridiculous. I don't do the happily-ever-after thing. You know that."

"It's not so bad. Maybe you should consider it."

If Tom had suggested they both take up skydiving, Ricky couldn't have been any more stunned. "This from a man who bolted from a marriage practically before the ink was dry on the license."

"*I* didn't bolt. *She* did. And we're talking about you, not me."

Despite the denial, Ricky thought he detected something wistful in his friend's expression. "Is there something going on with you and Nikki? Have you seen her?"

"Last night," Tom admitted grudgingly.

"Intentionally or did you bump into her someplace?"

"No, I stopped by."

"Really?" Ricky barely hid his surprise. He thought they hadn't seen or spoken to each other in months, despite his mother's attempts to push them back together. "And?"

"And nothing."

"Nothing happened? She kicked you out? What?"

"We talked for maybe five, ten minutes. Then her date showed up."

"Geez, I'm sorry, *amigo*."

"The man was wearing a pin-striped suit, for Pete's sake," Tom continued. "He's an accountant, you know, for one of those muckety-muck firms. A real nine-to-fiver. How boring is that?" He tried valiantly to achieve an air of disdain, but his hurt was evident.

"I'm sorry," Ricky said again. "Do you think it's serious?"

"Hey, he's exactly what she says she's always wanted."

"But did it look serious?" Ricky persisted. "Sparks flying, that kind of thing?"

"What difference does it make? If this jerk is what she thinks she wants, she'll find a way to talk herself into having a relationship with him."

"Then you'll just have to find a way to talk her back out of it," Ricky told him. "You know anybody with a better gift of gab than you? Present company excluded, of course."

Tom seemed to take heart from the reminder. "Hell, no," he declared.

"Well, then, if you want her back, fight for her. Do you want her back?"

Tom's expression turned miserable again. "I can't be a damned desk jockey, not even for her."

"Maybe there's a compromise."

"Such as?"

"I don't know. That would be up to the two of you."

"Well, if one exists, I can't think what it is," Tom said. "Let's talk about you and the beautiful Allie instead. Where is she?"

"Napping."

"She's in bed and you're out here? You are slipping."

"Go suck an egg," Ricky grumbled.

"Is that the response of a mature man?" Tom taunted.

"No, it is the response of a man who's at the end of his rope. I say I go in and take a shower, and you and I go out on the town. How about it?"

"Fine by me. I got nothing better to do."

"Good. That's settled then." A night on the town would prove to him that he wasn't really hooked on Allie. He'd probably find a dozen other women before the night was out who'd be more gorgeous, more willing, and less vulnerable. Leggy brunettes with sultry smiles.

Unfortunately, when he stepped inside the back door, he found Allie bending over in front of the oven. The view was too alluring to ignore. He enjoyed it for a full, uninterrupted minute, and every thought of leggy brunettes fled.

When she finally stood up and caught sight of him, she jumped, clearly startled.

"Sorry," he apologized, his voice husky.

"I didn't know you'd come in."

"I keep forgetting about sneaking up on you. What's in the oven?"

"Dinner. I found a roast in the freezer. I made pot roast."

He frowned. "I thought you were resting."

She scowled right back at him. "I was and now I'm not."

"You should have said something. Tom's here. We were going out."

If she was disappointed, she hid it well. "Fine."

"If I'd known you were cooking, I would have told you," he said, feeling defensive.

"It's not a problem. I'll have some of this tonight. You can eat the leftovers whenever you feel like it."

He didn't like it that she was letting him off the hook so easily, as if what he did didn't matter two hoots to her. "I suppose we could eat first and then go out," he said grudgingly. "Is there enough for Tom?"

"There's enough for an army, but don't stay on my account. I should have checked with you first."

"We'll stay," he said at once, wondering what Tom was going to make of the sudden turnaround.

"Fine. I'll set another place. Should I go out and tell him or will you?"

"I'll do it," Ricky said. If his friend was going to start laughing when he learned of the change in plans, Ricky didn't want Allie to wonder why. "How long till we eat?"

"A half hour."

"Perfect. I'll tell Tom, then take a shower and change."

Tom's reaction wasn't exactly what Ricky had anticipated. "Pot roast?" he echoed, staring longingly toward the back door. "The real thing. Not a frozen dinner?"

"The real thing."

"Damn, buddy, if you don't marry this woman, I might."

Ricky scowled. "Not in a hundred million years," he said fiercely.

Tom feigned shock. "Are you warning me off?"

"Isn't that what it sounded like?" Ricky retorted. "If not, I must be slipping."

"Message received," Tom said dutifully, but his eyes were full of mischievous sparks.

Ricky had the distinct impression he'd better take that shower and get back to the kitchen in record time. He wasn't quite sure whether he needed to be there to protect Allie…or his own interests.

Chapter 9

Aside from Ricky's vigilance, the only thing that kept Allie from returning to work on Thursday was the unexpected arrival of her boss from the speech and hearing clinic, first thing in the morning.

Looking smug, Ricky ushered Gina Dayton into the kitchen while Allie was sullenly sipping her third cup of coffee and glowering over the top of the paper. She felt her spirits improve the instant she spotted the energetic woman who ran the clinic.

"Gina, I had no idea you were coming," Allie said, signing for the woman's benefit.

Gina had been born deaf, but she had never considered it a detriment to achieving her dreams. She had been a grade-A student in high school, had graduated from college at the top of her class and had started her own cutting-edge clinic in her hometown of Miami.

With her energy and her boundless optimism, she was a role model to her clients and her staff.

"Your friend called me last night and told me you were getting restless," she said, gesturing toward Ricky. "He seemed to think the only way to keep you at home would be to get you an update on your students. I decided to come in person."

"I'll leave you two to catch up," Ricky said, after surveying the scene with apparent satisfaction.

Allie reluctantly met his gaze. "Thank you."

"No problem. Enjoy yourselves. Gina, would you like some coffee before I go?"

Gina signed her response, clearly startling Ricky.

"Gina doesn't speak," Allie told him, "except with sign language. She said she'd get her own coffee if you'd point her in the right direction."

"But I spoke to her on the phone," he said.

Gina grinned and signed a response. Allie translated for him. "She says you actually spoke to her assistant, who acted as an interpreter for her."

"So the words were hers, but the voice was her assistant's?"

Allie nodded. "Exactly."

"But Gina reads lips?"

Gina tapped his arm, grinning. "I do."

Ricky gave her one of his devastating smile. "Okay, then. The coffee's over there. And I picked up some guava pastries this morning."

Gina's expression turned rapturous as she signed, "Heaven."

Ricky grinned. "I think I got that. Let me know if you need anything."

As soon as he was gone, Gina regarded Allie with obvious fascination. "Girl, what have you landed yourself in? The man is a certifiable hunk. And he's the one who rescued you? How did you end up living with him? No wonder you didn't want to stay at my place with a man like him waiting in the wings to take you in." Her fingers flew as she signed the barrage of questions.

"He's not bad," Allie responded cautiously.

"Are you blind, too?" the other woman inquired, patting one hand over her heart. "My pulse is still racing."

"Because you don't get out enough," Allie told her. "You work all the time."

"So do you," Gina responded. "Let me know if you decide not to keep him."

Allie wanted to explain that he wasn't hers to keep, but she couldn't quite bring herself to do it. Ricky might not be hers, but she couldn't see herself handing him over to another woman, especially someone she knew. Just the thought of bumping into him with someone else made her stomach churn.

She frowned at her friend. "You're married and the mother of a new baby."

"But I have friends," she said fervently. "They would be in my debt forever if I brought a man like Ricky to them. I was very impressed when he called the other day to express his concern about you. And when he called back to arrange this visit, I knew I had to get a good look at him for myself."

Even though Allie said nothing, Gina apparently got the message. "Hands off, huh? Okay. But if you spot any more like him, let me know."

"Will do," Allie promised. "Now tell me what's happening at the clinic."

"Your patients all miss you like crazy. They sent cards," Gina said, drawing a stack of brightly colored pictures from her briefcase.

Allie accepted them, but the first one of a little girl's face with a tear on the cheek brought such a lump to her throat that she put them aside to study later, when she was alone.

"They love you," Gina signed, then gave Allie's hand a squeeze. "We are all grateful that you weren't hurt any worse than you were, and we can't wait for you to get back."

"I could come in tomorrow," Allie said eagerly.

Gina held up protesting hands. "Not on your life. I've already been warned by your friend in there that you are not coming back till Monday. Period."

"Ricky Wilder does not run my life."

"But he has your best interests at heart. Listen to him." She grinned. "Besides, if a man that gorgeous offered me an incentive to stay around the house, you can bet I wouldn't budge."

"That's what you say because you have a choice," Allie complained. "He's not giving me any choice at all."

"It's a few more days," Gina reminded her. "This ordeal has been a shock. It's not just the physical injuries you must deal with, but the emotional harm it did. Have you even been back to your house?"

Allie shook her head. Even at the risk that looters would take anything salvageable, she wasn't ready to face it yet.

"You must go," Gina told her. "Put it behind you. You know better than most the importance of moving on."

The allusion to the weeks during which she'd raged about her loss of hearing, rather than accepting the reality, brought that whole, awful, wasted time back to her. "I know you're right, but I'm afraid memories of the hurricane will overwhelm me. It was terrifying."

"Have you thought of talking to a psychologist about it?"

"No. I'm coping. It will get better with time."

"And if it doesn't?"

"Then I will see someone. I promise."

Gina stayed for a few more minutes, sharing gossip about the staff, reporting triumphs of the patients. "We need to talk about Kimi Foley," she said referring to one of Allie's more troubling cases. "She's not doing as well as we'd like, but we'll discuss that when you come in on Monday."

She eventually plucked a few articles and reports from her briefcase and passed them along.

"Reading material," she said. "And some paperwork. But don't do any more than you feel up to."

"Thank you," Allie said fervently. Maybe she wouldn't feel so cut off, so completely useless, if she could at least do a little of the endless paperwork her job entailed.

She walked Gina to the door, gave her a hug, then stood watching her drive away, unable to hide the wistfulness she was feeling.

She felt Ricky slip up beside her. He draped a comforting arm across her shoulders.

When she glanced up to meet his understanding gaze, he reminded her, "Only a few more days."

She sighed. "I know."

But it seemed as if she'd already been stranded in limbo forever.

With Allie settled more happily at the kitchen table with her paperwork, Ricky congratulated himself on the brilliance of his idea to get Gina Dayton to drop by.

After casting one last look at her, he stripped off his shirt and went outside to try to tame some of the shrubbery that was threatening to take over the front lawn.

He was hard at work, when he sensed he wasn't alone. Allie was sitting on the front stoop, arms around her legs, chin resting on her knees. She looked totally downcast again. He set aside his clippers and dropped down next to her.

"I didn't mean to distract you," she said.

"Then what did you mean to do?" he teased. "Get an eyeful of the scenery?" He deliberately glanced down at his gleaming chest.

Allie reacted with predictable embarrassment. "Of course not. I was just..." Her voice trailed off.

"Restless again?" he inquired sympathetically.

"Not exactly." She met his gaze. "I've been thinking."

"About?" he prodded when she didn't continue.

"I think I need to go back to my house."

He stared at her incredulously. "What? No way!"

"I have to do it. Your sister mentioned it the other day and today Gina brought it up."

He shot to his feet and began to pace. "They're both nuts," he declared. "Why would they suggest something like that?"

He felt Allie snag his hand and pull him to a stop, her expression frustrated.

"What?" she demanded.

He repeated what he'd said, then added flatly, "It's not a good idea."

"I think it is," she said with a determined jut to her chin. "Maybe some of my things can be salvaged. And even if they can't, I have to deal with what happened that night. I have to face it and move on. Will you take me?"

He struggled with the wisdom of what she was suggesting and his own fear that she wasn't ready to face that night. "Allie, I don't know."

"I'll find some other way to get there, if you don't."

He knew she would do it, too. Unlike the idle threats she'd made about sneaking back to work behind his back, he sensed that this time she'd made up her mind. She would go with him or without him. There was no way he would let her face it alone.

"I'll take you," he finally conceded. "When?"

"Now," she said with grim determination. She stood up to emphasize her declaration.

Ricky sighed. "Okay, now it is. Just give me a minute to clean up and put on a shirt."

"It's not like we're going someplace fancy," she protested. "We'll probably get filthy."

"Give me a minute," he insisted.

Inside, he made a quick, desperate call to Jane. "Do you think she's up to this?"

"If she says she is, you don't have a choice. I'll meet you there," the elderly woman said decisively.

"Want me to pick you up on our way?" Ricky offered.

"No, then she'll know you called. It'll be better if I just show up."

"Thanks, Jane. You're an angel."

"You can buy us both lunch when this is over. I have a craving for a nice, thick pastrami on rye with some kosher pickles."

"You've got it," Ricky promised. "See you soon."

To allow time for Jane to make her way back to

her old neighborhood via public transportation, Ricky opted for a shower, rather than the quick cleanup he'd intended. He took his own sweet time about drying his hair and getting dressed, then shaved, too. By the time he went outside, Allie was prowling the yard impatiently.

"It took you long enough," she grumbled.

"Is that the thanks I get for making myself beautiful?" He leaned in close. "See, I even smell good."

A reluctant grin tugged at her lips as she sniffed his aftershave. "Very nice. Something tells me it's going to be wasted on the vermin likely to be crawling over the remains of the neighborhood, though."

"As long as it's not wasted on you," he said agreeably and headed south.

The closer they got to Allie's old neighborhood, the more her anxiety increased. She had knotted her hands so tightly in her lap that the knuckles had turned white and there were lines of tension around her mouth. Ricky made the turn off the highway, then pulled into the parking lot of what had once been a small strip mall. Now the roof was gone, and the few remaining windows were covered with graffiti-decorated boards. He put his hand over Allie's.

"You okay? We don't have to do this now."

"Yes, we do," she said tightly. "Right now. Just keep going."

The deeper they drove into the area, the more devastation they saw. At first only trees were down, with the occasional boarded-over windows, but then house after house began showing signs of being ravaged by what was now presumed to have been a hurricane-spawned tornado.

"Oh, God," Allie murmured, a hand covering her mouth, her eyes stricken. "I'd forgotten. Where you live, it's like the storm never happened, so I told myself it couldn't have been as bad as I'd remembered." Her devastated gaze met his. "But it is. It's worse, in fact. There's nothing left."

"We're turning back," Ricky said, reaching a decision. He couldn't bear the pain in her eyes.

"No, please. Let's just get it over with."

He hesitated, but the unyielding expression on her face never wavered. "Okay, fine," he said and turned onto her street.

The only way to be sure which house was Allie's was to count the piles of rubble from the corner. When he pulled to a stop, her dismayed gasp quickly gave way to a sob.

"Oh, baby," he whispered, reaching for her. He pulled her into his arms and let her cry, helpless to think of anything more he could do to comfort her.

He held her until a tap on the car window startled him. He glanced out to find Jane studying them anxiously. Her flushed complexion worried him. He beckoned to her to get into the backseat so she'd be out of the heat.

Allie shifted, staring in surprise when the door opened and Jane climbed in. Jane took one look at Allie's ravaged face and managed to lean over the seat to give her a comforting hug.

"It's worse the first time you see it," she consoled her. "Then you just have to start thinking about how exciting it will be to have a brand-new home where the old one stood."

Allie's wounded expression didn't brighten at all at the prospect.

"Why don't you two stay here in the air-conditioning?" Ricky suggested. "Let me rummage around and see if I can find anything worth keeping."

"I'll come, too," Allie said at once.

Jane exchanged a look with Ricky, then clasped Allie's hand. "Stay here with me for just a bit. It was terribly hot out there. I need a few minutes in this cool air."

Allie immediately regarded her with concern. "Are you okay? Would you like something to drink? I brought along some cold, bottled water."

"That would be wonderful," Jane said.

Ricky seized the opportunity to slip out of the car. He wasn't especially hopeful that he would locate anything of value in the debris, but it would probably be less stressful for Allie not to have to sift through things she had once loved that were now broken or caked with mud.

It was a thankless task. He found a photo album, but water had all but destroyed the pictures inside. He put it aside on the chance that one or two photos could be saved. He discovered a jewelry box, but even before he pried open the lid, he knew that anything valuable had been taken by looters. Inside, he found an old Sunday school attendance pin and a high school ring, but whatever else Allie had owned was gone.

As he sifted through the debris, he found the occasional shoe—but never its mate—a few unchipped dishes, a cast-iron skillet and an assortment of stainless steel knives, forks and spoons. He found one drape relatively unscathed, but the other in tatters. Sofas, chairs, her television were completely ruined.

He had just picked up a teddy bear, its fabric caked with dried mud, one eye missing, when Allie joined him. She reached for the bear with fingers that trembled, then hugged him to her as tears streaked silently down her cheeks.

"He'll look better when he's had a bath," Ricky said optimistically. "And I'm pretty sure Maria can replace the eye. The boys were always destroying their stuffed animals, then sobbing till she patched them up again."

"I got this bear when I was in the hospital when I lost my hearing," she said, her voice choked. "Brownie and I have been through a lot together."

"And you've both survived," Ricky reminded her.

"A little the worse for wear," she said, tenderly smoothing the bear's mud-caked tummy. She shook her head. "I don't know what I expected, but it wasn't this."

"You weren't exactly in any condition to check out the scenery when we got you out the other day," he reminded her. "You were in shock."

"Yes, I suppose I was." She visibly struggled to pull herself together. "Have you found anything else?"

"I put a few things over here," he said, showing her.

She held it together until she saw the photo album, but then her shoulders shook with sobs. "It's like losing my entire past, as if it never existed."

"Don't be silly," Jane said briskly, stepping in when Ricky couldn't find a single word of consolation to utter. "They were just pictures. The memories are in your heart. You'll never lose those. And I imagine some of those pictures were taken by other people who very well might still might be able to give you a copy. We'll call your parents, some of your old friends, and put the album back together again."

Allie gave her a watery smile. "Thank you."

"For what?" Jane said dismissively. "I haven't done a thing."

"You came over here today. I know it wasn't an accident. Ricky called you, didn't he?"

"He might have mentioned you were thinking of heading over here," Jane conceded. "You should have told me yourself."

"It was an impulsive decision. Not a very good one, either."

"You're wrong," Jane told her. "It was a very brave decision. It's always better to get the things we dread over with, so we can move on."

"Amen," Ricky said. "Now I propose we all get out of this steam bath and go to lunch. A deli, perhaps?" He winked at Jane.

"Definitely," she said at once.

After casting one last, lingering look over her shoulder, Allie drew in a deep breath and led the way to the car, still clutching her bear. Ricky put the other items in the trunk, then drove them to a deli about a mile away.

Jane ordered her pastrami on rye and plucked a pickle out of the jar on the table, even before he or Allie could take a good look at the menu.

When Allie ordered a cup of chicken soup, Jane stared at her in horror.

"That's not enough to keep a bird alive. Eat something that will put a little meat on your bones," she advised Allie. "You have to keep your strength up."

To Ricky's surprise, Allie deferred to her friend.

"What would you suggest?"

"Potato pancakes with apple sauce and sour cream," Jane said at once, then grinned. "I'll split it with you, and you can have half of my sandwich."

"Done," Allie agreed.

As they ate, Ricky watched with relief as the color came back into Allie's cheeks and her eyes lost that dull lifelessness. She was actually laughing again—albeit not very wholeheartedly—by the time they left.

At Jane's place she gave the older woman a fierce hug.

"I'll be over to see you this weekend," Jane promised. "We'll get started on those calls. You make a list of everyone you'd like me to contact. Till then you keep a stiff upper lip."

"I'll see to it," Ricky promised.

Jane gave him a hug, too. "I'm counting on it, young man. Our Allie needs you."

Ricky knew it was true, but in the back of his mind, he couldn't help wondering if the neediness was only temporary. And what would happen to the two of them when she was back on her feet again?

How crazy was it to dread the time when she would be ready to move away and begin her life over again? he asked himself.

When he got home from Pedro's excruciating concert later that night, he sat in the backyard as Allie slept and wondered how she had gotten under his skin so quickly. Today certainly told part of the story. He didn't think he'd ever met anyone more brave. He was in awe of her strength.

It was that strength that would take her away from him in the end, and he would have to let her go, because if ever there was a woman who needed to stand on her own two feet, it was Allie.

But maybe, in time, if he was very lucky, she would let him stand beside her.

Chapter 10

Allie sat on a chaise longue in the backyard and cast surreptitious glances at Ricky, who was stretched out on the lounge chair next to hers. He was feigning sleep. She was sure of it. What she couldn't figure out was why. He'd been brooding and distant ever since they'd returned from their visit to what was left of her house the day before. She'd been relieved when he'd finally left to go to Pedro's concert.

Apparently, whatever was on his mind hadn't resolved itself by the time he returned, because he'd spent most of the night outside. She knew because she'd glanced out the window several times and seen him sitting right where he was now, a beer on the table beside him.

When she'd come downstairs first thing this morning, the bottle had been right where she'd seen it during the night and it was barely half-empty.

"You don't have to babysit me," she said eventually.

She saw his lips move slightly, but no word was formed. She interpreted that to be the equivalent of an acknowledging "Hmm?"

"I said I will be perfectly fine if you want to go out."

He opened his eyes then and glanced toward her. "Who said anything about going out?"

"You must be getting restless," she said.

"Not especially."

"Well, I certainly am."

He stood up so quickly she was sure he intended to seize the opportunity to take off.

"You're absolutely right," he said, and held out his hand. "Let's go."

"Go where?"

"Come on," he said, his eyes twinkling with a challenge. "Trust me."

Before she could second-guess herself, she jumped up. She told herself her eagerness was natural. She was sick of sitting around doing nothing. She'd finished every piece of paperwork Gina had brought by dinnertime the night before. Anything he had in mind would be an improvement. She ignored the little voice that taunted that this man could tempt her into doing things she would otherwise never consider. Her enthusiasm was all about being with him, not being active.

Before she could ask a single question, he'd grabbed her purse, a bottle of suntan lotion and their sunglasses.

"Are we going to the beach?" she asked, hurrying to keep up with him.

"You'll see."

En route to whatever their destination was, he pulled up to a small gourmet shop, ran inside and emerged with a cooler. "Lunch," he explained when she eyed it with curiosity.

Fifteen minutes later they pulled into a marina. Ricky led the way along a dock until he reached a small fishing boat. He stepped in and held out his hand.

"Yours, I hope," she said as she joined him.

"Tom's, but I have a key. There are fishing poles stashed on board. Let me get this food into the refrigerator down in the galley, and we'll take off." His gaze narrowed. "You don't get seasick, do you?"

Allie grinned. "It's a little late to be asking, isn't it?"

"It would be too late if we were a mile offshore. Here there are still options."

"As far as I know, I don't get seasick."

"As far as you know," he repeated. "Does that mean you've never been out on a boat?"

"You've got it," she confirmed.

"Well, luckily, the water's like glass today. You should be fine. Do you swim?"

"In a pool," she said.

"I'll get you a life jacket while I'm down below," he said dryly.

Minutes later he started the boat's engine, cast off the lines and eased away from the dock. Allie stood at the railing and watched the marina disappear as they headed out into the bay. The breeze smelled of salt and maybe seaweed or mangroves. The kiss of the air against her bare skin counterpointed the sun's heat. Though the Miami skyline was never out of sight, it was as if they'd retreated into their own world. When they were a mile or so offshore, Ricky cut the engine.

The boat bobbed gently on the water as he came to stand beside her.

"This is the first thing I do when I get back from a rescue operation overseas," he said.

She saw the ever-present worry lines in his face begin to ease. Without thinking, she reached up and touched his cheek. His skin was warm from the sun and rough with the beginning stubble of his beard. She'd never felt anything so masculine.

She wasn't sure of the precise moment when she became aware of the flare of heat in his eyes, but rather than withdraw her hand, she tentatively traced the outline of his mouth. A muscle in his jaw worked.

Then before she knew what he intended, he captured her hand where it was and drew one finger into his mouth in a slow, provocative move that made her heart leap in her chest. His gaze never left hers. Allie felt as if her entire world consisted of the blazing heat in his eyes and the sensation of his tongue against her finger.

"Do you have any idea what you do to me?" he murmured, releasing her hand with obvious reluctance.

Because she didn't think she could speak past the lump in her throat, she shook her head.

"I want to kiss you," he told her.

"Then do," she said, already feeling her breath hitch and her pulse begin to pound in anticipation. "Please."

His mouth claimed hers at once, almost as if he feared she might change her mind. Hot, throbbing need ricocheted wildly through her. She tried to get closer, but he held her a careful distance away, allowing only their lips to touch with the kind of intimacy she craved.

"Why?" she murmured restlessly, desperately wanting something he seemed unwilling to offer.

She felt his lips move against hers and knew he was responding. She wanted to know the answer, but she needed the kisses more. Sweet, tender kisses. Urgent, demanding kisses. The pattern was unexpected, unpredictable and relentless. She had never known that kisses could be so shattering, so utterly magnificent in their own right. She was practically quivering with need by the time he stepped back and released her.

Blinking against the brilliance of the sunlight and the sudden abandonment, she stared at him. "Why?" she asked again.

He shoved his hands in his pockets and faced her with grim determination. "Because I didn't bring you out here to seduce you."

"Plans change," she said, forcing a light note into her voice.

A grin appeared and disappeared so quickly she almost missed it.

"Not this time," he said, his expression unyielding.

Still fighting the aftereffects of his kisses, she struggled for a cavalier attitude. "Mind telling me why?"

"I am not taking advantage of you, of the situation," he declared, seemingly to remind himself as well as to enlighten her.

She felt her temper stir. "That's very noble, but why do you get to make the call?"

"Because you're not thinking clearly."

"Oh?" She managed the word with deadly calm, but the pounding of her blood told another story.

"Don't look at me like that. You've been through a very traumatic time."

"But my brain still functions fairly well," she retorted. "I think I'm capable of making rational decisions."

"Rational ones, perhaps," he agreed. "But this isn't about rational. It's about hormones. The two are mutually exclusive."

The superior tone grated. "Okay, let me get this straight," she said, hanging on to her fury by a thread. "You—intelligent male creature that you are—can make a *rational* decision about seduction for both of us, but I—a mere female—cannot be counted on to do so for myself. Have I got that right?"

He scowled. "I don't see why you're getting so worked up. I'm trying to do the right thing here."

"What *you* consider to be the right thing," she corrected. "If that isn't the most ridiculous, most patronizing, *male* logic I have ever heard in my life, I don't know what is."

"Now, Allie…"

"Don't you 'Now, Allie' me!" she shouted. "I just might be inclined to do something irrationally female and knock you overboard."

He stared at her with obvious shock. "You wouldn't."

"Don't test me," she snapped.

She whirled around, stepped gingerly toward the stairs leading belowdeck and retreated to the galley. She found herself a cold drink, popped the top and took a long, slow swallow, hoping to cool her parched throat and hot temper.

The man was a macho idiot. She'd been weak-kneed and willing, and he had rejected her. She didn't know which irritated her more—that he had been able to resist her, or that he'd actually thought she didn't know her own mind. Either way, it would be a cold day in hell before he got a second chance.

Women! Ricky sat on deck and wondered if he would ever understand the female of the species. He figured it was pretty doubtful, even for a man who'd grown up with four very perplexing sisters.

Frankly, up until the last week, his inability to grasp the complexities of the female mind hadn't mattered to him all that much, but for some idiotic reason he wanted to know what made Allie tick.

He was pretty sure he knew what ticked her off, though. What he viewed as honorable behavior apparently riled her no end. He had a hunch he could explain from now until they were both rocking in an old folks' home and she still wouldn't get it. He was beginning to wonder himself if he wasn't out of his mind. He'd had a woman who made him ache ready and willing to relieve that ache and he'd stopped her. Maybe he *did* need to have his head examined.

He would have given anything right now for something cold to drink, but it would take more than an insatiable thirst to make him wander belowdeck to cross paths with Allie. She was clearly in an unpredictable mood, and he was no saint. The next time she offered, he might not be nearly so concerned with what was right and honorable and decent.

He heard her footsteps coming up the stairs and forced himself to keep right on staring out to sea, his eyes shaded by very dark sunglasses. He almost jumped out of his seat when he felt the sprinkles of ice water on his chest.

"Damn, Allie," he muttered and looked up into eyes glinting with satisfaction.

"I thought you might want something to drink," she said sweetly.

"I'd rather have it in me than on me," he grumbled under his breath, but he accepted the can of soda, which was still dripping from being submerged in the cooler of ice. "Thank you."

"You're welcome," she said just as politely. "If you're hungry, I could bring up lunch."

He regarded her uncertainly. Was she trying to make amends for her overreaction? Or did she intend to find some way to spoil the food and poison him? Because he wasn't entirely sure, he said, "Not just yet." He wanted a little more time to get a fix on her mood.

He gestured toward the seat next to him. "Want to sit?"

"I'll stand."

"Whatever."

Unfortunately, her decision to stand put her legs at eye level. He couldn't seem to drag his gaze away from her bare, lightly tanned thighs. He wondered what she did to get that kind of muscle tone. He wondered how her skin would feel, how it would taste.

He wondered too blasted many things he had no business thinking about, he told himself sternly.

He looked up and saw that she was studying him with a frown.

"Everything okay?" she inquired.

"Perfect," he retorted irritably. "Everything is just perfect."

"Yes, it is, isn't it?" she murmured with a smug smile.

Then she turned and strolled to the bow of the boat, hips swaying. That sway was deliberate, Ricky concluded, as was that entire encounter. Apparently his sweet, vulnerable, brave Allie was dead set on revenge.

Ricky was pretty sure that the day, which had started with such promise, couldn't get any worse, but he was wrong. When he and Allie arrived at his house just after five—still barely speaking—he found the place crawling with people. Apparently his family had tired of waiting for an invitation to meet Allie and had decided to come calling.

If he was appalled by the timing, it was obvious that Allie was alarmed. When she spotted Maria and the boys, she clearly guessed the identity of the others. She cast a frantic look at him.

"Couldn't we run away?"

"We tried that once today and it didn't go so well," he pointed out. "It won't be so bad."

"Easy for you to say. It's your family."

"Which means I'll catch the brunt of the inquisition," he said. "They'll be nice to you."

He wasn't nearly as sure of that as he tried to appear. The gleam in his mother's eye as she approached the car was not reassuring. He'd seen that look before, directed at the men who were now his brothers-in-law.

His mother ignored him and headed straight for the door on Allie's side of the car.

"You must be Allie," she said, all but dragging Allie from the car and embracing her in a hug. "I am Enrique's mother. I've been so anxious to meet you, but my son kept telling me that I must wait until you have recovered. It is when you are *not* recovered that you

need family around you, is it not? Men do not understand such things."

Allie cast a desperate look in his direction. "I suppose," she murmured, clearly not knowing what to
make of this stranger who was already treating her
like a member of the family.

"Come, meet the others," his mother commanded,
not giving Allie much choice in the matter as she led
her up the walk.

The two women disappeared inside the house, and
Ricky breathed a sigh of relief. He exited the car slowly,
grateful for his own reprieve. There was nothing he
could do to save Allie, anyway. If he could just sneak
around back, he might be able to hide out until the
worst of the visit was over.

"Sorry, little brother," Maria said, joining him as he
rounded the corner. "Inside. Allie needs you."

"Actually, she's not very happy with me at the moment."

"Oh? Why is that?"

"Long story and not one I'm inclined to discuss.
Suffice it to say that the timing of your arrival sucks."

Maria laughed. "Maybe not. By the time Mama ex-
tols all your virtues, Allie won't be able to resist you."

Of course, her susceptibility to him wasn't exactly
the issue, not the way his sister meant. Again, though,
he refrained from explaining.

"Everyone's here?" he asked.

"Every single one of us, kids included," she said
with a disgusting amount of glee. "Not to worry,
though. Mama brought enough dinner for an army,
with plenty for leftovers."

"You're all staying?"

"Well, of course. Mama's not about to cut short a chance to get to know a prospective daughter-in-law. She's been waiting for this day for too long."

Ricky wondered if it was too late to bolt. He could run faster than Maria, though her speed had improved somewhat since she'd started chasing after four active sons. He sighed and gave up on the idea. Allie would never forgive him if he abandoned her. He might not understand a lot about women, but he knew that much with absolute certainty.

He turned to his sister. "One hour," he declared firmly. "You get them all out of here in one hour. Allie needs her rest."

Maria chuckled. "Nice touch. All that concern is very sweet, but something tells me it's not Allie you're worried about. You want us gone before we start planning your wedding."

"Bite your tongue," he snapped, then stalked inside.

He found Allie sitting on the sofa between his mother and his father. His sisters were planted in the remaining chairs, while their husbands stood uneasily surveying the scene—probably recalling when they'd been in similar uncomfortable circumstances.

Nine children, all under the age of ten, were racing from room to room, enthusiastically chased by a barking Shadow, who rarely had an opportunity for such indoor antics. For once Ricky almost envied Allie her deafness. The noise level was earsplitting.

"Shadow, sit!" Ricky commanded. The dog flopped down at his feet at once, tail wagging. Unfortunately, the effect of the command did not extend to the children. He frowned at them and pointed toward the door. "Outside."

Maria's husband, Ben, winked at him. "I'll go with them. I know you want to stay right here in the center of things."

"Not especially," Ricky said, watching enviously as his brother-in-law made a hasty escape.

He turned his attention back to Allie. She looked a little dazed by the barrage of questions being flung at her.

"You must have been terrified during the storm," Elena said sympathetically. "Had you been here before during a hurricane?"

At the same time, Margarita was saying, "I understand you're a teacher. So am I. We'll have to have lunch one day and compare notes." She patted her huge belly. "I'll have plenty of time off once these babies get here."

"That's what you think," Daniela said. "You might not be at school, but you'll wish you were." She shuddered visibly. "Two babies at once. I can't imagine it."

"She will have me to help," his mother said.

His sisters exchanged a pained look.

"What?" his mother demanded indignantly. "An *abuela* will be in the way?"

Margarita lumbered to her feet and planted a kiss on her mother's cheek. "No, Mama, you will be a godsend. I couldn't manage without you."

"Then why do I get these looks from your sisters?" she demanded.

"Because they are ungrateful beasts," Margarita said. "They know I am your favorite."

His mother clucked her disapproval. "You know I do not have a favorite."

"Except Enrique!" they all chimed in a well-rehearsed chorus.

He frowned at the whole lot of them, his reaction as familiar as the ribbing.

The chatter continued fast and furiously. It was peppered with Spanish. Allie sat amid the hubbub, blinking rapidly and trying to keep up, but Ricky could see from the way her head bobbed from person to person that it was a lost cause. Too many people were talking at once, much of it in a language she didn't understand.

Oddly, though, she didn't seem to be as frustrated as he would have expected. In fact, her lips had curved into a half smile and her eyes sparkled with delight. When she caught sight of him, the smile faded.

"Uh-oh," Maria murmured behind him. "You really are in trouble, aren't you?"

"I told you I was."

"Why don't I rescue Allie and take her into the kitchen? She looks as if she could use a breather from all the commotion. She and I can put out the food, while you fend off the inquiring minds. Mama's got that look in her eye, the one she reserves for unsuspecting potential mates. My Ben still shudders when he sees it. Says he'd never been so terrified in his life. Allie is definitely no match for that look and the questions that come with it."

"Fantastic idea," Ricky said gratefully. "In fact, why don't you take her right on out the back door and go to some nice quiet restaurant for dinner? You can bring her back after everyone's gone home."

"And have Mama on my case for a month? I don't think so."

Maria crossed the room and bent down to speak to

Allie. She nodded at once and stood up to follow the older woman. When their mother started to rise, Maria shot her a warning look that kept her in place.

After Allie and Maria had gone, the attention that had been riveted on Allie turned to Ricky.

"I've got nothing to say on the subject," he announced before they could start in. He looked straight at his father. "How about those Dolphins? Think they've got any shot at the Super Bowl this year?"

"Football," his mother said derisively. "If you think we came over here to discuss football, you are *loco*."

He planted a smacking kiss on her cheek. "I know it's not what you came to discuss, but Allie is off-limits. You'll scare her out of her wits."

"She was not frightened by us," his mother said.

"Overwhelmed, then. Do you realize that with all of you talking at once, she couldn't possibly know what you were saying? She can only read one set of lips at a time. Didn't you wonder why she never answered a single question?"

His mother's expression faltered. "Oh, I am so sorry. I never even considered." She leaped to her feet. "I must apologize."

"Leave it alone for now," Ricky advised. "Give her some time with Maria."

His mother looked torn. She clearly hated the thought that she might have inadvertently offended Allie, when her intentions had been only to welcome her into the family.

"Do as he says," his father advised, tugging on his wife's hand until she relented and sat back down.

"Thanks," Ricky said, a little surprised to have his

father's backing. Usually his father went along with whatever his beloved wife wanted.

"So," his mother said, her expression determined in light of their objections. "How about those Dolphins?"

Her daughters erupted into laughter. "Mama, do you even know who the Dolphins are?" Elena asked.

"Of course I do," his mother said indignantly. "But why anyone would choose to watch American football, rather than soccer is beyond me."

It was an old argument and one his family settled into readily. Satisfied that they were temporarily distracted, Ricky wandered into the kitchen just in time to hear Allie ask plaintively, "Do you think there's something wrong with me, besides my hearing, I mean?"

Maria caught a glimpse of him hesitating in the doorway and scowled before reassuring Allie, "There is nothing wrong with you. My brother is a dolt."

Ricky concluded that he was out of favor in the kitchen. He had two choices, he could go in there and defend himself for the second time that day, or he could go back to the living room and risk having the conversation shift from football back to his marital intentions. He opted for the kitchen, dangerous though it was.

"Need any help?" he inquired as he joined his sister and Allie.

"Everything's under control," Maria said. "I'll just start putting things on the table in the dining room. We'll do this buffet-style, since your table's not big enough for all of us to sit around it. The kids can eat outside."

She deliberately turned her back on Allie before adding, "Use this time alone with Allie to bail yourself out of trouble, baby brother. I don't know what you did, but it's obvious you hurt her."

"I don't think it's something that can be fixed in a few minutes," he said.

"Try," she ordered, letting the kitchen door swing shut behind her. "She's the best thing that ever happened to you. Don't blow it."

When they were alone, Allie regarded him nervously. "I like your family," she said.

"I'm sorry if they bombarded you with too many personal questions. It's a nosy crowd."

"I didn't mind." She grinned. "They didn't wait for answers, anyway. To tell you the truth, I had trouble keeping up with what they were saying."

"They didn't realize—" he began, but she cut him off.

"I'm used to that. You don't have to apologize. It's better sometimes when people forget I'm deaf. For a few minutes, even though I'm left out of the conversation, I feel almost normal."

"Allie, you *are* normal," he said fiercely, recalling the plaintive question she'd just asked Maria. "Just because you can't hear doesn't mean there's anything wrong with you."

She stared at him, clearly surprised by his vehemence. "You really mean that, don't you?"

"Well, of course I do," he said emphatically. "You're an amazing woman. Most of the time I completely forget that you can't hear. I have to remind myself that in certain circumstances you are at a disadvantage."

To his dismay, tears welled up and spilled down her cheeks. He knelt in front of her and brushed them from her cheeks. "What is it? What did I say?"

She clasped his hand and pressed a kiss to his palm. "You said everything just right," she whispered. "Most people, men especially, are too solicitous. They never forget that I have a disability and, because of that, they never let me forget it, either. There's no ignoring the fact that I can't hear, but once in a while it is so amazing to be able to pretend that it doesn't matter."

"It doesn't matter, not to me," he said. "My only regret is that you are missing some of the things you used to love, like your music. I can't even imagine how difficult that must have been for you to accept. It's no wonder you were so angry that I just walked away from my art."

"Yes, because you could do it and you don't."

"It's not in my soul, the way music was in yours. It's something I enjoy, something I'm good at, but it's not my passion."

"Sometimes I can still hear the music in my head," she told him, her expression filled with sorrow. She reached out and touched a finger to his lips. "Do you know what I really regret?"

He shook his head.

"That I've never heard the sound of your voice."

Ricky felt the sting of his own tears burning at the back of his eyes. "Oh, *querida,* you hear everything that's important."

Maybe one day he would even risk letting her hear what was in his heart.

Chapter 11

Allie declined an invitation from Ricky's mother to join the family for Sunday dinner. Her emotions were still ragged from the afternoon on the boat, the surprise visit of his family and from the things he'd said to her in the kitchen. She had the uneasy feeling that she was tumbling head over heels in love with a man she barely knew. Until she understood their relationship more fully, she didn't dare risk falling for his family, too.

"I don't understand," Jane said, when Allie tried to explain it to her. "You're crazy about him. He's crazy about you. Where's the problem?"

"It's too soon," she said stubbornly. "How can I trust what I'm feeling? Ricky certainly doesn't. He flat-out told me that I can't possibly know my own mind."

Jane chuckled. "How did you react when he suggested that?"

"I was furious."

"I can imagine."

Allie regarded her plaintively. "But what if he's right? What if the circumstances are just so volatile that I would have fallen for any man who plucked me out of that rubble? It's possible."

"Did you fall for Tom?"

She frowned at the absurdity of the question. "No, of course not."

"He was there, too," Jane said.

"But he wasn't the one who was talking me through it. He wasn't the one who actually brought me out."

"But if he had been, you would have fallen for him instead?" Jane asked, her skepticism plain.

Allie tried to envision herself falling for the sweet, gentle giant who was Ricky's partner. She'd spent a little time with him since the storm and hadn't felt so much as a tingle of attraction, though he was more classically handsome than Ricky.

"No," she admitted slowly. "He's a very nice man, but he doesn't do anything at all for me."

"Now we're getting somewhere." Jane regarded her with a sly expression. "Are you the first woman Ricky has ever saved?"

"No," Allie conceded.

"As far as you know, has he ever invited any of the others to live with him?"

"I'm not living with him," she argued. "I'm just staying here temporarily."

Jane rolled her eyes. "Whatever. Has he done this sort of thing before?"

"I don't think so."

"Then why do you suppose he picked you?"

Allie frowned. "If I knew that, this would be a whole lot less complicated."

"Sometimes love is only as complicated as we choose to make it."

"Whatever that means."

"It means, my darling girl, that love itself is simple. Resisting it is what makes it tricky. You're busy finding excuses for not being in love, instead of seizing it as the wonderful gift it is."

"Don't two people have to seize it at the same time?"

Jane grinned at the plaintive question. "That does help," she agreed. "Maybe I'll explain the concept to Ricky when he drives me home later this afternoon."

"Don't you dare. I don't want him to think we've spent the whole day sitting around talking about him."

"But that is exactly what we have done," Jane said.

"Then it's time to change the subject. How are things with you and your sister?" she asked, knowing it was a question that was guaranteed to send Jane off on another tangent. "They can't be too bad, because you look fabulous. You've even got a new haircut. Very flattering. You look ten years younger. You let the hairdresser put a blond rinse on it, too, didn't you?"

"I know what you're doing," Jane responded pointedly, even though she looked pleased by the compliment. "But I'm not going to forget about this business with Ricky."

"Then I suppose I'll just have to come along when he takes you home so I can protect my own interests."

"Suit yourself," Jane said easily. "As for my sister, the woman is flat-out crazy. Do you know what she's done now?"

Allie settled back for the tirade, relieved not to have

to defend her feelings for Ricky for the moment. Maybe things would be better after tomorrow. She intended to go back to work. They wouldn't be spending nearly as much time together. And soon she would move out.

That would be the real test, she concluded. If something were meant to happen between her and Ricky, then her moving to her own place wouldn't be the end of things. She resolved to start looking for a short-term rental the minute she finished up her first day back at the clinic on Monday.

Unfortunately, events conspired against her.

Her last patient was four-year-old Kimi Foley and she could see why Gina had expressed concern about the little girl. She wasn't keeping up with her sign language lessons nearly as well as Allie had hoped she would.

"Are you mad at me?" the child signed at the end of the session, her expression worried.

"Never," Allie reassured her, giving her a hug.

"But I keep forgetting."

"That's okay. You just need a little more practice at home."

Kimi's sweet little face fell. "How? Nobody at home will learn."

Allie bit back a curse. Jessica Foley was a good mother, but she was overwhelmed by the responsibility of four other children besides Kimi. Coping with Kimi's hearing loss was more of a burden than she'd been able to manage so far. Getting her daughter to the clinic for the twice-a-week sessions was about all she'd been willing to do. Staying for her own classes had been out of the question. She had flatly refused.

"I'll pick it up from Kimi," she had assured Allie, but the futility of that promise was increasingly evident.

As for Derrick Foley, he worked two jobs to try to provide for his family. He'd picked Kimi up on a few occasions and, though the love he had for his little girl was obvious, he still seemed to be in a state of denial that her disability was permanent and required any sort of adjustments on his part to help her deal with it. When he spoke to her, he raised his voice as if somehow that would help her to hear him.

The Foleys weren't the first family Allie had seen struggle to adapt to the needs of a hearing-impaired child, but it never failed to sadden her. As in her own case and Kimi's, it seemed to be worse when the hearing loss was sudden and unexpected.

"You and I will work harder," she told Kimi. "And I'll speak to your mom again about lessons. If she can't do it, what about your older sister. She's ten, right?"

The child's expression brightened at the suggestion. "Marty would do it. I know she would."

"Then I'll see if I can arrange it," Allie promised.

"I love you," Kimi signed.

"I love you, too," Allie told her. "Now let's go outside and see if your mom's here."

Mrs. Foley was sitting in her car, waiting at the curb. Allie walked Kimi to the car, but when she tried to speak to her mother, Mrs. Foley waved her off with the announcement that she was running late. She pulled away from the curb before Allie could say a word.

Allie sighed heavily and dragged back inside. Apparently, she wasn't nearly as recovered as she'd thought she was. She was exhausted, but she was determined to stick around for the weekly staff meeting.

Gina took one look at her and vetoed her plan. "You're pale. You need to go home."

"I'm back full-time," Allie insisted to her boss. "Give me five minutes to grab a cup of coffee, and I'll join you in the conference room."

She had assumed that Gina accepted her word as final, but apparently she was wrong. The meeting had barely started when it was interrupted by Ricky's arrival. Gina beamed at him.

"You made good time," she said.

"You called him?" Allie asked, stunned by the betrayal.

"We had a deal," Gina said. "I was to call if you resisted my commonsense advice. Now go home. Get some rest. We'll see you in the morning."

Sorely tempted to plant herself right where she was and refuse to budge, she changed her mind when she met Ricky's determined gaze. She could always quit just to express her displeasure, but she managed to leave the room without taking such a drastic step. She loved her job. And tomorrow she would tell Gina that she was perfectly capable of deciding whether she felt well enough to spend an hour at a stupid staff meeting.

Since that discussion had to wait, she settled for snapping at Ricky. "Why aren't you back at work?"

"I was. And I'll be there again as soon as I get you home. I have my beeper on, in case they need me in the meantime."

"I don't appreciate you barging in here like this," she said as she gathered up the work she intended to do at home that night.

"I didn't barge in," he said patiently. "Your boss called me."

"She had no business doing that."

"She cares about you."

"That's very sweet, I'm sure, but I can look after myself."

"Then do it. Go home and take a nap."

"I'm not tired," she said, perfectly aware that she sounded like a sullen child resisting bedtime.

"So you say," he retorted mildly.

Naturally, she had to go and prove him right. Five minutes in the car and she couldn't keep her eyes open. She wasn't even aware of arriving at the house. She woke up as he shifted her into his arms to carry her inside.

"What are you doing?" she demanded, struggling to get down.

It was a wasted effort. He merely chuckled and held on tighter, clearly unimpressed by her grouchiness. "Three guesses what I'm doing."

She pushed against the solid wall of his chest. "Put me down."

His gaze locked with hers. "Give me a break, Allie. Two minutes in my arms, maybe three. Is that so much to ask?"

Incredulity replaced indignation. "What are you saying, that you're enjoying this?"

He settled her a little more tightly against his chest. "What do you think?"

If she were forced to be totally honest, it wasn't so bad from her perspective, either. She sighed and relented, then looped an arm around his neck. "Go for it, Wilder. Enjoy yourself."

She had to admit that snuggling against him wasn't exactly a sacrifice. The only problem would be that when they got to her bed, he was going to unceremoniously dump her there and leave her all alone.

She pressed her face against his neck. But for two minutes, maybe three, she could pretend that he might not.

Ricky was pretty sure Allie Matthews was going to drive him out of his mind. Now that they were both back at work, they were uneasily struggling to fit into each other's routines. He'd actually believed that once they were both out of the house, life would be less complicated. He'd anticipated giving her a wide berth so he could keep his hormones in check, but it wasn't turning out quite that way.

She was on his mind night and day. He told himself it was because he hadn't slept with her. If they'd gotten that out of the way, he wouldn't feel this constant aching need. He would be halfway to being over her.

Instead, he was sex deprived and sleep deprived. With every moment that passed, he felt himself more and more drawn to Allie's amazing serenity, her strength and determination to recover fully and to reclaim her shattered life. Of course, her tendency to want to rush it annoyed him. She was going to have a relapse if she kept it up.

Monday had been a perfect example. When he'd gone to pick her up at school, it was plain that she was dead on her feet, but she'd still been furious because he and Gina had conspired to make her go home. If the woman didn't have sense enough to know when to call it quits, how was he supposed to believe she had sense enough to know her own mind when it came to him? Fortunately, he'd been smart enough not to ask her that. The memory of the last time he'd made that suggestion still burned in his head.

He sighed heavily, glanced up and suddenly realized he was surrounded by half a dozen grinning firefighters.

"What?" he demanded.

"Definitely a woman," one of them said with a knowing expression on his face.

"Has to be," another agreed.

"The beautiful Allie," Tom informed them. "She has our Enrique dancing at the end of a string."

He frowned at the teasing. "I am not…"

"Were you or were you not completely unaware that we have been standing here for the past ten minutes?" Tom asked.

"Yes, but—"

"Were you or were you not occupied with thoughts of your lovely houseguest?"

"I don't have to answer that."

Tom took a mocking bow as the others hooted. "I rest my case."

"You want to talk about women?" Ricky inquired lazily. "Shall we discuss the ex-wife who is never far from your thoughts? Shall we mention the fact that you have been dropping by her house, interviewing her damn dates?"

"I have not," Tom began, his face flushed with indignation. "Okay, I have been over there a few times."

"I rest *my* case," Ricky said.

"We're both a couple of saps," Tom concluded sorrowfully.

"Speak for yourself," Ricky retorted. "You've been there, done that. You ought to know better. I'm still feeling my way here."

"An interesting turn of phrase," one of his coworkers declared. "What do you suppose he means by that, men?"

"Oh, go to blazes," Ricky muttered.

"Not a suggestion to be made lightly in a fire station," Tom pointed out, then sighed. "But I understand the sentiment."

"What am I supposed to do?" Ricky asked.

"Like I would know," Tom responded woefully.

"Then leave me alone to think," Ricky pleaded. "I have to figure this out."

What was it about Allie? She was nothing like the women who usually attracted him. He was used to glib chatter and easy flirting. Allie got charmingly rattled at his teasing.

Moreover, he found that she expected—no, demanded—more, in her quiet, intense way. It was the way she looked at him, disappointment in her eyes, when he evaded a question or offered a less-than-truthful response. She always seemed to know, too, which was as disconcerting as it was flattering.

Then there was his family. They had taken to Allie as if she were one of their own. Each one of his sisters had called to express approval. His mother had taken him aside on Sunday to ask a million and one questions about his relationship with the woman living in his house. Even his father had commented at dinner that he considered Allie to be a keeper.

"The woman's got a good, level head on her shoulders," his father had told him. "You could do worse."

Even the kids had chimed in, his nephews declaring Allie to be "a real babe."

He frowned at each of the boys in turn. "What do you know about babes?"

"Hey, we're guys, too," Ray had declared, skinny little chest puffed out.

"And Mama says if we're not careful, we're gonna turn out to be flirts like you," Maria's oldest chimed in. "She says it as if it's a bad thing."

Ricky had glanced across the table at his sister. "A bad thing?"

"If all you do is flirt and never take any woman seriously, you'll wind up all alone in your old age," she said.

"Don't you think it's a little soon to be worrying about my old age?" he inquired.

"You're thirty, baby brother," Elena pointed out.

"By now you should have two or three children," his mother declared. "It's your responsibility to see that your father's name is carried on."

"Don't put pressure on him," his father said, in a rare contradiction of his wife. "Marriage is a big step. He shouldn't take it before he's ready."

"Somebody has to push him," Maria said. "Otherwise he'll still be dating when he's in the old folks' home."

"You're just jealous because I've been with more than one woman and you've spent your entire life with one man," Ricky had taunted.

His sister's cheeks had flushed, and she'd reached for her husband's hand. "When you find the best right off, there's no need to waste time sifting through second bests. Which reminds me, baby brother, you owe us a weekend of babysitting."

Ricky envied the love glowing in her eyes as she and Benny exchanged a long look. "I'll check my calendar, and we'll work it out," he promised. "Try to keep your hands off each other until then. There are children in the room."

"You're just jealous, *niño*."

"Okay, enough," his father declared. "Leave the man alone. He will do whatever he's going to do without our interference."

"Thank you, Papa," Ricky said.

"Don't thank me. I'm one of those who think you're a fool if you let Allie get away. I'm just not going to waste my breath trying to convince you."

As Ricky recalled the exchange, he felt the same pressure building up inside him. His family had too many expectations. By contrast, it appeared Allie had none. She hadn't asked for anything except a little honesty, a little less interference. Worse, he had a hunch she was gearing up to move out, and he had no idea how to stop her.

When his shift finally ended, he debated accepting Tom's invitation to stop off for a few beers but finally declined.

"Going home?" Tom asked. "Do you and Allie have plans?"

"No, no plans." Now that she was getting a ride home with one of her friends, he couldn't even be sure she would be there, but he wanted to head over there in case she was.

"What about later?" Tom asked. "Want to get together? Maybe go on a double date?"

Ricky regarded him with curiosity. "You have a date?"

"With Nikki," he confessed.

"That's a surprise. How'd you convince your ex to go on a date?"

"Actually, I told her you and Allie would be along to chaperone. She's anxious to meet the woman who has you tied in knots."

"What happens if we don't show up?"

"My goose is cooked. She'll probably refuse to leave the house," he said, looking totally dejected.

Ricky took pity on him. "Okay, I'll see what I can do. I'll call you at Nikki's in an hour."

Tom's expression brightened. "Thanks. I owe you."

"Yes. You do."

When he got home, he found Allie in the kitchen staring at the contents of the refrigerator. She was barefoot and dressed in shorts and a tank top. She'd scooped her hair into a careless ponytail. She looked as if she was barely out of her teens and sexy as sin, all at the same time. He had to resist the urge to sneak up behind her and press a kiss to her bare nape.

"I know you're there," she said, startling him. She turned slowly, her expression serious.

"How did you know that?"

A grin tugged at her lips. "It's probably best that I keep that little secret to myself. It comes in handy."

He decided that was worth further thought at another time. "You can close the refrigerator door," he said. "We're going out for dinner."

He wasn't sure what reaction he'd expected to his announcement. Even as he uttered the words, he realized he should have phrased it as a question. To his surprise she seemed relieved.

"Good thing. The cupboard is bare. Where are we going?"

For some reason her unexpected agreeability annoyed him. "That's it? Just okay and where are we going?"

She gave him a perplexed look. "Did you want an argument?"

"Not really, but I usually get one."

"You mean because you're usually issuing edicts, rather than inquiring about my preferences?"

He winced at the direct hit. "Pretty much."

She laughed. "Every once in a while your arrogance coincides with my own desires. Why waste time arguing when that happens? I don't fight with you just for the thrill of it."

"Funny. I was beginning to think that was how you got your kicks," he murmured, forgetting for a moment that just keeping his voice low wouldn't prevent her from knowing what he'd said.

To emphasize his mistake, she tapped his lips. "I saw that."

Her touch, as light and teasing as it was, set off all the pent-up hunger he'd been fighting for days. He reached for her and dragged her to him, his mouth closing over hers just as she uttered a little gasp of surprise.

He was only dimly aware that she wasn't struggling, wasn't even attempting to protest. He was too lost in the taste of her, in the way her body molded itself to his, the way one foot trailed up his calf as she fitted herself more snugly against his instant arousal.

Sweet heaven, the woman was a witch. Cool and

calm one minute, she drove him to a frenzy as he tried to get a reaction. The next minute she was all heat and heart-stopping temptation. How was a man supposed to cope with a woman who could change moods on a dime? A woman who could look like an angel and kiss like a sinner?

Right this second Ricky would have given everything he owned to be able to scoop her up and carry her off to his bed and take full advantage of everything she was offering. He doubted even his iron will and sense of honor could have prevented it. Only the very dim memory of his commitment to his best friend nagged at him, until he finally released Allie with a shuddering sigh of regret.

"One of these days we're going to finish this," he said on a ragged breath.

"Now seems like as good a time as any," she said, her expression dazed and hopeful.

"Tom's waiting for us."

She stared at him blankly. "Tom? What does he have to do with this?"

"He finally managed to convince his ex-wife to go out on a date."

"And that matters to you and me because…?"

"She'll only go if we go."

Allie regarded him with fascination. "Why is that?"

"She wants to meet you more than she wants to steer clear of Tom."

"Okay, back up. They're divorced, correct?"

Ricky nodded.

"Then why do they want to go out at all?"

"According to my mother, they're still in love."

"What do you think?"

"No question in my mind that he's still in love with her. I haven't spoken to Nikki, but my mother assures me that the feeling is mutual."

"Then why on earth did they get a divorce in the first place?"

"Because they're both too bullheaded to compromise. She wants him to quit his job and go to work in her father's business. He loves what he does as much as I do. We're both danger junkies."

All of the color seemed to drain out of Allie's face. She quickly turned away and started for the door, but not before he'd seen that something was terribly wrong.

"I'll get ready," she said, her voice a little too quiet, a little too subdued.

Ricky snagged her wrist. "Hey, what just happened?"

"Nothing," she said stiffly.

"Allie, talk to me. One minute you were full of questions about Tom and Nikki, the next you looked as if I'd kicked the stuffing out of that favorite teddy bear of yours."

She shook her head. "It doesn't matter. We'd better hurry if we're going to meet your friends."

This time when she pulled away, Ricky let her go. But he had a feeling it would be a long time before he could shake the questions stirred by her odd behavior. He had a hunch the answers were even more important than he could imagine.

Chapter 12

Allie wasn't sure why it hadn't sunk in sooner that what had been a rare and terrifying experience for her was something that Ricky did all the time. By his own admission, he thrived on taking risks. He hadn't built a career around saving lives because it was simply something that needed to be done or even as a way to prove to his father that he was macho as well as artistic. He did it because he loved the danger inherent in exploring collapsed buildings for survivors.

She had been caught by surprise, trapped in the rubble of her own home, alone and terrified for hours. He had considered rescuing her to be little more than a game, pitting his skill against Mother Nature's precarious aftermath.

Of course he was a well-trained expert. Of course he understood the risks and no doubt did everything in his power to minimize them. But the bottom line was he was the kind of man who would be easily bored by anything less than the extraordinary challenge of a dangerous profession.

How could he possibly be attracted to anything less in a woman? No wonder he'd never settled down with one woman. He needed the variety to avert boredom. As for her, she must seem incredibly dull, just an ordinary teacher, who couldn't even share in some of the activities most people took for granted, like music and dancing.

She realized glumly that these were definitely issues she was going to have to wrestle with, preferably sooner rather than later, and preferably without Ricky nagging at her for answers. She had hoped to get out of the kitchen without revealing her dismay, but obviously he'd noticed her reaction, even if he hadn't understood the reason for it. He wouldn't be satisfied with her evasion for long.

Thankful that they wouldn't be spending the evening alone, she rushed to get ready. She even managed to forget her own dilemma when they joined Tom and his ex-wife.

Allie liked Nikki at once. She had a warm smile and an exuberant personality. From the minute Allie walked through Nikki's front door, the other woman treated her as if they were old friends with a million things to catch up on.

"We have to talk," she told Allie, drawing her into the comfortably furnished living room of a Spanish-style home on a narrow waterway in Coral Gables. She gestured dismissively toward the men. "Let them fend for themselves. Tom knows his way around."

Tom looked disappointed, but he dutifully led Ricky off toward another part of the house.

Amused, Allie watched them leave. "I don't think this is what Tom had in mind," she suggested innocently.

"I'm sure it's not," Nikki agreed cheerfully. "I stopped doing what Tom expected on the day I divorced him. Actually before that. He didn't think I'd file to end the marriage in the first place. The man has a monumental ego. It serves him well in his work, but in his personal life..." She shrugged. "He needs to get over it."

It was an amazing display of bravado, but Allie didn't buy it. "You didn't think Tom would let you go through with the divorce, did you?"

Nikki stared at her in surprise. "How did you figure that out? No one else did. Well, except for Ricky's mother. She saw straight through me."

"And once you'd started the whole divorce thing, you didn't know how to stop it?"

The other woman sighed. "Pretty stupid, huh?"

"Not stupid. It was a drastic measure and it didn't work. I imagine you had your reasons for trying it."

"Oh, yes," Nikki said fervently. "That job of his scares me to death."

The response hit a little too close to what Allie had been thinking earlier. "But you knew what he did when you met, correct?"

"I thought he would be ready to stop once we started talking about having a family. I offered him an alternative, working for my father. I didn't care whether he did that or something else. I just wanted him to be safe. Instead of even trying to see my point, he accused me of trying to change him. He told me he wasn't cut out for a desk job and he never would be."

"And you couldn't live with that," Allie surmised.

Nikki shrugged. "I didn't think I could, but now that I've been through the alternative—living without him—I know it's worse. I still worry myself sick every single time he's raced off to some disaster. I still sit by the phone, then panic when it rings. Thankfully, so far it's been Tom checking in to let me know he's okay."

"He calls even though you're divorced?"

"Every night he's gone," she said.

"Have you told him what you've figured out? That the divorce didn't give you the peace of mind you'd expected it to?"

Nikki sighed. "No."

"Why not?"

"Too much pride, I suppose. I keep hoping that being without me will be just as hard on him. I'm pretty sure it is, too, but I haven't seen any evidence that he's willing to consider a compromise."

"And do what instead?" What would be the compromise between a desk job and slip-sliding into a mountain of debris that could kill a man with one false step?

"I wish I knew." She gave Allie a penetrating look. "What about you? Are you okay with what Ricky does?"

"To be honest, I don't think it sank in until tonight what he does. He said something that caught me off guard. It shouldn't have, but it did."

Nikki looked surprised by the response. "How can that be? You met when he rescued you."

"I know. I guess I was so wrapped up in the relief of being saved that I forgot all about the risks he took to get me out of there. And somehow I completely missed the fact that he does that kind of thing all the time, that it wasn't some sort of heroic fluke."

"Now that you've realized it, are you going to stick it out or bail?"

Allie's gaze strayed toward the direction in which the men had gone. "I wish I knew," she admitted candidly, then shrugged. "Of course, it's not exactly an issue. Ricky and I are just friends."

Nikki stared at her, then burst out laughing. "Oh, my," she said eventually. "Listen to the two of us. We're both delusional. I think my ex-husband is going to suddenly convert to some nine-to-five life and you think there's nothing going on between you and Ricky."

"There isn't," Allie insisted.

Nikki patted her hand. "Tell yourself that all you want. I saw the way he looked at you."

"How?"

A grin spread across Nikki's face. "The same way you looked at him, like a lovesick teenager."

Well, hell.

The evening wasn't going at all the way Ricky had anticipated. Even after they reached the club where they'd gone for drinks after dinner, Allie and Nikki had had their heads together every second, giggling like a couple of schoolgirls over jokes they apparently saw no need to share. Tom didn't seem to mind, but it was driving Ricky crazy. What the heck did they have to talk about? They'd just met.

He finally decided enough was enough. He stood up and put his hand under Allie's elbow. When she turned a startled look in his direction, he said, "Dance?"

"But I don't—"

"You can," he retorted, exerting a little pressure to encourage her to get to her feet. He glanced pointedly toward Tom and then Nikki. "I'm sure they'd like to dance, too."

Allie nodded at once. "Of course." She beamed at Nikki, who was regarding her ex-husband warily.

Before Allie could comment, Ricky urged her toward the dance floor. The music was slow, which was why he'd chosen that moment to insist on the dance. He could pull Allie close and demonstrate the rhythm of the song with the movements of his body.

For an instant she tensed against him, but then he felt her slowly relax.

"What's the song?" she asked, her gaze on his.

He told her the title of the old love song, and her expression brightened. He could hear her starting to hum the melody from memory. She found the rhythm on her own, without his guidance, then returned his gaze, her expression pleased.

"Told you so," he said.

"Told me what?"

"That you could dance."

"Because I remember the song," she said, then added wistfully, "I used to be able to play it on the violin."

"Have you played at all since you lost your hearing?"

She looked shocked by the question. "Of course not."

"Why not? You can still read music, can't you?"

"Yes, but—" Her expression faltered. Tears welled up. "I just can't. It would be too frustrating not to be able to hear it, not to know if I made a mistake."

He saw how much the loss of playing hurt her. "Some people would consider that an advantage," he said. "You could play in blissful ignorance. I'm sure Pedro would be happy to loan you his violin, and Maria would consider it a blessing if you'd keep it."

"No," she said fiercely. "Never."

He touched her cheek, tried to smooth away the lines of tension that had formed around her mouth. "I'm sorry. I was just hoping it might give you back something you'd lost."

"No. It would just make it a thousand times worse." She buried her face against his shoulder.

He wasn't quite ready to let the idea rest. He held her away from him and looked into her eyes. "Until tonight, you thought you'd never be able to dance again, but look at you now. It's something to think about."

To emphasize the point, he gathered her close and spun her around the dance floor in a series of intricate steps that she followed without a single stumble. The color rose in her cheeks and the sparks returned to her eyes. By the time the music stopped, she was laughing.

"Okay, okay, I can dance, but only if I hang on to you for dear life."

"And the problem with that is?" he asked, his gaze locked with hers.

Her bright-eyed expression faltered. "You won't always be here," she whispered so low that he could barely hear her over the music.

Ricky wanted to deny it, wanted to tell her that she would always be able to turn to him, but the commitment terrified him. The only thing that terrified him more was the prospect of losing her.

Yet over the next few days that was exactly what he sensed was happening. Allie was still sharing the house, but there was a growing distance between them, a distance he didn't understand and couldn't seem to bridge.

Her strength was back and she seemed to be settling into a comfortable routine that didn't include him. She spent her days at work and her evenings with friends or locked up in her room doing paperwork for the clinic. He'd spotted her studying ads for rental apartments on more than one occasion—though, thankfully, the rental market was tighter than ever because of the number of families displaced by the hurricane.

He was pretty sure he'd go nuts if he couldn't think of some way to shake that scary composure, that carefully polite facade that greeted him over the breakfast table.

He debated confronting her, asking why she'd suddenly withdrawn. He'd traced it back to the evening they'd spent with Nikki and Tom, but Tom was absolutely no help when Ricky questioned him about whether he'd noticed any reason why Allie might be ticked off.

"She seemed okay to me," Tom told him.

"And Nikki hasn't said anything?"

"Believe it or not, on those rare occasions when I actually spend time with my ex-wife, you are not the topic of conversation," Tom said.

Ricky heard the edginess in his friend's voice. "How is that going, by the way? Are you making any progress?"

"It depends on what you call progress," Tom said. "Her string of admirers seems to be dwindling, but she still gets all huffy when I suggest we go out. I'm running out of ideas and patience."

"Tell me about it," Ricky said grimly. He made up

his mind that he had to do something to break this un-spoken standoff between him and Allie.

He had a hunch based on past experience that a kiss would do it. He just had to find the excuse—or the right occasion—for stealing one.

Although his schedule at work could be unpredict-able, it appeared he had the weekend off. He concluded that Saturday would be the perfect opportunity for the two of them to spend some quality time together. He broached the subject over breakfast on Friday.

Reaching across the table, he tapped Allie's hand to distract her from the morning paper. "Do you have plans for tomorrow?" he asked when her startled gaze met his.

For an instant he actually thought he saw panic flare in her eyes, but she finally shook her head. "No. Why?"

"I thought we might spend the day together."

"You don't have to do that. I'm fine on my own now. I'm sure there are plenty of things you'd rather be doing than babysitting a houseguest who's probably overstayed her welcome."

The last part of her response snagged his attention. "You have not overstayed your welcome. Have I said anything at all to make you think that? If I have, I'm sorry. You're welcome to stay here as long as you want to. In fact, I insist on it."

She avoided his gaze. "You don't have to be polite. I know this was supposed to be temporary. In fact, I was thinking of spending Saturday looking at a couple of apartments."

Ricky felt his gut clench at the confirmation that she was itching to move out. The very thought of it made him crazy. "Don't be ridiculous," he snapped.

"Why should you spend money on an apartment when I have room here?"

"I must be cramping your style."

"Allie, where is this coming from?" he asked, barely curbing his impatience. "I thought we were doing okay here."

She regarded him guiltily. "I'm sorry. You've been wonderful. I just feel as if I'm imposing on you. I need to get back on my own."

"On your own? Or away from me? Why?"

She stood up, her movements hurried. "I have to get to work. Can we talk about this another time?"

She rushed out of the room, not waiting for a response. Ricky stared after her.

"Well, what the hell was that all about?" he murmured when she'd gone.

He grabbed the phone and punched out Nikki's number. "I need to talk to you," he said when she answered.

"Okay, talk, but if this is about Tom you're wasting your breath."

"It's not about Tom, though I could give you an earful on the subject. Another time, though. Do you have any idea what's up with Allie?"

"Allie? Is she okay?" she asked at once, sounding genuinely concerned.

"That's what I'm asking you. Ever since that night the four of us went out, she's been acting all weird. Do you know what that's about?"

"I might," Nikki responded thoughtfully. "But first let me ask you something. Are you in love with her?"

"I care about her," he said.

"That's not the same, is it?"

"No. What's your point?"

"She's a good person, Enrique. Don't mess with her head."

"For cripe's sake, Nikki, I am not messing with her head. I don't know where this is going. How am I supposed to find out, if she starts pushing me away?"

"Is that what she's doing?"

"It seems that way to me. She hasn't moved, but she's barely speaking to me. Did I do or say something to offend her?"

"You really are worried about this, aren't you?"

"Of course I am. That's why I called."

"Okay then, here's the deal. I can't say for sure, but I think it has to do with your job. We talked a little about how spooked I was by Tom's career. Allie seemed to be pretty much in the same place about yours. Apparently she just woke up to the fact that you put your life on the line on a regular basis."

"This is about my job?" Ricky echoed incredulously.

"I can't be certain, but that's my guess."

He groaned. He could fix a lot of things. He could talk his way out of just about anything. But what the hell was he supposed to do about his career? He loved his profession. It was who he was. Nikki had to be wrong. Just because she freaked out on a regular basis about Tom's job, she was probably projecting her own feelings onto Allie. He resolved to go straight to the source and he wouldn't wait until tomorrow. He'd do it tonight.

Allie came home to find the house lit by candles and dinner simmering on the stove. Picadillo, black beans and rice. She had a feeling they could thank

Mrs. Wilder or Maria for the food. She was less certain about the candles.

Ricky wandered out of the bathroom just then, a towel wrapped around his waist, his chest and hair still damp from a shower. It was not an image conducive to peace of mind. Her already-shaky resolve to fight the attraction she felt for this man took a solid hit, especially when his lips curved slowly into that irresistible smile of his.

"Hi." He gestured toward his barely concealed body. "I thought I had the place to myself."

Allie swallowed hard and tried to feign a nonchalance she was far from feeling. "It is your house."

A storm began to brew in his eyes. "Don't go there, Allie."

"I just meant—"

"I know what you meant," he retorted, his expression fierce. He seemed to be fighting a losing battle with himself. "Look, I'll be out in a few minutes. Dinner's almost ready. There's a bottle of wine on the kitchen counter. Pour yourself a glass, if you'd like one."

She was about to protest, to make an excuse and retreat to her room to avoid whatever unpredictable mood he was in, but she got the distinct impression he'd be infuriated if she tried.

"Thanks," she said instead. "I'll just put these papers away."

She had to brush past him in the narrow corridor to reach her room. He stubbornly refused to budge. She could feel the heat emanating from his body as she inched past. He smelled of soap and shampoo and pure masculinity. If she'd been another kind of woman, she would have reached out and given that precariously knotted towel a sharp tug just to see what might follow. As it was, she fought the impulse and made a dash for her room.

Closing the door behind her, she leaned against it and gasped for breath. "Oh, my," she murmured. She was in trouble. Knee-deep and sinking fast. More trouble than she'd ever imagined.

Worse, she thought, Ricky knew it. He might have turned up in the hallway wearing nothing but a towel and a smile by accident, but he'd lingered on purpose, enjoying her discomfort.

Why? That was what she wanted to know. What perversity had made him stand there and deliberately taunt her? Hadn't she been doing her best to steer clear of him ever since they'd gone on that double date with Tom and Nikki? Hadn't she practically told him by her actions that she considered them to be nothing more than casual roommates?

Hadn't she been lying through her teeth…to herself as well as him? She sighed heavily. She might as well admit it. She wanted Ricky Wilder, wanted him as she had never wanted another man, had never even been tempted by another man.

But he'd been right to warn her off. It would be a disaster. He was a flirt and a scoundrel, who took nothing very seriously except his work. She was serious and intense. When she finally got around to having a relationship, she intended for it to matter, for it to last. If that wasn't a doomed combination, what was?

She sighed again. She knew perfectly well that she couldn't hide out in her room. Ricky had already warned her against that. Surely she could spend an evening with him without acting on all of these raging impulses he stirred in her. She just had to get a grip and remember who he was, who *she* was.

When she finally emerged and headed for the kitchen, she was relieved that he wasn't there. She poured herself a glass of red wine and took a sip. Warmth cascaded through her. She felt better at once. Braver. She took another sip, then warned herself that continuing down that particular path would be folly.

She moved to the stove, lifted the lid on the picadillo and stirred the mixture of meat and spices, savoring the rich scent. Suddenly she felt Ricky's hand in the middle of her back. Her gaze shot up and met his as he leaned around her to check on the simmering pot of black beans. She couldn't seem to catch her breath.

"Hungry?" he inquired mildly, stepping back and pouring his own glass of wine.

Allie's pulse scrambled. Every sense was on full alert, and all he cared about was food. That ought to tell her something.

"Starved," she said, proud that she managed to get the word out without choking.

"Me, too. Have a seat. I'll fix our plates."

Allie sat, because her knees were threatening to buckle anyway. Ricky put a full plate in front of her, set one at his own place, then dimmed the lights, leaving the room bathed in the glow of half a dozen candles.

Allie automatically tasted the food, but it might as well have been sawdust. She had to fight the urge to cast surreptitious glances at the man seated opposite her. Something was going on here that she didn't understand. His solicitous behavior, the candles, that little scene in the hallway, all of it pointed toward a man intent on seduction. Not that she had a lot of experience in that area, but she was pretty sure this wasn't the way casual roommates behaved.

She could let the evening take its own course or she could ask a few questions and take charge of it herself. She'd vowed a long time ago not to let circumstances control her life. The next few minutes might be awkward, especially if she'd gotten it all wrong, but at least she would know.

"Ricky?"

He regarded her with a questioning expression.

"What's going on here?" she asked.

"We're having dinner."

"Besides that?"

His lips twitched ever so slightly, but his eyes were serious as they clashed with hers. "What makes you think something's going on?"

"You." She gestured toward the candles. "This."

"You have a problem with the ambiance?"

"I don't have a problem with it," she said, not even trying to hide her exasperation. "Not exactly."

"What then?"

She wanted to smack the innocent expression off his face. She thought maybe a little bluntness would do the job.

"Are you trying to seduce me?" she asked.

This time his lips curved into a full-blown grin. "Yes," he said, taking the wind out of her sails.

Allie stared at him, openmouthed. She hadn't expected him to admit it. Now that he had, what was she supposed to say? What was she supposed to do? Tell him to forget it? Get all huffy and indignant and stalk away from the table? Out of the house, she corrected.

She would have to get very far away, if she was to change the course he'd set.

The trouble was, her breath seemed to have lodged in her throat. Her body was shouting, "Hip hip hurray!" and all but daring her to say yes.

"Do you have a problem with that?" Ricky inquired lazily.

Allie swallowed hard and tried to muster up the protest that her brain assured her was appropriate.

"No," she whispered finally. "No, I don't have a problem with that."

His grin spread. "Good."

He reached over, picked up her hand and pressed a kiss to her palm. A shudder rolled through her.

"Eat," he advised. "You're going to need the energy."

Allie wanted to make some clever, snippy little comment about his ego, but she didn't. She picked up her fork and ate. It was hard to concentrate on beans and rice, though, when all she could think about was dessert.

Chapter 13

Ricky had taken a huge risk when he'd admitted to Allie that he intended to seduce her. He almost expected her to bolt from the room. For a minute, in fact, she'd looked as if she wanted to.

Then, to his amazement and relief, she met his gaze evenly and said, "Yes." He hadn't tasted another bite of food after that.

Still, he'd been determined not to rush her. He wanted to give her a little time to get used to the idea. He even wanted her to have time to change her mind, though he was pretty sure he would die if she did.

They even managed to carry on a conversation during the rest of the meal. He couldn't recall now what it had been about, but it had seemed brilliant enough at the time.

Finally, when the table had been carefully cleared

and the dishes dutifully done, she looked up at him, her heart in her eyes, and asked, "This seduction of yours, is it going to be tonight?"

Ricky swallowed hard, fighting the need that made him want to reach out and claim her. "Are you still okay with that?"

He lasted until she gave him the slightest nod and then his lips settled against hers. He'd lectured himself for the past hour to go slowly. He'd assured himself that he could.

But one taste of her had him reevaluating. Need slammed through him, hot and urgent. Still he kept the kiss light, persuasive and coaxing, rather than demanding. She whimpered against his mouth, clearly wanting more. His blood roared in his ears, insisting that he go along with her.

He fought that urge and all the others that tugged at him, settling instead for the sweet torment of a slow burn. Oh, he was on fire for her, all right. He'd never known anyone like her, a woman who offered everything. The complete surrender was as unexpected as it was exciting. It washed away all of the doubts that had made him hold back for weeks now. He promised himself he would make sure she didn't regret her decision, not tonight, not ever.

His mouth was still locked with hers when he scooped her up and cradled her against his chest. Even as small as his house was, it seemed to take forever, but he reached his bedroom eventually after stopping along the way to blow out each and every candle. The firefighter in him was unwilling to trade safety for ambience. Then he closed the door, leaving a disappointed Shadow on the other side. He heard a whimper as he carried Allie to the bed, then the thump of the dog's body settling against the door.

He lowered Allie gently to the bed. "Allie, are you sure?" he asked one more time as he stood staring down at her.

Dazed, dreamy eyes met his. "About what?"

"About this?" he said. "Making love?"

She stretched languidly, then scooted onto her knees and put her hands on either side of his face. Her gaze was clear, her expression determined. "Very sure," she assured him, then slanted her mouth across his and plunged her tongue inside in a way that removed all trace of doubt.

Ricky felt something inside him shatter. Later he would have to figure out what the sensation was, but for now he knew only that touching Allie was more thrilling than anything he'd ever experienced, in bed or out. He couldn't seem to get enough of the feel of her soft skin as he slowly removed first her top, then her bra, noting as he did that it was one of the sexy ones he'd picked out for her. Then he feasted on the sight of her bared breasts, the dusky peaks, the pebble-hard nipples. For now it was enough just to drink in the sight. Touching, tasting would come later.

When he'd satisfied himself with that vision, he slid the zipper of her pants down, then trailed his fingers along satiny flesh until he reached the silky barrier of her panties. He paused, then moved on. Her eyes widened with surprise, then pleasure as he touched the hot, slick core of her. She gasped when he stripped away her panties and touched the same place with his tongue. Her hips rose off the bed as she strained toward his touch and toward an elusive release.

"Not yet, *querida*. Not yet," he murmured, shifting his attention to her breasts, which were peaked with arousal. Her cries pleased him, but he wanted more. He wanted to give her an experience she would never forget, never equal.

She stirred restlessly when he pulled away. She reached for him, but he slipped out of reach, letting the sensations die to a simmer before stirring them back up again with a slow caress, a tender kiss, a deliberate slide of expert fingers deep inside her. She bucked against him, once again begging for a release he refused.

There was a sheen of perspiration on her body, an undeniable tension to her muscles. He felt that tension mirrored in his own body, which was hard and aching from the long denial.

"Please," she whispered, her voice hoarse with need.

Ricky guessed that she was at the end of her rope, *knew* that he was. He slipped out of the shirt that she had tried to remove, then shed his jeans. Her avid gaze fell on his arousal. She reached out tentatively, then drew one finger along the hard shaft. Ricky thought he might explode. He doubted she understood the danger, so he guided her hand to safer territory, but even her touch against his chest had him tensing with desire.

Once again he began to explore her body, partly to distract her from her own exploration, partly to begin the last slow climb to the peak he'd denied her time and again tonight. Satisfied at last that she was at the top, at the edge, he knelt between her legs and entered her in one fast, urgent thrust.

She shattered at once, her contractions hard and deep. He waited, perfectly still, until they slowed, and then he began the age-old rhythm that would take them both to the top yet again. She cried out as the sensations tore through her, and this time, with her cries echoing in his head and her slick heat surrounding him, he joined her in a shuddering release.

His breath came back eventually. His heartbeat quieted to a normal pace, but he couldn't bring himself to move. Something had happened to him tonight, something he'd never expected, never imagined. He'd made love, in every sense of the phrase. He couldn't deny it. He'd had a lot of experience with sex and none with making love. He could tell the difference. This, *this,* had been something special, something he would never get enough of, something he was reluctant to end.

He rolled over, bringing Allie with him, still joined in the most intimate way possible, still bound by that inexplicable bond that he'd wondered about but had spent a lifetime doubting.

She sighed heavily and stirred. When she would have moved away from him, he held her tight. He didn't want to talk, didn't want to gaze into her eyes to see if she felt the same way. He put his life on the line all the time without a second thought, but he didn't want to risk this moment, this magic. Damn, she had him thinking like a blasted poet, all soft and mushy and romantic. It wasn't his style. Permanence sure as hell wasn't his style.

But that's exactly what he wanted. Forever. He finally dared a glance at Allie's face. He saw satisfaction there, maybe even joy, but he thought he also detected a glint of determination in her eyes. He couldn't figure out what that was about, but something told him it couldn't possibly be good.

"Okay," he said warily. "What's on your mind?"

"The truth?"

"Always." Even when it hurt, and he was pretty sure this was going to.

"You're so good at this and I'm… Well, I'm not exactly experienced."

His mouth gaped. She needed reassurance? The woman who'd all but destroyed him? "Are you fishing for a compliment?" he asked.

"Of course not," she protested. "I'm trying to be honest."

"Allie, if you were any better at this, we'd collapse from exhaustion."

Her lips tilted up, but the smile faded before it could blossom. "But all those other women…"

"There are no other women. Not like you."

She continued to regard him doubtfully. Ricky couldn't think of any other way to persuade her except to show her in lingering, tormenting detail.

He wasn't entirely sure how convincing he was, but at least when he was through, she was way too breathless to argue. Good thing, too, because he really, really needed some time to figure out what he was going to do about the discovery he'd just made that he was falling in love with Allie Matthews.

Allie was pretty sure her brain must have been starved for oxygen while she was under her collapsed house. Not only had she moved in with a virtual stranger, but now, a scant few weeks later, she was sharing his bed. Maybe Ricky had been right after all, and she was incapable of clear thought. She was certainly behaving more impetuously than was her habit.

The proof? Tonight's lovemaking had happened after she had very firmly told herself that Ricky Wilder was not the kind of man she wanted in her life. She wanted someone solid and dependable, someone who didn't have a history of loving and leaving every woman he'd ever known.

Okay, she couldn't exactly accuse Ricky of not being solid and dependable, could she? After all, he had saved her life.

But he was also an outrageous flirt, a fact confirmed by everyone who knew him and that he himself had never bothered to deny. Despite his reassurances that she more than measured up to all those other women in his life, he hadn't exactly given her any reason to believe their relationship would be any more lasting than the others had been.

Moreover—and here was the real problem—he didn't think twice about putting his life on the line. Every time she thought of what he did for a living, she shuddered. She wanted a man who would be home every night, whose greatest risk was negotiating I-95 on his way to work. Life could be unpredictable enough without deliberately taking chances. She knew that better than anyone.

As if to prove her point, Ricky suddenly shifted away from her and reached for the phone. Allie glanced at the clock. It was the middle of the night. A ringing phone at two in the morning was never about something good. She tensed, watching his face for clues about what was being said on the other end of the line.

"I'll be there," he said at last, casting an apologetic look her way.

"What is it?" she asked, when he had hung up.

"An earthquake in El Salvador. It happened about an hour ago. The epicenter was only a few miles from San Salvador. It's a bad one, Allie. We have to go."

She swallowed hard against the longing to tell him to stay. This was his job. He had no choice. She knew that, but of all nights, the disaster couldn't have come on a worse one. She felt bereft as he moved out of her arms and began quickly and methodically getting ready to go, his mind already clicking through some long-established mental checklist.

She huddled in the bed, sheets drawn up to her chin as she watched him transform himself from lover to professional rescue worker in the blink of an eye. The brisk movements and grim expression banished any signs of the tenderness she had experienced in his arms just moments before.

He was showered and ready in minutes. He paused by the bed.

"I'm sorry. If there was any choice, I would stay here with you."

"I understand," she assured him. And it was true. She did. But that didn't seem to stop the knot of fear that was tightening in her belly or the dull thud of her heart or the images of him broken and bloody that formed in her head.

"Will you be okay?" he asked. "I mean with this." He gestured toward the tangle of sheets, still warm from their frenzied lovemaking.

"We'll talk about it when you get back," she said. "I know you need to go. Take care of yourself."

"Always," he said as he touched his lips to hers in a fleeting, distracted kiss.

His head was already somewhere else. She could

tell, and it hurt somewhere deep inside to know that he had left her behind even before walking out of the room.

He stopped at the door. "I'll get word to you when I can."

"How?" she asked, thoroughly frustrated by the realization that he couldn't just pick up the phone and call her on a whim as he might any other woman.

"It's okay," he soothed, clearly picking up on her anxiety. "A lot's going to depend on phone lines there being up, but I'll think of something. I'll get word to the clinic and have someone give you a message, or I'll have Maria or my mother come by."

She nodded, relieved that she wouldn't have to endure the days or even weeks without knowing what was happening or whether he was safe. "Thank you."

As he opened the door, she saw Shadow standing, ready and alert, as if he sensed that he, too, was on duty. And then they were gone.

Her spirits sank the minute the two of them disappeared from sight. She crept out of bed, tugged on Ricky's shirt just to be surrounded by the scent of him, then went into the living room to stare out the window as his car pulled away. She watched until the taillights vanished in the darkness.

More than she ever had before, she regretted her inability to hear. She desperately wanted to be able to call someone like Nikki, who would share her anxiety, who could commiserate with this sense of fear and abandonment. The latter, of course, was worse because of the timing of that fateful call. It had ripped Ricky out of her arms, taken him from their bed just as they were discovering the overwhelming tide of sweet passion that could carry them away. She had waited so long for that moment, convinced herself it might never happen. To have the joy of it cut short was a painful reminder that a life with Ricky would always be uncertain, that it could be cut short in the blink of an eye.

Because she couldn't sleep anyway, she showered, dressed and settled in front of the TV in the living room, tuned in CNN and watched the reports just beginning to come out of the ravaged city of San Salvador. The reports contained raw footage just sent in via satellite, the pictures graphic and uncensored. Allie had no idea what information accompanied the images, because the anchor was off camera. She just knew that her heart climbed into her throat when she tried to imagine Ricky arriving in the midst of that devastation.

She was almost relieved when it was time to leave for work. She desperately needed the break, but the first thing Gina asked when she saw her was whether Ricky had had to fly to El Salvador.

Allie nodded. "He got a call about two in the morning."

Gina studied her with a penetrating look. "How do you feel about that?"

"Scared," she admitted.

"Maybe it will get easier once you've been through a few disasters."

Allie considered that, then shook her head. "I don't think so."

"Is there anything I can do for you to make it easier?"

"I can't think of anything, but he might call here to let me know how things are going."

"I'll get you the second he does," Gina promised.

"Maybe you should get the same phone equipment at home, so he can call you there. You had it at your place, didn't you?"

Similar to email, the equipment transmitted the caller's written words on a screen for the benefit of the deaf. It also had a blinking light to indicate when a call was coming in.

"I had it before the storm, but I was going to wait till I got settled before replacing it."

"I think it's too important," Gina chided, signing emphatically. "You need to be able to communicate, not just with him but with other people, as well. Let me see if I can't make arrangements for it to get set up."

"Thank you," she said, grateful for the nudging. She realized she had been resisting installing the equipment at Ricky's because she didn't want it to seem as if she was settling in on a permanent basis. Now, though, she was sure he would understand how vital it was. He would probably even be grateful that she wouldn't be cut off from the outside world when he wasn't there.

Over the next week, her life took on a surreal quality. When she wasn't at work, she was glued to the television news, hoping to catch a glimpse of Ricky. A local station had a news crew on the scene and often featured interviews with the rescue crew from Miami.

Some nights Nikki did come over and they watched together. On other nights Maria or her mother dropped by, sometimes with messages from Ricky.

Allie was grateful to all of them, not only for the company, but for the information they were able to pass along.

"This must be so hard on you," Maria said. "I know

it's driving Ricky crazy not to be able to talk to you. Usually he's totally focused, when he's on one of these assignments, but now when he calls he has a million and one questions about you. I've never known him to care enough about a woman that she even crosses his mind while he's working."

Maria grinned. "I think that's wonderful, by the way. It's about time he found a woman who could put up with him and maybe put a little balance into his life."

But what if I can't? Allie wanted to ask, but didn't. How could she explain to Ricky's sister that she wasn't at all sure she could live with what he did for a living. Her own near tragedy was still too fresh in her mind to allow her to be complacent about the dangers he was intentionally facing every single second of every exhausting day. The possibility that she might be a dangerous distraction was far from reassuring.

She was able to voice her fear to Nikki, though. She saw the same tight lines of tension in her friend's face as she saw reflected in the mirror when she was dressing in the morning.

"It never gets any easier," Nikki said, tearing her gaze away from the television when the news switched to another story.

"What are you going to do?" Allie asked her. "You were thinking of going back to Tom before this happened, weren't you?"

Nikki nodded, her expression miserable. "If I thought for one single second that I could get through the rest of my life and never think about Tom again, I would move on, find some nice, boring accountant and raise a family. Unfortunately, Tom is the man I love, the man I've always loved. I could marry somebody else and move to Alaska and I still think I'd panic every time I heard about a natural disaster."

She shrugged. "Given all that, I might as well marry the man and have whatever time together that God grants us." Her expression brightened. "One of these days he's going to be too old to do this for a living. He'll be around the house, underfoot, and I'll be the one grumbling about the good old days when he was halfway around the world taking risks."

Allie tried to imagine such a time, but couldn't. She would thank her lucky stars to have Ricky underfoot. Whatever adjustments that would require were bound to be better than this fear that hadn't left her since the minute he walked out of the house.

He had been away for two endless weeks, during which she had never gotten remotely used to his absence, nor to accepting the reason for it with any sort of equanimity. It was the most frustrating experience of her life. It was also all the proof she needed that she was with the wrong man. There was no way she could live with this sort of unnerving uncertainty.

But when she drove into the driveway on Saturday morning after a trip to the grocery store, she saw his car parked in front of the garage, and her heart began to race. Then the front door opened, and he stepped outside. She flew out of the car and straight into his arms.

Relief and desire replaced tension and exhaustion. His mouth on hers was eager and demanding, his touch reassuring. In the heat of their reunion, she managed to forget all about her reservations.

It was hours later before she remembered the groceries. Laughing, she retrieved once-frozen food ruined by the heat, bread that had been baked a little too long by the sun and milk that had been spoiled. It seemed like a small price to pay for having Ricky back and for sharing his bed.

"Gina's getting the phone equipment so I won't be so cut off the next time you go away," she told him as she warmed up leftovers from the meal Maria had dropped off the night before.

"I was thinking about that," Ricky said, his expression thoughtful.

"Any ideas?" she asked.

"We could get a couple of computers and chat on-line. That would work. Or at least we'd be able to email each other. I just know we have to do something," he said, his gaze locked with hers, his hands settled on her waist as the food simmered unnoticed on the stove behind her. "This was the most frustrating two weeks I've ever had on the job. Not being able to check in with you directly was making me crazy."

It helped to know that his frustration had been as great as her own.

But that night as Allie snuggled next to him, his arm draped across her stomach, her hand resting against his chest, the sense of relief she felt at having him back safely took a backseat to the awareness that there would always be a next time and then another and another. All of the fear came flooding back, robbing her of the little bit of serenity she'd been able to reclaim.

She was quiet on Sunday. She spent most of the day inventing chores that took her away from the house, so she could be alone to think. It was ironic really. Being alone had grated on her nerves for the past two weeks, but now she sought out the solitude.

That night Ricky called her on it.

"What's up, Allie? You've been avoiding me all day."

"I've needed to think."

"About?"

She returned his gaze, feeling miserable and torn, but knowing what she had to do. "Us," she admitted finally. "This won't work, Ricky. It can't."

He stared at her in openmouthed astonishment. "What exactly are you saying—that you want to end this?"

"Yes," she told him. "I think it would be best if I move out."

His expression turned stoic. "Mind if I ask why?"

"It's because of what you do," she admitted. "For the past two weeks I have been almost sick with worry. I don't think I could do that for the rest of my life, just sit here and wait while you risk your life."

"The rest of your life?" he asked, looking incredulous. "You've done it exactly *once.* You and I, we're just starting to find our way. We don't know what's going to happen between us a week from now. Don't you think it's a little soon to start worrying about the rest of our lives?"

She was taken aback by the suggestion that she'd been unfair, that she'd leaped way too far into the future. "I just know how I feel," she said defensively. "Why drag it out?"

His expression darkened. "This is Nikki's doing, isn't it? She spent too much time here while I was gone, filling your head with nonsense about how dangerous my job is."

"It's not nonsense," Allie said. "And don't blame

Nikki. I felt this way before the last trip even happened. The trip just crystallized what I was feeling. You're the kind of man who obviously needs to live life on the edge. I'm not knocking you for making that choice. What you do is important and you're incredibly brave. I'm just saying I can't live with it."

"And you know that, after I've been on one assignment? It doesn't take much to scare you off, does it?"

She saw the mounting frustration in his expression, caught the flare of anger building in his eyes, but she couldn't figure out a way to make him understand.

"I lived through a disaster all too recently," she began.

"You survived, thanks to me," he pointed out.

"Yes, thanks to you," she said quietly. "That's why I admire what you do. I respect you for it. I'm grateful that there are men like you who are willing to take the risks, but nobody knows better than I do just how great that risk is. The minute you walked out that door, I was back under that rubble again, trapped in the dark, terrified that I was going to die there. I know that with time the memories of that will dim, but how can they if I have to relive them over and over every time you go on an assignment?"

His anger visibly faded as her words sank in. He reached for her and pulled her close, his expression shattered. "I'm sorry. When you put it like that, it makes a horrible kind of sense to me. I hate it, but it's true."

She lifted her gaze to his. "I have to move out," she told him. "I don't see any other choice."

A sigh shuddered through him. She could feel it as her cheek rested against his chest, but he didn't argue.

Much later, when he released her, she saw only sorrow and regret in his eyes.

"If you can wait until tomorrow evening, I'll help you find a place of your own," he offered.

"You don't need to do that," she said, pretty sure she would find it unbearable to have his presence indelibly linked to whatever house or apartment she rented.

"Let me do that much," he said, his expression set stubbornly.

Allie finally, reluctantly, nodded agreement because it clearly meant a lot to him. She just had to keep reminding herself that when the apartment hunt was over, she would have the rest of her life to get over the pain of walking away. But how long would it be before she knew if day-to-day serenity was a fair trade for losing a lifetime with the man she was beginning to love?

Chapter 14

Jane was beside herself when she heard what Allie intended to do. Apparently Ricky had filled her in, because she turned up at the clinic at lunchtime with a determined glint in her eye and a picnic hamper filled with Allie's favorite foods.

"Why are you here?" Allie asked warily.

"To talk some sense into you."

"Why are you siding with Ricky on this without even listening to how I feel?"

"I am on your side, always, which is why I'm here. I doubt, though, that there's anything you could say that would convince me that you're not throwing away a real chance at happiness."

She reached in the hamper and drew out a container of pasta salad. "Here, eat some of this."

Under her friend's watchful gaze, Allie took the

salad and a fork and automatically began to eat. There were bits of ham, cheese and bell peppers in the salad, just the way she liked it, just the way her mother had always made it. It was comfort food and Jane knew it.

"It's very good. Thank you."

"Now try this," Jane said, handing over a freshly baked brownie. "I brought more for the rest of the staff."

"They'll love you forever. Your brownies are always a big hit around here."

"I'm delighted to hear it," Jane said, though her expression remained grimly determined.

Allie took her time savoring the rich, moist brownie, which was filled with chocolate chips and walnuts, because she sensed that the minute Jane was satisfied that she was well fed, she was going to launch into a lecture. That was her way. She figured people were always more sensible with a full stomach.

Sure enough, the minute Allie had eaten the last crumb, Jane said, "Now then, let's get back to this lunacy about you moving out of Ricky's."

Allie bristled. "Telling me I'm nuts is not likely to make me receptive to whatever else you have to say."

"I call 'em as I see 'em," Jane retorted, hands on hips. The tough-woman effect was somewhat lessened by the pink sneakers and flowered baseball cap. "Live with it."

A grin tugged at Allie's lips, despite her determination not to be swayed by anything her former neighbor had to say.

"Look, I know Ricky must have called you. Did he mention why I thought it was important to get my own place?"

"Well, of course he did. He even said he could understand it."

"Then there's not a problem, is there?"

"Well, I don't understand it," Jane said. "I've seen the two of you together. If ever two people belonged with each other, it's you. If your mother were here, she'd tell you the same thing. Since she's not, I figure it's up to me."

"Actually, my mother doesn't have an opinion about this, one way or the other. She's not aware that my roommate is a man."

Jane stared incredulously. "How on earth can that be? Don't the two of you talk? Hasn't Ricky ever answered the phone?"

"Actually she prefers letters," Allie admitted stiffly.

"Why because she doesn't want that phone equipment around to remind her that you're deaf?"

"Something like that."

Jane muttered something. Allie figured it was just as well she hadn't been able to see her lips. She doubted it had been complimentary. She tried to head off any more discussion.

"Jane—"

"Enough about your mother. I'll keep my opinion to myself about that," she said, cutting off Allie's comment. "Now let me share something with you, Allie. I was married for thirty years. You never met my husband, but he was a lot like Ricky. He had a sense of honor and commitment to other people. We met when we were teenagers, before I had any idea that he was going to be a policeman. I was so proud of him the day he graduated from the police academy, but there wasn't a single day after that when I wasn't terrified that he might not come home to me." She leveled a look straight into Allie's eyes, then added pointedly, "Not one single day."

Allie got the message. By comparison, Ricky's risks were far less frequent. Allie was behaving like a coward in not accepting the risks as a small price to pay for a love that could bring her joy. Unfortunately, she also knew how the story ended.

"In the end your worst fears were realized," she reminded Jane gently.

"Yes, they were," she admitted, her eyes swimming with tears even after twenty years without her beloved husband. "He died in the line of duty, and I was devastated. But at least I knew I'd had thirty years with the best man on the face of the earth. If I had given in to my fears, I would have had nothing. No memories to cherish. No children or grandchildren. Ricky is a rare man, my dear. He's compassionate and brave. And he deserves a woman who can appreciate that."

"I do," Allie said fiercely. "That's what makes this so hard. I know what a wonderful man he is."

"Then don't let the fear win," Jane advised. She gathered up the empty food containers, then patted Allie's cheek. "Think about it. That's all I ask. And listen to your heart."

Allie had no problem at all hearing her heart. What terrified her was that it was going to wind up broken.

When Ricky came home and found Allie packing, he told himself it was for the best. He wasn't after permanence, never had been. Helping her to look for a new place to live would have just dragged out an already awkward situation.

"Where are you going? Did you find a place this afternoon?" he asked.

She avoided looking directly at him when she answered. "I'm going to stay with a friend temporarily."

Since there hadn't been a friend who could take her in when she left the hospital, he couldn't help wondering who it might be.

"Mind telling me who this friend is?" he inquired casually. "In case I need to reach you or forward your mail or something."

Her expression turned defiant. "Maria."

Ricky felt his blood begin to heat. "You're moving in with *my sister?* How the hell did that happen?" And how was he supposed to get over Allie, if she was living in the midst of his damn family?

"She came over, found me packing and refused to let me go to a motel."

"Well, isn't that just downright sisterly of her," he muttered bitterly.

Allie sank down on the side of the bed, her defiance slipping away. "I'm sorry. I know this is awkward. I tried to get out of it, but you know Maria," she said with a resigned shrug.

"I most certainly do," he said grimly, imagining exactly how the conversation had gone. Allie might be a more-than-even match for him, but she was definitely not equal to his big sister when Maria was on a mission. The only question was what she considered that mission to be. He whirled around and headed for the phone. He wasn't especially surprised when his sister answered on the first ring.

"Expecting my call?" he asked sarcastically, grateful that the portable phone allowed him to pace.

"Something like that."

"What are you up to?"

"You're not the only one in the family who can help a friend in need," she retorted. "Allie needed a place to stay. We have a guest room. I offered to let her use it."

"Why not let her move into a motel or her own apartment, the way she intended?"

"I could ask you the same question. Isn't that how she wound up at your house in the first place?"

Frustration coiled deep inside him. "Maria, you're not helping."

She chuckled at that. "I may not be helping you, but I'm pretty sure I'm doing Allie a favor. Come to think of it, I'm also pretty sure that one day you'll thank me."

"For what?"

"For not letting her get away."

"It's not as if she was planning to move to California," he pointed out. "I could have found her if I'd wanted to."

"But this way you won't have to waste time looking," Maria said cheerfully. "Gotta run. The kids want to watch a movie. Tell Allie I'll be expecting her over here in time for dinner. You can come, too, if you want."

"Don't expect me."

"Suit yourself," she said blandly.

He sighed heavily.

"Enrique?"

"Yes, what?"

"I love you."

"I know that."

"So does Allie."

He thought he had known that, too, but the past

twenty-four hours had made him question it. He hung up on his sister and went in search of his soon-to-depart houseguest…his lover, he reminded himself. He found her in the foyer, surrounded by her luggage. Shadow sat at her feet, watching her quizzically.

He noted that she hadn't acquired all that much while living with him. Just some clothes, a few essentials…and his heart.

"Did Maria answer all your questions?" she inquired politely.

"Not to my satisfaction, but she tried."

"Well, I'll be going now."

"Allie, you don't have to do this."

Her sad gaze met his, then darted away. "Yes," she said softly. "I do."

Ricky didn't know what else to say. He couldn't tell her the one thing she wanted to hear, that he would quit his job and do something less risky. Instead he just picked up her luggage and carried it out to her car, watched as she got settled behind the wheel.

"Since you'll be at Maria's, I imagine we'll bump into each other once in a while," he said.

"I'll try to make sure that doesn't happen," she said, gazing up at him through the open window. "I don't want you to feel uncomfortable about visiting your own sister."

"I won't be uncomfortable," he insisted. Just miserable.

"Whatever. Thank you for everything."

"You're welcome," he said, chafing at the exchange that made them sound like polite strangers.

Because he couldn't stand the distance a second longer, he bent down and captured her lips in a greedy, demanding kiss meant to remind her—remind them both—of what they were giving up.

She looked shaken when he finally pulled away, but that didn't stop her from reaching for the key to start the car, turning it with fingers that visibly trembled. Then she hit the power button to close the window between them, shifted the car into reverse and eased away from him, distancing herself from his life.

Watching her go was the hardest thing Ricky had ever had to do. The instant the car disappeared from sight he knew that he was making the worst mistake he'd ever made.

He shouted her name, then ran to the end of the driveway, Shadow barking alongside him. He slammed his fist into the mailbox in frustration when he realized what a wasted gesture the shout had been. How could he even tell her he loved her, when he didn't know the right words and she couldn't hear them even if he did?

He could think of only one person who would totally understand what he was going through. He called Tom, only to learn that Nikki was with him.

"She's agreed to think about getting married again," Tom exulted. "I really think we're going to make it work this time. She's dropped that whole thing about me working for her dad."

"What have you had to give up in return?"

"I've promised that I'll think about changing jobs in five years. I'll be thirty-five then. I'll probably be ready to do something that doesn't take me on the road so much, especially if we have kids."

"Sounds like you've got it all worked out," Ricky said, fighting to hide the bitterness in his own voice.

It wasn't Tom's fault that *his* love life was working out while Ricky's was going to hell.

"Why did you call, Enrique? You don't sound so good."

"It's nothing. You enjoy your evening with Nikki, okay? You two deserve it." He hung up before he could dump all of his problems on his friend.

He didn't miss the irony that the woman he'd blamed for instilling her own fears into Allie had somehow managed to get past those very same fears. Well, good for her, he thought sourly. And good for Tom.

Since he refused to wallow in self-pity, he changed clothes and went into the garage, picked up his hedge clippers and began to chop the hell out of an overgrown bougainvillea.

He was still at it two hours later when his mother arrived. She took one look at him and at the practically denuded flowering shrub and yanked the clippers away from him.

"Are you *loco?*" she demanded.

Ricky had the distinct impression that she was questioning more than his rampage with the clippers.

"Leave it alone, Mama." He stalked past her and headed for the kitchen. He pulled out a beer, popped the tab and chugged down a long, thirst-quenching swallow.

Hands on hips, she stood in the doorway and scowled at him. "I taught you better than that."

"Better than what?"

"To turn your back on a woman like Allie."

"I didn't turn my back on her. It was her choice to move out."

"But you let her go."

"What choice did I have? She said she worried too much about my safety, that she couldn't live with the thought of something happening to me."

"You think I don't understand such fear?" his mother said.

"But you've never asked me to give up the career I love."

"Of course not. Did she ask such a thing?"

"No. She just packed up and bailed."

"Then get her back."

Ricky regarded her with mounting frustration. "How do you suggest I do that?"

"If you can't figure it out, then you are no son of mine."

He wasn't particularly impressed with the threat. "You've been disowning me my whole life, every time I do something to displease you. I don't take it seriously anymore."

She muttered a string of Spanish epithets he hadn't even realized his mother knew. He stared at her in shock. She scowled right back at him.

"Well, what do you expect?" she snapped. "Your father and I agree that Allie is the best thing that ever happened to you and you let her walk away. Did you even fight to keep her here? Did you tell her how you feel?"

"I don't know how to tell her any more clearly than I have."

His mother's gaze narrowed. "Then you do realize that you love her?"

"Of course," he retorted. "It's the words I don't know, the ones that will convince her."

"Convince her of what? That she means the world

to you, that you want to take care of her and love her, have babies with her?"

"Yes, those words."

She rolled her eyes. "What is wrong with the ones you have just spoken to me?"

"You said the words," he pointed out. "I just agreed."

She stared at him, visibly exasperated. "Saints protect me, do I have to propose for you, too?"

"If you want there to be a wedding, it might not be a bad idea."

She cuffed him gently upside the head. "You are a man. A foolish one, but a man, nonetheless. Tell the woman what is in your heart. She will hear you well enough."

Overnight he thought about what his mother had said. Would mere words really make a difference? Hadn't he tried already, only to be rebuffed? He scoffed at the idea that one try was enough, given what was at stake. His mother was right. He owed it to both of them to try again…and again, if necessary.

On Saturday morning he decided to brave his sister's likely amusement, his nephews' interference and his brother-in-law's taunts. He arrived at Maria's to find the entire family gathered around the breakfast table, Allie included. She and Ramón were having a heated discussion about baseball versus soccer. Apparently Allie was a huge Florida Marlins fan, something Ricky hadn't discovered while she stayed with him though the T-shirt she'd worn when he rescued her should have been a clue. How many more things were there that he didn't know about her?

"Pull up a chair," his brother-in-law offered. "I think

there's enough batter left for a few pancakes. Maria thought you might be by."

"Did she now?" Ricky asked, casting a scowl in his sister's direction.

"Just optimistic," she said with a smile. She clapped her hands together to get the attention of her sons. "Boys, outside. Let the grown-ups have some peace and quiet."

The boys didn't waste a second scrambling to get away. If only getting rid of Maria and her husband would be as simple, Ricky thought wistfully. Unfortunately, they poured themselves second cups of coffee and settled back to watch him eat his pancakes while they waited to see what transpired between him and Allie. She looked as if she wanted desperately to bolt right behind his nephews.

Ricky studied her. She didn't look any more rested than she had when she'd left his place. Apparently, the serenity she'd craved had remained elusive.

"Are you settling in okay?" he inquired.

"Maria and her family have been very gracious," she said.

"That's good. How's work?"

"Fine."

"And Jane?"

"She's doing okay. I'm surprised you haven't talked to her."

"I'm planning to see her tomorrow. In fact, I've invited her to Mama's for Sunday dinner."

That got a reaction. "You have?"

"I thought you might want to come, too."

She looked tempted, but she shook her head. "No, thanks."

Maria heaved an impatient sigh, then turned to her husband. "Obviously, they don't intend to get into any of the good stuff as long as you and I are in the room. Want to take the kids and go to the beach?"

"Sounds good to me," Benny agreed, grinning at Ricky. "But you're going to owe us."

"I usually do," Ricky said.

As soon as they were gone, he faced Allie. "I've missed you."

"Ricky, don't. Please."

"Don't what? Don't be honest?"

"Not when there's no point to it."

"There's always a point to being truthful. Before you throw away what we have, I want you to see the whole picture."

"What whole picture?" she asked warily.

"I'll admit that it comes as a shock to me, but I see a future for the two of us. I see us married, living in my place for now, but eventually in someplace bigger, maybe with a pool in back. I see us having a family. Maybe two boys and a girl. I see us growing old together."

Suddenly she was blinking back tears. "Stop," she pleaded. "That's the part of the picture I can't see."

He knew precisely where she had stumbled. "Getting old together?"

"Yes. Every time I try to get past the here and now, to see into the future, I see something terrible happening to take you away from me."

He tried to think of some way to put her fears to rest, but the truth was it could happen exactly as she feared. But wasn't life filled with that kind of uncertainty. He could get killed in an accident on I-95 as easily as he could doing his job.

"Life doesn't come with guarantees no matter what you do for a living," he pointed out. "I love you. Doesn't that mean anything?"

"It means everything," she said, but her eyes were still filled with sorrow. "But I can't marry you. I need someone who will always come home to me."

"But I will," he insisted.

"You can't promise that, not and continue doing the job you love."

"The job that brought us together," he pointed out.

She touched a hand to his cheek. "And it is a part of who you are and why I love you," she said sadly. "But it's also the reason I can't marry you. I simply can't live with that kind of fear."

Ricky didn't begin to understand, but he saw the determined glint in her eyes and knew that she meant what she said. He leaned down and pressed a kiss to her lips, then to the dampness on her cheeks, before turning and walking away.

A week later, at the site of another earthquake, he took a dangerous misstep and found himself buried in rubble. Concrete and steel shifted precariously, slamming into flesh and bone. It was an uneven match. The pain was agonizing, but not nearly as agonizing as the realization that he was the one who'd been at fault, endangering not just himself, but others at the site.

He hadn't been concentrating, not the way he needed to. He wanted to blame Allie, blame the fact that he couldn't get her out of his head, but the truth was he'd been rushing, anxious to get the work over with so he could go back home again. He'd been entirely focused on proving to Allie that he would always come home.

Now it seemed, as he swam in and out of consciousness, he might have proved exactly the opposite. He had enough medical training to know that things weren't good. Blood was flowing from the injury to his head, which pounded like a jackhammer at the slightest movement. A shaft of metal had penetrated his thigh, too darned close to a major artery by the looks of it. He retched at the sight, then forced himself to take slow, deep breaths, head turned away.

He could hear Shadow's frantic barks, knew that Tom and the others would be conducting the slow, tedious excavation necessary to reach him where he was trapped.

As he drifted in and out of consciousness, he imagined what it must have been like for Allie to be trapped like this and terrified, her fate in the hands of strangers. It was little wonder that she didn't care to repeat the experience, albeit vicariously.

Even for him, knowing that his life was in the hands of experts whose skill was unquestionably the best, there was a sick feeling in the pit of his stomach that his luck might have run out. Trusting Tom and the other members of his crew didn't seem to figure into it, when he was too blasted close to bleeding to death, too much at risk of being crushed at any second.

Worse, he kept imagining Allie's reaction to the news. His frustration mounted with each second that dragged on, with each moment of uncertainty she must be facing. He hated himself for putting her through it, yet he knew if a choice had to be made, he would do it again. What he did was important, necessary work and he was good at it. Most of the time, anyway.

He had to resist the desperate desire to begin his own frantic excavation. For one thing, he knew he had to conserve his strength. For another, every movement caused blinding pain. He had to put his faith in the men he knew like brothers.

As he waited for help to come, he cursed his injuries, not because of the pain, but because Allie would see them as more proof that she had made the right decision. He cursed the fact that there were news crews on the scene to report every detail back home.

When the frustration and pain got to be too much, he concentrated on staying calm, staying alive. It wasn't just survival instinct that kept him going. It was Allie. He'd made her a promise and he had to fight with everything in him to be sure he kept it.

He was not going to die, buried in the very rubble from which he was supposed to rescue others, not now, not when he'd finally found the best possible reason for living: a woman he loved with all his heart.

Chapter 15

Allie hadn't been able to concentrate all day. She had an uneasy sense that something terrible had happened. She told herself she was being ridiculous, but she couldn't shake the feeling.

She felt a light pat on her hand and gazed into Kimi Foley's tear-filled blue eyes. The four-year-old was still struggling to master sign language, and today's lesson had been frustrating for both of them. Allie's attempts to get either of her parents involved had failed miserably. The Foleys had also been reluctant to let their oldest daughter step in and take the lessons so that she could help Kimi.

"What's wrong with me?" she signed, her expression miserable.

"Oh, baby," Allie whispered, then signed, "Nothing is wrong with you. You are very special."

Kimi's hands moved hesitantly, then fell still as she searched for some way of expressing her feelings. Tears rolled down her cheeks. Even without the words, Allie understood.

"Sweetheart, you are going to have all the words you need one of these days. I promise."

"My friends," she began, then stopped, clearly struggling to go on.

"What about your friends?" Allie encouraged.

"They don't play with me," she signed with a weary little sigh, then crawled into Allie's lap for comfort. Her arms crept around Allie's neck.

Choked up by the child's obvious pain, Allie wondered if her parents had any idea what they were doing to her. If the isolation of sudden silence was overwhelming for a nineteen-year-old, as Allie had been, what must it be like for a little girl who'd lost her hearing when she was barely able to speak and whose vocabulary was limited?

She glanced up to find Kimi's father standing in the doorway, his expression anguished.

"What's wrong?" he asked. "Is she okay?"

"She says her friends won't play with her," Allie told him. "Most likely it's because they don't know how to talk to her, so they just stay away."

"My God," he whispered, then tapped Kimi on the shoulder and held out his arms. His daughter scrambled into them and buried her head on his shoulder. He looked at Allie. "What do I do?"

"It would help if you and your wife, maybe even your children, would take the sign language classes. At least Kimi would be able to communicate at home."

He nodded. "We'll do it. I hadn't realized how she

must feel. I wanted so badly to pretend that she was normal."

"She *is* normal," Allie said fiercely. "She just can't hear." She regarded him intently. "Do you think I'm normal?"

He looked dismayed by the question. "Of course."

"One day Kimi will be able to communicate just as well. Although she may not have the verbal skills, because she was so young when she lost her hearing, she will have compensated in other ways. But she needs your help now for that to happen."

"She'll have it," he said with grim determination. "I'm not sure how we'll manage it, but we will."

Allie walked with them to the front door, then smiled at him. "I will do whatever I can to accommodate a schedule that works for you." She tucked a finger under Kimi's chin. "See you soon," she signed.

Kimi mimicked the gestures. And, his big hand awkward, her father did the same. A slow smile spread across Kimi's face.

As the father and daughter left, Allie breathed a sigh of relief. For the first time in weeks, she felt confident that things were going to work out.

When she turned to go back to her office, she found Gina waiting for her.

"Come with me," her boss signed, her expression somber.

"My next patient's due in a few minutes."

"Carol's taking her," Gina said.

Alarm flared at once. Allie's heart began an unsteady rhythm. Although the instructors occasionally backed each other up with patients, Gina usually preferred the same therapist to work with each one.

Unless there was an emergency.

Allie's pulse was racing by the time Gina closed her office door.

"What is it? Is it one of my parents?"

Gina shook her head.

"Oh, my God," she said, sinking onto a chair. "It's Ricky, isn't it? The earthquake in China. Maria told me he had to go. What's happened?"

"There was a cave-in at the building he was searching. He was trapped in it."

Tears spilled down her cheeks. "Is he...?" She couldn't even bring herself to complete the question.

"Tom called Maria. He says Ricky is alive, but he's been pretty seriously hurt. The doctors over there are still checking him out. There could be internal injuries, but the worst of it seems to be a blow he took to the head from a steel beam that shifted. He's been unconscious since they pulled him out. They'll know more in a few hours. Tom's been at the hospital the whole time. He's keeping in touch with Maria. If you want to be at home with the family, we'll cover for you here."

Obligations warred with the terrible need to know whatever news there was the instant it was available.

"I should stay," she began, but Gina cut her off.

"You should be with Ricky's family, at least until you get some further word. You can decide tomorrow if you're ready to come back in."

Dazed, she nodded. "Yes, that's probably best. I'd be useless this afternoon, anyway."

"Call me and let me know what's happening," Gina said. "I'll be praying for him."

Allie nodded, then raced to get her purse and head for Maria's.

The whole family had gathered there by the time she arrived. No one seemed the least bit surprised by her rush to be with them. First Maria and then Mrs. Wilder pulled her into a tight embrace.

"He's going to be fine," Mrs. Wilder said, her expression set stubbornly. "Our Enrique is strong."

"Of course he is," Allie agreed. "Hardheaded, too."

That drew a smile from the older woman. "Who should know that better than you and I, right, *niña*. He loves us, and that will make him fight to come back to us."

Allie glanced at the TV, saw that it was tuned to a station that was reporting the tragedy. There was a clip showing the efforts to get Ricky out of the building, then another one as they loaded his still body into an ambulance. Filled with dread, Allie turned away.

Don't you dare die, she raged inside. *You have to come back to me. You have to!*

Suddenly she understood the decision that Nikki had reached to take Tom back into her life. Allie realized it wouldn't matter whether she married Ricky or not. She would always be terrified when he was away, would always wait anxiously until he came back home. If that was true, then why let her fear cost them whatever precious time they might be allowed? She just prayed she would have a chance to tell him.

A few minutes later Nikki arrived, along with an official from the fire department. Mrs. Wilder and Maria headed for the kitchen and began cooking. Allie followed them, needing their presence as reassurance that everything would turn out okay. Those two women, more than anyone else in the house, believed it with all their hearts. Allie wanted to share their faith, but the arrival of the fire department official scared her. She was fearful that he had come because he was anticipating bad news.

"Sit," Maria ordered. "You're pale as a ghost."

Allie did as she was told and accepted a glass of brandy, even though she almost never touched alcohol. Still, she took a sip of the amber liquid and felt the heat spread inside her.

One sip was enough, though. She put the glass aside, aware that Maria was studying her worriedly.

"I'll be okay," she assured her.

"Of course, you will," Mrs. Wilder said, patting her shoulder. "It's just that this came as a shock."

Tears welled up and spilled down her cheeks. "What if…?"

"None of that," Mrs. Wilder commanded. "The phone is going to ring and Tom will tell us that Ricky is awake and complaining like always."

She left the kitchen with a plate of sandwiches before Allie could respond. Allie stared after her with admiration. "She has such faith," she said to Maria. "I envy her that. I'm scared to death."

"Don't let her fool you. So is Mama, but she believes in God's mercy and in His goodness. She's counting on that to bring her son home safely."

"I pray she's right," Allie said.

"What will you do when he gets here?" Maria asked, her expression troubled. "I see the love shining in your eyes, but everything that has happened today has confirmed your worst fears, hasn't it?"

Allie nodded, grappling with the emotions that had welled up inside her since the minute Gina had delivered the terrible news. "But it's also proved something else," she said slowly, wanting to tell Maria about the decision she'd made.

"Proved what?"

"That I don't want to lose a single second of whatever time I could have with him. Nikki realized that about Tom. And Jane always knew it about her husband. I didn't understand what they meant when they first told me, but after today, I think I do."

Just then, her timing impeccable as always, Jane walked into the kitchen, her colorful attire like a ray of sunshine in the gloomy atmosphere. She opened her arms and gathered Allie close. "I saw on the news and came right over."

"We're not going to lose him," Allie said with a surprising surge of conviction. "He has too much to live for."

"Does he?" Jane asked, studying Allie with a penetrating look.

Allie nodded.

"That's news that will definitely get him back here," she said, winking at Maria. "Don't you think so?"

"Absolutely," Maria said just as the phone rang. She grabbed it. Her expression brightened almost at once. "Well, if it isn't my baby brother."

A sense of relief washed over Allie, and then Maria was pulling her close. "My brother would like to hear the sound of your voice."

Allie swallowed hard. "Enrique Wilder, you scared us half to death," she scolded.

Maria grinned at the response on the other end of the line, then said, "I will not tell her that."

"Tell me what?" Allie demanded.

"He says he didn't come back from the dead just to have you yell at him."

Allie chuckled, then spoke into the phone. "If you think that's yelling, just wait till I see you in person." Her voice faltered then as it sank in just how close she had come to losing him. "I love you," she whispered. "Just come home soon."

Then she turned away, put her head on Jane's shoulder and let the tears fall.

I love you. Just come home soon.

Ricky clung to Allie's words over the next few days. Impatient to get home and see her, he had to battle the doctors for permission to make the trip.

"Being with my family will be the best medicine," he told them, but to no avail. They were determined not to let him go until they had completed a dozen different tests, repeated them, analyzed the results and concluded that he wouldn't die en route. He could have told them that there was no way he was going to die, not when Allie was waiting for him half a world away, but he doubted they would buy his assessment of his prognosis.

It was Tom who finally persuaded them to let him go, but only after mustering the resources to get Ricky onto a medical transport flight that would take him home with a nurse in attendance.

"Thank you," he told his best friend.

"Hey, nobody's more anxious than I am to get you back to the States. You are not a good patient. I'm more than ready to turn the hovering over to Allie and your mom."

"You're staying?"

Tom nodded. "The job's not done. Give Nikki a kiss for me and tell her I'll be home to help her plan that wedding soon."

Ricky grinned. "Maybe we can make it a double ceremony."

"Why Allie would want to marry a stubborn cuss like you is beyond me, but if she does say yes, we'll give it a shot," Tom agreed. "Maybe that way at least one of us will actually remember our anniversary and keep the other one out of trouble."

"Now that *is* an incentive," Ricky agreed. He regarded his longtime partner soberly. "I owe you, pal. I know you moved heaven and earth, just about literally, to get me out of there. I wouldn't be here if it weren't for you."

"The whole team was there every second. You're one of us. We weren't about to lose you. Now go home and get well so I don't have to shoulder your load the next time we get a call."

Soon after Tom left the plane, the nurse brought Ricky the pain pills he'd been refusing for days now. She persuaded him to take them by reminding him that it was going to be a long flight and he'd want to be well rested when he got back to Florida.

"You don't want to scare your family half to death when they see you, do you?"

Because the jostling he'd taken en route to the airport had sharply reminded him of every single ache and pain in his body, he gave in. A couple of pain pills would wear off long before they reached home. He intended to be wide-awake and fully alert when he saw Allie. He wanted to remember every single thing about their reunion. Not only that, if he proposed and she said yes, he didn't want her to be able to claim later that he'd asked while in a drug-induced state.

He was out of it for most of the endless flight, but the minute the pilot informed them that they were an hour out of Miami, Ricky called the nurse over.

"Can you help me shave?"

"You want to look pretty for your wife?" she asked with a grin.

"I'm hoping she'll agree to be my wife."

She laughed. "Then you really do need a little sprucing up. Let's see what we can do."

There was only so much improvement that could be made because of the bandages, but Ricky thought the bright-turquoise Florida Marlins cap gave him a jaunty look. Given how Allie felt about the team, maybe it would help his cause.

As soon as the plane was on the ground, he spotted his entire family on the tarmac waiting for him, along with an ambulance ready to take him to a Miami hospital to be checked out thoroughly before he could be permitted to go home to his own bed, where he desperately wanted to be.

His gaze frantically searched the gathering before finally coming to rest on Allie. She was so beautiful, she took his breath away. She was the reason he'd survived, the thought that had kept him fighting to stay alive. Her words on the phone had given him hope. Not just the admission that she loved him, but the promise in her voice that she wouldn't take that love away ever again.

Of course, once she got a look at him, all broken and bandaged, she might have second thoughts. He turned to the nurse. "What do you think? Can I get the girl looking like this?"

"Sugar, you'll sweep her off her feet. Just try to get past the black-and-blue stage before the wedding. It'll look lousy with the tux."

Ricky wished he could walk off the plane, but it was out of the question. He was carried out on a stretcher, the transporters pausing at the base of the steps to let his family surround him. His sisters hugged him gingerly, tears spilling onto his face.

"Hey, cut the waterworks," he pleaded. "I'm not dead, and you're ruining the outfit."

"Move out of my way," his mother chided her daughters, shouldering them aside to bend down and press a kiss to his cheek. She murmured to him in Spanish, then crossed herself and added a quick prayer.

"I'm going to be okay, Mama."

She winked at him. "I never doubted it. You have a reason for living. *Sí?*"

Ricky's gaze met Allie's and he nodded slowly. "Yes, I definitely have a reason for living."

"We will leave you with Allie now and see you later at the hospital," she promised, then leaned down to whisper. "Don't waste a minute, *niño*. I think she is ready to say yes."

Ricky grinned. "I hope you're right, Mama."

Allie looked from him to his mother. "Right about what?"

His mother patted her cheek. "It is not polite to eavesdrop."

After the others had gone, Ricky gazed into Allie's eyes. "Come here," he commanded quietly.

She stepped closer, her eyes bright with unshed

tears, and took his one unbandaged hand in hers. "You had to go and prove me right, didn't you?" she chided.

"*I* was right," he contradicted. "I told you I'd always come home, no matter what."

"Then I guess you win," she said.

Hope rose up inside him. "Oh?"

"That is if you still want me."

The pain, which had been dulled for a while by the pills, came back full force, but he fought it. The moment was too sweet to let anything ruin it. He drew in a deep, relaxing breath and focused on her. "You're saying yes?"

"I thought I was the one who couldn't hear," she teased.

He reached up and touched her cheek gently. "Can you hear what my heart is saying now?" he said, his gaze locked with hers.

She rested her hand against his chest, where she had to be able to feel the steady, reassuring beat of his heart.

"I believe I can," she said.

"It's beating because I knew I had to get back to you, because I promised. You're the reason I'm alive. Now we're even."

Her tears spilled over. "I was so scared," she whispered.

"I can't swear to you that it will never happen again," he told her honestly. "But I love you, Allie. I want us to have years and years together with kids of our own who are as smart and brave as their mother."

She gave him a watery smile. "Smart, maybe," she teased. "But brave? I don't know about that. You're the strong one."

He tucked a finger under her chin. "No. It's always harder being left behind than it is to be taking the risks. I know that."

"And I know that it wouldn't be any easier if I walked away now. I would always wonder and worry. You're in my heart, Enrique Wilder, for better or for worse."

"Tom wants to have a double wedding," he told her. "What do you think?"

"Anytime, anyplace," she said. "I don't want to waste another minute."

As if to prove it, her mouth settled lightly against his. Ricky was pretty sure that kiss could heal whatever injuries he had. It definitely would be a potent incentive for never taking an unnecessary risk.

"Ricky," she murmured when she pulled away, looking a little dazed. "I think you've given me back my music."

"Oh?"

A smile spread across her face. "I'm pretty sure I heard bells."

He laughed. "I know I did, *querida*. I know I did."

Epilogue

Allie still couldn't get over the way her mother had gotten into the spirit of the wedding preparations. She had insisted on taking off the spring semester and coming to Miami a month ahead of time. She had taken up residence in the guest room at Ricky's. She'd made no comment at all about the fact that Allie was living in the master bedroom with her fiancé.

In fact, she seemed to approve of her prospective son-in-law from the instant they met. Allie constantly found them with their heads together, looking through the replacement photo albums she'd brought, filled with some of the same pictures that had been lost in the hurricane. Allie knew that Ricky and Jane had had a hand in the creation of those albums and she was touched. Her mother couldn't have brought a better wedding present.

But if the instant bond between her mother and Ricky was a surprise, more shocking was the immediate connection the very staid Grace Matthews had formed with the exuberant Mrs. Wilder. They had designated themselves in charge of the planning for the double ceremony, leaving little for Allie or Nikki to do. Once in a long while, her mother consulted Allie about her preferences for this hors d'oeuvre or that one, but in general she seemed to be having the time of her life.

Allie observed all this with mounting confusion. What had happened to the woman she knew, the woman who preferred faculty teas to family dinners, the woman who had difficulty expressing her feelings?

Finally she insisted on taking her mother to lunch to get an explanation. Her mother seemed startled and vaguely insulted by her questions.

"You're my only child. Why wouldn't I want to be involved in your wedding?"

Allie struggled to come up with an explanation for her confusion that wouldn't hurt her mother's feelings. "Ever since I moved down here, you and Dad have been... I don't know how to put it. Distant, I suppose. After the hurricane you seemed almost relieved when I told you it wasn't necessary for you to come down to take care of me."

Despite her careful wording, her mother looked crushed. "Oh, darling, I am so sorry you felt that way. We were just so terrified of hovering the way we did when you first lost your hearing. We thought that would make things worse for you. And when you said you were doing fine, we felt we had to take you at your word."

Tears filled her eyes. "Don't you know that it was

agony for us to have you in the hospital so far away after such a tragedy? When you told us you didn't need us? It would have been so easy to insist you come home where we could look out for you or to rush down here to coddle you. But if we'd done that, you might never have fought so hard for your independence." She managed a faint smile. "You might never have gotten involved with Ricky."

Allie was stunned by the explanation. "You did it for *my* sake? I mean not just lately, but staying away when I first moved here?"

"Well, of course. Why else?"

"I was afraid you were disappointed in me, maybe even ashamed. I thought you were glad I'd gone so far away."

The tears in her mother's eyes spilled down her cheeks. "Allison Matthews, your father and I could never be disappointed in you," she declared indignantly. "We were devastated when you lost your hearing. We blamed ourselves for not taking better care of you. Of course it saddens us that you lost your music, but for *your* sake, not ours. We've loved you from the instant you were born. And we have never been more proud of you than we are now."

She swallowed hard, clearly struggling for composure. "You're remarkable, Allie. Can't you see that? Years ago you took a great tragedy and turned it into a challenge, which you have more than met. You did that again after the hurricane. You've found a truly wonderful man who obviously loves you. I expect we'll have gorgeous grandchildren we can dote on in no time. I've never seen you look happier. What more could a parent possibly want for a child?"

Her own eyes stinging with tears, and suddenly feeling as if her entire world was right again, Allie reached across the table and squeezed her mother's hand. "I love you, Mom."

In an afternoon of surprises, her mother responded in sign language. "I love you, my darling daughter."

That night as she snuggled close to the man who would be her husband in a few days, Allie recounted the story.

"I'm happy for you," he said. "I know how much you wanted your family around, even though you stuck that brave little chin of yours up in the air and declared it didn't matter if they were."

"My hunch is that if we give them a grandchild, we'll have a hard time getting rid of them."

He pulled her astride him, then grinned as he began to move inside her for the second time that night. "By all means, then, let's give them what they want."

Ricky stood next to Tom at the front of the church his family had attended his entire life, tugging at the tight collar of his fancy shirt.

"Remind me never again to wear one of these things," he grumbled.

"You say that at every wedding," Tom pointed out.

"Well, thank goodness there are no more sisters or best friends to get married. I should be safe."

"Only till all those nieces and nephews grow up," Tom retorted just as the music began.

Ricky turned to watch as his sisters started down the aisle in their pastel bridesmaid gowns. Nikki and Allie had agreed that they both wanted the Wilder women as their attendants. In fact, they had agreed on every single detail. He had a hunch that all Nikki cared about was getting Tom's ring back on her finger. She hadn't even batted an eye when Allie had insisted on having Jane as her matron of honor. As for Jane, she had been moved to tears by the request.

Now as Jane reached the front of the church, she gave Ricky an impudent wink, then took her place as the music swelled and everyone turned to watch for the brides. He peeked at Jane's feet, but, for once, to his disappointment, she wasn't wearing her bright sneakers.

Then his attention was riveted to the back of the church as the organist shifted into the familiar notes of "Here Comes the Bride."

Nikki came down the aisle first, wearing a simple white satin cocktail-length dress and carrying a bouquet of orchids, her gaze locked with Tom's all the way.

Then Allie appeared in the arched entryway, resplendent in a simple gown of white silk with tiny pearls around the scooped neckline. The narrow skirt fell to the floor, then extended in back to a short train. Rather than wear a tiara and veil, she had opted to have a strand of pearls woven into her upswept hair. Ricky hid a smile as he spotted the errant curls that had already escaped the tamed style to caress her cheeks.

"I might not hear the words, so I want to see everything very clearly," she had told him. "A veil would just get in the way."

He watched as she glanced up at her father, who gently patted her hand where it was looped through his arm. Then she focused all her attention on the cadence of Nikki's steps. Her lips pursed, and he knew she was humming the music as she began her walk down the aisle on her father's arm, a sweet-smelling bouquet of roses and camellias clutched in her hand. Misty-eyed, her father kissed her cheek before he released her into Ricky's care.

Ricky hadn't told her in advance what his intentions were, but he saw the joy begin to shine in her eyes when the minister accompanied the words of the ceremony with sign language. Ricky repeated his own vows, not only speaking them but signing them.

"So you will hear them well," he told her. "And keep them in your heart forever."

"Next to the love I have for you," she told him.

Then her voice rang out clearly in the old, Spanish-style church, promising to love, honor and cherish him, "all the days of our lives. Whether they be many or few, I will be grateful for each one."

And then, to his surprise and his family's evident delight, she repeated the vow in halting Spanish.

She made the commitment with such love shining in her eyes, such a solemn tone to her voice, that Ricky knew he would do everything in his power never to let her down.

"We'll be together through eternity," he mouthed softly, and saw her lips curve into a smile.

That smile said more than a thousand words.

At the reception after the ceremony, Tom and Nikki took them aside. Tom looked as if he were in shock.

"We have something to tell you," Nikki said, her face radiant. "I just told Tom after the ceremony, so excuse him if he seems a little dazed."

"What?" Allie said, her gaze intent on her friend's face. Nikki beamed. "I'm pregnant."

"Oh, my gosh," Allie said, a grin spreading across her face. "You must be ecstatic."

"I am," Nikki confirmed. Her expression sobered a little as she glanced at her new husband. "I'm not so sure about him."

"It's still sinking in," Tom said. "Me, a father? I can't believe it. I guess this means I'm about to change jobs."

At Ricky's startled look, he shrugged. "I promised her I'd do it when we started a family. We're just a few years off our timetable."

"You actually don't seem all that upset about it," Ricky noted.

Tom's expression turned thoughtful. "You know, I can't honestly say that I am. After what happened to you on that last trip, I began to see why Nikki was so shaken every time I left home. You scared the dickens out of me, too. I've been thinking the last few weeks that maybe I've had enough thrills and lived to tell about it. There's no point in pressing my luck, not when I have so much to live for."

Ricky gave Nikki a kiss, then hugged his friend. "Congratulations, you two. I'm really happy for you. I'm going to miss you at work, though. It takes a long time to find someone you're willing to trust with your life."

"There are plenty of guys on the team ready to step into my place. You'll be fine."

Ricky glanced at Allie and knew her doubts were being magnified a hundredfold by Tom's announcement. When the other couple had walked away, he tucked a finger under her chin.

"Hey, don't look so worried. I made you a promise. I intend to keep it."

"You'd better," she said fiercely. "I expect to have years and years with you. Besides, it takes time to have all those kids we've been talking about."

He grinned. "Want to sneak out of here and get started?"

She gestured toward the cake, which still hadn't been cut, and the band, which was just getting ready to start playing. "I think we'd be missed. Besides, you promised to teach me to tango tonight."

"The tango is a very seductive dance," he pointed out. "I could give you an even more amazing lesson in the privacy of the bridal suite upstairs."

"No band."

He slipped his arms around her waist and pulled her close. "We won't need one."

"Hey, it's bad enough that one of us can't hear the music," she teased.

"Not true," he said, his gaze locked with hers. "The music's in here, *querida*." He tapped his chest. "And I can hear it loud and clear."

Her lips curved slightly, and she tilted her head as if listening intently. "Come to think of it, so can I."

* * * * *

SHELTER
FROM THE STORM

RaeAnne Thayne

To Darcy Rhodes, for sharing your singing and your smiles, for changing diapers and telling jokes and helping us take unforgettable journeys we once thought were impossible. You'll always be part of our family!

Chapter 1

"Would you take your shirt off, please?"

Under other circumstances—and from just about any other woman—Daniel Galvez might have been tempted to take those words as a rather enticing request.

From Dr. Lauren Maxwell, he knew all too well she meant nothing suggestive—as much as he might wish otherwise.

He sighed, detesting this whole ordeal, even as he knew he had no choice but to comply. His right hand went to the buttons of his uniform and he wrestled them free, uncomfortably aware of her watching him out of those intense blue eyes that seemed to miss nothing.

He had to work hard to hide a wince as he shrugged out of his shirt, mentally bracing himself for the moment she would touch him with those cool fingers.

The pain didn't worry him. He had coped with much

worse than a little scratch on the arm. Handling Lauren and the feelings she always stirred up in him was another matter entirely.

She watched him take off his shirt, her eyes veiled as they always seemed to be in his presence, and he wondered what she saw. The dirt-poor Mexican kid on the school bus in the fraying, too-small jeans and the threadbare coat? Or the harsh, hard-as-nails cop she must hate?

Those cool, lovely features didn't reveal even a hint of whatever she might think of him. Just as well, he thought. He had a feeling he was better off not knowing.

"Sorry to come in so late," he said as he pulled his blood-soaked shirt away. "I wouldn't have stopped if I hadn't seen the lights on as I was driving past."

She raised an eyebrow, though her attention remained fixed on his reason for being in her examination room of the Moose Springs Medical Clinic. "That's quite a nasty laceration you've got there, Sheriff. What were you going to do about it, if you weren't going to stop here? Stitch it up yourself?"

If he were capable of such a feat, he probably would have tried rather than finding himself in this uncomfortable position. "I figured I would catch a minute to run into the emergency clinic in Park City later."

That was still his preferred option. But since he was missing two deputies this weekend in a department that was already understaffed, he didn't have that luxury.

This was his third night of double shifts and he just couldn't spare the personal leave to drive the half hour to Park City, sit in the emergency clinic there while he waited his turn for a couple hours among all the banged-up skiers and tourists with altitude sickness, then drive a half hour back to Moose Springs.

With the ski season in full swing, Park City in January was crazy anyway—throw in an independent film festival that drew thousands of Hollywood types and their entourages, and he would just about rather chew tire spikes than spend time there if he didn't have to.

Even if that meant baring his chest for Lauren Maxwell.

"You know I'm always on call for you and your deputies if you need me," she said. Though her voice was low and polite, he still felt a pinch of reprimand.

She stepped forward, close enough that he could smell the subtle, intoxicating scent of jasmine and vanilla that always seemed to cling to her. She didn't touch him yet, just continued to study the jagged three-inch cut on his upper arm that was beginning to throb like hell.

"How did you say you were injured?"

"Bar fight down at Mickey's. Some joker from out of town got mad when Johnny Baldwin kept playing 'Achy Breaky Heart' on the jukebox."

"Uh-oh. He and Carol are fighting again?"

"Apparently. By about the sixth go-around, the tourist had had enough of Billy Ray and tried to physically prevent Johnny from putting in another quarter."

"I hope you didn't arrest him for that. Sounds like justifiable assault to me."

A muscle twitched in his cheek at her dry tone, though it was taking most of his concentration to keep his mind on the story and away from how incredible it felt to have Lauren Maxwell's hands on him, even in a clinical setting.

"Most of the bar probably would have backed the guy up at first. But of course he had to go and push his luck. He went just a bit too far and insulted both Johnny and any woman stupid enough to go out with him in the first place. And of course three of Carol's brothers happened to be sitting at the other end of the bar and they didn't take too kindly to that. By the time I got there, everybody in the place was having a good old time throwing punches and smashing chairs. I was trying to take the tourist into custody, mostly for his own protection, when his buddy came after me with the business end of a broken beer bottle."

"I'm sorry."

He lifted his uninjured shoulder. "Hazard of the job."

"Should I be expecting more casualties?"

"From what I could tell, the damage seemed to be mostly bloody noses and a couple of black eyes. The paramedics showed up just in case but I appeared to get the worst of it."

"I imagine Mickey's not too crazy about having his bar ripped apart."

"You know Mickey. He was right in the middle of it all."

She probed the edge of his wound and he couldn't hide a grimace.

"Sorry," she murmured, stepping away. "I'm going to have to clean it up a little before I can put in any stitches. Sit tight while I grab a suture kit and some antiseptic."

"No problem."

The moment she left the room, he huffed out the breath he hadn't realized he'd been holding. Okay, so this hadn't been one of his better ideas. He should have just accepted his fate and driven into Park City, to hell with the jam it would put in his schedule.

Being here alone in the medical clinic with Lauren after hours was far too intimate, much too dangerous for his peace of mind.

He sighed, frustrated once again at this tension that always simmered between them.

It hadn't always been this way, but the events of five years earlier had changed everything. Lauren was still cordial, unfailingly polite, but she didn't treat him with the same warmth she gave everyone else. Every interaction between them seemed awkward and tense.

Though they grew up a few blocks away from each other, they may as well have been on different planets when they were kids. For one thing, she was three years younger. At thirty and thirty-three, now that didn't seem to make much difference. But when he was thirteen and trying his best to find his place in the world, a ten-year-old girl held about as much interest to him as learning the fox-trot.

Beyond that, they had been worlds apart demographically. She had been the smart and beautiful daughter of the town mayor—his dad's boss—and he had been the son of Mexican immigrants who never had enough of anything to go around but love.

He had tried to cross that social divide only once, the year he finished out his football scholarship and graduated from college. He had come home to work construction at her father's company for the summer before starting his police-officer training in the fall and he suddenly couldn't help noticing smart, pretty little Lauren Maxwell had grown into a beautiful college freshman, home for the summer between terms.

One night she had stopped by her father's office at the same time he dropped in after a job to pick up his paycheck. They had talked a little, flirted a little— though in retrospect, that had been one-sided on his part—and he had ended up asking her to dinner.

She had refused him firmly and decisively, almost horror-stricken, leaving him no room at all to maneuver around his abruptly deflated ego.

He could survive a little rejection. Hell, it had probably been good for him, a college jock far too full of himself.

If that had been the end of it, he imagined they could have salvaged at least a casual friendship over the years, especially after they both returned to settle in Moose Springs. She was the town's only doctor and he was the sheriff, so they were bound to interact sometimes.

But what came after had effectively destroyed any chance he had of claiming even that.

There was too much history between them, too many secrets, for anything but this awkwardness.

He wasn't sure how much she knew. Enough, obviously, for her to simmer about it. If she knew the whole truth, she would despise him even more. Somehow that knowledge did nothing to squash the attraction that always seethed under his skin, the edginess he couldn't seem to shake.

The door opened suddenly and she returned carrying a tray of bandages and suture supplies. He must have done a credible job of hiding his thoughts. She gave him a smile that almost looked genuine—until he saw the murkiness in her blue eyes.

"You'll have to sit down so I can reach your arm. You can rest it on this table."

He hesitated only a moment before he sat down where she indicated and thrust out his arm. The cut was jagged and ugly and still stung like hell, but he knew it looked worse than it really was.

Still, he winced when she pulled out a needle to numb the area. He would far rather face a dozen broken beer bottles than a needle. She caught his expression and gave him a reassuring smile. "It will only sting for a minute, I promise."

Feeling foolish and itchy at her nearness, he stoically endured the shot, then the gentle brush of her hands as she washed off the blood with Betadine and went to work stitching him up. He finally had to focus on a painting on the wall of two children on a beach eating ice cream and couldn't help wishing for a little cold refreshment to offset the heat of her fingers touching his skin.

"You're very good at that."

She didn't look up from her careful suturing. "Thanks. I considered a surgical specialty when I was in med school but I decided I wanted to see more of my patients than their insides."

"Lucky for us, I guess."

She didn't answer and the silence stretched between them. He scrambled around for another topic of conversation and grabbed the first one that came to him. "How's your mother?"

This time her gaze did flash to his, her expression unreadable. "Good. The warm St. George climate agrees with her. She's become quite a rabid golfer now that she can play all year."

He tried to picture soft and prim Janine Maxwell ripping up the golf course and couldn't quite get a handle on it. But then he never would have pictured Lauren Maxwell choosing to practice in quiet Moose Springs, when she could have gone anywhere else in the world.

Oddly, she seemed to follow his train of thought. "Mom wants me to sell the clinic and open up another one in southern Utah."

He didn't like the sudden panic spurting through him at the thought of her leaving. "Will you?"

Her hair brushed his arm as she shook her head. "Not a chance," she said firmly. "Moose Springs is my home and I'm not going anywhere."

He didn't miss the defiance in her voice and he fully understood the reason for it. Things couldn't always be easy for her here—he knew there were some in town who would rather drive the thirty-five minutes to Park City for their medical care than walk through the doors of any clinic run by the daughter of the town's biggest crook.

The good people of Moose Springs hadn't taken R. J. Maxwell's embezzlement of more than a million dollars of their hard-earned money very kindly. Even five years after his death, there were those who still carried a pretty hefty grudge.

Most people in town didn't blame the daughter for the father's sins, but he had heard enough whispers and veiled innuendos to know *most* didn't mean *all*. A certain percentage of the population wasn't as fair-minded.

If the full story ever emerged, he knew that percentage would probably increase dramatically.

Lauren's own mother had been quick to escape Moose Springs after the scandal broke. He couldn't understand why Lauren seemed determined to remain in town despite the ugly blotches on her family's laundry.

"That should do it," she said after a moment, affixing a bandage to the spot. "I'll write you a prescription for a painkiller and an antibiotic, just to be on the safe side."

"Just the antibiotic," he said, shrugging back into his ruined uniform shirt.

"That's a nasty laceration. You might be surprised at the residual pain tomorrow."

"I'll take an aspirin if it gets too bad."

She rolled her eyes but before she could speak, his communicator buzzed with static and a moment later he heard his dispatcher's voice.

"Chief, I've got Dale Richins on the line," Peggy Wardell said. "Says he was driving home from his sister's in Park City and blew a tire."

"He need help with it?"

"Not with the tire. But when he went in the back to get the spare, he found a girl hiding in the camper shell of his pickup."

He blinked at that unexpected bit of information. "A girl?"

"Right. She's beat up pretty good, Dale says, and tried to escape when he found her but she collapsed before she could get far. She only *hablas* the *español*, apparently. Thought I'd better let you know."

He grabbed for his blood-soaked coat, sudden dread congealing in his gut. One of the hazards of working in a small town was the fear every time a call like this came in, he didn't know who he might find at the scene.

He knew just about everyone in the growing Latino community around Moose Springs and hated the possibility that someone he knew—someone's *hija* or *hermana*—might have been attacked.

"Thanks, Peg. Tell Dale I can be there in five minutes or so."

"Right."

He headed for the door, then stopped short when he realized Lauren was right on his heels, passing a medical kit from hand to hand as she shoved the opposite hand into her parka.

"What do you think you're doing?" he asked.

"I'm coming with you," she said, that Lauren stubbornness in her voice. "Sounds like you've got a victim who will need medical care and if I go with you, I can be on scene faster than the volunteer paramedics."

He didn't want to take the time to argue with her—not when a few seconds consideration convinced him the idea was a good one. Lauren was more qualified to offer better medical care than anything the volunteer medics could provide.

"Let's go then," he said, leading the way out into the drizzling snow.

Daniel drove through the slushy roads with his lights flashing but his siren quiet, at a speed that had her hanging on to her medical kit with both hands.

She gritted her teeth as he hit one of the town's famous potholes and her head slammed against the headrest.

"Sorry," he said, though he barely looked at her.

Nothing new there. Daniel seldom looked at her, not if he could help himself. She was glad for it, she told herself. She didn't want him looking too closely at her. He already knew too much about her, more than just about anyone else in town—she didn't want him aiming those piercing brown eyes too far into her psyche.

She gripped her bag more tightly as he drove toward the scene, trying not to notice how big and hard and dangerous he seemed under these conditions.

Sheriff Daniel Galvez was not a man any sane person would want to mess with. He was six feet three inches and two hundred and ten pounds of pure muscle. Not that she made note of his vital statistics during the rare times she had treated him or anything—it was just hard to miss a man so big who was still as tough and physically imposing as the college football player he'd been a decade earlier.

Beside him, she always felt small and fragile, a feeling she wasn't particularly crazy about. She *wasn't* small, she was a respectable five feet six inches tall and a healthy one hundred and fifteen pounds. It was only his size that dwarfed her. And she wasn't fragile, either. She had survived med school, a grueling residency and, just a few months later, crippling shock and disbelief at the chaos her father left in his wake.

She shoved away thoughts of her father as Daniel pulled the department's Tahoe to a stop behind a battered old pickup she recognized as belonging to Dale Richins. The old rancher stood behind his camper shell, all but wringing his hands.

He hurried to them the moment Daniel shut off the engine. "The little girl is inside the camper shell of my truck. I had a horse blanket in there. I guess that's what she was hiding under. Looks like you brought medical help. Good. From what I can see, she's beat up something terrible."

He looked at Lauren with a little less suspicion than normal, but she didn't have time to be grateful as she headed for the back of the pickup. Daniel was right behind her and he didn't wait for her to ask for help—he just lifted her up and over the tailgate and into the truck bed.

He aimed the heavy beam of his flashlight inside as she made her careful way to the still form lying motionless under a grimy blanket that smelled of livestock and heaven knows what else.

She pulled out her flashlight, barely able to make out the battered features of a Latina girl.

"She's so young," Lauren exclaimed as she immediately went to work examining her. Though it was hard to be sure with all the damage, she didn't think the girl was much older than fourteen or fifteen.

"Do you know her?" Daniel asked, leaning in and taking a closer look.

"I don't think so. You?"

"She doesn't look familiar. I don't think she's from around here."

"Whoever she is, she's going to need transport to the hospital. This is beyond what I can handle at the clinic."

"How urgent?" Daniel asked from outside the pickup. "Ambulance or LifeFlight to the University of Utah?"

She considered the situation. "Her vitals are stable and nothing seems life-threatening at this point. Send for an ambulance," she decided.

She lifted the girl's thin T-shirt, trying to look for anything unusual in the dim light. She certainly found it.

"Sheriff, she's pregnant," she exclaimed.

He leaned inside, his expression clearly shocked. "Pregnant?"

"I'd guess about five or six months along."

She moved her stethoscope and was relieved to hear a steady fetal heartbeat. She started to palpate the girl's abdomen when suddenly her patient's eyes flickered open. Even in the dim light inside the camper shell, Lauren could see panic chase across those battered features. The girl cried out and flailed at Lauren as she tried to scramble up and away from her.

"Easy, sweetheart. Easy," Lauren murmured. Her skills at Spanish were limited but she tried her best. "I'm not going to hurt you. I'm here to help you and your baby."

The girl's breathing was harsh and labored, but her frantic efforts to fight Lauren off seemed to ease and she watched her warily.

"I'm Lauren. I'm a doctor," she repeated in Spanish, holding up her stethoscope. "What's your name?"

Through swollen, discolored eyes, the girl looked disoriented and suspicious, and didn't answer for several seconds.

"Rosa," she finally said, her voice raspy and strained. "Rosa Vallejo."

Lauren smiled as calmly as if they were meeting for brunch. It was a skill she'd learned early in medical school—pretend you were calm and in control and your patients will assume you are. "Hello, Rosa Vallejo. I'm sorry you're hurt but an ambulance is on the way for you, okay? We're going to get you to the hospital."

"No! No hospital. Please!"

The fear in the girl's voice seemed to hitch up a

notch and she tried to sit up again. Lauren touched her arm, for comfort and reassurance as much as to hold her in place. "You've been hurt. You need help. You need to make sure your baby is all right."

"No. No. I'm fine. I must go."

She lunged to climb out of the truck bed but Daniel stood blocking the way, looking huge and imposing, his badge glinting in the dim light. The girl froze, a whimper in her throat and a look of abject terror in her eyes. *"No policía. No policía!"*

She seemed incoherent with fear, struggling hysterically to break free of Lauren's hold. Daniel finally reached in to help, which only seemed to upset the girl more.

"Hold her while I find something in my kit to calm her," Lauren ordered. "She's going to injure herself more if I don't."

A moment later, she found what she was looking for. Daniel held the girl while Lauren injected her with a sedative safe for pregnant women. A moment later, the medicine started to work its calming effect on her panicked patient and she sagged back against the horse blankets just as the wail of the ambulance sounded outside.

Lauren let out a sigh of relief and started to climb out of the truck bed. When Daniel reached to lift her out, she suddenly remembered his injury. She ignored his help and climbed out on her own.

"You're going to break open all those lovely stitches if you don't take it easy."

"I'm fine," he said firmly, just as the volunteer paramedics hurried over, medical bags slung over their shoulders.

"Hey, Mike, Pete," Lauren greeted them with a smile.

"You trying to take over our business now, Doc?" Pete asked her with a wink.

"No way. You guys are the experts at triage here. I happened to be stitching up the sheriff at the clinic after the big brawl at Mickey's bar. When he received this call, I rode along to see if I could help."

"Busy night for all of us. What have we got?"

Daniel stepped closer to hear her report and Lauren tried not to react to his overwhelming physical presence.

She gave them Rosa's vitals. "I have a young patient who appears to be approximately twenty weeks pregnant. It was tough to do a full assessment under these conditions, but she looks like she's suffering multiple contusions and lacerations, probably the result of a beating. She appears to be suffering from exposure. I have no idea how long she's been in the back of Dale's pickup. Maybe an hour, maybe more. Whether that contributed to her hysteria, I can't say, but I do know she's not very crazy about authority figures right now. Seeing the sheriff set her off, so we may have to use restraints in the ambulance on our way to Salt Lake City."

"You riding along?" Mike Halling asked.

"If I won't be in the way."

"You know we've always got room for you, Doc."

She stood back while he and Pete Zabrisky quickly transferred the girl to the stretcher then lifted it into the ambulance.

"I'm guessing she must have climbed in the back of the truck in Park City, or wherever Dale might have stopped on the way. Though I'm pretty sure the attack didn't happen here, I'm going to put one of my deputies to work processing the scene," Daniel told her while they waited in the stinging sleet for the paramedics to finish loading Rosa into the bus.

"All right," she answered.

"I won't be far behind you. I'd like to question her once she's been treated." He paused. "I can give you a ride back to town when we're done, if you need it."

She nodded and climbed in after Mike and Pete. Maybe she had a problem with authority figures, too. That must be why her stomach fluttered and her heart-beat accelerated at the prospect of more time in the company of the unnerving Daniel Galvez.

Chapter 2

Watching Dr. Lauren Maxwell in action was more fascinating to him than the Final Four, the World Series and the Super Bowl combined. As long as she wasn't working on him and he didn't have to endure having her hands on him, Daniel wouldn't mind watching her all day.

As he stepped back to let the ambulance pull past him, with its lights flashing through the drizzle of snow, he could see Lauren through the back windows as she talked to the paramedics in what he imagined was that brisk, efficient voice she used when directing patient care.

In trauma situations, Lauren always seemed completely in control. He never would have guessed back in the day that she would make such a wonderful physician.

He still found it amazing that the prim little girl on the school bus with her pink backpacks and her fake-fur-trimmed coats and her perfectly curled blond ringlets seemed to have no problem wading through blood and guts and could handle herself with such quiet but confident expertise, no matter the situation.

She loved her work. It was obvious every time Daniel had the chance to see her in action. Medicine wasn't a job with Lauren Renee Maxwell, it was more like a sacred calling.

In the five years since she'd come back to Moose Springs and opened her clinic, he had watched her carefully. Like many others, at first he had expected her to fail. She was the spoiled, pampered daughter of the man who had been the town's wealthiest citizen. How could she possibly have the stamina to cope with all the gritty realities of small-town doctoring?

Like almost everyone else, he had quickly figured out that there was more to Lauren than anybody might have guessed. Over the years, her clinic had become a strong, vital thread in the community fabric.

They were all lucky to have her—and so was that young girl in the back of the ambulance.

"What am I supposed to do now?" Dale Richins asked, his wide, grizzled features concerned.

"We're going to need a statement from you. The address of your sister's house in Park City, any place you might have stopped between there and here. That kind of thing."

"I can tell you where LouAnn lives. She's on the edge of town, the only part the old-timers can afford anymore, with all the developers trying to buy everybody out. But I can tell you right now, I didn't stop a single place after I left her house. Headed straight home. I don't know if I even would have known that girl was back there if I hadn't stopped to fix the flat. She would have likely froze to death."

"You did the right thing, trying to help her."

"What else was I supposed to do? Little thing like that." He shook his head. "Just makes me sick, someone could hurt her and leave her to find her own way in the cold. Especially if she's pregnant like the doc said. It's got to be only eight or nine degrees out here. I can't imagine how cold it was in the back of that drafty old camper shell while I was going sixty-five miles an hour on the interstate. It's a wonder that little girl didn't freeze solid before I found her."

"Yeah, it was lucky you found her when you did."

"Who do you figure might have done this to her?"

"I couldn't guess right now until I have a chance to talk to her. I imagine she was probably looking for some way to escape when she stumbled onto your truck and camper shell. The lock's broken, I see."

"That old thing's been busted since before you quit your fancy job in the city and came home. But yeah, that makes sense that she was looking for a way out."

"So either she was injured somewhere near your sister's house or she stumbled on your truck sometime after the beating. I'll know better after I can interview her."

Dale cleared his throat. "You let me know if she needs anything, won't you? I can't afford much, but I could help some with her doctor bills and whatnot."

He couldn't help being touched at the crusty old rancher's obvious concern for his stowaway. Most of the time, Dale was hard-edged and irascible, cranky to everyone. Maybe Rosa reminded him of his three granddaughters or something.

"Thanks," he answered. "That's real decent of you."

"Least I can do."

"There's Deputy Hendricks," Daniel said as another department SUV approached. "She'll take a statement from you with the particulars of your sister's address and all, and then she can drive you home when you're finished."

"What the hell for? I can drive myself home."

"I'm sorry, Dale, but we're going to have to take your truck to the garage down at the station to see if we can find any evidence in the back. It's standard procedure in cases like this."

The rancher didn't look too thrilled with that piece of information. "Don't I have any kind of choice here?"

"You want us to do everything we can to find out who hurt that girl, don't you?"

"I suppose…"

"You'll have it back by morning, I promise."

That didn't seem to ease Dale's sour look, but the rancher seemed to accept the inevitable.

"You heading to the hospital now?" he asked.

At Daniel's nod, he pointed a gnarled finger at him. "You make sure R.J.'s daughter treats that girl right."

Though he knew it was a foolish reflex, Daniel couldn't help but stiffen at the renewed animosity in the rancher's voice. How did Lauren deal with it, day after day? he wondered. Dale wasn't the only old-timer around here who carried a grudge as wide and strong as the Weber River. She must face this kind of thing on a daily basis.

It pissed him off and made him want to shake the

other man. Instead, he pasted on a calm smile. "Dale, if you weren't so stubborn, you would admit Lauren is a fine doctor. She'll take care of the girl. You can bet your ranch on it."

The other man made a harrumphing kind of sound but didn't comment as Teresa Hendricks approached. Daniel turned his attention from defending Lauren—something she would probably neither appreciate nor understand—and focused on the business at hand.

"Thanks for coming in on your first night off in a week," he said to his deputy. "Sorry to do this to you."

"Not a problem. Sounds like you had some excitement."

He spent five minutes briefing her on the case, then suggested she drive the rancher home and take his statement there, where they both could be warm and dry.

"I'm going to follow the ambulance to the hospital and try to interview the vic," he said. "If anything breaks here, you know how to reach me."

The snow seemed to fall heavier and faster as he drove through Parley's Canyon to the Salt Lake Valley. It was more crowded than he would have expected at eleven at night, until he remembered the film festival. This whole part of the state was insane when all the celebs were in town.

By the time he reached the University of Utah Medical Center, his shoulders ached with tension and he was definitely in need of a beer.

At the hospital, he went immediately to the emergency room and was directed down a hallway, where he quickly spotted Lauren talking to a man Daniel assumed was another doctor, at least judging by the stethoscope around his neck.

The guy was leaning down, and appeared to be hanging on every word Lauren said. He was blond and lean and as chiseled as those movie stars in their two-thousand-dollar ski jackets up the canyon, trying to see and be seen around town.

Daniel immediately hated him.

He took a step down the hallway and knew immediately when Lauren caught sight of him. She straightened abruptly and something flashed in her blue eyes, something murky and confusing. She quickly veiled her expression and it became a mask of stiff politeness.

Just once, he would love the chance to talk to her without the prickly shell she always seemed to whip out from somewhere and put on whenever he was near.

"Sheriff Galvez," she greeted him, her delicate features solemn. "Have you met Kendall Fox? He's the E.R. attending tonight. Kendall, this is Daniel Galvez."

The doctor stuck out his hand and Daniel shook it, though he couldn't escape the impression they were both circling around each other, sizing up the enemy like a couple of hound dogs sniffing after the same bone.

He didn't miss the dismissal in the doctor's eyes and for the second time that night, he had to fight the urge to kick somebody's ass. He wouldn't waste his energy, he thought. Lauren was too smart to go for the type of smooth player who couldn't remember the name of the woman he was with unless she had it tattooed somewhere on a conveniently accessible portion of her anatomy.

"How's our victim?" he asked.

"She's gone to Radiology for some X-rays," Lauren spoke up. "The tech should be bringing her back in a moment. Kendall... Dr. Fox...and I were just discussing the best course of action. We think—"

Dr. Jerk cut her off. "She has a little frostbite on a couple of her toes, an apparent broken wrist and some cracked ribs."

"How's the baby?" Daniel pointedly directed his question back to Lauren, ignoring the other man.

She frowned, looking worried. "She's started having some mild contractions right now. We've given her medication to stop them, but she's definitely going to need to be closely observed for the next few days."

"She give any indication who put her here?"

Lauren shook her head. She had discarded her parka somewhere, he observed with his keen detective eye, and had put surgical scrubs on over the pale blue turtleneck she had worn when she treated his shoulder. Her hair was slipping from its braid and he had to fight a ridiculous urge to tuck it back.

"She clams up every time we ask."

"I was afraid of that. She's got to be frightened. It would sure make my job easier if she could just give me the name, age and last-known address of the son of a bitch who put her here. Of course we have to do this the hard way. Can I talk to her?"

"You cops. Can't you even wait until the girl gets out of X-ray?" Fox asked.

Daniel slid his fists into his pockets and pasted on that same damn calm smile that sometimes felt about as genuine as fool's gold.

He really hated being made to feel like a big, dumb Mexican.

"I didn't mean this instant," he murmured. "But I would like to talk to her as soon as possible, while the details are still fresh in her mind."

The doctor looked like he wanted to get in a pissing match right there in the hallway, but before he could unzip, a nurse in pink scrubs stuck her head out of one of the examination rooms.

She didn't look pleased to find the E.R. doctor still standing close to Lauren, a sentiment with which Daniel heartily concurred. Her reaction made him wonder if the good doctor was the sort who left a swath of broken hearts through the staff.

"Dr. Fox, can you come in here for a minute?" the nurse asked. "I've got a question on your orders."

The doctor's handsome features twisted with annoyance but he hid it well. "Be right there."

After he walked down the hall, a tight, awkward silence stretched between Daniel and Lauren. He found it both sad and frustrating, and wondered how he could ever bridge the chasm between them.

He wasn't exactly sure how much Lauren knew about the events that led up to her father's exposure and subsequent fall from grace. If she knew all of it, she must blame him for what happened next.

He sure as hell blamed himself.

"How's your arm?" she asked.

The blasted thing throbbed like the devil, but he wasn't about to admit that to her.

"Fine," he assured her. "Sorry I wasted your time on that. If I'd known I would have to make a trip down here to the city, I could have just had them fix me up here while I was waiting to interview our beating victim. But then, I doubt anybody on staff here can claim such nice handiwork."

She blinked at the compliment and he watched a light sprinkle of color wash over her cheekbones. "I... thank you," she murmured.

"You're welcome."

They lapsed into silence again.

"How's Anna these days?" Lauren asked after an awkward moment. "I heard she was in the Northwest now."

Grateful for the conversation starter, he smiled at the thought of his baby sister. "She loves Oregon. She runs a little gift shop and gallery in Cannon Beach that seems to be doing well. I took a few days and drove up there last year and she seems happy."

"She's not married?"

Some of the tension between them seemed to ease as they talked and he wanted to prolong the moment indefinitely. "No. Marc's the only one of us to bite the bullet so far. He and his wife live in Cache Valley. They have twin boys we all spoil like crazy."

"And Ren is still in Central America?"

"Right. We can't get him away from his sea turtles."

She opened her mouth to answer, but cut off the words as a hospital worker pushed a gurney around the corner.

"Here's Rosa," she said.

The beating victim looked even younger here in the harsh glare of the hospital lights and her bruises showed up in stark relief against the white linens. Daniel studied her features, trying hard to find any hint of familiarity, but he was certain he didn't know her.

He helped push the gurney through the door into

the examination room, earning a censorious look from Lauren for the mild exertion. He returned it with a bland smile, though he had to fight down a spurt of warmth. He liked her worrying about him far too much.

"How did it go, Riley?" she asked the kid, who looked young for an X-ray technician, as his hospital ID identified him.

"Good. She fell asleep while I was waiting for the films and I didn't have the heart to wake her. Poor thing."

"She's been through a terrible ordeal. She must be exhausted."

Lauren took the films from him and slid the first of several into the light box hanging on the wall. She studied it, then exchanged it for another and finally a third, a frown of concentration on her lovely features.

"Just as we suspected," she said after a moment. "She's got three broken ribs, a fractured ulna and a broken nose."

"Somebody did a real number on her." He was angry all over again at the viciousness behind the attack. "How's the baby?"

Lauren studied tape spitting out from a machine that was attached to a belt around Rosa's abdomen. "The contractions have stopped. That's a good sign. We did an ultrasound earlier and the fetus seemed healthy. It's a miracle. She's a dozen different shades of black and blue on her abdomen. My guess is somebody kicked her hard at least two or three times in an effort to induce abortion."

Daniel had a feeling this was one of those cases that would grab on to him with rottweiler jaws and not let go until he solved it. "Can I talk to her?" he asked.

Lauren pursed her lips. "My instincts say to let her sleep for a while, but I understand your urgency. You likely have to return to Moose Springs as soon as possible."

"I do. I'm sorry. We're shorthanded tonight." He paused and met Lauren's gaze. "It's not just that, though. I want her to tell me what happened. The quicker she identifies whoever did this to her, the quicker I can lock the bastard up."

Though he spoke with a hard determination that didn't bode well for the perpetrator, Lauren didn't feel so much as a twinge of sympathy for whoever had done this. They deserved to feel the full wrath of Daniel Galvez, a terrible thing indeed.

"I'm right there with you on that sentiment," she told him. "In fact, if you gave me half a chance, I'd like to be the one twisting the key in the lock."

"I've got to catch him first and I can't do that until I talk to Rosa."

Lauren sighed. "All right. Why don't you wait in the hall while I wake her, though. She might panic if you're the first thing she sees when she opens her eyes."

He raised an eyebrow. "Am I really that scary?"

She felt her face heat and regretted her fair coloring that showed every emotion to the world like a big neon billboard. "I meant your uniform," she answered stiffly, though she had to admit, she found the man absolutely terrifying.

Could he tell? she wondered, hoping it wasn't as obvious as her blush. She wasn't afraid he would physically hurt her, though he was big and powerful and all large men tended to make her uncomfortable on some instinctive level.

With Daniel, though, she was more wary of her own reaction to him and all the feelings he sparked in her, emotions she would rather not be experiencing for someone with whom she had such a tangled, complicated relationship.

To her relief, he let the matter drop. "Yell when it's safe for me to come in, then," he murmured, slipping out of the room with far more grace than a man his size should possess.

The room immediately felt about three times bigger without his overwhelming presence filling it. Lauren let out the breath she always seemed to hold around him and moved to her patient's bedside.

"Rosa? *Niña,* I need you to wake up."

When she didn't respond immediately, Lauren gently shook her shoulder. "Rosa?"

The girl's eyes blinked open and she looked around in wild confusion, panic blooming in her dark eyes. Her gaze shifted to Lauren and a light of recognition sparked there. "*Doctora.*" She covered her abdomen with her hands. *"El bebé. Está bien?"*

"Sí. Sí. Está bien." She smiled, wishing she had a little better command of Spanish. If things weren't so tensely uncomfortable with Daniel, she might ask for private lessons. But of course, that was impossible, so for now she would have to muddle through.

"Rosa, the sheriff is here to talk to you about who hurt you."

The panic returned to her features. *"No. No policía."*

Lauren sighed. The physician in her wanted to urge her patient to rest, to promise her she could have this difficult interview later when her body had a chance to begin the healing process.

She couldn't, though. Daniel had a job to do—a job she very much wanted to see him conclude with an arrest. She just had to trust that he would handle a frightened girl with both tact and compassion.

"I'm sorry, Rosa," she answered in Spanish. "But you must tell him what happened."

The girl shook her head, her hands clasped protectively around her abdomen as if she feared Daniel would snatch the child from her womb. Lauren gave her a reassuring pat. "It will all be all right. You'll see. Sheriff Galvez only wants to help you."

Rosa said something in Spanish too rapid for Lauren to pick up on. She had a feeling she was better off not knowing.

She went to the door and opened it for Daniel. "She's upset and doesn't want to talk to you," she said in an undertone. "I honestly don't know how much she'll tell you. I'm sorry. I can give you a few moments but if I think you're upsetting her too much, I'll have to kick you out."

"All right."

When he entered the room, Rosa shrank against the bed linens, her fine-boned features tight with tension. Daniel pulled out one of the guest chairs and sat on the edge of it. He moved slowly, like someone trying to coax a meadowlark to eat birdseed from his hand.

He spoke Spanish in a low, calm voice. She couldn't understand him well, both because he pitched his voice low and because he spoke too quickly for her limited comprehension skills.

After a moment, Rosa answered him quickly, reluctance in every line of her body.

Lauren found it a surreal experience trying to follow their conversation when she only understood about one word in five. Even without a perfect command of the language, she could hear the compassion ringing through his voice.

He genuinely cared about Rosa, Lauren thought. The girl might be just a stowaway he had never seen until an hour ago, but he wanted to get to the bottom of things. She suddenly knew Daniel would go to any lengths to protect the girl. Fate had dropped her into Moose Springs, and she had become one of his charges.

She had a feeling his sincerity wasn't translating for Rosa. She shook her head vehemently several times, and Lauren could at least understand the most frequent word the girl employed. "No" sounded the same in English and in Spanish.

After several moments of this, Rosa turned her head against the wall, a clear message that she was done talking to him. Daniel said something, his voice low and intense, but Rosa didn't turn around.

At last Daniel stood with a sigh, his big handsome features tight with frustration. He tucked a business card in Rosa's hand. The girl closed her fingers around it, but didn't even look at either the card or at Daniel. With another sigh, Daniel nodded to Lauren and left the room.

She followed him. "She won't talk?" she asked when the door closed behind them.

"She claims she doesn't remember what happened to her."

Lauren frowned. "She has no head injury that might

account for a loss of memory. I suppose it might be some self-protective psychological reaction to the trauma…"

"There *is* no loss of memory. She remembers perfectly. She's just not telling."

"Doesn't she understand her safety and that of her baby is at stake here?"

"I think that's exactly what she's thinking about. I think she just wants to pretend none of it happened. 'I'm fine, the baby's fine. That's all that matters,' she just kept saying over and over."

"I'll talk to her. She'll be under my care and the attending's here for at least the next two or three days. I want to consult with the high-risk ob-gyns on staff here and make sure we monitor her closely to ensure no lasting harm to the fetus from her injuries. I don't know that it will do any good, but I'll try to persuade her she has to talk to you, or whoever did this to her will get away with a double attempted murder."

"Thanks, Lauren. I'll try to stop back in first thing in the morning. Maybe she'll change her mind about talking to me by then."

"You put in long hours, Sheriff."

He smiled and the sight of those white teeth flashing in that darkly handsome face sent her stomach trembling. "I could say the same for you, Doc."

She gazed at him for far longer than was probably polite, until he finally cleared his throat.

"You still need a ride back to Moose Springs?"

Chill, she chided herself. This was Daniel Galvez, the one man in town who shouldn't rev her motor. She would be better off with a player like Kendall Fox. At least he just annoyed her. Being with Dr. Fox never left her feeling like she had just stood in a wind tunnel for two or three days.

"If it's not too much trouble."

"No trouble," he assured her, though she couldn't help feeling he wasn't being completely truthful.

"Just give me a few more moments to wrap things up with Kendall and I should be ready."

"Here comes the good doctor now."

She turned and found Kendall walking purposefully down the hallway.

"The sheriff is my ride back to Moose Springs since I came in the ambulance," she said quickly, hoping to deflect any more flirtation. "Do you mind if I leave my patient in your care?"

"We'll take good care of her until they can find a bed for her on the medical floor."

"I'll be back first thing in the morning to check on her," she said. "I want a phone call in the night if her condition changes at all. Make sure the nurses know that when they admit her upstairs. Any change at all, I want to hear about it."

"I'll take care of her, I promise." Kendall gave her the full wattage of his lady-killer smile. "I'm on until seven in the morning and I expect doughnuts and some decent coffee out of the deal."

"Done."

As her interactions with Dr. Fox went, this one was fairly innocuous. She could only hope she would get through the hour-long drive with Daniel Galvez as painlessly.

Chapter 3

The slushy snow of earlier in the evening had given way to giant, soft flakes as the temperature dropped. Daniel drove away from the U. toward the canyon that would take them back to Moose Springs through the feeder streets along the foothills. Roads here were mostly clear, though he knew the canyon would probably be dicey.

He was painfully aware of Lauren sitting beside him and wondered if they had ever been alone like this. He was so conscious of her that it took all his powers of concentration to keep his attention on driving as he took the exit to I-80 through the canyon.

Still, he was aware of every movement from her side of the SUV. When he caught her covering a yawn, he risked a look at her. "Go ahead and sleep if you need to. I've got a pillow in the back."

"I'm all right. It's been a rather long day. I imagine you know all about those."

"This week, I certainly do." He signaled to change lanes around a car with out-of-state plates going at a crawl through what was just a light layer of snow.

The scanner crackled with static suddenly and he heard radio traffic of somebody in Park City reporting a drunk-and-disorderly patron at one of the popular restaurants on Main Street.

"I'm sure that's not the first one of those they've had this week," Lauren said.

"Yeah, and it won't be the last until Sundance is over. The detective I spoke to tonight on the way here sounded just a little frazzled."

"Things are busy enough in Park City in the winter with all the skiers. Throw in the film festival and it's a nightmare."

"Have you been to any screenings this year?"

She shrugged. "I don't have a lot of free hours to go to movies. You?"

"No. I caught a few screenings last year but I'm afraid this one is going to pass me by. Too much work."

"We're pathetic, aren't we? Sounds like we both need to get a life outside our jobs."

"I'd love to," he deadpanned, "but who has the time?"

She laughed out loud at that, the low, musical sound filling all the cold corners of his Tahoe. "*We* are pathetic. I was thinking the exact same thing. By the time I finish a twelve-hour shift at the clinic, I'm lucky to find the energy to drive home."

"You need a vacation." He pushed away the image of

her on a white sand beach somewhere, a soft sea breeze ruffling her hair and her muscles loose and relaxed.

"Funny, that seems to be the consensus," she said. "You'll be surprised to find, I'm sure, that I'm actually taking one next week. Coralee and Bruce Jenkins are going on a cruise. Rather than hire a temp to be the office manager for a week, I decided to close the whole clinic and just give everyone the time off. My staff needed a break."

"Good for you!"

"The town got along without any doctor at all for a long time. I'm sure a few days without me will be bearable."

"What are you doing with yourself?"

"I haven't decided yet. Mom's bugging me to come down and visit for a few days. I might. Or I might just stick close to home, try out some new cross-country ski trails, maybe take in a movie or two in Park City."

"I'm sure Dr. Fox would be happy to take you to a screening if you just said the word."

He immediately wished he had just kept that little statement to himself. Out of the corner of his eye, he saw Lauren's eyes widen with surprise. Even from here, he could see color flare on her delicate cheekbones. "Kendall? I don't think so."

He knew he should let it rest but he just couldn't seem to make himself shut up. "Why?" he pressed. "He's good-looking, successful, probably loaded. Seems like a good catch."

"Maybe *you* should date him," she said tartly.

"I'm not the one the good doctor couldn't take his eyes off."

"You're delusional. I'd be happy to refer you to a doctor who can prescribe something for that."

He laughed, but figured he should probably change the subject before he revealed too much, like the attraction he had done his best to hide for more than a decade. Before he could come up with a conversational detour, she beat him to the punch.

"What about you?" she asked. "I heard rumors of wedding bells a few summers ago when you were dating little Cheryl White."

"She wasn't little," he muttered.

"Not in physical assets, anyway. But wasn't she barely out of high school?"

He had to admit, he was a little stung by her implication that he might be interested in jailbait. At the same time, he had to wonder why she noticed who he dated. "Cheryl was twenty-one when I started dating her. She didn't even have to use fake ID to get into Mickey's."

"That must have been a relief for you. It probably would have been a little awkward to have to arrest your own girlfriend."

It must be late, if she could tease him like this. The tension usually simmering between them was nowhere in sight as they drove through the snowy night. He savored the moment, though he was fairly certain it wouldn't last.

"For the record, Cheryl was never my girlfriend. We only dated a few times and we never discussed wedding bells or anything else matrimony-related. You ought to know better than to listen to the Moose Springs gossips."

Even without looking at her, he could feel her light

mood trickle away like the snow melting on the windshield.

"You're right. Absolutely right." Her voice cooled several degrees in just a few seconds. "Who gossips *to* you will gossip *of* you, isn't that what they say? And I certainly don't need to be the subject of any more whispers in Moose Springs."

The ghost of her father loomed between them and all the usual tension suddenly returned. He would have given anything to take his heedless words back, but like those snippets of gossip spreading around town, they couldn't be recalled.

His hands tightened on the steering wheel and he made some innocuous comment about the weather. She responded in a quiet, polite voice, as if those shared moments of intimacy had never been.

It was nearly midnight when he pulled up in front of the clinic. Three or four inches of snow had fallen while they had been in the city and her aging Volvo was buried.

He reached across the space between them to his jockey box for his window scraper. The movement brought him closer to her and he was surrounded by jasmine and vanilla.

His mouth watered and his insides gave one big sigh, but he did his best to ignore his automatic reaction. He pulled out the scraper and returned to the safe side of the vehicle—but not before he heard a quick, indrawn breath from Lauren.

He chanced a look at her. The SUV was parked under a lamppost and in the pool of light, he found her blue eyes wide and her lovely features slightly pink.

He wasn't quite sure what to think about that so

decided to put it from his mind. "Wait here where it's warm," he ordered.

Her forehead furrowed with her frown and now any flush that might be on her features turned to annoyance. "Are you kidding? I just put seven stitches in your arm, Daniel. *You* wait here where it's warm. Better yet, go on home and rest. I don't need a police escort to scrape the snow off my car."

"Wait here," he repeated, in the same no-nonsense voice he used with the prisoners at the jail.

Her sigh sounded exasperated, but he didn't let that stop him as he stepped out into the blowing cold that soaked through the layers of his coat to settle in his bones.

Nights like this made him feel all his thirty-three years—and more—and he couldn't help but remember every single hit he took as a running back at Wyoming. He ignored the aches, especially the throb and pull of the stitches in his arm, as he brushed the snow off her car then scraped the thick ice underneath.

He wasn't particularly surprised—just annoyed— when she joined him in the cold. She slid into the driver's seat of her vehicle and turned over the engine. After a chugging kind of start, the motor engaged. A moment later, she emerged with another window scraper and went to work on the other side of the vehicle.

When the windows were clear, she stood back. "Thank you for your help," she murmured. "And for the ride."

He didn't want it to end, he realized, as tense and uncomfortable as things became at the end there.

How pathetic was that?

"Don't you have any gloves?" he asked. "Your hands are going to be freezing by the time you get home."

"They're around somewhere. I keep buying pairs and losing them between here and my house."

He reached into the pocket of his parka. "Here. Take mine. I've got an extra pair in the squad vehicle."

Her mouth lifted slightly. "No offense, Sheriff, but your hands are a little bigger than mine." She waggled delicate fingers that would be dwarfed by his gloves and he felt huge and awkward. "Thank you for the offer but it's only half a mile. I should be fine."

"Good night, then," he said. "Thanks again for your help earlier stitching me up."

"You're welcome. Be careful of those sutures."

She smiled a little and it took all his willpower to keep from reaching between them, tucking her into his warmth and kissing the tired corner of that mouth.

She climbed into the Volvo and he returned to his Tahoe as she slowly pulled out of the parking lot into the deserted streets, her tires crunching on snow.

He pulled out behind her and they seemed to be the only fools out on the road on a cold January night. Everybody else must be snuggled together at home.

Okay, he didn't need that image in his head. Suddenly the only thing he could think about was cuddling under a big quilt with Lauren in front of a crackling fire while the snow pelted the windows, her soft body wrapped around him and jasmine and vanilla seducing his senses.

Reality was light-years away from fantasy—so far it would have been amusing if he didn't find it so damn depressing as he followed her through the snowy streets.

She lived on the outskirts of town, in a trim little clapboard house set away from her neighbors, the last house before the mountains. When they reached it, Lauren pulled into her garage and slid from her Volvo. In the dim garage light, he could clearly see her exasperated look as she waved him on.

He shook his head and gestured to the house. He waited until the lights came on inside and the garage door closed completely before he drove off into the snowy night.

She stood at her living room window watching Daniel's big SUV cruise slowly down the street.

How very like him to follow her home simply to ensure she made it in safely. It wasn't necessary. The distance between the clinic and her house wasn't far. Even if her ancient car sputtered and gave out on the way, she could easily walk home—in good weather, she walked to and from work all the time.

Yet Daniel had been concerned enough to take time out of his busy schedule to follow her home. A slow, steady warmth spread out from her core as she watched his taillights disappear in the snow.

She shouldn't feel so warm and comforted by his simple gesture, as if those big, strong arms were wrapped around her. It was foolish to be so touched, but she couldn't remember the last time someone had fussed over her with such concern.

Just his nature, she reminded herself. Daniel was a caretaker. He always had been. She could remember watching him on the bus with his three younger siblings, how he had always stood between them and anybody who might want to bully them. He wouldn't let anybody push them around, and nobody dared. Not if they had to run the risk of incurring the wrath of big Danny Galvez.

Oh, she had envied them. His sister had been in her grade and Lauren used to be so jealous that Anna had an older brother to watch out for her. Two of them, since Ren was just a year younger than Daniel.

She had longed for a noisy, happy family like the Galvezes. For siblings to fight and bicker and share with.

Siblings. Her mouth tightened and she let the curtain fall, hating the word. She shouldn't feel this anger at her father all over again but she couldn't seem to help herself.

She had siblings as well. Three younger brothers from her father's second family, the one she and her mother had known nothing about until after R.J.'s suicide and all her father's dark secrets came to light.

A few years ago she had met them and their mother—a woman who had been as much in the dark about her husband's other life and Lauren and her mother as they had been about her. They had all seemed perfectly nice. Children who had adored R.J. as much as she had and a widow who had still seemed shell-shocked.

They hadn't wanted any further relationship. Just as well, because Lauren didn't know if she quite had the stomach to continue being polite to the innocent children who had been the cause of R.J.'s relentless need for cash. Maintaining two households couldn't have been cheap and her father's way of augmenting his income was dipping into the public till.

She sighed and pushed thoughts of her half siblings

away, focusing instead on Daniel Galvez and his care-taking of the world.

She shouldn't feel singled out simply because he followed her home to make sure she arrived safely. This wasn't any kind of special treatment, just Daniel's way with everyone.

Imagining it meant anything other than politeness would be a dangerous mistake.

She turned away from the window and the dark night. Returning to her empty house late at night always depressed her, highlighting the lonely corners of her life. She needed a dog, a big friendly mutt to lick her chin and rub against her legs and curl up at her feet on the rare evenings she was home.

With her insane hours, she knew that wouldn't be fair to any living creature, though perhaps she should get a fish or something, just for the company.

She turned on the television for noise and headed for the bathroom. A good, long soak in hot water would chase away the tension of the day and perhaps lift her spirits.

She had no reason to be depressed. She was doing the job she loved, the one she had dreamed of since she was a young girl in junior high biology class. If she had no one to share it all with, that was her own fault.

She was lonely. That was the long and short of it. She longed for someone to talk to at the end of the day, for a warm body to hold on a winter's night.

Too bad her options were so limited here—eligible single males weren't exactly thick on the ground in a small town like Moose Springs—but she was determined to stay here, come hell or high water.

What other choice did she have? She owed the town

a debt she could never fully repay, though she tried her best. She couldn't in good conscience move away somewhere more lucrative and leave behind the mess her father had created.

The best cure for loneliness was hard work and she had never shied away from that. And perhaps she ought to stay away from Daniel, since spending any time at all with him only seemed to accentuate all the things missing in her life.

Her gray mood had blown away with the storm as she drove through the predawn darkness the next day through town. Her clinic hours started at nine but she figured if she left early enough, she could make it to see Rosa at the hospital in Salt Lake City and be back before the first patient walked through the door.

She felt energized for the day ahead as she listened to *Morning Edition* on NPR. The morning was cold and still, the snow of the night before muffling every sound. She waved at a few early-morning snow-shovelers trying to clear their driveways before heading to work.

Most of them waved back as she passed, but a few quite noticeably turned their backs on her. She sighed but decided not to let it ruin her good mood.

This area was settled by pioneer farmers and ranchers and for years they had made up the bedrock of the rural economy. But for the last decade or so Moose Springs had become more of a bedroom community to workers in Park City and Salt Lake City who were looking for a quiet, mostly safe place to raise their families.

She was glad to see newcomers in town and figured an infusion of fresh blood couldn't hurt. Still, she hoped this area was able to hang on to all the small-town things she had always loved about it.

The interstate through the canyon was busy with morning commuters heading into the city, but the snow had been cleared in the night so the drive was pleasant.

As she had promised, she stopped at her favorite bakery not far from the hospital to pick up a dozen doughnuts and several cups of coffee for Kendall and the floor nurses.

Juggling the bag, the cup holder and her laptop, she hurried inside the hospital and went straight for the E.R., hoping she could catch the nurses who had helped with Rosa before their shift changed in a half hour. She had learned early in her career that nurses were the heart and soul of a hospital and she always tried to go out of her way to let them know how much she appreciated their hard work.

She found several nurses gathered at the station. They greeted her with friendly smiles.

"No sexy sheriff with you this morning?" Janie Carpenter, one of the nurses she had worked with before, asked her.

If only. She shook her head. "Sorry. I'm on my own. But I brought goodies, if that helps."

"I don't know." A round, middle-aged nurse grinned. "Between doughnuts or a hottie like that, I'd choose the sheriff every time. I was thinking I just might have to drive to Moose Springs and rob a bank or something. I certainly wouldn't mind that man putting me under arrest."

"Or under anything else," Janie purred. "Think he might use handcuffs?"

Lauren could feel herself blush. She wanted to tell

them Daniel was far more than just chiseled features and strong, athletic shoulders. But maybe he enjoyed being drooled over. She pulled one of the doughnuts out and grabbed the last cup of coffee in the drink holder.

"I owe this to Dr. Fox. Is he around?"

Janie rolled her eyes. "Haven't seen him for a while. He's probably flirting with the nurses on the surgical floor. I'll be happy to set it aside for him, though."

She handed over the stash, not believing her for a second. Oh, well, she tried. It was Kendall's own fault for being such a player.

She waved goodbye to the nurses and headed up to Rosa's floor. Nobody was in sight at the nurse's station on this floor except a dour-looking maintenance man haphazardly swirling a mop around.

Served her right for coming just as the nurses were giving report. She could hear them in the lounge as the night shift caught the fresh blood up on their caseload.

She smiled at the janitor but he still didn't meet her eye so she gave up trying to be nice and began looking for Rosa's chart. Probably in with the nurses, she realized, and went to the lounge to ask if they were done with it.

"Here it is. She had a very quiet night," a tired-looking nurse said, handing over the chart. "No more contractions and I peeked in on her about an hour ago and she was sleeping soundly."

"Thank you."

When Lauren returned to the desk, the janitor was gone. She spent a moment flipping through the chart, pleased with what she saw there. Her vitals were stable and her pain level seemed to be under control. The few times she had awakened, she had seemed calm and at ease.

Lauren didn't want to wake her patient, but she also didn't want to leave after coming all this way without at least checking on her.

As she paused outside the door to her room, a strange whimpering noise sounded from inside and her heart sank. Despite what the night nurse had charted, maybe the mild painkillers Rosa had been treated with weren't quite cutting it.

She pushed open the door to check on the girl, then gasped.

The horrific sight inside registered for only about half a second before Lauren started screaming for security and rushed inside to attack the man who was trying to smother her patient.

Chapter 4

After that first instant of disoriented, stunned panic, everything else seemed a blur. She rushed the man, almost tripping over the mop and bucket on her way toward him as she yelled for him to stop and for security at equal turns

With no coherent plan, she slammed into him to knock him away from her patient. The force of her movement knocked them both off balance and they toppled against the rolling bedside table, sending it crashing to the floor and the two of them after it.

The man scrambled to his feet to get away and Lauren lunged after him, barely registering the coarse fabric of his janitor's uniform as she grabbed hold of it. For some wild reason she was intent only on keeping him there until security arrived, but he was just as intent on escape.

He shoved her to get her away from him, hissing curses at her in Spanish as he fought her off. Finally he just swung his other beefy fist out and slugged her, the blow connecting to the cheekbone and knocking her to the ground.

White-hot pain exploded in her skull. In an instant he was gone. She couldn't have stopped him, even if she hadn't been forced to release him when she fell.

Lauren's vision grayed and her stomach twisted and heaved from the pain. She wanted to curl up right there on the floor, but Rosa was clutching her throat and still gasping for air. Lauren forced herself to keep it together for her patient's sake. Using the bed for support, she pulled herself to her feet and hurried as fast as possible to the terrified girl's side.

"Come on, sweetheart," Lauren urged, grabbing the oxygen mask from the wall above the bed and placing it as gently as possible over Rosa's mouth at the same time she hit the emergency call button.

"Take deep breaths. That's the way. You're fine now. Nobody's going to hurt you."

Though she forgot all about the language barrier and spoke in English, Rosa seemed to understand her. The shaken girl made a ragged, gravelly sound deep in her throat and Lauren handed her the water glass by the side of her bed just as the first nurses rushed in.

"What is it? What happened?" the first one asked. "Are you okay?"

Lauren was shaking, she realized, and her head throbbed like it had been crushed by a wrecking ball. "No. I'm not okay. A man just attacked my patient. Call security. Have them block all the exits and entrances. They need to look for a Latino male in his mid-twenties. He was wearing a maintenance worker's uniform but it was too short for him so I'm guessing it wasn't real."

"You're bleeding!" the nurse exclaimed.

"Forget about me," she said harshly. "Just call security!"

The nurse rushed out and Rosa gave a strangled whimper. Lauren saw she was inches away from hysteria. She slid onto the bed and gathered the girl to her, as much to comfort her as to find a safe place to sit for a moment before her legs gave out.

"You're okay. You're safe now."

"Mi bebé. Mi bebé."

"Okay, okay. We'll check everything out but I'm sure your baby is all right."

As the adrenaline spike crested, Lauren had to fight to hold on to her meager breakfast. It wasn't easy.

She had been physically attacked only once before in her life and finding herself in this situation again brought back all those long-dormant feelings of shock and invasion she thought she had worked through years ago.

She didn't know what was stronger, the urge to vomit or the urge to crawl into a corner and sob.

"Rosa. Is that the same man who hurt you?"

The girl hesitated, though Lauren could tell she understood her fractured Spanish.

"The only way you can be safe is to report what happened so he can be arrested."

The gross hypocrisy of her words struck her, but she couldn't worry that now. Not when her patient's life was at stake.

"Rosa, you're going to have to tell someone what

happened. You have no choice anymore. Will you talk to Sheriff Galvez?"

Rosa let out a sob and curved both hands over her abdomen. After a moment, she gave a long, slow nod.

He was bone-tired, so tired all he wanted to do was pull over somewhere, put his hat over his face and doze off for a few decades.

A smart man would be home in bed right about now dreaming soft, pleasant dreams that had nothing to do with crimes or accident reports or people in need.

He, on the other hand, had decided on a wild hair to drive into the big city after his shift ended to check on their assault victim. He could only hope a night in the hospital had changed her mind about talking to him about what had happened to her.

He worked out the kinks in his neck as he parked his SUV and headed for the front entrance of the hospital. Four security guards and a Salt Lake City police officer stood just inside, a pretty heavy security force. Maybe they had beefed up security for some kind of high-profile patient. His guess was that some kind of A-list movie star from the film festival had broken a leg on the slopes or something.

He recognized the city cop as Eddie Marin, an old friend from police training. "Hey, Eddie. What's going on?"

The officer greeted him with familiar backslapping. "Galvez, long time no see."

"What's with all the uniforms?"

"Incident up on the medical unit. Some dude tried to off a patient. We've sealed off the entrances but the guy seems to be in the wind. We can't find any trace of him." He gave Daniel a considering look. "Not saying we don't appreciate all the help we can get, but isn't this one a little far out of your jurisdiction?"

"I'm off duty, just following up on an assault victim dumped in my neck of the woods. What does your suspect look like? I'll keep an eye out for him on my way up."

"We had an eyewitness who caught him in the attack and was hurt trying to fight him off. She was pretty shaken up but Dr. Maxwell described a Latino male in a janitor uniform, five feet eleven inches, one hundred ninety pounds, half his left eyebrow missing from a scar. Only problem is, we can't find the bastard anywhere in the hospital."

Daniel registered none of the description, too caught up in the words preceding it. "Did you say Dr. Maxwell? Lauren Maxwell?"

"I think that's her name. You know her?"

"She was injured?"

Eddie blinked at his urgent tone. "Perp punched her and knocked her to the floor. She's pretty banged up and needs a couple stitches but she won't leave her patient."

"What room?"

Eddie gave him a careful look. "You okay, man?"

"What the hell room are they in?"

The officer told him and Daniel didn't bother waiting for the elevator, he just raced for the stairs, his heart pounding.

He wouldn't say he was intimately familiar with the sprawling hospital but he had been here many times on other cases. He knew his way enough to find the room Eddie had indicated, and in moments he reached the medical wing.

Even if the officer hadn't given him the room number, he would have known it instantly by the crowd of people milling around. His own uniform seemed to smooth the way as he fought his way through until he made it to the room.

He found Lauren just outside the doorway, gesturing to another Salt Lake police officer he didn't recognize. She was holding a blood-soaked bandage to her cheek and her face was pale and drawn. Rage burned through him at whatever bastard might have hurt her and he wanted to fold her against him and keep her safe from the world.

She cut off her words the moment she saw him.

"Daniel!" she exclaimed, shock and relief mingling in her voice. Before he quite knew how it happened, she seemed to slide into his arms, pressing her uninjured cheek against the fabric of his uniform and holding on tight.

She felt delicate and fragile against him and despite the layers of his coat, he could feel the tiny shudders that shook her frame.

She sagged against him for only a moment, just long enough for him to want to tighten his arms and hold on forever. After entirely too short a time, she pulled away, a rosy flush replacing the pale, washed-out look she had worn when he first saw her.

He wanted to pull her back into his arms but he knew they didn't have that kind of relationship. The only reason she had turned to him in the first place was likely because he represented a familiar face, comfort and security amid her trauma.

Already, he could see her replacing the defenses between them and once more becoming the cool, controlled physician who could handle anything.

"What happened?" he asked.

She let out a breath. "It was terrible. Absolutely awful. I walked into the room to check on Rosa about half an hour ago and found a janitor with his hands around her neck, choking the life out of her. Only he obviously wasn't really a janitor. She says he was the same one who attacked her."

"How is she?"

Her eyes softened and he had the impression that had been exactly the right thing to say, though he wasn't quite sure why.

"Petrified and shocked. She keeps saying *mi bebé* over and over. Physically, I don't think she was injured by the latest attack but she's severely traumatized by it."

"And you?"

"I'm all right. He got in a good punch. I tried to hold him until security got here but he…he was bigger and stronger than I was."

Her shoulders trembled again. To hell with this, he thought, and pulled her back into his arms, whether she wanted to be there or not. He didn't know if the move was for her comfort or his own, he only knew he couldn't let her stand inches away from him and suffer.

This time she stayed a little longer before she slid away from him. "I'm okay. I am. A little shaky but I'll be fine. I'm glad you're here."

He knew she meant on a professional level, but the words warmed him anyway. He was grateful to be there, too, and had to wonder what higher power had inspired him to drive to the hospital this morning, exactly when he would be needed.

If he hadn't stopped for coffee on the way, though, he might have made it in time to stop the bastard. The thought haunted him.

"Do you think after this latest attack, Rosa might be ready to tell us what's going on?"

Lauren sighed heavily. "I think she's realizing she doesn't have any other choice if she wants to stay alive. I asked her and she agreed she would talk to you."

He didn't want to leave Lauren, but a nurse approached them. "Dr. Maxwell, the surgeon is ready for you."

"Surgeon?" he exclaimed.

She made a face, then winced at the motion. "Plastic surgeon. It's stupid but the hospital insisted he be the one to stitch up my cheek."

"Careful of the needles. I hate those things."

She gave him a half smile, which was all she seemed to be able to manage with her battle scars. "How can a man who played football against three-hundred-pound linebackers be afraid of a tiny needle?"

"What can I say? I'm a wimp."

She smiled again, looking noticeably more calm than she had when he arrived.

"Go take care of your face," he urged. "I'll go see if I can persuade Rosa to talk to me."

When he walked into the hospital room this time, Rosa didn't look surprised or frightened to see him, only resigned. Such fatalism in features as young and battered as hers was disconcerting.

He greeted her in Spanish. "How are you feeling?" he asked.

"Like I've been kicked by twenty donkeys," she answered quietly.

He met her gaze intently. "You have to tell me what is going on, Rosa. You know that, don't you?"

One hand was in a cast, but the other fingers tightened on the blanket and she suddenly seemed painfully young. "I am afraid."

"I understand that. Anyone in your position would be. But we can't help you unless we know who is trying to hurt you and your baby."

She closed her eyes, one hand resting on her abdomen. When she opened her eyes again, the raw fear in them twisted his heart.

"Rosa?" he prompted.

She sighed as if the entire weight of the world rested on her narrow shoulders. "His name is Gilberto Mata."

"Is he your baby's father?"

She looked down at the tiny mound beneath the covers. A spasm of emotion that almost looked like shame tightened her mouth. "I don't know. Maybe. It could be him or...others."

Her lip trembled and she wouldn't meet his gaze. He had to wonder if she might feel more comfortable with a female investigator, but he didn't want to interrupt the flow of her story by asking her, not when she seemed willing to tell him what had happened.

"Is that why he hurt you?" Daniel asked. "Because you had been with other men?"

She gave a harsh laugh and this time she did look at him, a deep, horrible bitterness in her eyes. "No. He was there when I was with the other men. He stood by laughing while all three of them, they raped me. And then he took his turn."

Madre de Dios. What the hell kind of trouble was this little girl mixed up with? He fought the urge to squeeze her hand and tell her everything would be all right.

"I am so sorry, Rosa," he finally said, abashed at the inadequacy of the words. "Maybe you had better start at the beginning."

She wiped away a single tear. "The beginning seems another lifetime ago. Six months ago I was working in Tegucigalpa. My mama, she died two years ago. I tried to stay in our village but there was no work and I had no money. I went to the city with my friend Consuela and we found work in a factory sewing clothes."

"How old are you?"

"I will be sixteen years on July sixth," she said, looking a little surprised by the question.

Daniel tried to put the years together. If her mother had died two years ago, she would have been about fourteen when she took a factory job.

"Consuela and I, we did not make much money but it was good, honest work. One day some men came to the factory. They talked to some of the girls and said we could find work in America and they would help us. They filled our stupid heads with stories of the riches we would find here and the good life we would have, like in the movies we see. I did not believe them, but Consuela, she wanted to try. The men flattered her, told her she was beautiful, that she would find good work. I tried to talk her out of it but she would not listen. She begged me to go with her and I finally agreed. I just wanted to protect her, and without her I had no one left in my country."

She bunched the blanket in her uncasted hand. "For

five days Consuela and I and a dozen other girls rode in the back of a closed truck, with no food and only a little water. It was so hot and we thought we would die. At last we arrived in Texas but for some of us, our journey was not done. They told us they had good work for us in Utah. Stupid fools, we believed them."

Another tear trickled down her cheek and he handed her a tissue from a box by the bed. "What happened when you got here?"

"I soon realized what kind of work we were to do. Prostitutes. Whores. They told us if we did not do what they wanted, we would be killed. I would not do it. I was a good girl in Honduras. So the bosses, the men who brought us here…they forced me. Gilberto, he is the worst. We were all afraid of him."

Daniel clamped down his fury, doing his best to hide it so he wouldn't frighten Rosa. He couldn't conceive the kind of animals who would force young, innocent girls into a dark, ugly world of prostitution. That such things were happening only miles from his safe, quiet town seemed an abomination.

"I was lucky. Because I cried so much when…when they made me do those things, I only had to wash the dishes, do the laundry and scrub the floors."

"Do you know where this all happened?"

"Six of us work above a bar in the town of Park City. The Lucky Strike. The others, including my friend Consuela, are in Salt Lake City somewhere. I do not know where."

"What happened to make Gilberto want to hurt you?"

"It was my fault. A few months ago I discovered I was pregnant from…from that first week. I was angry at first and hated what was inside me as much as I hated whatever man had put the baby inside me. But after some time, I knew I couldn't blame the baby, that nothing was her fault. I tried to hide it and find a way to escape. They watch us carefully and lock us in at night but I thought I might be able to sneak out the window. I didn't know where I would go after that but I knew I must get away. They would kill my baby. They had made one of the other girls have an abortion and I knew they would do the same to me."

She shivered. "Last night I tried to escape but Gilberto, he found me. He...he beat me and was going to rape me again. Then he saw I was pregnant and he started calling me names, hitting and kicking me, trying to make me lose the baby, too. I fought him and knocked him down the stairs, then ran as fast as I could. It was a big crowd on the street and somehow I got away from him. I ran and ran until I had no more breath. I thought I would die, I hurt so much. I didn't know what to do, then I saw a truck parked in front of me. I could see a blanket inside, and the back, it was unlocked. I climbed inside and pulled the blanket over my head to hide from Gilberto. The next I remember, the man with the white hair opened the truck and found me there. And that is all."

An understatement if he ever heard one. Human smuggling, rape, forced prostitution, attempted murder. There were more class-A felonies in this girl's story than he sometimes dealt with in six months.

"I thought I was safe now, until I woke up in the hospital and found Gilberto in my hospital room. Again, I expected to die and then the pretty doctor, she came rushing in and fought him off."

She sniffled a little and he handed her another tissue. "I am sorry she was hurt. I did not believe Gilberto would find me here."

"That's a good point. How *did* he find you? Did you call someone and tell them you were in the hospital?"

"No. No one. Who would I call? I told you, my friend Consuela, I do not know how to reach her now. They separated us and she is working in Salt Lake City. The other girls at the bar, we did not talk much. They kept us apart most of the time. I know no one else."

It didn't make sense. He supposed they could have been monitoring police traffic on a scanner when they had called for an ambulance to transport her here. It was the only explanation he could come up with, though it seemed a stretch.

"Why does Gilberto want you dead badly enough to come here and try to finish the job?"

"Because I am a fool." She wiped at her eyes again. "Do you know what it is like to be afraid and filled with anger at the same time? When Gilberto was hurting me and…and trying to hurt the baby, I… I told him to stop, that if he did not, I would go to the police, I would tell them everything that had happened to us here since we left Honduras. I had more freedom than the other girls because I cleaned the rooms. I do not snoop, but I see things and I knew the names of the men who hurt me and who made the other girls do those things."

"Everyone?"

"Except the big boss. I do not know his name and I have not seen him, I only know he is Anglo. But I lied. I told Gilberto I did. I should not have said that but I only wanted him to stop hitting me. I thought if he was afraid of being arrested he would let me go."

She covered her face. "I was stupid. An imbecile. He only hit me harder and I knew he would kill me."

"You can't blame yourself, *niña*. None of this is your fault."

She started to weep then, huge, wrenching sobs, and Daniel leaned forward and squeezed her shoulder. The next moment, she threw herself against him, sniffling against his uniform in much the same place Lauren had done.

He patted her hair awkwardly, wishing he had some words that might make this miserable situation all better. Before he could come up with anything, the door opened and Lauren came in. She paused in the doorway, a soft, arrested look in her eyes he didn't quite understand.

She had a stark white bandage on her cheek, but the color had returned to her features, he was grateful to see.

"I'm sorry to interrupt, but Rosa is overdue for pain medication and I don't want her to get behind. How are you?" The last words were in Spanish, directed at the girl.

"Better," Rosa said shyly. She laid back against the pillow, her gaze on Lauren's bandage. "I am sorry you were hurt by Gilberto Mata. He is a bad, bad man and would have killed me if not for you. You saved my life."

Lauren blinked a little at her gratitude, then smiled. "Daniel, will you tell her I didn't go to all the trouble to fix her up only to lose her again to this Mata character?"

Daniel complied.

"How long will I stay here?" Rosa asked.

"I can't answer that right now," Lauren said, and

Daniel translated for her. "At least tonight, I'm thinking. They're going to move you to a more secure location in the hospital."

"Are you leaving?" Daniel asked.

"My clinic is supposed to be opening—" she checked her watch "—right now. I can reschedule some of my patients but not all of them. Tell Rosa I'll be back later this afternoon after I'm through at the clinic."

Rosa yawned suddenly and Daniel thought she must be exhausted after her ordeal of the morning and by the retelling of her story.

Lauren picked up on it as well. "Get some rest. They should be moving you sometime this morning, but rest until then." She paused. "Sheriff Galvez, may I have a word with you?"

Curious, he nodded and followed her from the room.

"Did she tell you what this is all about?"

He nodded. "She and several other girls have been smuggled out of Central America to be used as prostitutes and unpaid labor."

"Slavery?" She looked appalled.

"It's alive and well in the underground," he said. "And a much bigger problem than many people realize. Rosa tried to escape when she realized she was pregnant as a result of rape in her early days in the country. She was caught and beaten because of what she knows and because she threatened to go to the police. I don't think they'll stop with one attempt on her life, especially now that they know for sure she's here."

"We can't leave her here unprotected with some maniac on the loose. I've talked to the hospital and they're going to put full-time security outside her room but

I'm not sure some rent-a-cop will be enough. What else can be done?"

"I'll make sure there is adequate protection. You do realize, this is bigger than the Moose Springs Sheriff Department can handle. I'm going to have to call in the FBI on this one and I'm sure they'll set up a multijurisdictional task force."

"Good. I hope they find the bastards who did this to her and string them up by their *cojones*."

He blinked at such fierceness coming from the cool, collected Dr. Maxwell. But then he looked at the bandage marring the soft loveliness of her features and couldn't help but agree.

Chapter 5

Lauren was an hour and a half late for her first appointment of the day and spent most of the morning trying her best to catch up without sacrificing the personalized time she liked to spend with each patient—all while her mind seemed stuck on a courageous young girl recovering in a hospital miles away.

One of the things she enjoyed most about being a small-town doctor was the sheer variety of patients she saw, everything from prenatal visits to setting broken arms to pulling slivers out of tiny fingers. Every day was different, full of new challenges to test her abilities.

Just now she was seeing one of her favorite patients, Cameron Vance. Cam had epilepsy and though he regularly saw a neurologist at the children's hospital in Salt Lake City, she was still his primary care provider and saw him for routine visits.

Just now he was suffering from a case of the sniffles that had lasted for ten days.

"Besides the gross runny nose, how's everything else going with my favorite climber dude?" she asked him.

Cameron grinned. "Awesome. Me and Cale are gonna go to Jackson Hole and climb the Grand Teton this summer. We're in training."

At that surprising bit of information, Lauren raised an eyebrow to his mother, Megan, one of her good friends.

Megan shrugged. "What can I do?" she said. "Cale assures me Cameron has the climbing skills to handle it. He'll be ten by then and is certainly experienced enough for it. I can't really say no, especially since he hasn't had a seizure since the big one last summer."

Lauren knew just which *big one* Megan referred to. In August, Cameron had been lost in an abandoned mine in the foothills above Moose Springs and had gone without his seizure medication for more than thirty-six hours. He had been rescued in the middle of a prolonged grand mal seizure by Cale Davis, one of the FBI agents assigned to his case, just seconds before a mine cave-in would have trapped them all.

At Christmastime, Megan had married the man who had rescued her son and Lauren was thrilled to see them all so happy.

"Cale will take care of him," she assured Megan now. "He won't take Cameron anywhere it's not safe. He's a great stepdad."

"He is, isn't he?" Megan glowed when she talked about her husband and, as happy as she was for her friend, Lauren couldn't help the little spurt of envy.

It was small of her, she knew. Megan hadn't had an easy time of things. Cam and his sister, Hailey, had lost their father a few years ago when he was killed fighting in Afghanistan. Megan had raised her children alone, dealing with all the emotional and physical strain of Cameron's epilepsy. She deserved every slice of happiness she could find and Caleb Davis was a great guy who was obviously crazy about her.

Lauren was thrilled for her. But in comparison to Megan's newfound joy, her own personal life fell somewhere between dry and excruciatingly dull.

"What do you recommend for Cam?" Megan asked now and Lauren jerked her mind away from her own private pity party and focused on her patient, as she should have been doing all along.

"I'm guessing with the duration of his symptoms, we're looking at a sinus infection here."

"That's what I thought, too."

"You don't need me, do you?" She smiled at Megan.

"Yes, I do," Megan said firmly. "I don't know what we would do without you and your clinic so close."

She might not have a personal life, but she did have a pretty darn good professional one, Lauren reminded herself. "I'm going to write Mr. Monkey here a prescription for an antibiotic that should be fine with his other medications. As to the cold symptoms, I know you're leery about giving him some of the over-the-counter decongestants because of the chance they may trigger a seizure. The best thing I can recommend is some good old-fashioned chicken noodle soup. If you want, I can email my favorite recipe with plenty of garlic and onions. That should help clear him out."

"Definitely. I'm always looking for soup recipes."

She made a note reminding herself to send it as soon as they finished. "If his symptoms don't improve in a couple of days, call me back and we'll try to figure something else out."

"More garlic, maybe?"

Lauren smiled. "It couldn't hurt."

She turned to Cam. "Let me know when you and Cale head off for the big climb. I'm going to want pictures of you on top of the Grand to hang in my office. And let's hope your nose has stopped running by then, because that would just be gross at high altitude."

They shared a grin as Megan took the scribbled prescription from her and stuck it in her purse.

"Thanks, Lauren," she said on her way out the door.

As they were her last appointment before lunch, Lauren walked them out to the waiting room.

Her office manager held up a hand to stop them. "You're probably getting a bit on the old side for a sticker," Coralee said to Cameron. "But can I interest you in a sour ball?"

"Heck, yeah," he exclaimed. At a chiding look from his mother he rolled his eyes. "Yes, ma'am," he corrected. "Thank you."

Coralee grinned and was pulling out her secret stash of candy when the low chime on the door rang. Lauren looked up and was startled to find Daniel standing in the doorway, looking big and tough and intimidating.

To her dismay, her pulse quickened and everything inside her seemed to sigh in welcome.

He looked exhausted, she thought. His eyes were bleary and he needed a shave, and she had to wonder when he had slept last.

"Sheriff Galvez!" Cameron exclaimed and bounded

over to Daniel. At the sight of the boy, he straightened and seemed to lock away his exhaustion. The two of them greeted each other with a series of high fives and handshakes that looked as complicated as it was well choreographed.

"Hey, Cam. Megan. Two of my favorite people. How's everything at the Vance-Davis compound?"

Megan hugged him. "Good. When are you coming to dinner again? You owe us, since you bailed the last time."

"Sorry." He made a rueful face. "That was the night we had that bad accident out on Barrow Road, wasn't it?"

"That time. Before that, it was the structure fire at James Woolstenhume's barn and the time before that was a traffic stop that turned into a drug bust, I think. The next time we invite you to dinner, do me a favor and try to keep the emergencies to a minimum, won't you?"

He smiled with affection at her teasing. "I'll do my best. Can't make any promises."

"That's the trouble with you law enforcement types." Megan nudged his shoulder. His good one, Lauren was relieved to see. "Next week, okay? Which night works for you, Friday or Saturday?"

"Uh, I'll have to check my schedule and get back to you."

"Lauren, you should come, too. I've been meaning to have you out again. We'll make it a party."

Megan gave her a guileless smile, but Lauren could swear she felt the tug of a matchmaking web.

She flushed and didn't dare look at Daniel. "I'm supposed to be on vacation next week."

"Good, then you'll have plenty of time to get ready." Megan didn't wait for an answer as she herded Cameron toward the door. "I'll call you both in a day or two to work out the details. Thanks again for the prescription. Let's hope it takes care of this kiddo's runny nose."

"I...you're welcome."

After the door closed behind him, the room seemed to steady as if they had all just been caught in the eye of a cyclone. She finally risked a look at Daniel and found him looking as nonplussed as she felt. She was about to ask him about Rosa when he turned away from her and headed for the reception desk.

"What's this I hear about you heading out on a cruise, Coralee? When do you sail?"

Lauren's office manager was always eager to talk about her trip. "Next week. I've already got my bags all packed, waiting by the door."

"You'll have to forgive me," Daniel drawled, "but I'm having a real tough time picturing Bruce on the beaches of Tahiti, soaking up the sun in a Speedo."

"Oh, heaven forbid!" Coralee made a face. "He says he's just coming along for the food and the fishing. Though I'm sure he won't mind seeing the island girls in their hula skirts."

"How's Sherry?" he asked, launching Coralee into her second favorite topic after her upcoming vacation—her grandchildren. Lauren stood back and watched them, marveling that he could make small talk with all the heavy matters that must be weighing on his mind.

This was part of the ebb and flow of a small community, stopping and talking and asking after loved ones.

Daniel seemed comfortable talking to everyone in town, which was one of the things that made him such a good sheriff. He was respected and well liked by all segments of Moose Springs, from kids like Cameron to the low-income families to the town leaders.

He appeared to get along with everybody in town—except her.

She sighed, wishing that thought didn't depress her so much. Watching his easy rapport with Megan and Cameron and Coralee only reinforced how stiff and uncomfortable he always seemed with her.

"Sorry to drop in like this without an appointment," he said, and she realized with a start he was talking to her. "I was wondering if there's any chance you could take a look at my arm? Something doesn't quite feel right about it."

He wanted *her* to look at his arm? This, from the man who had endured her ministrations the night before like she was shoving bamboo shoots under his fingernails?

He had just come from a morning spent at the University of Utah Medical Center. If his arm was bothering him so much, why didn't he just have someone there check it out?

"Of course," she managed through her shock. "I can do it now. We were just about to go to lunch."

"Do you want me to stick around?" Coralee asked.

"No, that's all right. I know you're meeting your sister for lunch at the diner. Go ahead."

Lauren led Daniel to an exam room. "Uh, do you want to unbutton your shirt?" She could feel her face flush at the question and prayed he didn't notice.

He leaned against the exam table and folded his

arms across his chest—including the injured one in question. "No. I just used that as an excuse so I could talk to you without Coralee overhearing our conversation. I didn't realize she would be leaving anyway or I wouldn't have had to come up with a good story."

"Right. Coralee is harder to lie to than my mother."

"You lie to your mother, Dr. Maxwell? I'm shocked."

"I know. I'm a terrible person."

A muscle twitched in his cheek but he didn't give in to a full-fledged smile. "What did you tell Coralee about the bandage?" he asked.

"The truth. Or mostly the truth. I told her I had an accident at the hospital while checking on a patient."

"I think that's wise. I know she can be discreet, but the fewer people who know what's going on, the better."

"It wasn't really that. I just didn't want to worry her. Coralee is a bit of a mother hen, especially with my own mother living six hours away now." She paused. "While you're here, you might as well let me take a look at your shoulder."

He looked less than enthralled at the idea. "That's really not necessary. I'm fine."

"Humor me. I want to make sure you're not starting with any infection. You can tell me what happened this morning at the hospital while I check you out. Your injury, I mean."

She wanted to bite her tongue for adding that last part so quickly, especially when he gave her a long, measuring look. She geared up for an argument about her demand, but either he was too tired to put up much of a fuss or his arm really *was* bothering him.

After a moment, his fingers went to the buttons of

his uniform shirt and he started working them free. Lauren refused to acknowledge the ripple of her insides as he started baring all that smooth skin and hard muscles. He was a patient, for heaven's sake. She had to treat him with all the professionalism and courtesy she showed all her other patients.

She pulled the bandage away to find a little redness and swelling around the wound site.

He flinched when she touched it and she chewed her lip. If she needed a reminder to keep her mind away from him as a very attractive man, there it was. He obviously didn't like her touching him, even in a professional capacity.

She needed to remember that and forget about how her hands itched to smooth over him.

By the time she finally stepped away from him and shoved her hands into the pockets of her plum-colored sweater, Daniel was sweating and light-headed from holding his breath the whole time she had her hands on him.

He tried to hide his deep inhale behind a cough.

"Everything looks fine," she said. "A little red and swollen, but that's not out of the ordinary. If you notice any of that starting to spread at all, make sure you let me know."

Her voice was cool and brisk and he did his best to match it.

"I'll do that," he said. He fumbled with his buttons with fingers that felt big and awkward, as if they were bandaged, too.

He sure as hell hoped his arm healed soon because he couldn't endure her touching him again.

Okay, there was a lie he knew he couldn't sneak past either Lauren's mother or Coralee Jenkins. The bare-bones truth was just the opposite. He *did* want her hands on him, just not in any kind of medical setting.

"Now tell me how Rosa is doing?"

He cleared his throat, shifting gears back to what he knew he should be focusing on. "She was fine when I left an hour ago. Exhausted, since she didn't get much sleep before Cale and Gage McKinnon showed up and she had to go through it all again."

"Cale and his partner are handling the case?" Lauren asked. "That's a relief."

"Her imprisonment, rape and attempted murder definitely fall under their jurisdiction in the Crimes Against Children Unit," he answered. "We don't know if all the possible victims are under the legal age, but since Rosa will be the star witness and she's only fifteen, CAC will be spearheading the investigation."

"Great. With you or Cale both on the case, whoever did this will be behind bars in no time."

"I hope so, but I'm afraid it's not going to be that easy. The real reason I stopped by was to let you know she's been moved to a more secure location in the hospital. Even though you're the physician on record, you're going to need the access information before the guards will let you in. Assuming you're still planning to stop by, anyway."

"Of course."

He nodded, not at all surprised. Lauren was a dedicated doctor, completely committed to her patients. He would have been surprised if she *hadn't* been planning to drive to the city again that night.

"It's still not the ideal situation. I don't believe this

Mata or the people he's working with will just give up trying to shut her mouth, but for now this is the best we can do, moving her to a more secure location and keeping security posted at her room at all times."

"I hope it's enough. What about when she's released?"

"We're still trying to work that out." He fought back a yawn. "The FBI is trying to find a good placement for her. She'll have to stick around to testify to the grand jury while the FBI gathers enough evidence to break up the smuggling and prostitution ring so they can make arrests. How much longer do you think Rosa will need to stay in the hospital?"

"Under normal circumstances, I would probably keep her at least a few more days, probably through the weekend. She hasn't had prenatal care throughout the pregnancy. That complicates things. I would recommend careful monitoring for the rest of her pregnancy, especially given the nature of the assault and the fact that she's already had some early contractions."

"I'll give the FBI a call and let them know they should plan on having a new placement for her by the day after tomorrow, at the latest."

"Will you let me know how things are going?" she asked.

"Of course."

He shrugged into his coat and was putting on his hat to leave when she touched his arm. "Daniel, how long since you slept last?"

As if her words finally pierced whatever force of will was keeping him functioning, he was suddenly so tired he wanted to lean his forehead against her and fall asleep right there.

"Yesterday morning, six a.m.," he admitted.

"You need some rest. I'm sure you don't need me to tell you that. You've been an athlete and you know it's not at all healthy for you to burn yourself out like this."

He hadn't had anyone fuss over him for a long time. He wasn't quite sure how to handle it. "There have been a few unusual circumstances the last twenty-four hours keeping me awake. But I'm heading home now. I have high hopes I'll be able to fall into my big, warm bed and not wake up again until my shift tonight."

She still look worried but she managed a smile. "Do that. We need you strong and healthy."

He wasn't at all sure why color rose on her delicate cheekbones, but he found it fascinating.

"The town, I mean," she said quickly. "If you wear yourself out, you're bound to compromise your immune system and leave yourself open to all kinds of infections."

"Right. We wouldn't want that, would we? Don't worry about me. You've got enough on your plate taking care of the whole town. I'll be fine."

Did she have any kind of drugs he could take that would give him a stronger immune system when it came to her? he wondered as he finally left her clinic and drove toward home. Something that would keep her from invading his thoughts and completely taking over?

He had told her these last twenty-four hours had been full of unusual circumstances. Right at the top of that list was the fact that he had spent more time in her company since he walked into her clinic yesterday evening than he ever had. Even when he hadn't been with her physically, she hadn't been far from his mind.

Was it wishful thinking on his part to think perhaps she wasn't completely immune to him, either? He had sensed several times last night and again this morning that she might be softening toward him. Things between them seemed easier, somehow. Slightly more comfortable.

He liked it. More than liked it.

He drove past her massive childhood home, the biggest house in town, all wrought iron and elegant cornices and perfectly groomed grounds. She had sold the place after her father's death to a young couple from Utah County. Nice people. The husband commuted to Orem every day to work in the state's own version of Silicon Valley and the wife volunteered in the little Moose Springs library.

A few blocks later, he reached his own house, the same four-room clapboard house where his parents had raised their family. He had fixed it up before his mom lost her fight with cancer, added a family room off the back and another bathroom, but it was still a small house on a tiny lot.

Daniel sighed. Here was the hard reminder he needed. Lauren had been raised in luxury and comfort, the pampered only child of two doting parents. He had grown up fighting for one minuscule bathroom with two brothers and a sister.

The biggest obstacle between them wasn't really his humble upbringing or her socially elevated one. He might see that as a glaring difference, but he had a feeling Lauren really wouldn't care about that.

She *would,* however, care about his role in her father's downfall and subsequent suicide.

No amount of wishing on his part could change that.

Chapter 6

She was ready for a vacation.

Friday morning dawned stormy and cold as she drove the busy canyon from Moose Springs to the hospital in Salt Lake City. Her wipers worked steadily but they couldn't keep the big, juicy flakes off the window and she was grateful for the all-wheel-drive of her car.

Lauren had grown up driving in snow but she still wasn't crazy about it. She always found it stressful and demanding. Winter driving wasn't so bad in tiny Moose Springs, where she never encountered more than a few other cars on the road, but the early-morning commute into the city was another story altogether.

By the time she pulled her Volvo into the parking lot at the hospital, her shoulders were tight and her fingers ached from gripping the steering wheel. She climbed out of her vehicle and stepped into four inches of snow that hadn't been scraped off the parking lot yet.

Maybe later in the week when things were settled with Rosa, she ought to give in to her mother's pressure tactics and head to southern Utah for a few days. Soaking up the sun in St. George seemed like a lovely idea right about now.

A week of leisure time would be a decadent luxury. She hadn't had a break longer than a quick weekend in five years and the grim truth was, she wouldn't be taking this one if not for Coralee and her anniversary cruise.

A little respite would be good for her, a chance to recharge and remember why she started in medicine in the first place. And some sunshine right about now might lift her spirits out of this funk.

She walked through the door, stomping snow off her boots. The first person she saw in the lobby was Kendall Fox, talking to a couple of women in scrubs. He looked ruggedly handsome, with that sun-streaked blond hair and skier's tan, and she had to admit her ego enjoyed a nice little boost when his eyes lit up with pleasure at the sight of her.

He excused himself from the other nurses and headed toward her. "Lauren! I was hoping I would bump into you today."

"Oh?" Why couldn't she summon a little attraction for vivid blue eyes and a man who knew just what to do with them? Instead, all she could think about were Daniel's eyes, dark and warm and solemn.

"Yeah. Don't ask me how I did it but I scored an invite for one of the huge after-screening parties up at Deer Valley tonight. I need to find a gorgeous woman to escort, and of course I thought of you. What time can I pick you up?"

She had to admit to a flicker of temptation. When he wasn't hitting on anything that moved, Kendall could be funny and charming and attentive. She was tired of living like a nun. Was it wrong to want a little diversion from the solitude of her life?

A moment's reflection was all she needed to reinforce what a lousy idea that would be. She wasn't at all interested in a player like Kendall, who probably had the cell phone numbers of every available female at the hospital and a few unavailable ones as well.

If she went out with him and had to spend the evening fighting off his inevitable moves, she would be left more depressed than ever.

"Sorry. I've got plans tonight," she lied.

"Break them. Come on. How often do you get to mix with the Hollywood glitterati in your little Podunk Cow Springs?"

"*Moose* Springs. You're right, almost never. And yet somehow I still manage to lead a rewarding, fulfilling life."

"You want fulfillment, I can provide it beyond your wildest dreams," he murmured in her ear.

She barely restrained from rolling her eyes. Okay, forget lousy idea. Going out with Kendall Fox, even for the sake of a little conversation, would be a nightmare of epic proportions. She would spend the whole night fighting off his wandering hands and wishing she were somewhere else. Or at least that *he* was *someone* else.

She started to answer—or at least tell him to back off and give her a little room to breathe here—but the words died in her throat. Some instinct had her looking up and she was horrified to find Daniel standing ten feet away from them, watching her out of those dark eyes of his that suddenly didn't look remotely warm.

"Daniel!" she exclaimed. She had no reason to feel so absurdly guilty but that didn't keep hot water from washing over her cheekbones.

She quickly stepped away from Kendall.

"Lauren. Dr. Fox." She couldn't tell if that reserve in his voice was politeness or disdain.

She forced a cheerful smile. On the one hand, she was grateful to have a ready excuse to escape Kendall's persistence. On the other, she would have preferred anyone other than Daniel be the one to ride to her social rescue.

"I imagine we're here to see the same person," she said brightly. "I'll walk up with you."

An instant of surprise registered in his eyes, but he quickly veiled it. "All right."

Kendall's features tightened with annoyance. He opened his mouth but she cut him off. The last thing she needed right now was for Daniel to be standing nearby when she told Kendall she wasn't interested in ever going out with him.

"Have a good time at your party," she said, hoping her refusal was firm and clear, then led the way through the hospital lobby toward the bank of elevators.

She and Daniel were the only two people taking the elevator. In such close quarters she was acutely aware of his size and how small and fragile she always felt next to him.

He look rested, she thought. Or at least not quite as exhausted as he had two days earlier in her office, when she had seen him last.

"We need to talk," he said abruptly, when the doors

glided closed. He smelled of soap and clean male and he was freshly shaved. It was all she could do not to run her hand along that strong, hard jawline.

She blinked. "Okay."

"Are you planning to write discharge orders today?"

Right. Rosa's case. What else would they have to talk about? "I can't know that yet until I have a chance to look at the chart and see how her pain level was during the night and whether she's had any repeat contractions. If she had a quiet night, I don't really have any reason to keep her longer. Unless you think she's safer in the hospital."

"I don't," he said as the elevator lurched to a stop on Rosa's floor. The doors opened and Lauren was vastly relieved to step out into the hall, where she could breathe without inhaling his delicious scent.

"I got a call from hospital security this morning that there was a suspicious man lurking around here last night just as visiting hours were closing," he went on. "He walked down the hall, saw the security guard outside Rosa's room, then backtracked. They tried to detain him for questioning but he disappeared. I have to believe they'll try again."

Her hands tightened on her laptop case. "Does Rosa know?"

"Not unless security or the FBI told her. Cale is meeting me here this morning to talk about a safe house situation for her."

"It's good of them to keep you in the loop."

"I'm making sure they do on this one. She trusted me enough to tell me what was happening and I won't betray that trust by just turning her over to the FBI without making sure they have a good placement for her."

When they reached the secured unit, they found Cale and his partner Gage McKinnon standing at the nurse's station. Lauren had met Gage the summer before during the search for Cameron Vance. She smiled a greeting and asked after his wife, Allie, and his daughters and infant son, whom she had met at Megan and Cale's wedding.

They exchanged small talk for a moment, then Lauren excused herself. "I need to check in on my patient," she said.

Rosa was sitting up eating breakfast and watching Spanish soap operas when she walked in. The girl smiled at her. Three days after her attack, the bruises and swelling were beginning to fade and Lauren could see the fragile loveliness begin to emerge.

She greeted the girl in her painfully precise Spanish and asked how she was feeling.

"Good. Better," Rosa said with a shy smile.

"I see that. You're looking good," Lauren said. "Did you sleep well?"

Rosa shrugged and said something quickly in Spanish that she didn't quite catch.

"Sorry. Slower, please," Lauren begged.

Rosa repeated her statement and this time Lauren caught the key word. *Nightmare.*

"I'm sorry," she said softly. "Those will fade in time, I promise."

This, she knew from experience. Her own had faded some time ago, though once in a while they still reared their ugly head. Two nights before—the night after she had caught the man in Rosa's hospital room smothering the life out of her and he had struck her—Lauren's own nightmare had returned for the first time in a long time.

In her dream she had been eighteen again, trapped and helpless and frightened.

This time she had fought back, as she hadn't dared do then, and had kicked and clawed and finally stabbed her attacker with a conveniently placed scalpel.

If she had the right words in Spanish, she would have told Rosa that nightmares could sometimes be empowering, could sometimes alert a woman to the amazing truth that she had grown past her fears into a capable, strong woman.

She didn't have that kind of command of the language, though, so she only squeezed her shoulder. "It will get better," she promised again.

She finished her exam of the girl and then returned to the hallway, where Daniel stood talking to the FBI agents.

"What's the verdict?" Cale asked. "Do you think she's in any condition to be released?"

Daniel wasn't the only one who felt protective toward the girl. She folded her arms across her chest. "Before I'm prepared to answer that, I need to know if you have a safe place for her to go."

"You sound just like Dan. I'll give you the same answer I gave him. Not yet, I'm afraid. At least not any option I'm all that crazy about. Our best possibility is a safe house we use down in the Avenues, close enough that we can get her to the hospital in just a few minutes if we need to."

"Sounds perfect," Daniel said.

"Only trouble is, it's not available right now and it won't be for another few days," McKinnon said.

"What's behind Door Number Two?" Lauren asked.

"You won't like it," Cale predicted.

"Try me."

"We thought maybe we could check her into a hotel near the hospital until she testifies to the grand jury next week."

Lauren narrowed her eyes. "No way. You can't possibly be considering dumping a frightened, pregnant girl who doesn't speak English into a cold, impersonal hotel somewhere."

"I know that. That's the dilemma we're facing. We have agents and safe houses in other states where we could send her, but we need Rosa close for her grand jury testimony. Are you sure she's ready to be discharged?"

She wanted to tell him no, that Rosa should stay right where she was, but she couldn't lie in good conscience, not when the bed should be used for someone who really needed it.

"There's no medical reason for her to stay," she admitted. "Her condition is stable and she is recovering nicely from her injuries. But I'm telling you right now that if you plan to abandon this girl in some seedy motel somewhere, I will damn well make something up to keep her here!"

Daniel had to smile as Lauren's impassioned words rang through the hallway, drawing the attention of several nurses at the desk. He knew she was a good doctor, but this was the first time he realized how committed she was to the welfare of her patients.

No, he didn't want to cheer. He wanted to pull her into his arms and kiss her until they were both breathless.

"Do you have any other suggestions?" McKinnon asked.

"Yes," Lauren said firmly. "She can stay with me."

"What?!" Daniel and both of the FBI agents exclaimed the word at the same time.

"I'll take her to my place in Moose Springs until your safe house is ready. After today, I'm off for a week and I can stay with her and watch over her, keep her company, monitor her for more contractions. I can give her one-on-one attention."

"Absolutely not," Daniel snapped.

Lauren lifted her chin, apparently not at all intimidated by three menacing males. "Why not? It's a perfect solution. She'll be absolutely safe at my house. Who would ever think to look for her there? And I can care for her far better than any FBI agent stuck in a safe house with her!"

"It's completely out of the question. Isn't that right?" he demanded of the FBI agents.

He was stunned when he glanced at Cale and found his lips pursed as if he were giving the idea serious consideration. "I don't know. It's certainly an option."

"It is *not* an option." He wanted to shake Lauren and Cale both. And maybe McKinnon for good measure, even though the other FBI agent hadn't said a word. "How can you even consider putting a civilian in that kind of danger?"

"What danger?" Cale asked. "It makes a lot of sense. Rosa needs a safe place where her medical condition can be closely monitored. This seems like a good solution and if we handle this right, the smuggling ring would have no way to connect Rosa with Lauren."

"Other than the minor little fact that Lauren is her *doctor,* for hell's sake!"

He was apparently talking to himself. Lauren ignored his objections—and so did the FBI agents, whom he had always considered reasonable men before this.

"We would need to figure out a way to sneak her out of the hospital in case they're watching the entrances and exits," McKinnon said. "Your address isn't in public record, is it?"

"No," Lauren said. "I use a PO Box for all my personal correspondence and everything else comes to the clinic."

"This could work," Cale said. "We'll have to run it past the brass to get their input but I think this could definitely work as a temporary option for only a few days until our safe house is available and our staffing issues resolve a little. What do you think, Gage?"

"It can't hurt that your house is just a mile away from Dr. Maxwell's, for additional support if it's needed."

"True."

Before he could say anything else, a cell phone rang suddenly. The two agents exchanged looks and McKinnon answered his phone in a low voice. A moment later, he hung up.

"Sorry, we've got to run," he said, heading toward the door. "We just got a break in another case we're working."

"What about Rosa?" Daniel asked. "We need to settle this!"

"We'll make a few phone calls and see if we can put the wheels in motion," Cale said. "We'll get back to you later today."

To his intense frustration, they both hurried toward the elevator before Daniel could raise the whole host of objections crowding through his mind. He and Lauren were left standing alone.

"You don't have to stand there glaring at me like I just ran over your foot or something," Lauren said. "I think it's a good idea."

"I think you're insane. And I think Davis and McKinnon are right there with you in Crazy Town."

"I didn't see *you* coming up with anything else! You know they can't just toss her into a hotel somewhere. She's been raped and abused and nearly strangled. She's frightened and alone and she needs friends more than anything else. Right now, we're the only people she knows and trusts in the entire country!"

"What if they figure out where she is somehow and follow you to Moose Springs?"

"They won't."

"What if they do?" he pressed, his attention on the stark white bandage on her cheek. "You've already been hurt once watching out for her. You have no idea what kind of resources these people might have. They found her here, didn't they? I sure as hell don't need that kind of trouble in my town."

He could see the temperature in her eyes drop well below freezing. "Since when is Moose Springs *your* town? I don't believe I need your permission to invite a guest to my home."

"In this case, you do," he snapped. "Despite their misguided enthusiasm for the idea, Cale and Gage and the others at the FBI will never agree unless I give the final okay. I'm the local law, I get the last word. That's the way it works. I can make all kinds of trouble for them until they decide maybe it's not such a great plan after all."

"You would do that? Put up a fuss, just so you can keep your town clear of the riffraff?"

He didn't think he had ever seen her so angry. Hurt, yes. Devastated, definitely. When he and the chief of police had shown up at her big, ornate childhood home to tell her and her mother about R.J.'s suicide in jail, she had been desolate with grief.

Now, she was just pissed. He couldn't quite understand it.

"Why is this so important to you?" he asked. "You've treated other crime victims, plenty of them. I've brought more than my share to your clinic myself. You always treat them with compassion and professionalism, but not to the point where you want to take them home with you. Why are you so invested in Rosa's situation?"

He thought he saw something flicker in her eyes, something murky and dark, but she quickly veiled it.

"She's my patient," Lauren said briskly. "Beyond that, Rosa is a courageous young girl who has survived a terrible ordeal. I want to help her. Right now, this seems like the best way I can do that. With the clinic closing next week, I have plenty of time to spend with her. It works out all the way around."

Daniel knew Lauren was devoted to her patients, the kind of rare doctor who was available in case of emergencies 24/7.

This was the perfect example of her dedication, that she wanted to go so far, possibly put herself in harm's way for the second time in a week, to help a young girl she had only met a few days earlier.

"You should be taking a vacation, not babysitting a patient. What were you planning to do before this came up?"

Lauren shrugged. "I thought about following the sun and going to southern Utah for a few days to visit my mother," she admitted. "But I can do that anytime, really. Over a long weekend, even. I couldn't go right now and have a good time, knowing that I left Rosa huddled in some cold, impersonal hotel room with strangers who probably don't care what she's been through or how much strength it took for her to come forward and report what happened to her."

She tempered her tone. "You're the one who said you wouldn't turn her over to the FBI unless they had a good placement for her. They don't and so I'm coming up with my own."

In a twisted kind of way, the idea *did* make sense. Moose Springs was completely off the beaten track, a quiet little town no one would ever suspect as the safe haven for a key federal witness in a human smuggling case.

He had to admit, Rosa would probably do better if she spent her first few days out of the hospital with someone who could watch her carefully for any signs she might be overdoing things—and she would definitely do better with people who cared about her than distant FBI agents more concerned about their case than a young girl's bruised psyche.

He sighed heavily, already regretting what he was about to do.

"All right. If you want to go ahead with this crazy idea. I won't stand in your way. On one condition."

"What condition?" she asked, her voice wary.

"I'm part of the deal."

She stared at him, shock widening her eyes. "You what?"

"You can call it chauvinism, you can call it machismo, you can call it whatever the hell you want. But I'm not letting the two of you stay out at your place alone when Rosa has already twice been targeted for murder and you've been injured. You want to take her home with you, fine. But I'm coming, too."

Chapter 7

Several hours later, Lauren stood just inside her storm door, watching in the light cast from her porch light as Daniel helped Rosa out of the backseat of a nondescript sedan she didn't recognize.

It wasn't his, she knew. On his personal time, Daniel drove a big white pickup truck that only served to make him seem more darkly gorgeous behind the wheel.

Maybe it belonged to the sheriff's department. Or perhaps the FBI had provided transportation, since they weren't able to provide much else in the way of support.

What had she done? Daniel Galvez was coming to stay at her house for at least a day or two, possibly longer. He would eat at her table, he would use her shower, he would fill every corner of her little house with that huge presence.

She hadn't really planned out her impulsive offer

for Rosa to stay at her house back at the hospital this morning. The words had escaped her mouth before she had fully considered the ramifications.

If she had taken the time to think it through, she might have anticipated that Daniel would insist on stepping forward to provide protection for Rosa—and for *her.*

If the thought had even crossed her mind, she probably would have rescinded her suggestion and consigned poor Rosa to a hotel.

No, she thought as she watched them make their careful way up the walk she had just finished shoveling. She still would have demanded Rosa stay here. She just would have been better prepared to tell Daniel all the reasons his presence was not required—not required and certainly not at all good for her sense of self-preservation.

She watched him lift Rosa over a rough section of sidewalk, the solid bulk of his shoulders not even flexing at the effort, and her insides ached.

She held the door open for them, giving Rosa a wide, welcoming smile. She did her best to keep that welcome on her features when she faced Daniel, but she guessed some of her reservations must have filtered through when his mouth tightened and his dark eyes grew cool.

"Come in," she said in Spanish. "I'm so pleased you are here." Lauren tried to include both of them in that statement, even though that self-protective part of her nature wanted to shove Daniel back onto the porch and lock the door behind him.

"Gracias," Rosa said quietly. She looked tired, Lauren thought with concern.

"Come. Sit," she urged, and led them both to the open living area off the kitchen. In the rare hours she was home, this was the space she tended to utilize the most.

A fire crackled in the fireplace and the room was several degrees warmer than the rest of the house. She settled Rosa in her own favorite chair by the fire and tucked a blanket around her.

"How was your drive?" she asked Daniel.

"Long. We traded vehicles three times in case anybody followed us and we took the most complicated route possible."

"Did you see anyone?"

"I never saw a tail, except Gage and Cale. They followed us to Park City and then turned around. I don't think anyone saw us leave. We borrowed an ambulance for the first leg of the journey and sneaked her out in that."

Worry creased his features. "Just because we made it here safely doesn't mean we're out of the woods yet, though. This whole situation makes me itchy."

"I know." The gravity of his expression gave her pause. She prayed she wasn't putting Daniel in harm's way. She couldn't back out of this now, no matter how much she dreaded several days of enforced intimacy with him.

She turned her attention to her patient. "Rosa, how are you feeling?" she asked in Spanish.

The girl tried to smile, but Lauren could see the circles under her eyes and the strained exhaustion tugging down the corners of her mouth. She murmured something in a low voice that Lauren didn't quite catch and pointed to her head, but the doctor in her didn't need the words to know what her patient was communicating.

"Your head hurts? I can give you something for it, something safe for the baby. I've made some dinner for you, but I think you should rest first until you feel better."

"Sí." Relief flickered in her dark eyes. *"Gracias."*

Lauren helped her from the chair and showed her to the small guest room she kept ready for her mother's visits.

Since Janine had plenty of reason to hate coming back to Moose Springs and usually avoided the place as if everyone in it had a highly contagious form of leprosy, the room had rarely been used. As a result, it was rather sparsely decorated, just a bed with a pale lavender floral bedspread, a plain dresser and a bedside table.

Rosa gazed around wide-eyed, as if she were walking into the posh suite of a four-star hotel. Tears formed in her eyes and she whispered her thanks in Spanish several times.

Lauren's heart twisted for what this poor girl had endured. Impulsively, she hugged her. "I'm happy you're here," she murmured again in Spanish. "Rest. I will bring you something for your headache. The soup will wait until you're feeling better."

With a relieved sigh, Rosa nodded and sat on the edge of the bed. Knowing it would be a difficult task with the cast on her arm and the pain of her cracked ribs, Lauren knelt and helped her out of her shoes. She wore shiny white tennis shoes with pink stripes and Lauren wondered where they had come from.

All her clothes—even her parka—looked new and

Lauren was embarrassed she hadn't thought about what Rosa would wear from the hospital since the girl's own ragged clothes had been ripped and bloody after the attack.

She wondered if the FBI agents had the foresight to provide them, but some instinct told her exactly who had been thoughtful enough to remember such an important detail.

Daniel.

Her stomach gave a funny little flip when she pictured him in a shoe department somewhere picking out white tennis shoes with pink stripes on the sides.

Pushing away her silly reaction, she settled Rosa into bed, drawing the fluffy comforter around her, then went in search of her medicine.

When she returned from giving it to Rosa, she found Daniel in the entryway stamping snow off his boots and carrying a large dark duffel in one hand and a small blue suitcase in the other.

"This is the rest of Rosa's stuff." He handed over the suitcase.

"Did you buy it for her?" she asked, though she already knew the answer.

He shrugged. "There's not much in there but I tried to think of everything she might need. Toothbrush, a nightgown, socks, that kind of thing. One of the nurses helped me guess the sizes."

She imagined the nurses would help him with anything he might ask when he looked at them out of those sexy dark eyes that seemed to see inside a woman's deepest desires...

"Where do you want me to stow my gear?" he said.

"Oh. Right." Flustered, she drew herself back to the

conversation. "I have a small room I use as an office, right next to Rosa's. It has a couch that folds out. It's not the most comfortable bed in the world but I'm not really set up for a lot of houseguests. I'm afraid I don't have anything else."

Except for my bed.

The thought whispered through her mind with an insidious appeal she found both horrifying and seductive.

She was in serious trouble here if she couldn't go ten seconds without entertaining completely inappropriate thoughts about the man.

"I'm sure I've slept in worse places," he answered. "It will be fine, don't worry."

Easy for *him* to say. He wasn't the one who couldn't seem to focus on anything else but the way his broad shoulders filled her small entry, how his size and strength seemed to dwarf all the perfectly normal-sized furnishings in her house.

"You'll have to point the way."

She blinked. "The way?"

"To the foldout couch."

"Oh, yes. Of course. The office is the second door on the right. The first one is Rosa's room. Mine is across the hall and there's a guest bathroom next to that. I'll show you."

She led the way down the short hallway and opened her office door. He set his bag inside and she showed him the bathroom across the hall.

"It's a little small," she apologized, wondering if he would even fit in the shower.

As soon as the thought entered her mind, she shoved it away quickly. She did *not* need to go there.

"I'm sure it will be fine."

"There's room in the medicine cabinet for anything you need to put there. Razors, your toothbrush, whatever."

For some ridiculous reason, her face heated at that. It seemed terribly intimate to have a man here. How pathetic must her love life be if she could blush at having a man in her bathroom?

"Thanks," he murmured, and she had the oddest feeling he didn't find this whole situation any easier to handle.

"I, uh, fixed some soup earlier if you're hungry," she said after a moment. "It's all ready. Chicken and black bean."

"Sounds great. Thanks."

They returned to the kitchen and Lauren quickly went to the stove to stir the soup, then reached into the cupboard for a bowl.

"There is silverware already on the table. Just sit wherever you would like and I'll dish it for you."

He stood in the doorway. "You don't have to wait on me, Lauren. That wasn't part of the deal."

"You're a guest in my home," she said. "You might be an uninvited one, but you're still a guest."

He laughed a little abruptly at her tartness. "I guess that's plain enough."

"Sit down, Daniel. You can have some soup, even if you are on guard-dog duty."

A muscle twitched in his cheek. "Well, if you want the truth, I haven't had time to eat all day and whatever you're cooking smells delicious."

"I'm not much of a cook," she confessed, "but I do have a few good soup recipes."

He finally complied, though he didn't look happy

about it, and she filled two bowls with the steaming soup, flavored with cilantro, lime and jalapeño peppers.

"Here you go," she said, setting both bowls on the plates she had already set earlier. She gestured to the garnishes already on the table—shredded cheese, tortilla strips, sour cream, more jalapeños and cilantro. "You can put whatever garnishes you want in it. It's kind of a flavor-your-own deal."

"It looks great. I'm sorry you went to so much trouble."

"It wasn't any trouble."

It did look delicious, she had to admit. Just the thing for a snowy Friday night. She put a little grated cheddar in hers and a few baked tortilla strips, but she wasn't at all surprised when he piled on the jalapeños.

He seemed so close here at her small square table, huge and overpowering. She was acutely aware of the broadness of his shoulders and the blunt strength in his arms and the scent of him, leathery and male.

So much for enjoying the soup. She couldn't taste anything, she was far too twitchy just being this close to him.

This certainly wasn't the first meal they had ever shared. Moose Springs was a small town with very little in the way of entertainment except the annual Fourth of July breakfast and the August Moosemania celebration. Everybody turned out for those, and over the years she and Daniel had almost certainly shared a table.

They had many of the same friends in common—Mason and Jane Keller, Cale and Megan Davis. But even those times they had attended the same dinner parties or barbecues, there had always been others around to provide a buffer.

She couldn't remember ever sharing a meal with him alone like this. For some reason, it had all the awkwardness of a blind date—something she made it a practice to avoid at all costs.

"I was wrong," he said after a moment. "Your soup isn't delicious. It's divine."

She mustered a smile. "Thank you."

"This is the perfect thing to warm the blood on a cold winter night," he said, then winced at the inanity of his conversation. Not only was it a banal thing to say, it was patently untrue.

His blood didn't need any more temperature spikes. He only had to sit within a few feet of Lauren to be plenty warm. Before the evening was done, he was very much afraid he would be sweltering.

He was doing his best to focus on the meal in front of him and not on Lauren, with her soft blond hair pulled back in a loose ponytail and her slim feet in fuzzy socks and her skin rosy and flushed in the warm kitchen.

It was an impossible task. Even with the bandage on her cheek, she was so lovely here in her house, sexy and soft, and with every taste of soup she took, he wanted to whip the spoon out of her mouth, throw it against the wall and devour those lips.

His body ached just breathing the same air. How ridiculous was that? He had always known he had a thing for her, but these last few days had just demonstrated it was far more than a little unrequited crush.

He was powerfully attracted to her. He couldn't remember ever reacting this way to a woman, this wild heat in his gut. Every nerve cell in his body seemed to quiver when she was anywhere around and he couldn't seem to focus on a thing but her.

She sipped her water, and when she returned the water goblet to the table, a tiny drop clung to her bottom lip. He couldn't seem to stop staring at it, wondering what she would do if he reached across the table and licked it off.

"What do you usually eat?" she asked.

He blinked away the unbidden fantasy, harshly reminding himself he was here to do a job, to protect Lauren and her houseguest, not to indulge himself by wishing for the impossible.

He forgot what she had asked. "Sorry?" he managed.

"We keep the same kind of hours and I know you don't have much more time than I do. I just wondered if you eat every meal on the run or if you take time to cook a decent meal once in a while."

"I'm not a great cook but I do try to fix a few things on my days off. Whenever I can, I cook extra so I have things to warm up during the week. I think my deputies and Peggy and the other dispatchers think I live on nothing but cold cereal and frozen dinners. They must feel sorry for me, because it seems like somebody is always inviting me over for dinner."

"Like the department stray dog?"

He smiled. "Something like that."

She returned his smile. Daniel stared at the way it lightened her features, made her look not much older than Rosa. His breath seemed to catch in his throat and he did his best to remind himself of all the reasons he couldn't kiss that soft mouth.

"While Rosa and I are here, I really don't expect you

to wait on me. I'll do my share of the cooking. Why don't I take breakfast?"

"Since cold cereal is your specialty?" she teased.

"I can fix more than cold cereal," he protested. "For your information, Miss Doubter, I'm great at toast and can usually manage to boil water for oatmeal, too, without burning the house down."

"I hope so. I'm fairly fond of my house," she said.

The conversation reminded him of something he meant to bring up with her earlier. "If the FBI doesn't make the offer, my department will pick up the tab for the groceries Rosa and I use while we're here. Just keep a tally and send the bill to my office when this is over."

Her spoon froze halfway to her mouth, then she returned it to her soup bowl with a clatter. "Absolutely not!" she exclaimed.

He wasn't quite prepared for her vehemence. "Why not? Rosa is ultimately my responsibility. You're not obligated to pay for her room and board, my office should be taking care of that."

"Forget it, Daniel. I'm the one who insisted she stay here. She is a guest in my house and I will take care of feeding her."

"You didn't want me as part of the package."

"No. I didn't," she snapped, and though he knew it was crazy, he couldn't help feeling a little hurt. How could he burn for her so hotly when she didn't even want him around?

"Fine, we'll compromise," he said. "You can pay for Rosa's food and I'll pay my own."

"This is stupid. I've already bought enough groceries to last a week or more for all three of us. Just take your share out of the huge collective mental ledger everyone seems to be keeping, the one marked 'Maxwell family debt' and clearly labeled 'unpaid.'"

She clamped her teeth together as soon as the bitter words were out and looked as if she regretted saying anything.

Was that what she thought? That everyone believed she owed her heart and soul to Moose Springs, just because her father was a crook?

"There is no collective ledger, huge or otherwise."

"Right." She rose, her usually fluid movements suddenly jerky and abrupt as she started clearing away the dishes. He had been considering asking for a second helping, but he forgot all about it now, struck that she could entertain such a misguided notion.

"Everyone knows you're not responsible for what your father did, Lauren."

"Do they?"

He frowned at her pointed question. Okay, he had to admit there might be some validity in her bitterness. The other day with Dale Richins, he had experienced just a taste of what she might encounter in certain circles. The scorn, the disdain.

It suddenly bugged the hell out of him that anybody could blame an innocent girl for her father's crimes.

"In their hearts, everyone knows that. But some people in town are just more stubborn and pigheaded on this issue than they ought to be. How can it be your fault? You were only a girl when he first, uh…"

His voice trailed off and he wasn't quite sure how to couch his words in polite terms.

"Go ahead and finish it, Daniel. When R.J. first starting dipping his fingers into the city's meager financial well."

"Right. You were just a child. Anybody who can blame you for what R.J. did is being mean and stupid."

"Intellectually, I know that. It doesn't make the digs and slurs in the grocery store any easier to deal with it. My father paid for my medical school tuition out of stolen money—which means, in effect, that the people of this town paid for my education. Do you think I'm not aware of that every time I look at my diploma?"

He had no idea she tied the two things together, her father's embezzlement and her own medical school bills. Guilt spasmed through him at his own role in this whole thing. If she knew the truth, she probably would have added rat poison to the soup.

"Lauren—"

"This town owns me, body and soul. My father made sure of that. I can never leave here, no matter all the slights and slurs and whispers I have to endure. They paid for my education and I am obligated to damn well give them their money's worth."

She shoved a dish in the dishwasher with a clatter. "But you know, it doesn't matter what I do, how much I give. I can pour out my soul here in my practice, work twenty hours a day, treat anybody who walks through the door whether they have any intention of paying me or not. But I'll still always be crooked R. J. Maxwell's daughter."

"You can't change where you came from, Lauren, no matter how hard you try."

He should know. He had spent way too much time during his teenage years wishing he could belong to any other family in town except the dirt-poor Galvez family, with a mother who scrubbed toilets and a father who did every miserable grunt job that came along at

R. J. Maxwell's construction company, for usually half as much as anybody else on the crew, just because he didn't have a green card.

Now, it shamed him deeply that he had ever considered his family inferior to anyone else.

He used to ride his bike past Lauren's grand house on Center Street and want everything inside there—furniture that matched and didn't come from Goodwill, a soft, pretty mother who smelled like flowers instead of disinfectant, his own bedroom instead of the crowded, chronically messy one he had to share with two annoying younger brothers.

He used to think Lauren's life was perfect. She had everything—money, brains, beauty. He wanted the kingdom, and in his deepest heart, he had wanted the beautiful golden princess who came along with it.

Over the years, he had learned that the kingdom was built on sand, the king was a fraud and a cheat, and the castle had been sold long ago to pay his bills.

But the princess.

Oh, yeah, he still wanted the princess.

"I know I can't change what my father did," she said quietly. "I live with it every day."

"You've done more to make things right than anyone could ever expect of you, Lauren. Anyone who doesn't see that, who doesn't admire and respect the hell out of you for what you've done here, is someone who doesn't deserve even a moment of your time."

At his words, something about her seemed to crumble. One moment she was looking at him with defiance and bitterness and the next, her soft mouth trembled and she stared at him out of luminous blue eyes welling with tears.

"Ah, hell. I'm sorry. Don't cry, Lauren. Please don't cry."

He rose and pulled her into his arms. He couldn't help himself.

She sagged against his chest and her arms slid around him. To his vast and eternal relief, she sniffled a few times but she didn't let the tears loose. He held her close, burying his face in hair that smelled of jasmine and vanilla. After a moment, she stirred and lifted her face to his.

"I'm sorry. I try not to indulge in pity parties more than once or twice a month. You just caught me on a bad day."

"Don't mention it," he murmured, and then he couldn't help himself. He took what he had been fantasizing about since he walked into her house earlier.

Chapter 8

Her mouth was soft, delicious, like sinking into the best dream he had ever had. After one raw instant, his body revved into overdrive and he could focus on nothing but how incredibly right she felt in his arms.

He wanted to devour her, right there in her kitchen, just wrap his arms around her, drag her to the floor and consume every inch of her. Even as the wild need raged through him, ravaging his control, he forced himself to take things slow and easy, to hide his wild hunger behind a facade of soft, steady calm.

He hadn't been with a woman in a long time, but he knew that wasn't the reason why his vision dimmed and he suddenly couldn't seem to keep hold of a coherent thought.

That reason was simple, really. Lauren.

He couldn't quite believe she was here in his arms,

the girl who had been affecting him in a strange, baffling way since he was a kid.

Even when he had been sixteen and big for his age, the toughest kid in school, he had dreamed of sweet Lauren Maxwell. The mayor's little girl, with her shiny blond ponytail and her soft, pretty hands and her wide, generous smile.

It had mortified him, this fascination with her, and even then he had known anything between them was an impossibility.

The taste of her seemed to soak through his bones and he couldn't seem to get enough. This was stupid, he knew. Monumentally stupid. Playing chicken with an express train kind of stupid.

He had to reign in his hunger. If he didn't, if he gave in to it, how could he ever return to the stiff politeness that had marked their relationship since her father's death?

He drew in a ragged breath and did his best to clamp down on the wild need raging through him.

He might have even succeeded if he hadn't heard the soft, seductive sound of his name on her lips, against his mouth, and felt her hands tremble over the muscles of his chest.

They had come this far. One more kiss wouldn't hurt anything. That's what he told himself, anyway.

And a tiny portion of his mind even believed it.

She was sliding into an endless canyon of sensation, surrounded by the heat and strength and leashed power of Daniel Galvez.

Somehow, she wouldn't have expected his kiss to be so slow, so easy and gentle. Though she couldn't say she spent a great deal of time fantasizing about men and their kissing styles, if she had to guess Daniel's, she would have expected him to kiss a woman like the athlete he had been, fast and fierce and passionate.

Instead, he seduced her with softness, teasing and tasting and exploring. He nibbled her lips, he traced light designs on the bare skin of her neck with his fingertips, he rubbed his cheek against hers—and she found that light rasp of evening stubble against her skin far more evocative and sensual than a full-body massage.

He kissed her until every nerve ending inside her seemed to quiver, until she wanted to melt into him, to wrap her arms around his strong neck, press her body against his muscles and lose herself in him.

When she was young, she used to love it when Moose Springs held its annual celebration and the town paid for a small carnival for the children with giant inflatable slides and a Tilt-o-Whirl and enough cotton candy to power the midway lights on juiced-up kid power alone.

Her favorite was the pony ride. Once, when she was probably seven or eight, her father had slipped the carnival workers a few extra dollars to let her just keep riding that little horse around and around. She probably rode for half an hour and she had never forgotten the magic of that night, with the lights flashing and the screams of children braving the more terrifying rides and the smell of popcorn and spun sugar and spilled sodas.

This was far more exhilarating than any long-ago pony ride. She didn't want the kiss to end, she just wanted to lock the cold, snowy world outside her kitchen and stay right here in his arms forever with this wild heat churning through her insides and this fragile tenderness settling in her heart like a tiny bird finding a nest.

The only sounds in the kitchen were the soft soughs of their breathing and the low crackle of the fire in the other room. Finally, when she was very much afraid her legs weren't going to support her much longer, Daniel made a sound deep in his throat, something raw and aroused, and deepened the kiss.

She sighed an enthusiastic welcome and returned the kiss. He pulled her closer and she molded her body to his. This time she relished how small and delicate he made her feel next to his size and strength.

They kissed until she couldn't breathe, couldn't think, until she was lost to everything but Daniel, his taste and his scent and his touch.

Suddenly, over the sound of their harsh breathing, she heard something else. The rather prosaic sound of a toilet flushing somewhere in the house. Rosa.

Lauren froze as if she had stepped naked into that storm outside the windows. Jarred back into her senses, she scrambled away from him, her heart beating wildly.

What, in heaven's name, just happened here? Had she really just been wrapped around *Daniel Galvez?*

Her face flamed and it was all she could do not to press her hands to her cheeks. What must he think of her? She had responded to him like some wild, sex-starved coed. She had all but dragged him to the floor and had her way with him.

She was fairly certain she had even moaned his name a time or two. How could she ever look him in the eye again?

"Rosa must be awake," she said, keeping her gaze firmly in the vicinity of his chest, until she realized that probably wasn't the greatest idea since it only made her want to smooth her hands over those hard muscles once more.

"Sounds like," he said. Did his voice sound more hoarse than usual? she wondered.

She finally risked a look at him and could have sworn he had a dazed kind of look in his eyes—the same baffled, disoriented expression she saw in patients with mild concussions.

Had Daniel been as affected as she had by that shattering kiss? How was it possible? He disliked her. Okay, *dislike* might be a bit harsh. But he certainly never seemed interested in her on that kind of level.

Except once, she reminded herself—so long ago, it seemed another lifetime. More than a decade ago, he had asked her out and she turned him down. Quite firmly, if she recalled.

He had been the first guy to show any interest in her since the grim events of that spring and she had been far too raw and messed-up to even consider it. The very idea had terrified her. The details were a little hazy but she was fairly certain she hadn't been very subtle with her refusal, either.

In all those years, Daniel had never given her any indication he might be interested in her. Things between them were always strained, always slightly uncomfortable, though both of them did their best to be polite.

That kiss, though.

That was certainly not the way an uninterested man kissed a woman.

Her stomach muscles fluttered and she didn't know

what to think. She suddenly was desperate for a little space to figure out what had just happened between them.

Distance from the man was not something she would likely find in the next few days, she realized with considerable dismay. Her house was small but had always seemed more cozy than confining to her. With Daniel here—six feet three inches of him and all that muscle—she suddenly felt like the walls were squeezing in, sucking away every particle of oxygen.

"Uh, Lauren—" Daniel began, but whatever he started to say was cut off as Rosa came into the kitchen, looking much more rested than she had when they arrived.

She greeted them with a shy smile, apparently oblivious to the tense undercurrents zinging through the kitchen like hummingbirds on crack cocaine.

"How are you?" Lauren asked in Spanish.

"Better," Rosa answered.

"Sit. I'll get you something to eat. Would you eat some soup?"

She dipped her cheek to her shoulder, looking hesitant to put anyone to more trouble.

Daniel said something in rapid Spanish, too fast for Lauren to understand, and pulled a chair out for her at the table. Rosa's shyness lifted and she giggled a little and nodded, then obediently sat down.

"What did you say?" Lauren asked.

"I told her she had to have some of your delicious soup or I would end up eating it all and end up too fat to wear my uniform."

He gave an embarrassed smile and Lauren stared at it, an odd emotion tugging at her chest.

She was in trouble here, she thought as she hurried to the stove to dish Rosa a bowl of soup. Panic spurted through her and it was all she could do not to drop the soup all over the floor.

Oh, she was in serious trouble.

She could probably handle the physical attraction. But she suddenly realized she had no defenses against a man who had the wisdom to cajole and tease and look after a frightened young girl like she was his own little sister.

The evening that followed had to live on in her memory as one of the most surreal of Lauren's life. While Rosa picked at her bowl of soup, the storm that had been toying with this part of the state all day let loose with a vengeance. The wind lashed snow against the window and moaned under the eaves of her little house.

Daniel threw on his coat and made several trips to the woodpile out back so they had a good supply of split logs close to the house. Lauren gathered lanterns and flashlights just in case the power went out, as it often did during big storms like this that brought heavy, wet snow to knock out power lines.

While she cleaned the kitchen and loaded the dishwasher, Daniel checked in with his department.

She listened to his strong, confident voice as he reviewed emergency storm protocol with his lieutenant and she thought again how lucky the people of Moose Springs were to have him as their sheriff. He was wonderful at his job and truly cared about the people he served.

She knew her reasons for setting up her practice in

her hometown but why did *he* stay here? He could be working anywhere. He had spent his first few years in law enforcement as a Salt Lake City police officer and many had expected him to stay there and make a promising career for himself. Then his mother had fallen ill, his father was killed and he had returned home.

His mother had lost her battle with cancer shortly after Lauren returned to town. So why did Daniel stay all these years?

She enjoyed listening to him. It was silly, she knew, but she loved hearing him in action. Oh, she had it bad.

He ended the phone conversation just as she finished wiping down the countertops.

"If you need to go on a call or something during the night, I'm sure we'll be fine here," Lauren offered.

"I've got good people working for me and I'm sure they have everything under control. But if something comes up that nobody else can handle, one of my deputies can come here and relieve me for a while."

"Does everyone know you're staying at my house?"

His mouth tightened and his expression cooled. It took her a moment to figure out how her question must have sounded, as if she worried about her reputation.

He answered before she could correct the assumption. "No. Only Kurt Banning, my second-in-command, knows the entire story. As far as everybody else is concerned, I'm taking some personal leave. That should set your mind at ease."

"My mind is not at all unsettled."

Not about her reputation, at any rate. She was afraid she had none in Moose Springs.

She could have an entire orgy of sexy law enforcement officers camping at her house and people would just shake their heads and ask what else could they expect of R.J.'s daughter?

"Is there a free plug for my cell phone somewhere?" Daniel asked. "I want to make sure I've got a full charge while I can in case the power goes out on us."

"Yes. Of course. Good idea." She showed him an open plug, then spent a few moments digging out her own cell phone to charge in case she was needed on a medical emergency.

What if they were both called out on a crisis at the same time? she wondered, then decided to set her mind at ease, at least on that score. It was certainly possible, but she had no doubts Daniel would have thought of every eventuality.

The wind lashed the windows as Lauren went to join Rosa in the living area. The girl was curled up on the couch with a blanket over her, watching a comedy on the Spanish language channel. Lauren could only pick out half the words and she was just reaching for her latest lousy attempt at knitting when Daniel joined them and settled in the recliner.

He watched TV with Rosa for ten minutes until the show ended, though she had the feeling he was only pretending to pay attention.

Was he as off balance as she was by that kiss? she wondered. Even a half hour later, she could still taste him on her mouth.

She was wondering if she had any DVDs with Spanish subtitles, for the sake of distraction if nothing else, when Daniel suddenly jumped up from the recliner.

"Let's play a game or something."

"Okay," she said slowly. "What did you have in mind?"

"I don't know. What have you got? You have a deck of cards?"

"I'm sure I do somewhere."

"What about a card table?"

"In the garage against the north wall."

While he went in search of it, she finally unearthed a deck in her kitchen junk drawer that was probably left over from medical school study breaks. While she was searching, Daniel had found the card table and had set it up near the fireplace.

"What did you have in mind?" she asked after the three of them settled into the chairs he brought in from the dining room and he shuffled the deck.

"I don't know. I was trying to come up with some game that would transcend the language thing. What about Crazy Eights?"

She didn't believe she had played that game since she was about ten years old in summer camp. But she was willing to try anything that might keep her mind off that stunning kiss.

For the next hour, they played Crazy Eights and War and SlapJack, and a new one to her called Burro Castigado, similar to draw poker. Daniel must have been inspired with the cards, Lauren thought. As they played, Rosa giggled and smiled and seemed much more like a girl than a young woman who had survived a horrendous ordeal.

After a while, she moved to the kitchen to make some popcorn and she could overhear Daniel and Rosa speaking in Spanish. Daniel's low laugh drew her gaze.

She watched them together for a moment, a funny pang in her chest. He was so kind to the girl, just as he used to be to his own younger sister. She used to be filled with envy that Anna had three big, strong brothers to watch out for her. It had hardly seemed fair to Lauren, when she had none.

He turned suddenly and caught her watching him. Something flared in his dark eyes, something hot and intense. In her mind, she was in his arms again, savoring that strength around her and the flutter of nerves as her body seemed to awaken from a long, cold sleep.

Their gazes caught for a long moment, until the microwave dinged and yanked Lauren back to reality. She pulled the popcorn bag out and took her time shaking it into a bowl while she tried to force her pulse to slow again. She was never going to make it through the next few days if she didn't get a grip over herself here.

At last she felt in control enough to return to the card table, and pasted on a bright smile.

They played for another half hour, until she caught Rosa trying to cover a yawn. It was nearly eleven, Lauren realized with some surprise.

"You need to sleep," she said to the girl. "Come on, let's get you settled for the night."

Daniel had picked out a warm, roomy nightgown for her and Lauren showed her the toothpaste, washcloths and towels. Rosa bid her good-night with a smile that was growing more relaxed and comfortable.

When she returned to the other room, she found Daniel shrugging into his heavy coat once more.

She frowned. "I'm quite certain you brought in enough wood earlier to last for at least a week. There is no reason for you to go out into the storm again."

"I figured I'd shovel your walk before I turn in."

She was about to argue the sidewalk could wait until morning but some restless light in his eyes tangled the words in her throat. He looked like a man with energy to burn.

She could think of other ways to exhaust that energy, but she wasn't about to suggest them to him.

"Thank you," she said instead.

She picked up her pitiful knitting again while he was outside and tried to focus on the news, but it was a losing battle. All she could think about was the man out there braving the elements to shovel her sidewalk.

When he returned twenty minutes later, snowflakes were melting in the silky darkness of his hair and his cheeks were flush with cold, but he seemed far easier in his skin.

"It's a b-witch out there," he said, stomping snow off his boots and shaking it from his coat. "That wind chill coming from the north has got to be at least minus ten. I bet we get a foot or more."

She nodded. "Nights like this make me grateful to be home in front of the fire instead of driving through the snow on my way to an emergency somewhere."

"Makes me glad for insulated windows," he said, shrugging out of his coat. "When I was a kid, we used to stick blankets over all the windows in our house. They were all single-paned. I imagine they probably let in more cold than they kept out."

He laughed suddenly at a memory. "Ren used to put cups of water in front of them so we could measure how long it took for ice to form. He was always doing crazy things like that. First thing I did after I moved back was to replace them all with energy-efficient windows and blow better insulation into the walls. Made a hell of a mess and cost a fortune, but the house stayed about thirty degrees warmer in the winter."

Lauren couldn't help thinking of her own home, where her mother insisted on keeping the thermostat at seventy-three degrees and invariably had a fire going as well. R.J. used to complain about the heat bill, but never enough to make her mother turn down the thermostat.

Of course, her mother didn't know R.J. was heating another house somewhere.

"Would you like something warm?" she asked. "I've got several kinds of cocoa."

His raised eyebrow lifted even higher when she opened a cupboard to show the wide, varied selection inside. Orange chocolate, chocolate raspberry, chocolate mint, chocolate cinnamon, chocolate amaretto and plain old delicious milk chocolate. She had about every flavor of hot chocolate ever invented.

"I'm something of a cocoa junkie in the winter," she admitted ruefully. "Even in the summer sometimes, if I've had a bad day. Nothing comforts quite like it."

He watched her, a strange, unreadable light in his eyes. She didn't know what it meant, she only knew it made those blasted stomach flutters start all over again. After a moment, he shook his head. "Maybe tomorrow night I'll take you up on that."

She let out a breath. However would she endure so much time trapped here in his company, especially when she couldn't stop thinking about that kiss?

"I can help you pull out the couch in the office if you'd like."

"I was just thinking I would stretch out over there, if that's okay with you."

She gazed at the short couch near the fire, then at

his long, muscled body. The two things seemed a definite mismatch.

"Are you sure?" she asked. "It's no problem at all to make the couch into a bed."

"This is fine. That way I can be close to keep the fire going, just in case the storm knocks out the power in the night."

"I'll bring you some blankets and a pillow, then."

She pulled them out of her small linen closet, certain as she returned to the living room that she shouldn't find the idea of him watching over her and Rosa such a comfort.

She was a strong, independent woman. She certainly didn't need a man to take care of her, to bring in her wood and shovel her walks and tend the fire through the night.

She didn't need it, perhaps. But she couldn't deny that she found it very appealing to share the everyday burdens of life with someone else once in a while.

When she returned with the linens, she found him sitting on the recliner, gazing into the fire. He looked up at her entrance, and again she was surprised at the odd, glittery expression in his eyes.

"Here you go. Good night, then. If you need anything else in the night, let me know," she said.

"I'll do that," he murmured, and she could feel the heat of his gaze on her all the way through the kitchen and down the hall to her bedroom.

Chapter 9

Something woke him in the early-morning hours.

He instantly sat up, alert and on edge. The house was quiet, the only sound the low murmur of the fire flickering low, reduced now to just a log burned almost all the way through and a few red embers glowing in the dark.

His instincts humming, he looked around, trying to figure out what had awakened him.

The house was *too* dark. *Too* quiet.

It only took a moment for him to figure out why. As he and Lauren had both feared, the power must have gone out in the storm. The fire provided the only light in the house and the usual subtle sounds of a juiced-up house were nowhere in evidence. No buzz of a refrigerator, no whirr of a furnace kicking on. Nothing.

The only thing he could hear now besides the fire

was the wind hurling snow at the windows. He slid off the couch and threw another log from the pile onto the glowing embers. It crackled for a moment, but he had no doubt the coals were hot enough that it would soon catch.

Moving with slow caution, he eased to the window and peered out into the storm. He looked up and down her isolated road, but could see no other lights out there, not even the ambient glow from the concentrated lights of town he might have expected.

Though he knew from experience that any power outage was a major pain in the neck for law enforcement officials, the pitch-black set his mind at ease.

If the whole town had lost power, obviously Lauren's house hadn't been targeted specifically by someone cutting her juice for nefarious reasons.

He didn't know what kind of threat might lurk out there for Rosa, but he wasn't about to take any chances. Someone wanted her dead because of all that she knew. Melodramatic as it seemed, it wasn't wholly out of the realm of possibility that someone might cut Lauren's power to have better access to her house.

They had tried to kill Rosa in her own hospital bed. He had a feeling these bastards would certainly have no qualms about killing anybody else who got in their way.

He hated this whole damn situation. A pretty young girl like Rosa should be dreaming about her *quinceañera*, should be trying out makeup and giggling with her friends and discovering the vast world of possibilities awaiting her. Instead, she was battered and bruised and five months pregnant from a brutal gang rape, doing her best to stay alive.

And Lauren had put herself right in the middle of Rosa's troubles by bringing the girl home to recover.

He sighed, his mind on the woman asleep in her room just a few yards away. What a mess this assignment was turning into. In the first eight hours after bringing Rosa here, he had hurt Lauren's feelings, dredged up memories she didn't want and kissed her until he managed to forget his own name.

He could only wonder, with a strange mix of dread and anticipation, what the morning would bring.

In the soft glow of the fire, he could read the face on his watch. It was 2:30 a.m., which meant he had probably slept a grand total of maybe an hour and a half all night. And though he had slept, he couldn't say those had been the most restful ninety minutes he'd ever enjoyed.

He should have expected it. Lauren's house wasn't exactly conducive to a good night's rest. How could it be, with her subtle scent of jasmine and vanilla surrounding him and the knowledge that she was only a few footsteps away burning in his gut?

He couldn't stop thinking about that kiss, those incredible moments in the kitchen when she had been in his arms, all soft and warm and delicious. After all these years of wondering what it might be like to kiss her, to touch that skin and taste her soft mouth, he had to admit the reality had far surpassed any fantasy.

And reliving the moment over and over again sure as hell wasn't going to help him get any sleep.

He reached for his cell phone and dialed his dispatcher. Tonight, Jay Welch was on duty and as Daniel greeted him, he pitched his voice low so he didn't wake up Lauren or Rosa.

"Hey, Sheriff," Jay said. "I thought you were taking a few nights off, squeezing in a little R&R."

Rest and recreation. Right. There was absolutely nothing remotely restful about staying in Lauren's house, having to fight like hell to keep his hands off her.

And the only recreation he could seem to wrap his brain around was exactly the activity he knew he wouldn't be engaging in anytime soon.

"I'm still around," he murmured. "Just checking on the situation there with the power out."

"So far, so good. The backup generator kicked in right away. We're starting to get a few anxious calls from people wondering what's going on. The power company says a tree came down north of town and knocked out the power line. They expect to be back in business no later than an hour."

Without electricity, most furnaces couldn't turn on, even if they were natural gas- or oil-fueled. A house could get mighty cold during a January blizzard without heat for an hour. He thought of those single-paned windows in his childhood home and couldn't help a shiver, despite the little fire now burning cheerfully in the grate.

Most people around here had secondary heat sources like fireplaces or wood or pellet stoves, but he didn't want to take any chances with the health and safety of the people of his town. "I'll check in with you in an hour for an update. If it's not back up and running by the time the sun comes up, we're going to want to start welfare checks on some of the senior citizens who live alone."

"Okay."

He hung up and sat on the couch gazing at the dancing flames and wondering what he was supposed to do with all this restlessness burning through him.

Suddenly, he heard a noise somewhere in the house. He reached for his 9mm, thumbed off the safety and rose, alert and ready. An instant later Lauren's bedroom door opened.

She stood just outside the rim of light from the fireplace, but he didn't need illumination to know the sound he heard was her.

He slid the safety on and tucked the gun back under his pillow on the couch. "I hope I didn't wake you while I was on the phone," he said.

"You didn't. I think I woke when the power went out. That sounds silly, doesn't it?"

"Not *that* silly. I did the same thing."

They lapsed into silence and he wondered why she was out here instead of tucked into her warm bed.

"Everything okay?" he asked.

She stepped farther into the fire's glow and he could see the rueful expression on her face. "I just realized that even after I went to all that trouble to round up secondary light sources for a possible outage, I forgot to take a flashlight into my room when I went to bed. I was lying in bed wondering how I could sneak out here in the dark and grab one without waking you, then I heard you on the phone."

"I was just checking in with dispatch," he said. "Jay Welch has already talked to the power company and we're looking at about an hour before it's back online."

"It's good you had the foresight to keep the fire going," she said, grabbing a flashlight from the table where she had assembled them earlier in the night.

"What about Rosa? I wondered if I should let her sleep or wake her to let her know the power is out. I wouldn't want her to wake up in the middle of the night in the pitch-dark and be frightened."

"I can listen for her. If I hear sounds of stirring, I'll explain to her what's going on. Those bedrooms are going to get mighty cold without the furnace if the power company's estimate is wrong and it takes them longer than they figure to fix the problem. I'll have to wake you both up so you can come out here and bunk by the fire where it's warm."

"You don't have to stay up all night to watch over us, Daniel."

"I don't mind."

She tilted her head and studied him and he wondered again what she saw when she looked at him. "I know you don't. You watch over everyone, don't you?"

Was that how she saw him? He shrugged, uncomfortable. "It's my job to keep the people of Moose Springs safe. Go back to bed, try to get some sleep. I'll wake you if the power doesn't come back up in an hour or so."

"I couldn't sleep now anyway."

He should keep his distance from her. One of them should have a little good sense here. If he were smart, he would insist that she march right back into her bedroom and stay away from him.

Too bad he didn't feel very smart around the delectable Dr. Maxwell.

He sighed. "You might as well come in and sit down out here by the fire, then. We can keep each other company until the lights come back on."

She hesitated, just long enough for him to wonder if

the tug and pull between them unnerved her as much
as it did him. He couldn't have said which he would
prefer: that she go back to bed and leave him alone or
that she come in and sit beside him so he could indulge
his unwilling fascination a little longer.

She chose the second, pausing only long enough
to turn on the light switch so they would know when
the power was back on, then she sat in the armchair.

In the fire's glow, he could see she wore soft, lace-
edged cotton pajamas the color of spring leaves. He
did his best not to think about how they would feel
under his fingers.

When she pulled her knees up and wrapped her
arms around them as if she were cold, he lifted one of
the extra blankets she had brought him from the end
of the couch and tossed it to her.

"Thanks," she murmured. She snuggled into it,
tucking the edges around her feet. They sat for a moment, accompanied only by the low rumble of the fire,
their own breathing and the distant wind.

"When I was a kid, I used to love storms like this
when the power would go out," she said into the still-
ness. "That sounds crazy, doesn't it?"

"I guess it depends why you liked it."

"My dad would make it all seem like a big adven-
ture. When the power went out in the middle of the
night like this, he would pull out the sleeping bags
from the garage and start a fire in the big fireplace in
the great room and the three of us would roast marshmallows and pop popcorn and tell stories just like we
were camping out."

He had to admit that even after all these years, he
didn't like hearing anything positive about R.J. Max-

well. He had never quite understood how a woman like Lauren could come from such a bastard.

"Sounds great," he said politely.

"It was. Even when I was in high school, Dad would still drag us down there. When he was home, anyway. He was always so busy, off on his *business trips.*"

The resentment in those last two words left him acutely uncomfortable. He knew the real reason her father spent so much time away from him, but he wasn't sure if *she* knew he was one of the few who were aware of all the facts. They had never talked about this before, about the motives behind R.J.'s embezzlement and everything that went along with it. He wasn't sure he wanted to talk about it now, in the hushed peace of the night.

Before he could come up with a response, she shook her head slightly; and even in the darkened room, he could see regret flitter across her lovely features.

"Sorry. I didn't mean to sound embittered. I really do try not to be, but sometimes it slips through."

"You have a right to be angry, Lauren."

She had a right to be angry at *Daniel,* he thought. She just didn't know it—and he didn't know if he had the courage to tell her.

"Most of the time the whole situation just makes me sad." She gazed into the fire, avoiding Daniel's gaze. "If R.J. hadn't taken a coward's way out of the mess he created, the first question I would ask would have been why my mother and I weren't enough for him."

"He loved you, Lauren. He was always proud of his daughter."

"Right." After a moment she smiled, though it

looked strained. "Let's talk about something else, can we? I'm really not in the mood to dredge up any more of the past tonight."

What are you in the mood for? he wanted to ask. The question almost spilled out as images flashed through his mind of those heated moments in her kitchen earlier.

He forced his mind away from that dangerous line of thought. As much as he yearned to taste her and touch her again, he knew it was impossible.

"You want to pick the topic or should I?" he asked after a moment.

Her teeth flashed white in the dark as she smiled. "I will. I was wondering this earlier. What are you doing here, Daniel?"

"W-e-e-ll," he drew out. "It's a little cold sleeping out in my truck on a night like tonight. Your couch is much more comfortable for guard-dog duty."

"I don't mean here, right now. I mean, why did you stick around in Moose Springs? I know you came back to help your mother when she was sick. But after she died, why did you stay here when you could have gone anywhere?"

He hadn't been expecting the question and it took him a moment to formulate a reply. "I don't think there's any one answer to that. This is my home and I love it here. That's one reason, probably the easiest, most obvious one."

"What else?"

"I don't know." He shrugged. "Maybe I felt like I had something to prove."

Her eyes widened with surprise. "Why would you think that?"

"We grew up in different worlds, Lauren."

"Not that different. You lived three blocks away."

"In a shack that R.J. probably wouldn't have considered a fit place to store his riding mower."

In the glow from the fire, she looked flushed. "Your parents were wonderful people. Your mother was always so sweet. Every kid in town would save their allowance for weeks to buy those cherry empanadas she sold at Moosemania Days. And I don't think I ever saw your father when he wasn't smiling."

"I agree. They were great people. That didn't change the fact in a lot of people's minds that we were dirt-poor Mexicans."

As soon as the words were out, he heartily wished he hadn't said them. He didn't need to emphasize the differences between them. They were obvious enough.

"And so you wanted to show people you were more than that. That's why you worked so hard in school, why you pushed yourself at football, why you worked to become an indispensable deputy in the sheriff's office?"

"It started out that way, anyhow. Pretty pathetic, isn't it?"

"You had nothing to prove, Daniel. Absolutely nothing! Look at all you've achieved! Not only did you have a full-on football scholarship, but you were the high school valedictorian, as I recall, and Ren was the year after you. Anna would have had the same honor in our grade but, uh, someone else beat her to it. She had to settle for salutatorian."

"Don't worry. She doesn't hold a grudge against you. At least not much of one."

She laughed, as he had hoped she would. It echoed softly through the room and warmed him at least a dozen degrees.

"I don't know about Marcos, since he was a few years behind Anna and me. How were his grades?"

"He was third in the class."

"What a slacker!"

"We think it's because he was the baby and Mom and Dad took it easier on him than the rest of us."

She smiled, then tilted her head to study him. "You're a good sheriff, Daniel. Maybe the best Moose Springs has ever had."

He fought the urge to rub an embarrassed hand to the burn at the back of his neck. "I don't know about that. I can say, I never expected to enjoy it as much as I do. Being here, being home, feels right."

"Think you'll ever move away?"

"I don't know. I get offers once in a while. But it all comes back to me asking myself if I could really be happy anywhere else. I don't have a good answer to that so for now I'm staying."

"Good." She spoke barely above a whisper and the sound of her low voice strummed down his spine like a soft caress. His gaze met hers and she didn't look away.

Again, the memory of that kiss seemed to shimmer between them and he could think of nothing else, the sound of her murmuring his name when he kissed her, the taste of her as she opened for him, warm and welcoming, how perfectly *right* she had seemed in his arms.

He wanted more. Much, much more.

He could kiss her again. He knew it wouldn't take

much for him to lean forward and close the distance between them. The ache to touch her again was a physical burn in his gut.

Even as he started to lean forward, to take what he so desperately wanted, reality came rushing in like that cold wind out there and froze his muscles.

Things were tense enough between them. Was he willing to throw in another kiss that could never lead anywhere?

Yeah.

Hell, yeah.

But he wasn't sure where things stood between them. Though she responded the last time in the heat of the moment, she had looked stunned afterward and he was certain he had caught more than a glimmer of dismay in her gaze.

He let out a breath and the sound of it seemed to echo in the still room. "Lauren—" he began, not sure what he intended to say. *Kiss me before I die on the spot,* maybe.

Whatever it might have been was driven from his mind when the power came back on suddenly, an abrupt, jarring shift from dim to full, bright light.

He blinked a few times to adjust his vision. When he could see through the glare, he saw that in those brief moments she had drawn her arms tighter around her knees and all her defenses were firmly in place.

Just as well. The seductive intimacy of those few moments alone in the dark with her could never survive the harsh glare of light.

She was relieved, Lauren told herself firmly. The power switching back on at just that moment when he had been gearing up to kiss her—and she had so desperately wanted him to—must have been some kind of an omen, a karmic warning that she was messing in dangerous things she damn well ought to stay clear of.

She might be able to sell that argument to her intellect. Her body was another matter entirely, and all she seemed able to focus on now was the deep well of disappointment inside her.

The furnace kicked in and she knew it would be blowing its warmth through the house any moment now.

"Looks like we're back in business," she murmured, mostly to fill the sudden awkward void between them.

"For now. Let's hope it stays on."

She shouldn't regret the loss of that quiet intimacy between them. She knew it was dangerous, knew it filled her mind with all sorts of treacherous thoughts, but she couldn't help feeling as if she had lost something rare, something precious.

"I suppose I'll say good night, then."

"Try to get some rest."

"Same to you."

She rose, self-conscious now about her favorite threadbare pajamas. She hadn't given them a thought when the power was out, but now she wished she'd thrown a robe on before wandering out.

In her bedroom, she closed the door behind her and leaned against it, just for a moment.

It was foolish, she knew, but she wanted the electricity to blink out again. She wanted to be sitting out there with Daniel in the dim firelight, to be listening to his deep voice and feeling the strength and heat of him. A few more moments. Was that too much to ask?

Too bad she had learned the bitter lesson long ago that a girl couldn't always have everything she wanted.

Chapter 10

Two days later, Lauren was just about ready to climb out of her skin. She was beginning to understand the frustrated restlessness of a mouse in a cage.

After forty-eight hours in her house with only Daniel and Rosa, she was edgy and out of sorts and needed some sort of physical outlet. If the snow wasn't still howling out there, she would suit up and jog around the block. The idea tempted her, despite the blizzard, but she decided she really wasn't in the mood for the inevitable argument with Daniel about it.

She had to settle for the mild but distracting exertion of cooking dinner for the three of them.

Not wanting to bother Rosa and Daniel in the adjoining room, she tried her best not to bang pots and pans around as she pulled out the frying pan she needed to sauté chicken.

They didn't even look up from their movie as she set it on the stove and added olive oil to begin heating.

They were watching a DVD of a comedy with Spanish subtitles and every once in a while she could hear their laughter echo through the little house. She was pleased to hear Rosa relaxing, but each time she heard Daniel's bass laugh, she felt as if he had reached across the distance between them to stroke her neck with strong fingers.

Outside, the wind continued to lash snow against the window, as it had much of the day. The blizzard had continued on and off for two days and Daniel had been on the phone a great deal, coordinating his department's response to the storm.

She didn't find much consolation that this enforced isolation was tough on him as well, especially in the midst of a weather crisis. Some time ago, she tried to convince him she and Rosa would be fine here alone for a few hours if he needed to get out in the middle of the action with his deputies.

She thought it had been a reasonable enough suggestion. Daniel just raised one of those expressive eyebrows of his and assured her he wasn't going anywhere.

More's the pity. She sighed as she finished cutting up a chicken breast and slid it into the olive oil in the frying pan, filling the kitchen with sizzling heat.

Maybe he would let *her* go somewhere and help his department with the storm cleanup. True, she didn't know a blasted thing about directing traffic or cleaning up weather-caused accidents. But at this point, she was just about willing to do anything that would get her out of the house for a moment or two so she could regain a little psychic equilibrium.

She filled her large stockpot with water for the pasta, then set it on to boil while she tackled the fresh vegetables for another of her few specialties. She was slicing red and yellow peppers when Daniel laughed again at something on the show.

A shiver slid through her and she almost chopped her finger off. Oh, this was ridiculous. Still, she couldn't resist a quick peek into the other room. Rosa was stretched out on the couch while Daniel had taken over Lauren's favorite easy chair. He sprawled in it, wearing jeans and a rust-colored sweater. He looked rugged and masculine and so gorgeous, he made her insides ache.

She was in serious trouble here.

She grabbed the onion and started slicing it fiercely. Her eyes started watering profusely, but she didn't care. Damn him, anyway. For two days, she had done her best to ignore the thick tension between them, but she wasn't making any progress whatsoever.

He was just so…*there*. He seemed to fill every corner of her small house with the potent force of his personality.

She found everything about him fascinating. She enjoyed listening to him talk to his deputies with a firm voice that managed to convey authority and respect at the same time. She liked watching him with Rosa. He treated the bruised and battered girl with a gentle kindness that touched her deeply.

She also admired his deep reservoir of patience, this further proof that he was often quite literally the quiet spot in a storm to those around him. For a man with such an overwhelming personality, Daniel had an almost Zen-like calmness to him in the middle of a crisis.

Calm did not mean *detached*. Not in the least. Even now, when he appeared relaxed and at ease watching a movie, he never seemed to shed that subtle air of alertness about him, like some kind of predator constantly sniffing the air for prey.

Throughout the last two days, he had put on his winter gear several times to brave the storm, ostensibly to shovel the driveway or for more firewood, but she had the feeling he also used the opportunity to case her house and its surroundings, looking for anything unusual.

He was a dangerous man, she thought as she stirred the chicken. More so, she imagined, because it would be easy—and disastrous—for an opponent to mistake his outward calm for inward placidity. Anyone foolish enough to err so badly would have to overlook those sharp dark eyes that never seemed to miss anything.

She could only hope they didn't see *everything*. She would die of mortification if he guessed her attraction.

Oh, she had it bad. Now that it was out in the open in her psyche, she couldn't believe she had missed it all these years, all the reasons she was tense and uncomfortable around him.

Her attraction had always been this undefined thing in her mind, this awareness of him that was somehow lost in her frustration and sadness over the past.

How would their relationship change after this time with Rosa was over? How on earth could things ever return to the way they were before, that wary but polite accord?

She was checking the cookie sheet of breadsticks baking in the oven, their yeasty smell mingling with the spices in the chicken, when some sixth sense warned her Daniel had entered the kitchen behind her.

Even without turning around, she knew he was there by a sudden subtle vibration in the air, a stirring of the molecules, an alertness in her nerve endings.

Her pulse kicked up a notch, as it seemed to do whenever he was within five feet of her, but she pasted on a smile and turned around, only to find him watching her with an odd expression on his face, something dark and intense and unsettling.

He hid it quickly and moved to the coffeepot to refill his cup. "Smells delicious," he said, gesturing to the sizzling chicken. Did he sound more gruff than usual? she wondered, then dismissed the thought.

"Thanks," she murmured.

"You don't have to do all the cooking. I know we've talked about this but I should have been more proactive. Sorry to dump the burden on you. Things have been a little crazy, with the storm and all. To be honest, I forgot all about it, but I promise, I'll cook breakfast and dinner tomorrow."

"I really don't mind cooking," she assured him.

"It's only fair. And I don't mind it, either."

"Do you expect you and Rosa will still be here by dinnertime tomorrow?" she asked.

"I'm still waiting to hear from Cale on the status of their safe house situation. We'll know better after he checks in." He paused. "Whenever we get out of here, I imagine you'll be happy to have us out of your way."

"You're not in my way."

Much.

She was a lousy liar and his rueful half smile indicated he didn't believe her any more than she believed herself.

Not that she would be completely thrilled to have them gone. On the one hand, she would be vastly relieved when her life returned to normal and her clinic reopened. On the other, she was terribly afraid she would be lonely when this was all over.

She had a good life, she reminded herself as she added the pasta to the boiling water. Every day she tried to make a difference in the world, to help the people of her community live healthier, happier lives. She had no reason at all for this discontent simmering under her skin.

"You know," he said after a moment, "if Cale and McKinnon do find another placement for Rosa in the next day or two, you would still have time left of your vacation to go visit your mom in southern Utah."

"Maybe. I don't want to make any definite plans until things are figured out here."

The timer went off, indicating the breadsticks were done. She slid them out, aware of him watching her the whole time.

"Anything I can do in here?"

She wanted him out of the kitchen. How could she possibly concentrate on cooking with him crowding her psyche this way? "No. I just need to toss it all together. Go back to your movie. Everything should be ready in ten minutes or so."

"I can set the table, at least."

"All right."

For the next few moments, they worked together in silence, Daniel setting out plates and silverware while

Lauren brushed melted butter on the breadsticks and finished sautéing the vegetables.

She was concentrating so fiercely on trying to ignore him that she nearly caused a disaster. When she determined the pasta was done, she carried the stockpot to the sink to drain and almost collided with Daniel, who must have gone to the cupboard by the sink for glasses.

He caught her and steadied her, but a tiny amount of hot liquid spilled over onto the front of his sweater.

"I'm sorry!" she exclaimed. "Are you all right?"

"Fine. It's a thick sweater."

This time she was certain his voice sounded rough. She lifted her gaze from his shirtfront to his face and that jumpy, fluttery feeling twirled through her insides at the raw hunger she surprised in his expression.

"I... Good," she said breathlessly. They froze there in an awkward tableau, then he stepped away.

"You'd better drain that before you get burned."

The pasta. Right. She hurried to the sink, hoping he would attribute her sudden flush to the cloud of steam curling around her.

The doorbell rang just as the three of them were clearing the dinner dishes. The change in Daniel was rapid and disconcerting. One moment he was teasing Rosa in Spanish, the next he became alert, predatory.

"Stay here," he ordered, his voice hard and flat.

He headed toward the door, reaching for something under his sweater. He had a gun. Good Lord. She should have realized he would be armed. He was here for protection, for heaven's sake, she reminded herself. He couldn't very well face down Gilberto Mata with nothing but his fists, no matter how powerful they were.

Still, the sight of that stark, black weapon in his hand drove home the precariousness of the situation—and the dangerous edge to Daniel's nature he usually managed to cloak from view.

From the angle of the kitchen cabinets, she only had a sliver of a view into the entryway. She watched Daniel ease to the front window and barely twitch the curtains to look out on to the porch, just like a gunfighter in the Wild West.

She held her breath, but whatever he saw there must have set his mind at ease. He quickly holstered his weapon again and worked the locks on the door.

"It's okay. Everything's okay." She gave a Rosa a reassuring smile when she heard Daniel greeting Cale Davis.

A moment later, both men entered her kitchen, and the cozy room instantly seemed to shrink. Though Lauren knew Rosa had met the FBI agent when she was in the hospital, the girl seemed tense and anxious in his presence.

Seeing her reaction only reinforced to Lauren how very comfortable Rosa had become with Daniel. That thought was further validated when Daniel smiled at Rosa and she visibly relaxed.

"We've just finished eating," Lauren said. "There's plenty left. Are you hungry?"

He shook his head. "I'm fine, thanks. Megan's holding dinner for me at home so I can't stay long. Since your place is on my way home, I figured I would stop and see how things have been going."

"Quiet," Daniel answered.

"That's good. Just the way we like it. Sorry I haven't checked in with you before now. We've been in the middle of a big bust on another case. I think we've finally tied up all those loose ends and are ready to put all our energies into this case."

"Has there been any progress?" Lauren asked.

Cale glanced quickly at Rosa, who was hovering close to Daniel. "Some," he said. "We're closing in on the smuggling ring. With the information Rosa gave us, we've been able to find Gilberto Mata. We know who he is and we've got a tail on him."

"Have you arrested him?"

Cale shook his head. "Not yet. We're trying to track his movements, his known associates, that kind of thing, to see if we can figure out who else might be involved and find the other girls Rosa talked about. Her friend and the others. That's going to take some time. We know from her statement that she knows at least four other men were involved besides Mata, the three other men who raped her and who handled the day-to-day operations and another one who seemed to be calling the shots. There have got to be more than that if they're keeping the other girls somewhere—"

Rosa said something quickly in Spanish to Daniel, a questioning look on her fragile, half-healed features. She must have been asking him to translate the conversation. Since Lauren had spent the last two days trying in vain to follow the rapid conversations between Rosa and Daniel, she thought she understood how Rosa felt.

"Can I tell her what you said? She deserves to know what's going on," Daniel said.

Cale pursed his lips. "You're right. She does."

Daniel quickly explained what the agent had said

and Rosa nodded. Lauren actually understood her response as she asked him in Spanish why they hadn't already arrested the man who hurt her.

Cale apparently understood some Spanish as well. "Explain to her that we can't move too quickly on this and risk blowing the whole investigation by sending them all running back over the border. As I said, we're still trying to find the other girls she talked about. We need a few more days to make sure we can get them out safely when this all goes down."

Daniel translated his words to Rosa, who nodded solemnly.

"Federal prosecutors want to convene a grand jury by Tuesday or Wednesday so we can get some indictments. We would like to prep Rosa to testify as early as the day after that."

He looked at Lauren. "Do you think she'll be up to that?"

"Are you asking me as her doctor or as her friend?" she asked, and couldn't help the ridiculous little glow that blossomed inside her when Daniel gave her a wide smile of approval.

"Both, I suppose," Cale answered.

"I think you're going to need to ask her that. Medically, there's no reason she can't testify. She's rebounding remarkably well from a horrific beating. She still has pain and will for some time, but both she and the baby seem to be fine. Emotionally, she's suffered months of trauma and she's going to be healing from that for a long time."

Cale turned to the girl and asked her in Spanish if she would be willing to testify about what happened to her so the men who hurt her could be arrested.

She shook her head vehemently, her eyes wide and her expression taut with fear. Lauren instinctively went to her. But Daniel moved first. He squeezed her shoulder gently and spoke in a soft, reassuring voice.

At first, Lauren couldn't understand what he said. Only after she translated the words in her mind did his meaning become clear. He told Rosa she was strong and beautiful, courageous enough to handle this task they put before her, as hard as it would be, and he swore he would be with her the entire way.

Rosa swallowed hard, her fingers trembling as she twisted them together. She looked as if she wanted to run out the door and escape this whole situation, but after a moment she seemed to straighten her shoulders.

"If it will help the other girls to be safe and away from those bad men, then yes, I will tell what I know."

Daniel smiled at her with pride and affection. As Lauren gazed at those strong, handsome features, the terrifying truth poured over her like someone had just rushed into the kitchen and dumped a bucket full of snow over her head.

She was in love with him.

Instinctively, she fought to deny it. She couldn't be. It wasn't possible.

Yes, she was attracted to him. That was a normal physiological reaction to a powerful, gorgeous man. Yes, she admired his dedication and his commitment to his job and his town, his kindness and his compassion.

But *love*.

That was something else entirely.

Even as her mind tried to rationalize, to frantically search for some escape, the inevitable truth seemed to settle into her chest, seeping into her soul.

She was in love with Daniel Galvez.

How could she have missed it all these years? They had definitely been there, these feelings growing inside her. Looking back, she could see clear signs. She had always had a bit of a crush on him as a girl—just like all the other girls at school.

Daniel had been tall, dark, gorgeous, athletic—and slightly rough around the edges. All the things that twittered the hearts of silly teenage girls, and she had been no different.

She had put it out of her mind over the years, but since they both returned to Moose Springs as adults and she watched the kind of man that boy had grown into, these tender feelings had been growing inside her—untended and wild, but still somehow finding root.

Through her dismay, she realized Cale and Daniel were still talking about the case.

"What about the safe house situation?" Daniel asked.

"We should have everything set by tomorrow afternoon. We've got a couple female agents standing ready to stay with her. One of them is fluent in Spanish, too."

"That's good," Daniel said, relief in his voice. "I'll feel better if she has someone to talk to."

"Things will be easier with her in our place by the U. This way the prosecutors will have easier access to prep her for her testimony." Cale paused. "You two okay here one more night?"

"I'm good," Daniel said. "Lauren?"

No. She was *not* good. Didn't anybody else notice the sane order of her life crumbling around her feet?

"She can stay here as long as necessary," she managed.

"Thanks. Tomorrow should be sufficient."

Could she make it through one more day? she wondered as Daniel showed Cale to the door and she and Rosa resumed clearing the dishes from the kitchen table.

Oh, this was a complete disaster, she thought as she stood filling the sink with soapy water for the dishes that weren't dishwasher-safe. She was destined for heartache here.

She thought of the tension that was always there just below the surface when she was with Daniel. He didn't share her feelings. She had never picked up any kind of vibe like that.

Maybe she just missed it. She had been too stupid to realize her own feelings. But he had kissed her.

A fluke, she assured herself, a temporary aberration brought on by the heat and intensity of the moment.

Who would have guessed when she stepped up to offer a wounded patient a sanctuary for a few days that she would discover a grim truth about herself that would rock her to the core?

"Everything okay?"

She looked up from the sink to find Daniel had returned to the kitchen and was watching her with concern in his eyes.

"Much harder and you're going to scrub the nonstick coating right out of that pan," he said.

She stilled her movements, hoping the truth wasn't painfully obvious in her features.

"Yes. Of course. Everything's fine," she lied. "Just fine. Why wouldn't it be?"

Chapter 11

Something was wrong.

Daniel covertly studied Lauren throughout the remainder of the evening, trying to figure out exactly what had happened at dinnertime to make her so jumpy and out of sorts.

She tried to hide it, but he could see some kind of turmoil seething in her blue eyes. Though she went through the motions of watching another DVD with them, he didn't think she caught any of it. Half the time she wasn't even looking at the screen, she was gazing into the flickering fire or out the window at the snow. She seemed the proverbial million miles away.

Maybe this situation was harder on her than she let on. *He* sure as hell found it a nightmare.

Being this close to Lauren—living in her house, surrounded by her things, by her scent, by her sheer presence—was just about the hardest assignment he had ever endured.

He had gone undercover as a scumbag drug dealer for five months back on the job in Salt Lake City and had seen—and done—things that still made his gut burn. All for the greater good of busting up a crime ring that focused exclusively on hooking junior high and high school kids on methamphetamines.

The whole thing had been a miserable, soul-sucking time in his life. While the two dozen resulting arrests hadn't completely washed away the stink of it from his skin, they had certainly helped.

Sitting in Lauren's house, pretending a casualness he was far from feeling, seemed much harder than those five months.

He ached to touch her again. Every time he came within a few feet of her, he had to shove his hands in his pockets to keep from reaching for her.

Maybe that's why she was so twitchy, because she feared he was going to jump her again any minute now.

She didn't need to worry. He could have reassured her on that score. He had vowed to himself the night before that he would keep his hands off her for the duration of this assignment and he would damn well keep that oath, no matter how impossible it seemed at times.

The music on the movie swelled and he realized the closing credits were rolling. He hadn't paid much more attention than Lauren. He only hoped Rosa had enjoyed it.

"Do you want to watch another one?" Lauren asked in Spanish.

Rosa shook her head. "I'm tired," she said softly, her hand resting on her abdomen.

Lauren studied her with concern. "You're hurting, aren't you?"

Rosa started to deny it, then finally she shrugged.

Lauren turned to him. "Can you ask her if it would be all right for me to check her temperature and blood pressure? I'm afraid I don't quite have the language skills."

He repeated her question to Rosa, who shrugged again. She *did* look achy and upset and he admired Lauren's powers of observation.

She rose with her usual grace and left the room. When she returned, she carried her medical bag. She flipped up the lights they had dimmed for the movie and sat down next to Rosa on the couch.

As usual, he found watching Dr. Maxwell in action far more absorbing than anything on the silver screen. Despite her halting Spanish, she made Rosa completely comfortable with her quiet skill. After a quick check of temperature and blood pressure, she pulled out a small sensor from her bag, the same one she had used during her initial exam of Rosa.

"I'm going to check the baby's heartbeat, okay?" She patted her chest to pantomime a heart beating and pointed at Rosa's abdomen.

"Do you want me to leave?" Daniel asked.

"That's up to Rosa."

He repeated the question to the girl, who shook her head. "Just turn around," Rosa ordered.

He had to smile at the peremptory tone—something she was using more and more as she became more comfortable with them both. He complied, then was astonished a moment later to hear a rapid, steady heartbeat filling the room.

"Is that the baby?" he asked, amazed at the strength of it.

"That's her," Lauren said. "She's a fighter. That's a strong, normal heartbeat."

A moment later, the miraculous sound stopped. "You can turn around now," Lauren said.

When he shifted his gaze, he saw she was putting the monitor thingie away while Rosa pulled her shirt back down. Instead of looking thrilled to hear the heartbeat, she was looking increasingly distressed.

Lauren must have picked up on it, too. "What is it?"

Rosa shrugged but her chin gave an ominous quiver and her big dark eyes started to fill up with tears.

Daniel's first instinct—like that of any sane man— was to shove his chair back and run like hell. Lauren could handle it. She must know exactly how to deal with a young girl's tears.

She'd been one, after all.

He started to shift his weight forward to escape, but Lauren caught the movement. She impaled him in place with a glare.

"What is it? Everything is fine. Good. Are you hurting somewhere else?" she asked in her stilted Spanish.

He sighed. As much as he desperately wanted to escape any emotional outburst, he couldn't leave, not with the language barrier between Lauren and her patient.

Rosa pressed a hand to her chest. "Here," she said.

"You're having chest pains?" In her dismay, Lauren forgot herself and asked the question in English, then looked helplessly at him. He repeated the question in Spanish.

Rosa sniffled once, and then unleashed the floodgates. "My heart," she sobbed. "It aches inside me. I worry so much. What will happen to my baby? She did nothing wrong and I do not want her to die. I am glad she is a fighter, as Dr. Lauren says, that Gilberto Mata did not kill her. But I cannot love her. Who will take care of her?"

Daniel couldn't begin to imagine what she must be going through, pregnant as a result of rape, afraid for her life in a country where she didn't speak the language.

"What did she say?" Lauren demanded, frustration at the language barrier obvious in her features.

"She's worried about the baby."

"Her heartbeat was fine. Better than fine. It's great," Lauren said, clearly baffled.

"Not the baby's physical well-being. More about what will happen to her." He translated the rest of what Rosa had said and watched the anxiety in Lauren's eyes turn to soft compassion.

"Oh, Rosa," she said, and hugged the girl. *Big help there,* he thought, panicking more. Rosa only seemed to sob harder.

After a tense moment, she seemed to calm down and Lauren produced a tissue.

"The other day in the hospital, you said you wanted to give the baby up for adoption, remember? Rosa, there are wonderful couples with so much love to give a child. If that's what you decide, we will find the perfect home for your baby, I promise you. I'll help you. You can choose exactly where the baby goes."

He translated for Lauren, though he had the impression the girl understood the gist.

She twisted the tissue in her hands until it was mangled. "But what if my baby hates me for giving her away?"

"She won't. I promise." She squeezed the girl's hands, tissue and all. "I can tell you that from experience. I was adopted and I have never been anything but grateful to the woman who gave me life."

He stared at her, struck dumb at that unexpected bit of information. How had he never known that about her, in all his months of investigating R.J.? Or maybe he had learned it, he had just been so consumed with vengeance he hadn't internalized the information.

He suddenly remembered his translator duties and relayed what she had said to Rosa. Her words seemed to ease much of the girl's worries. Lauren spent a few more moments reassuring her, until the tears appeared to have dried up, to his vast relief.

"Come on," Lauren said. "The best thing for you right now is rest. You will feel much better about everything in the morning."

"Thank you," Rosa whispered. "Thank you for everything. You have both been so kind to me."

Lauren hugged her once more, then went with her to help settle her for the night.

She returned just as Daniel was throwing another log on the fire. She paused inside the room and again he caught the wild edge of restlessness in her stance.

"I don't believe I ever knew you were adopted," he said.

She blinked as if she hadn't quite been expecting his statement. "It wasn't some big dark secret," she said. "I don't think about it much, it's just part of who I am."

"What were the circumstances?"

"The usual, I guess. My parents were married for

five years and found out they couldn't conceive. This was in the early days of in vitro. They tried everything, apparently, without success. Finally they went the private adoption route."

"Do you know anything about your birth mother?"

"Only that she was young and pregnant and alone, like Rosa," she said. "That's all."

Was this the reason Rosa's situation seemed to affect Lauren so strongly? She had sympathized with the girl from the very beginning. He had asked her why she had insisted on bringing Rosa home with her to Moose Springs to heal. Perhaps this helped explain her actions somewhat.

"She chose my parents before the birth," Lauren continued, "but stipulated there be no contact between them. My mother and father never met her. I don't know anything more about her than that."

"Have you ever wanted to look for her?"

"When I was in high school, I was curious. I guess I grew out of it, right around the time I figured out only fools go borrowing trouble."

"How do you know it would be trouble?" he asked. "Maybe you would be friends."

"Maybe. I just figured she could find me if she wanted. She knew my parents' names and where they lived. She would only have to Google R.J.'s name to know the whole ugly story. It wouldn't be hard to find mention of his only surviving child in those stories. His only legal one, anyway."

Again, he heard the bitterness in her voice. He knew the reason for it and he ached for her. Before he could respond, she spoke again.

"We don't need to dance around this, Daniel. You

must know all the gory details. You worked in the sheriff's department at the time everything happened so I'm sure you were privy to all the juicy details that never made it into the papers."

If she only knew.

Before he could respond, Lauren forced a smile. "I'm sure you're wondering if my mother's inability to conceive had anything to do with the choices R.J. made later. The other family he kept in Salt Lake City. His three bouncing baby boys from another woman who thought she was happily married to a man who merely traveled more than she liked. I've certainly wondered the same thing. My mother was unable to give him a son and apparently he found someone who could."

Though she tried to hide it, he heard the raw pain in her voice and would have given anything to have the right words to ease it, as she had comforted Rosa.

"I do know the truth," he said carefully. "But you can be sure I'm one of only a few who do."

"I figured as much, otherwise everyone in town would know by now."

"Have you met them?"

She gave a humorless laugh. "Still more trouble I didn't want to go borrowing. My family tree is quite a wild tangle, isn't it? But yes, I have met my half brothers. Ian, Jamie and Kevin. And their mother. She's a very sweet woman who didn't deserve a betrayal like this."

"Neither did you or your mother."

"No, we didn't." She sighed. "I'm sorry. You must think I brood about the past constantly. I've talked about this more the last few days than I have since it all happened. I'm not sure why that is, but I would really like to put it behind me."

This was the perfect opening for him to tell her the truth he had been running from, the guilt that burned through him whenever they talked about the grim ghosts of the past.

He hesitated. If he told her, everything between them would be ruined, this fragile friendship that had begun to take flight the last few days. If he told her, she would loathe him. How could she not?

Perhaps he would be better to just let things stay as they were. No. He couldn't take the coward's way out, not about this.

He sighed. He had to come clean, and damn the consequences.

"Lauren, there's something I should tell you."

She studied him across the room, his darkly handsome features suddenly solemn, and her stomach jumped with nerves.

"Whatever it is, I don't want to hear it," she said immediately, jumping up from her chair. "Not tonight."

"Lauren—"

She cut him off. "I need to do something physical. If you need anything, I'll be in my room on my yoga mat in the downward-facing dog."

He studied her intently, until she flushed under the weight of it. She could only hope he couldn't see the wild chaos of emotions she was doing her best to hide from him.

"Why are you running away?" he asked.

"Who's running away?" she retorted, then sighed

at his raised eyebrow. "Okay," she admitted. "I'm running away."

"Why?"

She gave a short laugh. "I'm a physician, Daniel. In my world *we need to talk* is just about the most terrible thing I can say to a patient. The only time I ever use those words, I invariably follow them up with something really awful. Whatever it is you want to tell me about my father or anything else, I don't want to hear it. Not tonight. I don't care if that makes me some kind of an ostrich up to my eyeballs in sand. I just… I can't take any more right now."

Though she knew it was rude to a guest in her home, she left without waiting for an answer and retreated to her bedroom, where she quickly changed into workout clothes.

At first, she pushed herself through her asanas, but after ten minutes or so her body and mind relaxed and she could feel the long days of tension begin to seep out of her.

Thirty-five minutes later, she finished her usual poses and was asking herself why she hadn't tried this days ago to still the turmoil inside her, when she heard the outside door open and close.

Daniel must be outside shoveling snow, she assumed. This would probably be the perfect time for her to grab a bottled water from the refrigerator, something she had neglected earlier in her haste to escape from him.

For the first time in days, her mind wasn't churning and her muscles felt pleasantly loose as she went to the kitchen and opened the refrigerator. She found a bottle and was taking a long, refreshing drink when that sixth sense warned her she wasn't alone.

She turned and found Daniel standing in the doorway, his eyes shadowed.

Her relaxed feeling disappeared. Acutely conscious of her yoga clothes—a midriff-baring tank and stretchy capris—she swallowed hard, sincerely wishing she had never left her mat.

"Snow's stopped."

Her nerves tingled at the hoarse note in his voice.

"I... Good. That's good."

"I'd say we got at least a foot out of the storm. Maybe eighteen inches."

How could he possibly talk about the weather, with all the currents zinging between them? She couldn't even manage to string together a coherent thought.

"How'd the, er, low-down dog go?"

That strange note in his voice caught her attention again and she took a closer look at his expression. She finally saw the hunger there—hot desire with an edge of desperation.

She continued to stare at him, hypnotized by the twitch of muscle in his jaw. He was so big, so dangerously male, and all she could think about was how easy it would be to tug him into her bedroom right now and get her hands on all that hard strength.

He wanted her. She couldn't quite believe it, but she couldn't deny the evidence in his eyes.

"It's the, um, downward-facing dog." Her voice sounded hoarse as well. "I feel much better—all loose and relaxed. You should try it."

She took another swallow from the bottled water. When she lowered it, she found him staring at her mouth. Had she left a water droplet or two there? she wondered, sweeping her tongue across her bottom lip to be sure.

Daniel made a strangled sound. "You're killing me here, Lauren."

"I'm...what?"

"I have to kiss you again. I'm sorry."

She had only half a second to wonder why he seemed compelled to apologize for something she wanted with a fierce ache, and then she was in his arms.

His lips were cold from being outside and he tasted of mint. She shivered as he pressed her against the cabinet, his mouth hard and possessive. Oh, my. She wrapped her arms around his neck, relishing the strength of him against her curves. Raising her arms lifted her exercise tank another few inches, baring more of her midriff and she could feel the nubby texture of his sweater against her skin.

When he slid a hand to her bare back, under the cotton of her tank, and pulled her closer, she forgot all about it—forgot to breathe or think or do anything but exist in the heat of his arms. Raw sensation glittered through at the touch of his fingers on her bare skin, at his tongue stroking hers.

Oh, my.

He was so big and solid, like those mountains outside the window, and she wanted to melt into him.

Where their kiss two days before had been slow, easy as a sluggish creek on a hot summer day, this one was a raging, churning whirlpool. She feared if she wasn't careful, the urgent force of it would suck her down and carry her away.

Clinging wildly to the spinning edges of her sanity, she summoned every ounce of willpower and managed to wrench her mouth away from his long enough to come up for air.

She could feel his chest's rapid rise and fall, see the dazed desire in his eyes.

Had she really done that to him? It didn't seem possible that she could have that effect on someone who was usually so calm and unruffled under any circumstances.

"You taste just like I always imagined you would," he murmured.

It took a moment for his words to sink in. When they did, she raised disbelieving eyes to his. "You... imagined kissing me?"

He still held her, his hands on the bare skin of her back, and his low laugh rumbled against her chest. "Not much. Only just about every time I saw you for the last decade or so. Possibly more."

She managed, barely, to keep her jaw from completely sagging open. She swallowed hard. "You have not."

His expression suddenly guarded, as if he wished he hadn't said anything, he dropped his arms and stepped back. She instantly felt about a dozen degrees colder in her skimpy yoga clothes.

"I don't mean to argue with you, Dr. Maxwell, but I know my own fantasies, thanks very much."

Here was twice in one day she felt she had just entered some kind of alternate universe. He had fantasized about *her?*

She rubbed her chilled arms. "I... Why didn't you ever do anything about it?"

"Tried that once and you shot me down. Quite brutally, in fact. I didn't see the need to embarrass both of us by a repeat performance."

Disoriented and more off balance than she was in her most challenging yoga pose, she didn't know what he meant at first. It took her a moment to realize he must be referring to the time she had turned him down for a date, that terrible summer she had returned to Moose Springs between her freshman and sophomore year of college.

She would have felt threatened by any male who showed interest in her that summer. She was jumpy, skittish. Someone as athletic and virile and *overpowering* as Daniel would have sent her spiraling into panic.

But that had been years ago, another lifetime. All this time he had wondered about kissing her and he had given her absolutely no indication of it until now.

She couldn't quite fathom it—at the same time, she realized she probably hadn't exactly given him any encouragement to do more than wonder.

"I'm sorry. It wasn't you," she said lamely. "I…that was a crazy summer."

He leaned a hip against the counter. "It doesn't matter."

It did, she realized. She could tell by the studied casualness in his eyes. Somehow her rejection had bothered him very much.

All these years, she thought the subtle tension that always seemed to simmer between them stemmed from what her father had done. How foolish of her, especially when Daniel had made it clear many times that he didn't believe her responsible for her father's sins.

She didn't know whether to be relieved or dismayed that his discomfort might have more to do with her blunt rejection, that he thought she disliked him all these years, when she had been fighting her own attraction.

She let out a breath. How could she ever explain how messed up she had been that summer, what a blur those weeks had seemed?

She had to, though. She loved him. He deserved the truth, no matter how hard the telling of it might be for her.

"Daniel, I promise. It wasn't you. I had…reasons."

"Yeah?"

She sighed. She did *not* want to have this discussion in her workout clothes, probably smelling like that low-down dog he talked about.

"Give me a minute to change and I'll explain. Okay?"

She didn't wait for an answer, just made her escape.

Fifteen minutes later, he sat back on his heels after tossing another log into the fire and watched the flames consume it, trying fiercely to remind himself he was working here. He needed to keep his senses alert and vigilant to guard against any possible danger to the women under his care.

He couldn't risk losing control with Lauren, not with so much at stake. Maybe he would be better off if she just decided to stay in her room for the night. Temptation was far easier to resist when it wasn't gazing at him out of columbine-blue eyes.

But he had to admit, he wanted to hear what she had to say. More, he wanted to know if the desire he had seen in her eyes had been real or just a reaction to the heat of the moment.

He gave a heavy sigh. He had it bad. No surprise

there. He just needed to try like hell not to let her see how he burned for her. He still yearned for the pink-and-white princess in the castle.

No. He didn't want that fairy-tale dream. He wanted Lauren. The smart, dedicated doctor who poured her heart and soul into healing her patients, the one who showed such kindness and compassion to a frightened young girl, the courageous woman who faced down an entire town's whispers.

She came out a few moments later, her hair damp and curling at the ends. She must have taken time to shower before changing into soft jeans and a white blouse.

She looked beautiful, soft and warm and delicious. As he gazed at her in the fire's glow, the truth seemed to kick him in the gut like a pissed-off mule.

He was in love with her. Not because she took away his breath, but because of all those things he had thought about earlier. Her courage, her strength, her compassion.

Her heart.

His own chest ached and he fought the urge to rub his hand across it. He was in love with her and probably had been since those days he used to ride his bike by her house.

What the hell was he supposed to do with that?

"I'm going to make some hot chocolate," she said. "Do you want some?"

He wanted things to go back to the way before, when he thought he was just a stupid kid craving the pretty blonde princess who represented everything he didn't have.

"Sure," he mumbled.

"What flavor?"

As if he cared about that right now. "Anything."

She spent a few more moments in the kitchen. His mind churning with shock and dismay, he tried his best to keep his eyes off her as she bustled around boiling water, pulling out mugs, pouring, measuring, stirring.

Was Lauren the reason he was still thirty-three and single? He had come close to changing that a few times, but had backed away before things reached the sticking point. Those other relationships never felt quite right, no matter how hard he tried to make them so.

What a mess. He was in love with a woman who would despise him if she knew the truth about what he had done. He finally gave in and rubbed the ache in his heart.

When she returned, she handed him a blue mug with intricate silver snowflakes on the side. "It's cinnamon. I didn't know which one to pick for you but, um, I know you like cinnamon mints."

A rosy blush crept over her cheekbones and for the life of him, he couldn't figure out why. Was it because she had noticed the kind of Altoids he preferred?

"Thanks," he murmured.

She perched in the chair opposite him and sipped at her cocoa. He obediently tried his. Though he usually preferred the liquid jolt of coffee, he had to admit there *was* something comforting about sitting here in the night by a flickering fire sipping cocoa, despite the tension in his gut and the turmoil in his heart.

After a moment, she let out a sigh. "I don't know where to begin."

He set his mug down on a coaster on the coffee

table. "You don't have to say anything, Lauren. The past is done. Let's forget it."

She went on as if she didn't hear him, as if she had a script in her head and was going to get through it, no matter what.

"I'm very sorry I rejected you that summer. The truth is, I would have turned down any man who asked me out. But especially an athlete like you, someone big and tough and…overwhelming. It wasn't anything personal, I swear."

"It doesn't matter," he said again. "I just figured you weren't interested. No big deal."

"Any other time, I would have been."

He watched color rise in her cheeks again. She cast him a sidelong glance, then quickly looked away.

"Any other time except that summer I would have *definitely* been interested."

Chapter 12

At her words, he swallowed hard, a hundred different thoughts racing through his mind. He finally focused on the words that preceded her stunning declaration.

"What was different about that summer?"

"Everything. *Everything.*"

She paused, both hands wrapped around her cocoa mug. "You have to remember, I was young, barely seventeen, when I started college. Young enough and stupid enough to think I could handle any situation. I was wrong. Seriously wrong."

He knew with sudden certainty he didn't want to hear this.

"Near the end of my second semester, I had an… incident that threw me off. Oh, this is harder than I thought it would be."

Grim premonition in his gut, he wanted to tell her

to stop right there. But if she could be tough enough to talk about it, he damn well could hear her out.

She sighed. "I was attacked. Date-raped. He was an athlete, the captain of the rugby team and I can remember feeling so flattered when he asked me out. He walked me back to my dorm and my roommate was gone for the weekend. I let him in. I knew it was stupid, but I did it anyway. So we were talking and before I knew it, he was pushing me to do things I didn't want to do. He was bigger than I was, stronger than I was, and…wouldn't take no for an answer."

His hand fisted around his mug so tightly, it was a wonder the thing didn't explode into shards.

"Did you file charges?" the cop in him compelled himself to ask.

She shook her head. "I told you, I was young and stupid. I was so embarrassed that I'd allowed him in when my roommate wasn't home, that I had been stupid enough to think I was worldly enough to handle anything. I just wanted to come home to Moose Springs, to my mama. I thought everything would be okay if I could only come home. Somehow I made it through the last few weeks of the term and came back for the summer to work for my dad and try to get my head back to normal."

She blew out a breath. "And then I missed my period."

He jerked his gaze to her and found her cheeks pink and her eyes determinedly fixed on the fire. "As you can guess, it was a pretty terrible time. I was terrified to tell my parents, terrified of anybody with a Y chromosome who dared to talk to me. I couldn't believe this was happening to me and I just wanted it all to go away."

His throat tightened, imagining her as an eighteen-year-old girl, traumatized and frightened and alone. Like Rosa, he realized, with only a few more years under her belt.

Suddenly everything made sense. Her compassion for the girl, her insistence on bringing her home and caring for her, as Lauren probably wished someone had done for her.

That summer when he had burned with embarrassment at her blunt rejection, he convinced himself she was just some rich bitch, a country-club baby who didn't want to dirty her hands by being seen with somebody like him.

Now he was ashamed that he had even entertained the thought for a moment.

"What happened?" he asked gruffly.

"I had a miscarriage. Less than seven weeks gestation. In retrospect, it was a blessing but I felt terribly guilty at the time, as if I had somehow wished the pregnancy away. I ended up having to tell my mother and she got me help—a good doctor and a good therapist."

He didn't know what to say, what to do. What man would, after finding out some bastard had done such a thing to the woman he loved? His first instinct was to demand the man's name so he could find him and mete out some long overdue justice.

Finally, he said the only words he could. "I'm so sorry, Lauren," he murmured.

"I'm not a victim. Please don't treat me like one. I promise, I don't even think about it much anymore." She paused. "That's not quite true. Last week after I was attacked in the hospital, I dreamed about it again. About him." She smiled a little. "This time was different. In my dream, I stabbed him with a scalpel and, it felt great. I suppose that makes me sound vicious and bloodthirsty, doesn't it?"

"I'd like to do that to the bastard and more," he said quietly.

She stared at him for a moment and then she took a deep breath. "He *was* a bastard but I refuse to let a few moments out of my life a dozen years ago define me. I'm not a victim," she repeated. "I've had years to deal with what happened and I'm fine now. I wouldn't have even mentioned it except I wanted you to know why I was messed up that summer and why I treated you so coldly. It honestly wasn't you, Daniel."

"Good to know. I guess I can spend the next decade or so trying to heal my battered ego."

Her eyes widened with distress.

"Kidding, Lauren. I was kidding. I was a college jock way too full of myself back then. My ego could certainly stand being knocked down a peg or five or ten."

She smiled, then shifted her gaze back to the fire. "I don't know if this helps the healing process at all, but I should tell you that if you had asked me out any other time—before that summer or after I came back to Moose Springs—I would have jumped at the chance."

"You don't have to pretend anything, Lauren."

"Who's pretending? Why do you think I stutter and stammer and generally act like an idiot around you most of the time?"

"What are you talking about? You're never anything but professional and courteous."

"Is that what you call it when I all but jumped you in my kitchen?"

"Hey, I'm a big fan of professional courtesy."

She laughed, then rubbed her hands on her jeans. "So now that I've spilled all my secrets, where do we go from here?" she asked.

She might have spilled all hers, but he still had a few to go. He knew this would be another good opening to tell her about the investigation, but he couldn't seem to form the words. Not yet. He had to give her the truth but he couldn't bear the idea of that trust and affection in her eyes changing to hurt and anger.

"Uh, where would you like this to go?" he asked instead.

"That's up to you. If you asked me out again, I promise, I wouldn't say no this time."

"I'm afraid I wasn't very original back in the day. I think my master plan probably would have been pretty boring—to take you to dinner and a show and hopefully sit in the back row during the movie and neck."

She swallowed and that adorable pink flush crept over her cheekbones. "We've already had dinner. But I suppose we could watch a DVD."

His heart pounding like crazy, he stepped forward. "Or we could skip the movie and just head right on to the good stuff."

She smiled a little tremulously. "I was really hoping you would say that."

She sighed his name when he kissed her and he found it the most erotic sound he had ever heard.

Her mouth was soft and warm, and tasted like raspberries and chocolate, rich and sweet and addicting. He couldn't seem to get enough, especially when she sighed again and wrapped her arms around his waist.

This was as close to heaven as he had ever imagined,

Lauren in his arms, the fire popping and hissing in the background, this seductive heat swirling around them.

He kissed her until his blood jumped wildly through his veins, until they were both breathing hard and it was all he could do not to press her against the couch and rip her clothes off.

He pulled away to give himself a little room to catch his breath, but she wasn't having any of it.

"Don't stop," she murmured. What man could resist an invitation like that? Certainly not him. With a strangled groan, he kissed her again, lost in a haze of desire.

He wasn't aware of any conscious movement but before he quite realized how it happened, they were in her bedroom.

She had left a lamp on in her room and it illuminated a wide bed covered in plump, luxurious pillows and a downy comforter in salmon and pale green. Like the rest of her house, this room was warm and comfortable, a haven from the stress and tension outside her doors.

Her room smelled like her, that subtle scent of jasmine and vanilla that made him think of warm, moonlit nights. He kissed her again just inside the door, intensely aware of the bed just a few steps away, how easy it would be to carry her there and do everything he had ever dreamed of, and more.

"I like the necking part of your dating strategy," she murmured against his mouth, sending heat shooting straight to his groin.

"I'm pretty crazy about it, too, right about now. A guy's got to go with what works."

He felt her smile against his skin and his heart swelled. He wasn't just crazy about the kissing. He was crazy about *her*.

"What comes next?" she asked. "I hope you're not going to tell me this is the part where you drop me off with a kiss at my door."

He loved this playful side of her, especially because he had the feeling she didn't show it to many people. He was about to answer when she pressed her mouth to the curve of his jaw and he had to lean against the door just to keep from falling over at her feet.

"Are you kidding?" he said hoarsely. "I don't think I could go anywhere right now, even if your house caught on fire."

"Good," she murmured. "I want you right here."

She pulled him closer and he surrendered to the heat and the hunger. He didn't know if she led him to the bed or if he guided them both there. He only knew he wanted to be closer to her.

He wanted everything.

Her mouth was warm, welcoming. He slid a hand to her skin just above the waistband of her jeans. She had the most incredibly soft skin and he couldn't seem to get enough.

He dragged his mouth away from hers and trailed kisses down her neck, pausing just above the first closed button of her shirt, just a breath away from the slope of her breast. He could hear the rapid beat of her heart as he cupped her through the material and she arched against his fingers. He pressed his mouth to the exposed skin as he worked a button free and she shivered.

He paused, surrounded by her softness and the delectable scent of her and tried to catch hold of his wildly scrambling thoughts. "Everything okay?"

"Yes. Oh, *yes*."

She kissed him fiercely and his fingers fumbled with the rest of her buttons like some stupid, awkward kid in the backseat of his dad's car.

She wore nothing beneath her shirt but skin, a discovery he found as surprising as it was incredibly sexy.

He didn't pull her shirt off, just unfastened it, then eased back so he could see her. He didn't think he had ever seen a more arousing sight than her soft, pale curves against the dark comforter.

"Touch me," she begged. "Please, Daniel."

The entreaty in her voice seemed to wake him from a dream, some hazy wonderland where reality didn't exist, just the joy and peace he found in her arms.

A few more moments and they would both be naked, bodies entwined as they tangled up her pretty bed. That's exactly where this was headed. He wanted it, she wanted it.

But he couldn't do it.

He swallowed and felt like he had just taken a mouthful of glass shards.

He should have told her long before now about her father and his. Though he wanted to make love to her as he had never wanted anything in his life—with a hot, heavy ache in his gut, with every iota of his heart, body and soul—he knew it would be wrong.

Before they took this most beautifully intimate of steps together, his damn conscience demanded he had to give her the truth, no matter how painful the consequences.

It was the right thing to do. The decent thing. But right now he had to admit he wouldn't mind having a little more ruthlessness and a whole lot less conscience.

It seemed a Herculean task but he slid his hand away

from her skin and rolled over on the bed, gazing up at the ceiling fixture.

"We can't do this, Lauren. We have to stop."

With her shirt undone and her breasts full and achy from his touch, Lauren gazed at him in the glow from her bedside lamp, baffled and disoriented.

Why had he stopped? Had she done something wrong? He was as aroused as she was. She could see it in the slight unfocused look to his eyes, in the rapid, ragged edge to his inhalations.

She sat up, pulling the edges of her shirt closed and wishing she could pull her composure around her so easily. She didn't exactly have a lot of experience with this sort of thing.

"Is this because of what I told you? About what happened to me in college? I swear, I'm absolutely fine in that department. No lingering hang-ups whatsoever. Daniel, I want you to make love to me." She gave a rueful smile and held up a hand. "Look, I'm trembling with it."

An odd, pained expression twitched across his features, and then he stood up. "I want you, too, Lauren. More than I have ever wanted anything in my life. More than I want to breathe. You are the sexiest, the most incredible woman I know."

He sighed. "This has nothing to do with what happened to you. Or not what happened to you in college, anyway. That you had to endure such a thing makes me furious and sad and sorry. But it doesn't make me want you any less."

"I'm sorry. I missed something here, then. We both

are obviously on the same page, so why did you stop? Are you worried about Rosa?"

He blinked as if he had forgotten all about her houseguest and the reason for his presence here.

"Not until you said that," he admitted. "That should tell you a little of what you do to me. I've never forgotten the job before. It's not Rosa. It's…there are things you should know before we take this any further."

He sighed and took her hand and a vague premonition curled through her. "Lauren, I care about you. The last thing in the world I want to do is hurt you."

Her hand trembled in his. "But?"

"Earlier tonight I tried to tell you something. Something important. You said you didn't want to hear it. And while I can understand your reluctance, I can't in good conscience kiss you like this, touch you, until you know the truth."

More than a little nervous now, she worked the last few buttons of her shirt, wondering what this was all about. "So tell me."

He sighed. "I can't do this in here. You and a bed are too potent a combination in my mind. Do you mind if we go back in the other room?"

She shrugged and walked out into the living area. The fire had burned down while they had been in the bedroom and Daniel paused to toss another log on and stir the coals. She had the feeling he was trying to find the right words, and her nervousness ratcheted up a level.

Finally he turned to face her, his beautiful features shuttered, and their intimate embrace seemed miles away.

"I read a quote somewhere once, something about

how the past lies upon the present like a giant's dead body. That's what I feel like right now, that I can't even move until I try to pry free of this heavy deadweight of the past."

She didn't have any idea what he was talking about, but she could see by the solemn set to his features that this was serious.

He sighed. "I need to tell you what happened five years ago, things you have every right to know before this goes any further. Once you have the information, you may very well decide you don't want to see me again. I hope to God that doesn't happen. But whatever you decide, I have no choice but to deal, just as I've had to live with the consequences of the wheels I set into motion."

Five years ago. She didn't have to do the math to know what he referred to and a grim unease started in her stomach and spread. "I assume this has something to do with my father, then."

"Everything." He let out a breath. "It has *everything* to do with R.J."

To her surprise, he sat down on the sofa beside her and took her hand, absently holding her fingers as he spoke. "I have to start the story with my own father. You said you remembered that he was always smiling. He was. My father was a good man—a great man—who came to this country with nothing but a dream of making a better life for his family. That might be a cliché but it was absolutely true for Roberto Galvez. He was the most humble, hardest-working man I've ever known. He could find the good in anyone, no matter how poorly they might have treated him."

"I always liked him," Lauren said. "I was sorry to hear he died."

His fingers tightened on hers. "He was killed the summer before I came back to Moose Springs. I think you were starting your residency. How much do you know about what happened to him?"

She frowned, trying to remember. Those had been hectic days and she had been two thousand miles away in Chicago. "Not much. It was some kind of accident, wasn't it?"

"Right. An *accident*." He turned the last word into something harsh and ugly.

"What happened?"

"He was killed on one of R.J.'s construction sites in Park City, when the substandard materials Maxwell Construction was in the habit of using to cut corners collapsed. He fell eight stories. He was conscious the whole time until he died an hour later on the way to the hospital."

Nausea churned in her stomach and she pressed a hand there. She had seen construction fall injuries during her E.R. rotation. She knew exactly what kind of excruciating pain Roberto Galvez must have endured in that last hour of his life.

"I'm so sorry," she said, the most inadequate words in the English language. Here was one more truth about her father she had been sheltered from, another illusion laid to rest.

"My mother was lost without him," Daniel went on. "She was already sick herself with the cancer and she just couldn't function. My brothers and Anna and I knew one of us would have to come home and stay with her. They were all still in college and I couldn't ask them to walk away from their educations. Since I already had my degree and was working as a cop in Salt Lake—something I could do anywhere, including Moose Springs—I decided to come home."

This was only the setup to whatever he wanted to tell her. She knew it, could feel the tension rolling off him as he continued holding her hand.

"I was so angry when I came back. I had a million reasons to hate R.J. already. I blamed him for my father's death, for the decades of substandard wages he paid him, for the subtle but pervasive humiliation he heaped on a man just trying to support his family."

He let out a breath. "Then Maxwell Construction used my father's illegal resident status to somehow wiggle out of paying my mother any kind of financial settlement for his wrongful death or even paying his pension. When they cut off her insurance benefits— a widow fighting breast cancer—my anger turned to rage."

Oh, she hated this. She wanted her daddy back, the man who sat her on his lap and read her stories, who loved to tickle her with his whiskers, who roasted marshmallows with her in the fireplace when the power went out. She didn't want to know how ruthless and amoral he had been in his business dealings.

"Anyone would be furious," she managed through a throat that felt raw and bruised. "What happened was wrong."

"I knew the score in Moose Springs. I always had. Your father called the shots in town and everybody jumped to do what he wanted. I came back home with one overriding goal, besides taking care of my mother. To bring your father down."

At last he pulled his hand away as he rose and stood by the fire. "I became obsessed with finding dirt on R.J. It sounds melodramatic now, five years later, but I spent every waking moment of my off-duty time digging through garbage. I followed paper trails, I studied budgets, I combed through his financial records, trying to find any dirt I could to bury him."

She folded her arms tightly, chilled despite the warm fire. "And you found it."

"You could say that. I worked around the clock trying to put the pieces together. It was all I cared about. I was consumed with it. All I could think about was vengeance. I wanted him to pay. No, I wanted to bleed him dry."

How could this man talking about her father in such a harsh way be the same man who had held her so sweetly just fifteen minutes before?

"I had to take everything I found to the county attorney. When they finally filed charges and I was able to arrest him, it was the greatest day of my life, like finding the Holy Grail, Eldorado and the lost city of Atlantis, all rolled into one."

That nausea churned again in her stomach at his words.

"I destroyed your father, Lauren. It was calculated and deliberate and driven by my thirst for revenge. I set out to bring him down any way I could and I succeeded beyond my wildest dreams."

He reached for her hand. "I was looking for financial irregularities. That's all. You have to believe me. I never expected the rest of it, about his bigamy and his other family. That only came out during questioning after he was arrested."

He paused and squeezed her trembling fingers. "And I certainly never expected things to end the way they did."

She slid her hand away and folded her fingers together. "You were on duty at the jail the day my father killed himself," she suddenly remembered out loud.

"Yeah. I was the deputy who found him."

She stared at him, this man she loved, as a horrible suspicion took root. She didn't want to believe it of him, but she felt as if her whole world had been turned upside down and she had to ask.

"Did you have anything to do with it?"

He reeled back as if she picked up the fireplace poker and shoved it into his gut. She saw shock and hurt cross his features—and then she saw something else. Guilt.

"Not directly," he finally said.

She rose, desperate for air, for space. "Directly or indirectly. What difference do semantics make?"

"You're right. Absolutely right." He sighed heavily. "I have lived with this for five years, Lauren, wondering what I might have done differently. Should I have guessed R.J. would take that way out after he was arrested? I don't know. I knew your father, both personally and from the profile I created while running the investigation. I worked for him for three summers and my dad was an employee of Maxwell Construction my whole life. I knew the kind of man R.J. was and how important his image, his standing, were to him around here."

Her father loved being addressed as Mayor, even of a little town like Moose Springs. He had loved being the most important man in town, the wealthiest, the most powerful.

"I never expected him to end things the way he did," Daniel went on slowly. "But in retrospect, I should have taken better precautions. Put him on suicide watch."

"I'm sure you didn't exactly cry over his grave."

"Believe it or not, I found no satisfaction that he killed himself. Absolutely none. I wanted a trial. A public venue where all his wrongdoings could be aired for the whole world to know."

She drew in a ragged breath. "You hated me so much? Hated my *mother* so much?"

"Of course not! You and your mother were innocent of everything. That was clear from the beginning and I was sorry you were hurt peripherally by everything. What choice did I have, though? Once I started to discover the magnitude of what your father had done, his years of corruption and greed, I had to follow through. I was an officer of the law, Lauren. I couldn't let him get away with it."

"Of course you couldn't."

She was suddenly exhausted, utterly wrung out. The emotional roller coaster of the evening had taken a grim turn and she wanted the hell off.

She rose, desperate for space and distance. "You were wrong. I didn't need to know this. I could have lived quite well the rest of my life without knowing that the man I'm...that I have feelings for is the same man who destroyed my family."

His features twisted with pain. "Lauren—"

"Good night, Daniel."

She walked to her bedroom and closed the door gently, though it took every ounce of self-control not to slam the thing over and over to vent some of this consuming pain.

She sank down onto the bed—the very same bed where he had just touched her, caressed her—and buried her face in her hands.

She heard the echo of the harsh words he had said. *I wanted him to pay. No, I wanted to bleed him dry.*

All these years, she had assumed correctly the awkwardness between her and Daniel had something to do with her father's sins. She just never imagined what was beneath it all.

Would her father's crimes haunt her for the rest of her life? She thought tonight when she was in Daniel's arms that she might just have a chance at happiness. Once more, like that imagery Daniel had used, the dead giant of the past was crushing her, smothering her, sucking any trace of joy from her present.

Daniel had been the one to shine a magnifying glass onto R.J.'s actions, the catalyst to everything that came after. If he hadn't come home motivated by vengeance, perhaps none of the rest of it would have happened.

She pressed a hand to her mouth to hold back the sob there. The man who had kissed her with such aching tenderness seemed a different individual from the hard-eyed stranger in her living room who had spoken of revenge and hatred.

Intellectually, she knew she couldn't really blame Daniel for her father's death and for the circumstances leading up to it. R.J. had made his own choices, had created his own destiny with his arrogance and his greed.

He couldn't honestly have thought he could get away with stealing so much money forever, it was only a matter of time—and a dogged investigator—before he would be caught.

R.J. had made his bed and lined it with stolen taxpayer funds. He had lied and cheated and stolen his way to a fortune. The sheer breadth of his wrongdoing still took her breath away.

Circumstances had put Daniel in the role of that investigator. She understood he had been doing his job. And if not him, it would have been someone else on the police force or an auditor somewhere or another elected official with sharp eyes.

But it had been Daniel. He had known, all these years, that he had set the wheels in motion that had crushed her mother and her. His investigation had resulted in her father's last, horribly selfish act—leaving them behind to face the shambles he had created.

Lauren curled up on her bed, hugging her arms tightly around herself. She had given her heart to the man who had destroyed her father and her family.

She couldn't snatch it back. It was entirely too late for that. She loved him and she couldn't just stuff all those feelings back into her subconscious now that they had been set free to soar through her.

She loved him. Now she just had to figure out how she could get past the brutal truth.

And how she could spend another day trapped in this house with him, pretending her heart wasn't broken.

Chapter 13

She finally fell into a restless sleep shortly before dawn. When she woke gritty-eyed and achy a few hours later, her first instinct was to cower in her bedroom all day, just drag the blankets over her head and hide away from the world.

Or at least from Daniel.

She knew she couldn't. She had a guest in her home, a young, frightened girl who needed her. Lauren knew she couldn't abandon her—for Rosa's sake, she would have to walk out there and face him, no matter how much she dreaded it.

She didn't know what she could possibly say to him. She wasn't angry with him. Somehow in the night, the worst of her betrayal had faded and she was left with only this deep sadness in her heart.

Most of all, she hated that five years after his suicide, her father's legacy was still tainting everything good and wonderful she wanted. She loved Daniel. Nothing had changed that.

She loved him and as she had tossed and turned the night before, her mind raced through their interactions the last few days and she was fairly certain she saw signs that he might care for her in return.

Could she move beyond his revelation? she wondered. Or every time she looked at his strong, beautiful features, would she see his hunger for vengeance and the chain reaction of calamities it had wrought in her life?

She didn't know. She hated thinking about him toiling away, digging through her family's dirty laundry, and wondering at all the soiled linens he might have uncovered there

She was quite sure she still didn't know the full story of all that her father had done. She didn't really *want* to know, but she hated thinking Daniel might have all that information.

Lauren pushed the blankets away. She wasn't a coward. She never would have survived the rigors of med school and a grueling residency if she had been. She was strong enough to walk out there and pretend all was fine, even though she hated knowing she and Daniel would return to the tension that had marked their relationship before these last few days.

She took a long, hot shower and spent longer than usual getting dressed, driven to take extra pains with her hair and makeup as armor against the day and the awkwardness she knew waited for her.

Even with blush and more eye makeup than usual,

she still looked haggard and worn-out, but at least her hair looked good, falling in soft waves around her face.

She supposed a girl had to take what she could get.

Filling her lungs with a deep, cleansing breath, she pushed open her bedroom door and prepared to spend the day with a polite smile stuck to her face, as if she had taken a staple gun to it.

She followed the low murmur of voices and found Rosa in the kitchen talking comfortably in Spanish to another woman, with Daniel nowhere in sight.

Rosa smiled a welcome when she saw her, as did Teresa Hendricks, the only female deputy in the sheriff's office.

"Hi, Teresa," Lauren said. "This is a surprise."

"Morning." Teresa gave her wide, friendly smile that made everyone trust her, good guys and bad guys alike. "The sheriff had some business in the office that couldn't wait and asked me to come spell him for the morning. He should be back this afternoon. Hope you don't mind that I grabbed some cocoa out of the cupboard. You've got quite a collection."

"I…no. Of course not. Do you want coffee?"

"No. Cocoa will do me. I'm a bit of a fanatic, too."

That was Lauren. The crazy doctor who self-medicated with chocolate to heal all wounds.

She had a feeling she better stock up in the coming months.

She forced a smile for Teresa and joined them at the table. "So how are you? How are John and the kids?"

"Great. Just great. They keep me running every minute."

Lauren treated Teresa's two children at her clinic. They were great kids—Casey was ten and Mia was twelve and Lauren had been their primary care physician since she moved here five years earlier.

Envious of Teresa's fluency with the language, Lauren hauled out her halting Spanish to ask Rosa how she was feeling. She didn't need to hear the girl's answer to see that every day she seemed better.

Something was different about her today. Her bruises were fading, but that was only part of the conversion in her. Lauren tilted her head, studying the girl. There was a new light in her eyes, something that hadn't been there before.

Hope, Lauren realized with a little catch in her throat. Rosa no longer wore that lost, disillusioned look in her eyes. For the first time since Rosa opened her eyes in the bed of Dale Richins's pickup truck, she looked as if she was happy to be alive, as if she believed in a future.

She had a long, arduous journey ahead of her, Lauren knew. But she was on her way, and that was the important thing.

Rosa chattered something to Teresa and the deputy answered just as quickly.

"How did you learn Spanish so well?" Lauren asked.

"I spent a couple years in Guatemala on a church mission. I've lost a lot over the last fifteen years but I practice whenever I can."

Rosa said something and Teresa answered her and the two of them chattered away in Spanish for a moment, with Lauren catching one or two words in every sentence.

Though after several days, Rosa seemed comfortable talking to Daniel, Lauren had never seen her talk to him with such animation. She talked to Lauren, but always with Daniel as a go-between.

She must have been desperately missing the freedom of having another woman to converse with, Lauren realized. Had Daniel picked Teresa as his replacement for just that reason? she wondered. Because he wanted Rosa to have Spanish-speaking company to talk to?

"Sorry," Teresa said, making a rueful face after a moment. "Didn't mean to exclude you."

"Not a problem." She smiled. "To be honest, I'm glad you're here to talk to her. I'm sure she's frustrated with having to repeat everything she says to me a hundred times before I get it, or use Daniel as a translator."

With the deputy there and Rosa in such good hands, she could escape the confines of the house for a moment.

The thought whispered through her mind and suddenly she was desperate for a little air and to see something besides her own walls. "In fact, I have some paperwork at the clinic that I've put off longer than I should have. If you don't think it's unforgivably rude for me to leave, I would love the chance to run down there for an hour or so and try to gather some things to work on here at home tonight."

"No problem." Teresa smiled. "We'll just stay here and have a good visit while we dig into your hot chocolate stash."

"*Mi* cocoa *su* cocoa," Lauren said with a smile.

She grabbed a coat out of the closet and found her keys. Fifteen minutes later, she felt like a prisoner out on work release as she pulled her Volvo into the parking lot of the clinic. She paid a high school student to shovel off her parking lot every time it snowed. Brandon Tanner had a pickup with a plow on the front and took the job seriously, never missing a storm.

Lauren walked through the cleared parking lot and unlocked the door to her clinic. She was here often alone by herself. Usually it didn't bother her, but today the emptiness of it seemed to echo, giving her the creeps.

That's what happened when she was surrounded by people for three days. Rosa and Daniel had been a constant presence and she was just having a tough time adjusting to solitude.

Still, she shivered and headed straight for the thermostat. She had turned it down before she left three days earlier, keeping the temperature just warm enough to keep the water pipes from freezing, but certainly not a comfortable level for anyone but a penguin.

She turned it up, then walked to her office at the end of the hallway.

She was proud of what she had done here. She ran an efficient, effective operation. Though she still had her detractors, many more people in the community trusted her than didn't. She treated their grandchildren, their grandparents, and everyone in between.

She was good at her job and she loved her patients, something most big-city physicians couldn't understand. She was invested in their lives, in their health.

When Karen Elliot's cholesterol level dipped twenty points from her new exercise regimen, Lauren rejoiced as much as she did. When Dallas and Sara Fitzgerald's baby overcame a rough start as a two-pound preemie and learned to walk by eleven months, Lauren had been the first one standing in line to cheer her on.

She worried about them, she grieved with them, she celebrated with them.

This was her town. Her life. She loved it here, warts and all.

If not for her father's actions, she would have missed this. She stared at the closed door of her office, startled by the realization. Before R.J.'s arrest, Lauren had been fielding offers from medical facilities across the U.S. She had most seriously been considering an attending position at the Chicago hospital where she finished her residency.

After her father's suicide and all the horrible revelations began to jumble up one after the other, she had pulled her name from consideration. She had known she must return to Moose Springs. As she had told Daniel, she felt a huge obligation to the people of this community who had, in effect, paid for her education by default.

She had come home to help her mother try to pick up the pieces of their shattered world and face down the stares and whispers. In the process, Lauren had begun to build this clinic. She had created something good here—something that might not have existed if not for the chain reaction Daniel had started in his quest for vengeance.

Daniel. She was still going to have to face him at some point. Could they find their way past the rubble of their shared history?

She shook off the depression suddenly settling over her shoulders and pushed open her office door. Her voice-mail light was flashing. Big surprise there. The rest of the world didn't stand still just because she took a few days off.

She keyed through the lengthy list of missed calls on the caller ID menu. Only twelve missed calls—and six of those were from Kendall Fox. She sighed. The man didn't seem to understand the concept of rejection.

She turned on her computer to print out some files and was just about to hit the playback messages button on her phone when it rang, sounding abnormally loud in the empty clinic.

She intended to let it ring, since she absolutely didn't want to talk to a drug company salesman or an insurance rep right now. But out of curiosity, she checked the caller ID and groaned when she saw Kendall's name and mobile number.

This was ridiculous. She thought she had made her feelings clear the other day at the hospital, but apparently she would have to come down harder.

"Hello?"

There was a brief pause, as if he hadn't quite expected her to answer. "Lauren! I've been trying to reach you for days."

"I've been off. I just came into the office to catch up on some paperwork and saw that you had called."

"Only a half-dozen times. I would have called your home or cell but I couldn't seem to track down those numbers. Can it really be possible that I have failed to get the personal contact numbers of the most gorgeous doctor with privileges at my hospital?"

If she weren't so tired, she could no doubt come up with some brilliantly concise reply that would discourage him once and for all without being rude. But with her brain sluggish and slow, nothing came to mind.

"You found me now. What did you need?"

"Aren't you even going to ask me how the Sundance after-party went?"

"How did it go?" she asked automatically, hoping her complete disinterest didn't filter through her voice.

"Miserable. I was lonely and bored and missed you every second."

Which meant he probably had only one girl on each arm.

"Listen," he went on, "since you've been bragging about the cross-country skiing in your little cow patch, I decided to come up this way and see what you're talking about. I'm just outside town now. I figured I could take you to lunch, then you could show me the trails you're always talking about. What do you say?"

Just what she needed, for Kendall to show up and complicate everything.

She sighed. Last week, she turned him down because she wasn't interested in a flirtation with a co-worker. After the last few days spent with Daniel, she knew she could never go out with Dr. Fox, charming though he might be.

How could she even look at another man? She loved Daniel Galvez with all her heart.

"I didn't realize it was within my power to completely wow you into speechlessness."

Heat rose in her cheeks as she realized she had been woolgathering about Daniel instead of responding to Kendall's lunch invitation.

"Sorry. It's been a…strange few days. I'm afraid my mind is running in a hundred different directions. I'm sorry, but today isn't a good day for me."

"Are you saying that because you don't want to go with me or because it really isn't a good day?"

She thought of Rosa at home and the FBI agents who would be on their way to take her with them in a few hours. She should be there with her, she realized, and was ashamed of herself for taking a coward's way out and escaping to the office.

"It's not a good day."

"But if it were, you still wouldn't go, would you?"

She sighed. "I would have no problem showing you the ski trails around here, Kendall. And lunch would probably be fine, as long as you don't consider it a date."

"And if I did?"

"Then I would tell you no. It's nothing personal, I promise. I have the greatest respect for you as a doctor and I enjoy your company, but I just have a strict policy about not hooking up with other doctors I work with. I've had a few bad experiences where things became messy and it's easier all around to keep those parts of my life separate."

She paused. "And to be honest, I'm involved with someone right now,"

It wasn't precisely a lie. Her heart was involved with Daniel, even if they had yet to even go on an actual date.

"Let me guess. The big, bad cow-patch sheriff."

She blinked. Were her feelings that obvious? "I... why would you say that?"

"I don't know. A vibe I caught between you two. Am I right?"

She didn't know how to answer that. After a moment, he gave a short laugh. "I'm right. If you ever get tired of the tough jock type, you know where to find me."

"I'll keep that in mind."

"Hey, speaking of the sheriff, what was the deal with that girl we treated last week? I meant to stop by and see how she was doing, but she had more security around her room than a movie star hiding out from the paparazzi. Next I know, she was released. Any word on how she's doing?"

"She and her baby are both fine," Lauren answered. "She's an amazingly resilient young woman."

There was an odd pause on the line and she thought for a moment his cell call had dropped, before he spoke again. "She had some great doctors. Especially the extraordinarily talented one she had in the E.R."

"I'm sure that has had a great deal to do with her rapid recovery," Lauren said dryly.

He laughed, though it sounded oddly strained. "Well, since I'm already in town, the least you can do is tell me how to get to the ski trail you're always talking about."

"Right." She gave him directions to the trailhead for an easy-to-moderate groomed trail that led past pine and aspen to a frozen waterfall.

"You can just ski there from your house?"

"Right. I'm just a quarter mile down the road," she said absently. "The last house before you get to the trailhead."

"Good to know. Thanks."

He seemed in a hurry to hang up after obtaining the directions.

After she said goodbye and disconnected the call, she spent a fruitless twenty minutes answering email and trying to finish her paperwork. When she realized she had been staring at the same computer screen for ten minutes, she finally gave up, gathering the papers she needed and stuffed them in her briefcase.

She didn't want to be here, she wanted to be home with Daniel and Rosa. The irony didn't escape her—for three days she had balked at being stuck in her house, had felt trapped and isolated and restless, but now she didn't want to be anywhere else.

Would Daniel be back at her house yet? she wondered. And if he had returned, was she ready to face him?

Yes. The knowledge washed through her, warm and sure. She loved him. She loved his laugh, she loved his strength, she loved the deep sense of honor that had compelled him to tell her something painful at a time when any other man would have ignored his conscience and taken what he wanted and she had been more than willing to give.

That he had started the investigation that destroyed her father didn't matter. She sat up in her office chair, staring unseeing at the sage walls. She loved him. He was a loving son who had been grieving for his father and angry at the mistreatment of his mother. She couldn't blame him for wanting vengeance.

Daniel may have been the catalyst to the finale, but R.J. had been completely responsible for his own downfall.

She thought of the heat of Daniel's kiss, the tenderness of his touch, his kindness with Rosa. That was the man she loved.

She wanted what they had started the night before. No, she wanted more. With a deep, fierce ache, she wanted to see him, to tell him she was sorry for her reaction the night before and the cold words she had uttered.

Despite the anticipation spiraling through her at seeing him again and trying to make things right between them, she couldn't seem to shake a vague sense of unease as she climbed into her Volvo and headed back to her house. She couldn't quite put a finger on it, but something niggled at her, some dissonant tone to the music of her morning.

She was just tired, she assured herself as she neared her house. Exhaustion from her sleepless night was playing tricks on her.

All seemed quiet at her house as she pulled into the driveway. Smoke curled up from the chimney and sunlight glittered off the fresh snow. When she opened the garage door, she saw Daniel hadn't returned. Teresa Hendricks's personal SUV was still parked in the second bay.

She walked into the house and her unease ratcheted up a notch. Something wasn't right. The television was playing in the family room, but neither Rosa nor Teresa were anywhere in sight.

"Teresa? Rosa? Hello?" No one answered.

"Hello?" she called again, only to be met by more silence.

She grabbed her cell phone out of her coat pocket and punched 911. Just as she moved her thumb to hit the send button on her way to check Rosa's bedroom, she heard a low, anguished moan.

Warily, her heart pumping with thick urgency, she followed the sound to the entryway, then shock sucked the air from her lungs at what she found there.

Chapter 14

Daniel perused the duty roster for the week, his second-in-command across the desk.

With a department of only eight full-time officers, including himself, sometimes personnel issues and making sure everybody's schedules worked for the slot they were assigned was his biggest challenge.

"I still don't know what we're going to do about tomorrow night." Kurt Banning shook his head. "I've juggled and juggled but no matter how we shake it, we're still short a deputy and we're completely maxed out on overtime this month."

"Davis and McKinnon said they're coming for our witness this afternoon. That should free me up from guard duty so you can add me back on to the rotation. I can handle the graveyard shift tonight and a double shift tomorrow."

"You sure about that? Maybe you ought to take a few days off after your tough ordeal of sitting around Lauren's place all day drinking tea and watching movies."

"Ha ha. You're hilarious, Banning."

"So they tell me." His lieutenant and good friend grinned. Banning had given him a hard time today about his "easy" guard duty at Lauren's place. They probably would have a tough time believing he would rather have been out in the middle of a blizzard directing traffic than enduring more time in Lauren's company, knowing she despised him now.

"Just put me on the schedule. I don't mind the extra hours."

"Will do. So the feds are coming for the girl today, you said?"

"Right. In a few hours. They're moving her to a safe house in the city so they can start prepping her for grand jury testimony."

The deputy shook his head. "Hell of a case to fall into our lap, wasn't it? My heart just breaks for that little girl and for the others who came over the border with her."

"She's had a tough time of it, but she's hanging in. Tell me what's been going on with the Cole case."

They spent a few more moments discussing progress in some ongoing investigations and were just starting to wrap things up when they heard a shout from outside.

"Sheriff! You need to get in here now!" Peggy yelled from the dispatch desk.

He and Banning shared one quick look and his lieutenant's expression mirrored his own shock. Peggy had been dispatching for thirty years and she never lost her cool. The urgency in her voice moved them both to action and they rushed from the office.

She had put the 911 call on the speaker and his gut tightened with raw fear when he instantly recognized Lauren's voice.

"I need an air ambulance immediately at my house, Peggy. Officer down. Deputy Hendricks has been shot in the stomach. She's bleeding heavily and drifting in and out of consciousness. I need the local paramedics here with oxygen but call LifeFlight first and get them in the air."

"I'm on it."

"Where's Daniel?"

He rushed forward and picked up the mike. "I'm here, Lauren. Are you hurt? Where's Rosa?"

"I'm fine. I don't *know* where Rosa is."

Though he could tell she was trying her best to stay in control, he could hear the anguished panic filter through her voice and it ripped him apart. "I went to the clinic for a while. I was only gone maybe an hour. I just walked in the door and found Teresa on the floor and no sign of Rosa. I think they've got her. Please hurry."

"I'm on my way, sweetheart. Hang on."

He rushed for the door, strapping on his weapon and yelling orders as he went for Banning to let the FBI know, mobilize all deputies and call the county sheriff for reinforcements.

"We need to establish a search perimeter and block off all exits into and out of town. I don't know who we're looking for or how many suspects, but whoever it is, they're armed and dangerous. Do whatever it takes to protect yourselves and the girl."

Sick with worry and guilt, he rushed to Lauren's

house with his lights and sirens blaring. How the hell could this have happened? He should never have left her house. Skulking away that morning before she woke had been an act of cowardice, borne from a selfish wish to avoid seeing the disgust in her eyes.

As a result, a damn good deputy was injured and Rosa was missing and he didn't know how he would ever live with himself.

For the second time in his life, he had let his own emotions stand in the way of the job.

Put it away, he ordered himself. There would be time for recriminations and blame-slinging later. Now he needed to focus on the situation, on Rosa and Teresa.

He covered the distance between the sheriff's office and her house in record time and jerked his Tahoe to a stop in the driveway. Inside, he found Teresa on the floor of the entryway, with Lauren applying a pressure bandage to her blood-soaked abdomen.

She looked up at him with vast relief. "Daniel!"

"How is she?"

"Stable, for now, but she's losing blood fast. Peggy says LifeFlight is on its way. Our volunteer medics should be bringing oxygen."

Teresa blinked her eyes open when she saw him and struggled to sit up, but Lauren held her fast.

"Sheriff," Teresa mumbled, her eyes glazed. "Sorry. So sorry."

He had a narrow window of opportunity to obtain as much information as he could. Though his instinct was to let her rest and conserve her energy, he had to push. "What happened? Where's Rosa?"

Teresa groaned. "Don't know. She was in the bathroom when the doorbell rang. I told her to stay put there. Lock the door. Through the peephole, I saw a blond guy, looked familiar. Five-ten, five-eleven, maybe. Red SUV in driveway."

She coughed a little and Lauren changed compresses. His gut clenched and he thought of Teresa's two kids and John, her husband. If she didn't make it through this, he would never forgive himself.

"I shouldn't have answered the door," Teresa mumbled. "Rookie mistake. Knew better. Guy asked for Lauren. Said he was a friend. She's not here, I tell him. He says he'll wait and pushes his way inside. Next I know, he's got a weapon out, tells me not to move. Asks me where the girl is. I played dumb, just like we talked about, but he wasn't fooled. Knew she was there, he said. Told me to get her. I tried to draw my weapon, then he…shot me. Everything after that's blurry."

"Did he find Rosa?"

"I don't know, Sheriff. I don't remember. I heard him looking, tearing through the house, but then…the pain. I passed out."

Before he could ask her any more questions, the volunteer paramedics arrived, bringing oxygen and equipment.

Daniel forced himself to step back and let them do their job. His deputy was in good hands. Lauren would do everything possible for her here and that high level of care would continue after the chopper airlifted her to the University of Utah.

He needed to focus on finding Rosa. He headed to the bathroom. According to Teresa, Rosa had been there when everything went down.

The bathroom door had been kicked in, he saw immediately, careful not to disturb any forensics.

That matched Teresa's story. She said she told Rosa to lock the door. The perp would have checked every door, found this one locked and probably known immediately this was where he would find his prey.

Daniel looked around, then his gaze caught on something discordant. The hamper had been moved. He had showered in this bathroom for three days and he absolutely remembered it being against the other wall.

Now it was shoved in an awkward spot by the toilet—and directly under the small, high window.

His heart kicked up a pace as a small glimmer of hope shot through him. Rosa could fit through that window. She was petite, even with her pregnancy. If she heard a gunshot, would she have cowered in here like a frightened rabbit or would she have tried to run? He had to believe the latter. She had already proved her courage and strength. He couldn't imagine her just waiting in here for her fate.

He was convinced when CSU dusted the windowsill, they would find Rosa's prints there. It didn't mean she had escaped, he reminded himself. The shooter easily could have figured out the same thing and followed her. But at least it was something to hang on to.

The hot spurt of adrenaline in treating a trauma victim, especially one she knew and cared about, sustained Lauren through the next fifteen minutes as the air medics arrived and were briefed on Teresa's condition.

She stood back and watched them load the litter into the waiting helicopter for the short flight to the city.

"You riding along, Dr. Maxwell?" Jolie Carr, the flight nurse, asked her.

She thought seriously about it for maybe half a second, then shook her head. "Her condition is stable. You have things under control for the fifteen-minute flight and I know you don't need the extra weight. Since we have a possible kidnap victim out there somewhere, I'd better stick close just in case I'm needed here."

Jolie nodded and strapped down the gurney. "Understandable. We'll take care of her."

"I know you will. Have the attending at the trauma center page me if there are any questions."

"Will do."

She climbed in and closed the door behind her. Lauren stepped back and watched the chopper lift off, swirling the powdery snow in a cloud as it rose into the air.

She pulled her sweater closer around her, chilled to the bone by more than just the temperature and the chopper's vortex. She had done all she could for Teresa. Now she could only trust in the University of Utah trauma team and pray.

She blew out a breath and returned to her house, which bustled with activity. Cops and emergency workers from every nearby jurisdiction had already descended with remarkable speed.

Inside, she saw Daniel giving orders to several other men. He towered over them and even from here she could feel the air of command radiating off him.

When she looked beneath the surface, she had to close her eyes and whisper another prayer, this one for him. Under the layer of control and authority, she could just catch a glimpse of something else, something raw and dark, almost tortured.

Since she returned to town and opened her clinic,

she had seen Daniel in action in all kinds of tough circumstances. Bad car accidents, mine rescues, ugly domestic disputes. No matter what the situation, he always seemed to have an air of quiet competence about him. He was a deep pool of calm in a troubled sea.

Right now, despite his thin veneer of control, he looked adrift.

When he seemed to finish talking to the others and they left for their respective duties, she walked to him on impulse and laid a hand on his arm.

His dark eyes seared into hers with a raw emotion and her chest ached with the urge to wrap her arms around his waist and never let go.

"I think she's going to be okay, Daniel. She's tough and help arrived not long after it happened. That's a big plus in her favor."

If she hadn't followed impulse and returned to the house when she did, she feared Teresa would have bled to death right in her entryway, but she didn't tell Daniel that. His eyes burned with too much guilt already.

"This is my fault. I should have been here."

"Then you would have been the one with a bullet in your gut," she pointed out.

"I don't have two kids who need their mother." The anguish in his voice destroyed her. She squeezed his arm again.

"I think she's going to be okay," she repeated. "We just have to wait and see, but she's young and strong and has the thought of those kids to help her hang in."

He nodded, and she thought her words penetrated.

"Any sign of Rosa?" Lauren asked.

"There's a chance she may have gone out the bathroom window." He paused. "You saw her this morning, didn't you? Do you remember what she was wearing?"

She tried to picture Teresa and Rosa as they chattered around the kitchen table. "Jeans and a sweatshirt. The yellow one."

"What about shoes? I bought her a pair when I picked up the other stuff, but she hasn't worn them except that first day I brought her here."

Lauren shook her head. "I can't say. I didn't notice her feet this morning. I hope so. I hate to think of her out on the run somewhere in the snow with no shoes."

"Sure as hell beats the alternative," he said grimly.

She shivered. "You're right. You're absolutely right."

"If she's out there, we'll find her, Lauren."

"I know you will."

She paused, her mind racing with a hundred things she wanted to say to him. This wasn't the time for any of them. "Be careful," she murmured instead.

He nodded absently but before he could answer, Kurt Banning hurried over to them. "Sheriff, we think we may have something. Joe Pacheco, a mile or so down the road, called Peggy to report some movement in his horse barn. He thought he saw someone sneaking in there. He thought it might be a kid, by the size, but he thought with all the activity down this way, he should let us know."

"If it is Rosa, she's probably terrified out of her mind. We can't just run in there with guns blazing. She doesn't know who the good guys and who the bad guys are here."

"She knows you," Lauren said. "She won't be frightened if she sees you."

"You're right. Kurt, take charge here. I'll take a couple of the county deputies and see if we can roust her out. Lauren, she may need treatment for frostbite and exposure, especially if she ran a mile through the snow without shoes."

"Right. I'll go back to the clinic and meet you there."

He hurried away, that brief glimpse of emotion shielded now. All she could see was a tough, determined male. He would find Rosa, she assured herself. If anyone could bring her back, it was Daniel.

Her car was hemmed in by rescue vehicles so one of the deputies rushed her to the clinic before hurrying off to the roadblocks at the routes leading out of town.

She unlocked the doors and headed immediately to her treatment room to begin prepping it with any items she could think of that might be needed to treat someone with possible exposure.

She was putting clean blankets in the clinic's small warming unit and wishing for one of her nurses to help her with some of these details when she thought she heard the outside door opening.

That was fast, she thought. Amazingly fast! Such speed had to be a good sign, didn't it?

"Daniel?" she called. "I'm in the treatment room. Bring her straight back here."

No one answered, and she frowned. Had she been hearing things? She turned away from the warmer to investigate, then gasped and stumbled backward, just managing to stop before she burned herself.

To her shock, Kendall Fox loomed in the doorway, but this was a far different man than the polished charmer who flirted with every nurse in the hospital. His hair was messy, his clothes disordered, and he looked savagely furious.

Her heartbeat kicked up a notch. "Kendall!" she exclaimed. "What are you doing here?"

Even as she asked the question, somehow she knew. It wasn't possible, it couldn't be, but she couldn't come up with any other explanation.

Her mind raced, trying to piece together a puzzle that made no sense. Teresa had reported her shooter was a blond white male about five-ten, which described Dr. Fox perfectly.

"Where is she?" he demanded.

She played for time. "Who?"

"You know," he growled. "The stupid little bitch who is ruining my life. Where is she?"

Panic sputtered through her and her eyes darted around the room, frantically looking for some kind of weapon. Warm blankets wouldn't exactly cause lasting harm, she was afraid, and any sharp medical implements were wrapped in sterile packaging.

She had a feeling Kendall wouldn't sit patiently and wait while she peeled back the plastic on a surgical kit for something sharp.

Think, she ordered herself, but she couldn't focus on anything but her shock and fear.

"I don't know what you're talking about," she finally said.

"Don't play stupid. You suck at it. You know. The girl you've got staying at your house. If I'd had any idea she was one of ours the night you brought her in, you can bet she wouldn't have made it out of the E.R."

Icy cold blossomed in her stomach. "You don't mean

that," she said, sickened at the blunt claim, especially delivered in such a cold, emotionless voice.

"Don't I? No way am I going to let her testify to some frigging grand jury and destroy everything."

This couldn't be happening. She knew Kendall. She had talked with him—even laughed with him—just a few hours before. Could she really have been so blind as to have missed the darkness skulking inside him?

One of ours, he had said, and the implication behind the words sickened her further.

"You're the fifth man in the smuggling ring."

"I'm not the fifth anything. I'm number one, baby. The whole thing was my idea. You would not believe the kind of money a few stupid whores have put in my pockets."

"They're not whores, they're children! Young girls who had no choice about the things they were forced to do! What you've done is obscene. Despicable."

Rage spasmed over his features and he stepped closer. She had nowhere else to go, with the blanket warmer at her back. "Don't sit in judgment of me, Dr. Self-Righteous. I didn't have a rich, crooked daddy to put me through med school. I had debts. Big ones. I had to do something."

"By kidnapping girls and forcing them into prostitution? How does a med student go from the Hippocratic oath to peddling human flesh?"

"I'm not some kind of monster!"

Could he honestly think what he had done was anything *but* hideously monstrous?

"I went to med school in San Diego and my last year I started working a clinic over the border," Kendall said. "It was a legitimate job. But then I got the brilliant idea to make a little money on the side. I started packing a few things back over each trip I crossed the border. Prescription drugs, Ruffies, that kind of thing. After a while, I thought, why not people? And here we are."

She let out a breath. "Here we are. You've now moved from drug smuggling to kidnapping, enforced prostitution and attempted murder. Nice career move, Dr. Fox."

"Shut up," he snarled. "You don't know anything about this."

"You're the one who sent Gilberto Mata to Rosa's room at the hospital, aren't you? I wondered how he knew where to find her."

"What the hell else was I supposed to do? She was going to ruin everything. She said she was going to go to the police and tell them everything she knew. We couldn't just leave her running loose to flap her gums to anyone who would listen. We were screwed. Gilberto said he could take care of things. My only mistake was in trusting him."

"How did you figure out she was here in Moose Springs?"

"Lucky guess. I saw the way you hovered over her at the hospital. I figured you would at least know where they took her after she was released, all I had to do was charm it out of you. I never imagined she was in your own house until you told me."

She closed her eyes, sick to think she had led him right to Rosa. She had to find some comfort that Rosa was safe from him for now, or he wouldn't be here looking for her.

She, on the other hand, was in serious trouble. So

far he hadn't pulled out any kind of weapon, but she knew he must have one, the same weapon he had used to shoot Teresa. He wouldn't be telling her this if he had any intention of leaving her alive here.

She didn't want to die. She needed to get through this, if only to tell Daniel she didn't blame him for her father's sins, that she knew and understood he had done nothing wrong during his investigation of her father.

That she loved him.

She wanted a future—a future with Daniel, if he would give her a chance.

If she could somehow reverse their positions slightly, she might be able to pull the instrument tray behind her to give her enough time to escape. It was a long shot, but she had to do something. She refused to stand here and accept the fate he intended for her.

She shifted slightly, edging in a barely perceptible half circle. "How many girls are we talking about here?" she asked to distract him.

He shrugged. "Enough. We have two houses in Utah, but the real money is in Vegas and Phoenix."

She slid a little more to the left. She started to reach behind her for the instrument tray when she heard the outside door open.

"Lauren?" Daniel's voice called. She and Kendall gazed at each other for half a second, then she opened her mouth to call a warning. Before the words could escape, Kendall moved fast, grabbing her in a choke hold and shoving his hand over her mouth.

Here was the gun, she realized wildly as he pulled it out of his pocket and held it to her head. "Not a word," he hissed. "Or your sheriff is going to have a nice gunshot wound to the chest."

She choked back her tiny sound of distress, fear a hard, vicious ball in her gut. Her brain felt numb, sluggish with sudden dread.

She couldn't bear the idea of something happening to Daniel. If he walked through that door, she had no doubt Kendall would shoot him, just as he had shot Teresa.

She had to protect him. She *had* to, no matter what the cost.

Kendall eased them both behind the door and she felt the slick cold metal pressed against the skin at her temple.

She had one chance only. With a prayer for courage, she drew in a deep breath, then clamped her teeth as hard as she could on the flesh of his palm.

As she hoped, he instinctively moved his hand away, just far away for her to yell, "He's got a gun!"

"You stupid bitch," Kendall growled. He backhanded her exactly where her stitches were from the attack by Gilberto Mata, striking her so hard she whipped back and struck the wall.

For a moment, she was light-headed as pain exploded in her head and cheek. She reeled, her knees suddenly weak, and started to slide to the floor. He grabbed her before she could hit the ground and yanked her in front of him, the gun again at her temple, just as Daniel crashed through the door.

Chapter 15

A smart cop doesn't just run headlong into a room when somebody yells *gun*.

He takes a minute to case the situation, to call for backup, to devise a strategy.

Daniel knew all that, but he didn't give a damn. All he could focus on was the hoarse panic in Lauren's voice and the tiny yelp of pain he heard her utter right after her warning.

Before he had time to even wonder what the threat might be on the other side, he whipped out his weapon and plowed through the door.

What he found was worse than anything he might have imagined. A man had her in a choke hold and had jammed a big, ugly black Glock against her temple.

"Stop right there, Sheriff," the bastard holding her yelled, like something out of a bad Western. It took him only an instant to recognize the smarmy doctor from the emergency room who had been hitting on Lauren the night they took Rosa in, then a few days later in the hospital lobby.

Fox. Kendall Fox.

His mind registered a dozen things simultaneously—among them that she looked dazed, her eyes blurry with pain, and a tiny trickle of blood seeped from the bandage on her cheek.

He died a thousand deaths wondering what Fox might have done to her—and trying to figure out his own next move.

The bastard had already shot one cop. He had to be the one who had wounded Teresa. If Daniel played this wrong, he knew Fox wouldn't hesitate to shoot him, too, and then where would Lauren be?

And Rosa. Damn it all to hell. He should have at least taken the time to make sure she was safe before rushing in here.

"Let's all just take it easy." Daniel infused his voice with every ounce of calm he could muster, not an easy task when he wanted to rip the son of a bitch apart with his bare hands for hurting Lauren.

Fox was sweating, he saw, and the gun in his hand trembled ever so slightly against her head. "Shut up," he barked. "Just shut the hell up and drop your weapon or I'm going to shoot her."

This was the part where a good negotiator would placate the suspect, earn his trust, establish some sort of rapport. Daniel just couldn't do it. Not when Lauren was in danger.

"You hurt her more than you already have and you can be damn sure you won't take another breath," he promised, in that same calm, controlled voice he had to hope cloaked his gut-wrenching fear.

The doctor's hand trembled a little more on the weapon while Daniel forced his own hand to remain perfectly still.

Fox looked trapped, his eyes darting wildly around the room like some kind of wild creature looking for a convenient hole to slink into. It was obvious he was searching for any kind of escape from the mess he had created.

Daniel just had to make sure his way out didn't involve any more harm to Lauren.

He took his eyes off the suspect for half a second, just long enough to reassure himself that she was all right. She still seemed dazed and he saw fear in her eyes. But when she met his gaze, they brimmed with a deep reservoir of trust that humbled him.

"All I want is the little *puta*," Fox growled. "Where is she?"

He assumed the bastard meant Rosa. "I don't know. We haven't found her," he lied. No way in hell was he going to tell the man she was out in his vehicle wrapped in blankets with the heater going full blast.

Daniel had only come in first to make sure Lauren had an exam room ready before he carried Rosa inside to be treated for her mild hypothermia. Now he could only be grateful to whatever instinct had compelled him to leave her in the vehicle.

She was far from safe, though. He knew the dangers. He would rather she were miles away in the FBI safe house with Cale Davis and Gage McKinnon.

Heavy pressure dug into his lungs, the onus of

knowing he had to protect two women. He couldn't mess this up.

Fox hissed a pungent oath. "I don't believe you."

Daniel shrugged. "Believe what you want. She's not here. Who knows? She could be halfway to Juarez by now. It's just the three of us. Now why don't you let Lauren go so you and I can figure out a way to work this out. I know you don't want to hurt her."

His arm tightened around her throat and he dug the gun into her temple harder. Daniel's gut clenched. He could see the desperation in Fox's eyes, the grim realization of what he had done already and the implications of those actions.

He had shot a deputy sheriff. He had to be feeling any chance at a future that didn't involve serious prison time slipping away.

"This wasn't supposed to happen. This whole thing has been screwed up from the minute we brought that little bitch over the border. It's all her fault everything is falling apart."

Daniel hitched in a breath as he saw that Glock quiver again. The man was as twitchy as a polecat bedded down with a rattlesnake.

"Look—" he kept his voice slow, even "—let Lauren go and you and I can talk about this. I'm sure if we put our heads together we can figure out what to do from here. She doesn't need to be in the middle of this. I know you don't want to hurt her."

His arm clenched around her throat. Any tighter and he would be cutting off her air supply, Daniel feared.

"Here's a better idea. Drop your weapon nice and slow and Lauren and I will go for a little drive."

No way in hell. Fox wanted to use her as his ticket

out of here. As soon as she lost her usefulness as a bargaining chip, Daniel knew the bastard would have no qualms about killing her and dumping her body somewhere along his escape route.

His mind raced through his options. They were terrifyingly limited. Whatever he did, he didn't have much time. Already, Fox was on a knife's-edge of control, not thinking rationally. He had to know he was in far worse shit now than he would have been even if Rosa had testified to the grand jury about the smuggling ring.

The slightest misstep by Daniel would likely send Fox careening over that edge.

Daniel's options were limited and his window of opportunity was narrowing by the second.

"Come on, Sheriff. We can't stand here all day. Sooner or later, one of us is going to blink. You know you can't shoot me or you'll hit Dr. Maxwell here. You want to keep her alive, your best chance is to drop your weapon now and let us out of here."

He released a breath, knowing he had no choice. After a long, painful pause, he bent at the waist and placed his weapon on the floor.

Lauren gave a tiny, anguished whimper, the terror in her eyes ticking up a notch.

Trust me, he mouthed while Fox's attention was glued to his Beretta on the floor tiles between them.

"Good choice," the man said. "Now if you'll just step aside, we'll be on our way."

Adrenaline flowed through him as he tensed, ready to pounce, when suddenly he heard a noise from outside the treatment room. The outside door opening, he realized.

A moment later, he heard a small, concerned voice. "Daniel? Lauren? *Donde éstan?*"

Rosa. *Mierda!*

Kendall Fox froze at the voice, then a dark and ugly satisfaction spread over his too-handsome features.

"Your lover boy is a liar, Lauren," he purred. "Looks like I'll be able to take care of my little problem after all."

He drew the gun away from Lauren's head to aim it at the door and released her slightly. Daniel knew this was his only chance.

He hadn't played college football in more than a decade but he still knew how to take a man down. He used Fox's momentary distraction to charge. In an instant, he pushed Lauren out of the way and plowed into the other man.

They both toppled to the floor and Fox instinctively fired, but the shot went wild. Still, the other man managed to keep hold of his weapon and for what felt like an eternity, they grappled fiercely for it.

Daniel was desperate to wrest it away, but the doctor was just as determined to hang on. Though Daniel outweighed him by at least thirty pounds, the bastard was tougher than he looked, wiry and quick. It didn't help his concentration that he was painfully aware of Lauren and Rosa huddled together in the doorway.

He wanted to yell at both of them to get the hell out of there and call for help but he didn't dare even take his attention off Fox for an instant.

Finally, the tide began to turn. He was able to drive an elbow into the doctor's nose and when his head whipped back, Daniel grabbed hold of his wrist and slammed it with vicious force against the hard tile floor.

The weapon flew free, sliding across the floor. Breathing hard, adrenaline coursing through him like crazy, Daniel dragged them both to their feet and shoved Fox against the concrete wall. His head connected with a loud crack, and with a moan he sagged to the ground.

In seconds, Daniel yanked out his handcuffs and used only a little more force than strictly necessary to drag his arms behind his back.

The bastard had shot one of his deputies, was responsible for all the misery Rosa had endured, and had threatened the woman Daniel loved.

For the first time since he went through police officer training a decade ago, Daniel fiercely wished he wasn't a cop bound by laws and the Bill of Rights. He would give just about anything for the freedom to administer a little frontier justice right about now.

He read the dazed man his rights. Only when he was sure he wasn't going anywhere did Daniel pick up his own Beretta and Fox's weapon and turn to check on Rosa and Lauren.

Rosa was gazing at him with a wide-eyed kind of awe that left him highly uncomfortable. Lauren, on the other hand, looked ready to spit nails.

"Are you both okay?"

"We're fine," Lauren answered, her voice hard and tight. "You're bleeding."

He looked down and saw a red blotch spreading on his sleeve. He hadn't paid any attention to it in the heat of the moment, but now he realized his arm stung like hell.

"Did he shoot you?"

He flexed his arm. "Don't think so. I'm okay. I must have broken through my stitches from the other night when I was subduing him. I'll deal with it after I get Fox into custody."

Her mouth tightened. For a moment, he didn't quite understand the reason for her anger, and then he remembered everything, all he had told her the night before about her father's downfall and his role in it.

Of course. She hated him now. She was probably wishing Fox *had* shot him.

The satisfaction that churned through him at subduing and arresting Fox—at finding the man who had hurt Rosa and shot his deputy—dried up instantly and he was miserable once again.

She had never been so angry in her life.

The fury coursed through her like a thick, torpid creek and she couldn't seem to wade across it.

She managed to contain it while she treated Rosa for mild exposure and tried to follow the girl's story about what had happened earlier, about how she had heard a gunshot and climbed out the bathroom window and slogged through the snow as fast as she could looking for shelter.

She asked questions and made appropriate responses as best she could in Spanish, but the whole time she was afraid her fury would suck her under. The source of her anger was still in her clinic talking to Cale Davis and Gage McKinnon about what had happened.

She would have to give a statement soon, she knew, but right now her patient took precedence.

Rosa yawned suddenly in the middle of her story

and Lauren forced her attention back to her patient, tucking the warmed blankets closer around her.

"Rest now," she said. "You can tell me the rest of the story later when Daniel is here."

Daniel was apparently the magic word. Rosa was crazy about him. The events of the last hour only seemed to have solidified the girl's hero worship.

Rosa nodded. Lauren smoothed a hand over her hair and she smiled, closing her eyes. She stayed with her until she fell asleep, then dimmed the lights and slipped out of the room, leaving the door ajar so she could hear if her patient awoke.

Out in the hallway, she finally let down her guard and leaned against the wall, utterly exhausted by the strain of the day and the sleepless night that preceded it. Her cheek and her head both ached where she had slammed against the wall and she closed her eyes, trying to relax the tight grip of tension in her shoulders with a couple of breathing exercises.

They didn't seem to want to be soothed, especially when some sixth sense warned her she wasn't alone.

She jerked her eyes open and found Daniel standing five feet away, watching her out of those intense dark eyes that missed nothing.

He looked so big and comforting and wonderful and she had to grip her hands together to keep from sagging against that hard chest and holding on tight.

Until she remembered how angry she was with him.

"Everything taken care of with Kendall?" she asked, her voice deliberately cool.

"Yeah. Cale and McKinnon will be picking him up at our jail and taking custody. Your Dr. Fox isn't going to be seeing the light of day anytime soon."

"He's not *my* Dr. Fox. I hope he never gets out of prison for what he's done."

He looked a little surprised at her vehemence, which only seemed to make her angrier. Did he honestly think she would have a shred of sympathy for Kendall?

"You need to let me look at your arm."

He glanced down with a distracted look, as if he had forgotten all about it. "I think it's stopped bleeding."

"I still want to check it out. Come in here."

She didn't give him a chance to argue, just headed for the nearest exam room. After a pause, he followed, looking about as thrilled to be there as a two-year-old on the way to a booster shot.

"Would you take off your shirt, please?" she ordered. The words had an oddly familiar ring and she couldn't figure out why until she remembered she had made the same request of him the night Dale Richins found Rosa in the bed of his pickup.

Everything had changed in those few short days. She had kissed him, touched him.

Discovered how very much she loved him.

She huffed out a breath. She wasn't quite ready to surrender her anger yet by giving in to that soft twirl of emotion.

Still, she had to admit her insides shivered when he shrugged out of his uniform, baring that vast expanse of bronze skin and muscle.

She was a professional, she reminded herself. She shouldn't even notice. She stepped closer, and pulled the exam light over so she could look at his injury.

"The stitches still look good," she said after a moment while she rifled through a drawer of the exam table for the necessary supplies to clean off the crusted blood. "You must have just bumped it in a bad spot and started it bleeding again. I'm sure you were too busy being an idiot at the time to notice."

He raised an eyebrow. "Was I?"

"What else would you call it? You could have been killed, Daniel. He had a gun, in case it escaped your attention."

"I believe I was aware of that."

"What kind of idiot rushes toward a man holding a gun aimed at his chest?"

"It wasn't aimed at my chest when I tackled him, it was aimed at the door. I was well aware of the risks but I had everything under control. I had to take a chance, Lauren. I couldn't let him hurt you or Rosa."

"You were willing to sacrifice yourself for us!"

"It wouldn't have come to that. I wouldn't have let it."

Abruptly, all her anger seeped away, leaving only the echo of that raw, terrible fear she had endured watching him wrestle an armed and desperate man. She swallowed hard, hoping he couldn't see her hands tremble as she wiped gently around the edges of his injury.

"You could have been killed," she said softly. "I have never been so scared in my entire life."

To her horror, her voice broke on the last word. She took a breath, then another, trying to regain control, but it was too late. A sob escaped her and she dropped the gauze on the exam table and buried her face in her hands.

"Lauren," he murmured, then he wrapped those strong, wonderful arms around her and held her against his bare chest while she wept.

Those terrible moments replayed through her mind again and again, her fear and helplessness and the horrible dread when that single shot exploded through the room.

"Everything's all right now," he said. "We're all okay. You and Rosa are safe and that's the important thing."

Her hand curled into a fist and she struck out blindly, punching him in the chest, even though she was far too upset to put much force behind it.

"Don't you *ever* do that to me again, Daniel Galvez. I died inside when I thought he had shot you."

At her words, he froze, the hard, smooth muscles against her fist suddenly tight. After a charged pause, he covered her hand with his and drew it to his heart, squeezing tightly as if he didn't dare let go.

Her gaze lifted to his and the intense emotion there snatched away her breath.

"You did?" he asked, his voice low, shocked.

Her chin quivered as she nodded and wiped away a tear with her finger. Another one slipped out after it, but he dipped his head and absorbed it with a gentle whisper of a kiss.

"I'm sorry," he murmured, kissing away another and another.

"You'd better be," she replied, then she wrapped her arms tightly around his neck and drew his mouth to hers.

She kissed him fiercely, pouring every ounce of the emotion raging through her heart into her embrace. Love and anger and a deep, cleansing celebration of life.

Several long moments later, he lifted his head slightly, his expression dazed and his breathing ragged.

"You're going to have to take me back a few steps here, Lauren. I must be a little slow this afternoon. I thought you hated me. After what I told you last night, I figured you would never want to talk to me again."

"I could never hate you."

"Ten minutes ago you were furious with me."

"I was angry at you for rushing a man with a gun, for risking your life. I still am."

During those long, terrible moments, all she wanted was the chance to tell Daniel how she felt about him. Now that she had the opportunity, the words seemed to catch in her throat.

She swallowed hard, then drew a deep breath for courage. "Mostly, I was angry because I couldn't bear thinking you might have died before I could ever tell you I love you."

Had she really just blurted that out? *She* was the idiot here. With her pulse pounding loudly in her ears, she finally lifted her gaze to his and the raw emotion in his eyes sent that pulse racing into what she was sure couldn't be a healthy rate.

He looked thunderstruck at first, completely stunned, then a fierce joy leaped into his eyes.

"Say that again," he ordered, his voice hoarse, stunned.

She managed a watery smile, tenderness soaking through her. She wasn't afraid of this. With everything inside her, she loved this man. Somehow she knew he would never hurt her. He had risked his life for her. Risking her heart was a piece of cake compared to that.

"I love you, Daniel. I think I have for a long time, I just never realized it until these last few days. I love your strength and your courage and your goodness. I love the way you touch me and the way you make me feel inside, like I'm riding a roller coaster without a seat belt, and the amazing way you seem to believe I can do anything I set my mind to do."

Daniel heard her words but he couldn't quite comprehend they were coming out of her mouth. He was afraid to believe it could be real, especially after the long, miserable night he had spent lying awake on her couch watching the flames dip and sway and wishing away the past.

He hated to ask, but couldn't seem to contain the question. "What about your father? About the investigation? You don't blame me for what happened?"

She sighed, looking weary. "How can I blame you for doing your job? My father made his own choices, every step of the way. You had nothing to do with them. I've had to accept that his choices had a ripple effect in many, many lives. I just never realized until today that some of those ripples have helped shape and guide my life into a direction I can't regret. I have a great life here. Good friends, patients I care about, a growing practice. No. I don't blame you."

Relief poured through him and he wrapped her in his arms again, resting his forehead on hers. He was at peace as he hadn't been in a long time and he wanted to hang on to the feeling forever.

"I have one more confession," he murmured.

She looked wary suddenly and he smiled, kissing her hard. "I have to tell you that when I was a kid, you were everything I ever dreamed of, everything I wanted. I think I was in love with you, even back then. Nothing has changed."

He stopped and shook his head slightly. "No, that's

not true. *Everything* has changed. Before, I wanted this image I had of you, the perfect house and the pretty girl who went along with it. I didn't know that pretty girl would grow into this smart, incredible woman I love so much, someone who pours her heart and soul into healing others, who has this powerful sense of justice, a bottomless well of compassion in her heart. And a rather terrifying obsession with hot chocolate."

She laughed, though a faint wash of color danced across her cheekbones. He brushed his mouth across her soft, delicate skin. He couldn't believe this was real, that she was in his arms.

She loved him. It seemed a miracle, an incredible gift, and he was fairly certain his heart would burst with happiness. He smiled, not concerned in the least.

At least he would have a good doctor around when it happened.

Epilogue

"If you don't stop sniffling, she's going to hear you."

"I'm trying," Lauren whispered back to Daniel. She pulled out the handkerchief she had at least had the foresight to bring along, dabbed at her teary eyes, then shifted on the hard bleacher seats of the high school gymnasium trying to find a comfortable spot.

It wasn't an easy task for anyone—forget a woman who was six months pregnant.

Beside her, Daniel canted his hips slightly and tugged her against him so she could use his solid bulk as a backrest.

"Better?" he murmured as the commencement speaker talked of lessons learned and the road less traveled.

"Much." She leaned into him gratefully, feeling the tight muscles in her lower back ease. After three years of marriage, she still couldn't understand how he instinctively seemed to know exactly what she needed before she even figured it out herself.

He did this kind of thing all the time, these quiet acts of consideration that always seemed to take her breath away. Her heart bubbling over with emotion, she reached for his hand, linking her fingers through his.

She would never have believed she could come to love him so much. She thought of the aching loneliness in her life before that January that had changed everything, before she acknowledged the feelings that had been growing inside her most of her life. She thought she had been content building her medical practice, living her life as best she could, trying to repair all that her father had done.

The contrast of these last three years to her earlier life only illustrated how starkly empty that world had been. Marriage to Daniel had been filled with everything she might have wished—laughter and joy and the peaceful assurance that this strong, wonderful man was crazy about her.

Not everything had been easy. Their early months together had been tempered by heartache as she had helped Rosa deliver her baby and then a day later handed the beautiful dark-eyed girl to the adoptive couple Rosa had selected.

More tears bubbled out now as she remembered Rosa's courage—and pain. Lauren was a physician, trained to help people heal, and she had hated knowing she couldn't make everything right for Rosa. Giving the child up for adoption had been the right choice. She knew it. But it hadn't been an easy one for any of them.

As an adopted child herself, she knew Rosa had

been giving her daughter a better life than she could provide as a fifteen-year-old single mother with little education.

She and Daniel had talked long and hard about the possibility of adopting the girl themselves. In the end, Rosa made the decision for them, with a wisdom and strength that still amazed Lauren.

Here in Moose Springs, Rosa said, there would always be rumors swirling around her daughter. Everyone knew of the trial, of Rosa's violent rape and the attempts on her life. She wanted her child to grow up where she would never have to know the ugly circumstances that had created her, where she could be free to thrive and grow.

"My daughter is innocent of what happened to me and she should not have to live with that burden. No child should," Rosa had said firmly.

As it had been her choice, Daniel and Lauren stood by her and helped her find the right placement for the child. Rosa had finally selected friends of Daniel's sister Anna in Oregon, a wonderful, loving couple who had been childless for eight years.

Seeing their utter joy at their new daughter had eased some of the heartache, but not all. Still, the whole experience had given Lauren a new appreciation—both for the unknown woman who gave birth to her and for her own parents.

As the young speaker finished her speech with an enthusiastic plea to the graduates to grab all life had to offer, Lauren forced her attention away from the past back to the present.

"She's next," she whispered.

She didn't realize she was squeezing Daniel's hand

so tightly until he laughed slightly and slid his hand away to cover her fingers with his. "Easy, sweetheart. She'll be great."

Jim Fordham, the principal of the high school, stood to introduce the next speaker and Lauren's heart kicked up a notch.

"Every year the senior class at Moose Springs High School votes on the most inspirational graduate of the year," the principal began. "It has been a tradition at this school since I attended, back in the Dark Ages. Never before could I say how wholeheartedly I support their unanimous selection."

He smiled as the crowd applauded. "This student exemplifies courage and strength under difficult conditions. She came into this country with barely an elementary school education but in two years, despite her circumstances, she has thrived. She does not have the best grades of anyone in her graduating class, but every teacher she has ever had at this school tells me no one tries harder to succeed. She is never without a smile, she is kind to everyone she meets, and she will be greatly missed by students and faculty alike when she leaves to attend nursing school on a full scholarship in the fall. Your choice as inspirational graduate of the year, Rosa Vallejo."

The graduating seniors jumped up and began clapping. Beside Daniel, Lauren thought her heart would burst with pride as Rosa walked to the microphone, her long dark hair gleaming against the glossy white of her graduation robes.

The frightened, battered girl she and Daniel had found in the back of Dale Richins's pickup was now a strong, beautiful, confident young woman. Rosa smiled at the crowd, though Lauren thought her gaze lingered on them for just a moment as she waited for the applause to fade and the crowd to sit again before she launched into her speech.

As Rosa began speaking in her accented but clear English, Lauren followed along in her head with the speech they had practiced for two weeks. It was a wonderful message and though Lauren had heard it dozens of times, she was still touched as Rosa talked of life's challenges, and how people can choose to wallow along in their adversities or they can reach out to lift others. She talked of the bright future and of possibilities in a speech punctuated several times by applause.

Close to the end, Lauren waited for the big inspirational finish. Instead Rosa's voice faltered. She paused for several seconds, long enough that Lauren began to fear she had forgotten the words they practiced.

"I wish I had better English," Rosa said after a moment. "Maybe then I could find the words to thank the two people who have given me everything. They have given me help and courage, friendship, understanding, love. They have given me a home and they have stood with me through my darkest hours."

Rosa gave a watery smile and Lauren sniffled in response. Beside her, Daniel gripped her hand tightly. "Most of all, they have given me hope. My mother died in Honduras when I was thirteen. I did not know when I came to this country I would find two new parents but I have been so blessed. My heart is full of gratitude and love for them. To Daniel and Lauren Galvez, thank you. From the very, very bottom of my heart, I thank you. Because you reached out to help a stranger when you could have turned away, my future is a bright and wonderful place."

She stepped away from the podium and began to clap. Around them, others stood and clapped as well. This was her town, Lauren thought as she looked around at the smiling faces looking back at her. Her neighbors and friends and patients, and she loved them.

Daniel slid an arm around her and pulled her close and she risked a look at his strong, rugged features. Suspicious moisture leaked from his eyes and she handed the extra tissue she had brought along.

He would be a wonderful father to this child she carried. She had no doubt at all, because she had seen his quiet guidance with Rosa these last few years.

As the principal returned to the podium to begin reading off the names of graduates to hand out diplomas, Lauren touched her abdomen. Rosa was right. The future was a bright and wonderful place.

She couldn't wait.

* * * * *

We hope you enjoyed reading

A LOVE BEYOND WORDS
by #1 *New York Times* bestselling author
SHERRYL WOODS
and

SHELTER FROM THE STORM
by *New York Times* bestselling author
RaeANNE THAYNE

Both were originally Harlequin® Special Edition and Harlequin® Romantic Suspense stories!

Heart-racing romance set against the backdrop of suspense. Discover these stories of true to life women in extraordinary circumstances who are rescued by the powerful heroes of their dreams.

HARLEQUIN®

ROMANTIC suspense
Heart-racing romance, high-stakes suspense!

Look for four *new* romances every month from **Harlequin Romantic Suspense!**

Available wherever books are sold.

www.Harlequin.com

SPECIAL EXCERPT FROM

♦ HARLEQUIN®

ROMANTIC suspense

*Widow Penelope Barrington never thought she'd
speak to Reid Colton again, as he's the man she holds
responsible for her husband's death. But when she
finds evidence incriminating her father in his father's
disappearance, she's forced to team up with her teen
crush to find the truth...before it's too late.*

Read on for a sneak preview of Beth Cornelison's
COLTON CHRISTMAS PROTECTOR,
the final book in
THE COLTONS OF TEXAS *miniseries.*

"Reid..." she rasped.

He raised his head to look deeply into her eyes. "I want
you, Pen. I won't pretend otherwise any longer. But if this
isn't what you want, you can tell me to go to hell, and I'll
respect your feelings."

She opened her mouth to reply, but so many thoughts
and emotions battled inside her, she could only stare at
him mutely.

When she didn't reply, his expression darkened. He
levered farther away from her as if to leave, and she
tightened her grip on his shirt.

"Pen?" He angled his head, clearly trying to read her.

"I...need more time." Her heart thrashed in her chest
like a wild animal tangled in a snare. She felt trapped,
caught between loyalty to Andrew and a years-old lust for
Reid. Factoring in the mind-numbing twists her life had
taken, her father's deceit and the foggy road that was her

future, how could she know what was right? For both her and Nicholas, because she had to put her son's needs at the top of her considerations.

Reid bowed his head briefly, his disappointment plain. "More time. Right. Because we've only known each other for fifteen some years. Been friends for seven."

"Andrew—"

"Has been gone for over a year," he finished for her, his voice noticeably tighter. Pain flashed in his eyes, and he shoved away from her. "All right. I promised to respect your choice, and I will."

Freed of his weight and warmth, a stark chill sliced through her. Confusion or not, she didn't want to be without him. She did desire him, value the protection he offered, appreciate his friendship.

"Wait!" she cried before he could rise from the couch. She sat up, shifting her legs under her to kneel on the cushion beside him. "Reid, I'm still sorting out my feelings, but I want…" Her throat tightened. "I need…"

He arched an eyebrow to indicate he was listening, waiting.

She drew a slow breath, her body quivering from the inside out. She threaded her fingers through the hair near his ear before cupping the back of his head and drawing him close. "This…" she whispered as she slanted her mouth over his.

Don't miss
COLTON CHRISTMAS PROTECTOR
by Beth Cornelison available December 2016
wherever Harlequin® Romantic Suspense
books and ebooks are sold.

www.Harlequin.com

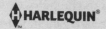

ROMANTIC suspense

Heart-racing romance, high-stakes suspense!

Save $1.00

on the purchase of
ANY
Harlequin® Romantic Suspense
book.

Available wherever books are sold, including most
bookstores, supermarkets, drugstores and discount stores.

Save $1.00

on the purchase of any Harlequin® Romantic Suspense book.

Coupon valid until January 31, 2017.
Redeemable at participating outlets in the U.S. and Canada only.
Not redeemable at Barnes and Noble stores. Limit one coupon per customer.

52614385

5 65373 00076 2   (8100)0 12228

NYTCOUP1116

Return to the beloved town of
Chesapeake Shores
in this special release of the series by
#1 *New York Times* bestselling author

SHERRYL WOODS

Available now, wherever books are sold!

THE WORLD IS BETTER WITH

Romance

Harlequin has everything from contemporary, passionate and heartwarming to suspenseful and inspirational stories.

Whatever your mood, we have romance when you need it, wherever you are!

HARLEQUIN®

A *Romance* FOR EVERY MOOD™

www.Harlequin.com

#RomanceWhenYouNeedIt